Diaries

MERLINE LOVELACE

First Published in Great Britain 2017
By Mills & Boon, an imprint of HarperCollins*Publishers*
1 London Bridge Street, London, SE1 9GF

THE DUCHESS DIARIES © 2017 Harlequin Books S. A.

The Diplomat's Pregnant Bride, *Her Unforgettable Royal Lover* and *The Texan's Royal M.D.* were first published in Great Britain by Harlequin (UK) Limited.

The Diplomat's Pregnant Bride © 2013 Merline Lovelace
Her Unforgettable Royal Lover © 2014 Merline Lovelace
The Texan's Royal M.D. © 2015 Merline Lovelace

ISBN: 978-0-263-92983-6

05-1017

Printed and bound in Spain
by CPI, Barcelona

MILLS & BOON®

Why shop at millsandboon.co.uk?

Each year, thousands of romance readers find their perfect read at millsandboon.co.uk. That's because we're passionate about bringing you the very best romantic fiction. Here are some of the advantages of shopping at www.millsandboon.co.uk:

* **Get new books first**—you'll be able to buy your favourite books one month before they hit the shops

* **Get exclusive discounts**—you'll also be able to buy our specially created monthly collections, with up to 50% off the RRP

* **Find your favourite authors**—latest news, interviews and new releases for all your favourite authors and series on our website, plus ideas for what to try next

* **Join in**—once you've bought your favourite books, don't forget to register with us to rate, review and join in the discussions

Visit **www.millsandboon.co.uk** for all this and more today!

A career Air Force officer, **Merline Lovelace** served at bases all over the world. When she hung up her uniform for the last time she decided to combine her love of adventure with a flair for storytelling, basing many of her tales on her own experiences in uniform. Since then she's produced more than ninety action-packed sizzlers, many of which have made the *USA TODAY* and Waldenbooks bestseller lists. Over eleven million copies of her books are available in some thirty countries.

When she's not tied to her keyboard, Merline enjoys reading, chasing little white balls around the fairways of Oklahoma and traveling to new and exotic locales with her handsome husband, Al. check her website at www.merlinelovelace.com or friend her on Facebook for news and information about her latest releases.

THE DIPLOMAT'S
PREGNANT BRIDE

BY
MERLINE LOVELACE

To my gorgeous niece Cori and Jane and the
rest of the crew at Clayton on the Park, in Scottsdale.
Thanks for the inside look at the ups and downs
of an event coordinator's life!

Prologue

I could not have asked for two more beautiful or loving granddaughters. From the first day they came to live with me—one so young and frightened, the other still in diapers—they filled the empty spaces in my heart with light and joy. Now Sarah, my quiet, elegant Sarah, is about to marry her handsome Dev. The wedding takes place in a few hours, and I ache with happiness for her. And with such worry for her sister. My darling Eugenia has waltzed through life, brightening even the sourest dispositions with her sparkling smile and care-free, careless joie de vivre. Now, quite suddenly that carelessness has caught up with her. She's come face-to-face with reality, and I can only pray the strength and spirit I know she possesses will help her through the difficult days ahead.

Enough of this. I must dress for the wedding. Then it's off to the Plaza, which has been the scene of so many significant events in my life. But none to match the delight of this one!

From the diary of Charlotte,
Grand Duchess of Karlenburgh

One

Gina St. Sebastian forced a smile to hide her gritted teeth.

"Good Lord, you're stubborn, Jack."

"*I'm* stubborn?"

The irate male standing before her snapped his sun-bleached brows together. Ambassador John Harris Mason III was tanned, tawny-haired and a trim, athletic six-one. He was also used to being in charge. The fact that he couldn't control Gina or the situation they now found themselves in irritated him no end.

"You're pregnant with my child, dammit. Yet you refuse to even discuss marriage."

"Oh, for...! Trumpet the news to the whole world, why don't you?"

Scowling, Gina craned her neck to peer around the bank of gardenias shielding her and Jack from the other guests in the Terrace Room of New York City's venerable Plaza Hotel. With its exquisitely restored Italian Renaissance ceiling and crystal chandeliers modeled after those in the Palace of Versailles, it made a fabulous venue for a wedding.

A wedding put together on extremely short notice! They'd had less than two weeks to pull it off. The groom's billions had eased the time crunch considerably, as had the miracle

worker Dev Hunter employed as his executive assistant. Gina had done all the planning, though, and she would not allow the man she'd spent one wild weekend with to disrupt her sister's wedding day.

Luckily no one seemed to have heard his caustic comment. The band was currently pulsing out the last bars of a lively merengue. Sarah and Dev were on the dance floor, along with the St. Sebastians' longtime housekeeper, Maria, and most of the guests invited to the elegant affair.

Gina's glance shot from the dancers to the lace-clad woman sitting ramrod-straight in her chair, hands crossed on the ebony head of her cane. The duchess was out of earshot, too, thank God! Hearing her younger granddaughter's pregnancy broadcast to the world at large wouldn't have fit with her notions of proper behavior.

Relieved, Gina swung back to Jack. "I won't have you spoil my sister's wedding with another argument. Please lower your voice."

He took the hint and cranked down the decibels, if not his temper. "We haven't had ten minutes alone to talk about this since you got back from Switzerland."

As if she needed the reminder! She'd flown to Switzerland exactly one day after she'd peed on a purple stick and felt her world come crashing down around her. She'd had to get away from L.A., had to breathe in the sharp, clean air of the snow-capped Alps surrounding Lake Lucerne while trying to decide what to do. After a day and a night of painful soul-searching, she'd walked into one of Lucerne's ultra-modern clinics. Ten minutes later, she'd turned around and walked out again. But not before making two near-hysterical calls. The first was to Sarah—her sister, her protector, her dearest friend. The second, unfortunately, was to the handsome, charismatic and thoroughly annoying diplomat now confronting her.

By the time Sarah had made the frantic dash from Paris in response to her sister's call, Gina's jagged nerves had

smoothed a little. Her hard-won poise shattered once again, however, when Jack Mason showed up on the scene. She hadn't expected him to jump a plane, much less express such fierce satisfaction over her decision to have their child.

Actually, the decision had surprised Gina as much as it had Jack. She was the flighty, irresponsible sister. The good-time girl, always up for a weekend skiing in Biarritz or a sail through the blue-green waters of the Caribbean. Raised by their grandmother, she and Sarah had been given the education and sophisticated lifestyle the duchess insisted was their birthright. Only recently had the sisters learned how deeply Grandmama had gone into debt to provide that lifestyle. Since then, Gina had made a determined effort to support herself. A good number of efforts, actually. Sadly, none of the careers she'd dabbled in had held her mercurial interest for very long.

Modeling had turned out to be a drag. All those hot lights and temperamental photographers snapping orders like constipated drill sergeants. Escorting small, select tour groups to the dazzling capitals of Europe was even more of a bore. How in the world could she have imagined she'd want to make a career of chasing down lost luggage or shuffling room assignments to placate a whiny guest who didn't like the view in hers?

Gina had even tried to translate her brief sojourn at Italy's famed cooking school, the Academia Barilla, into a career as a catering chef. That misguided attempt had barely lasted a week. But when her exasperated boss booted her out of the kitchen and into the front office, she'd discovered her apparently one real talent. She was far better at planning parties than cooking for them. Especially when clients walked in waving a checkbook and orders to pull out all the stops for their big event.

She was so good, in fact, that she intended to support herself and her child by coordinating soirees for the rich and famous. But first she had to convince her baby's father

that she neither needed nor wanted the loveless marriage he was offering.

"I appreciate your concern, Jack, but..."

"Concern?"

The handsome, charismatic ambassador kept his voice down as she'd requested, but looked as though he wanted let loose with both barrels. His shoulders were taut under his hand-tailored tux. Below his neatly trimmed caramel-colored hair, his brown eyes drilled into her.

Gina couldn't help but remember how those eyes had snared hers across a crowded conference room six weeks ago and signaled instant, electric attraction. How his oh-so-skilled mouth had plundered her throat and her breasts and her belly. How...

Oh, for pity's sake! Why remember the heat that had sizzled so hot and fast between them? That spontaneous combustion wouldn't happen again. Not now. Not with everything else that was going on in their lives.

"But," she continued with a forced smile, "you have to agree a wedding reception is hardly the time or place for a discussion like this."

"Name the time," he challenged. "And the place."

"All right! Tomorrow. Twelve noon." Cornered, she named the first place she could think of. "The Boathouse in Central Park."

"I'll be there."

"Fine. We'll get a table in a quiet corner and discuss this like the mature adults we are."

"Like the mature adult at least one of us is."

Gina hid a wince. The biting sarcasm stung, but she had to admit it wasn't far off the mark. The truth was she'd pretty much flitted through life, laughing at its absurdities, always counting on Sarah or Grandmama to bail her out of trouble every time she tumbled into it. All that changed about ten minutes after she peed on that damned stick. Her flitting

days were over. It was time to take responsibility for herself and her baby.

Which she would.

She would!

"I'll see you tomorrow."

Chin high, she swept around the bank of gardenias.

Jack let her go. She wasn't the time or the place to hammer some sense into her. Not that he held much hope his calm, rational arguments would penetrate that thick mane of silvery blond curls or spark a glimmer of understanding in those baby-doll blue eyes.

He'd now spent a total of five days—one long, wild week-end and and two frustrating days in Switzerland—in Gina St. Sebastian's company. More than enough time to confirm the woman constituted a walking, talking bundle of contradictions. She was jaw-droppingly gorgeous and so sensual she made grown men go weak at the knees, but also friendly and playful as a kitten. Well-educated, yet in many ways naive beyond belief. And almost completely oblivious to the world around her unless it directly impacted her, her sister or her dragon lady of a grandmother.

Pretty much his exact opposite, Jack thought grimly as he tracked her progress across the crowded room. He came from a long line of coolheaded, clear-thinking Virginians who believed their vast wealth brought with it equally great responsibility. Jack's father and grandfather had served as advisors to presidents in times of national crisis. He himself had served in several diplomatic posts before being appointed the State Department's ambassador-at-large for counterterrorism at the ripe old age of thirty-two. As such, he'd traveled to some of the most volatile, violent trouble spots in the world. Recently he'd returned to State Department headquarters in Washington, D.C., to translate his hard-won field knowledge into policies and procedures that would improve the security of U.S. diplomatic personnel around the world.

His job demanded long days and long nights. Stress rode on his shoulders like hundred-pound weights. Yet he couldn't remember any issue, any recalcitrant bureaucrat or political pundit, who frustrated him as much as Gina St. Sebastian. She was pregnant with his child, dammit! The child he was determined would carry his name.

The child he and Catherine had tried so hard to have.

The familiar pain knifed into him. The feeling wasn't as vicious as it had once been, but was still ferocious enough to carve up his insides. The lively conversation around him faded. The flower-bedecked room blurred. He could almost see her, almost hear her Boston Brahmin accent. Catherine—brilliant, politically savvy Catherine—would have grasped the irony in his present situation at once. She would have...

"You look like you could use a drink, Mason."

With an immense effort of will, Jack blanked the memory of his dead wife and turned to the new groom. Dev Hunter held a crystal tumbler in one hand and offered one to Jack with the other.

"Scotch, straight up," he said dryly. "I saw you talking to Gina and figured you could use it."

"You figured right."

Jack took the tumbler and tipped it toward the man who might soon become his brother-in-law. Not might, he amended grimly as they clinked glasses, would.

"To the St. Sebastian sisters," Hunter said, his gaze shifting to the two women standing with their heads together across the room. "It took some convincing, but I got mine to the altar. Good luck getting yours there."

The Scotch went down with a well-mannered bite. Jack savored its smoky tang and eyed the sisters. They were a study in contrasts. Dark-haired Sarah was impossibly elegant in a clinging ivory gown with feathered clasps at each shoulder and glowed with the incandescent beauty of a bride. Blonde, bubbly Gina was barely six weeks pregnant and

showed no signs of a baby bump. She was still slender but more generously endowed than her sister. Her flame-colored, body-hugging, strapless and backless sheath outlined her seductive curves to perfection.

Jack's fingers tightened on the tumbler. Six weeks after the fact and he could still remember how he'd positioned those seductive hips under his. How he'd buried his hands in her silky hair and lost himself in that lush body and those laughing blue eyes.

They'd used protection that weekend. Went through a whole damned box of it, as he recalled. So much for playing the odds.

"I'll get her to the altar," he vowed. "One way or another."

Hunter raised a brow but refrained from comment as his bride smiled and crooked a finger. "I'm being summoned. I'll talk to you again when Sarah and I get back from our honeymoon."

He handed his empty tumbler to a passing waiter and started for his wife, then turned back. "Just for the record, Mason, my money's on Gina. She's got more of the duchess in her than she realizes. And speaking of the duchess..."

Jack followed his glance and saw the silver-haired St. Sebastian matriarch thumping her way toward them. A long-sleeve, high-necked dress of ecru lace draped her slight frame. A trio of rings decorated her arthritic fingers. Leaning heavily on her cane with her left hand, Charlotte dismissed her new grandson-in-law with an imperious wave of the right.

"Gina says it's time for you and Sarah to change out of your wedding finery. You only have an hour to get to the airport."

"It's my plane, Charlotte. I don't think it'll leave without us."

"I should hope not." Her ringed fingers flapped again. "Do go away, Devon. I want to talk to Ambassador Mason."

Jack didn't consciously go into a brace but he could feel

his shoulders squaring as he faced Gina's diminutive, indomitable grandmother.

He knew all about her. He should. He'd dug up the file the State Department had compiled on Charlotte St. Sebastian, once Grand Duchess of the tiny principality of Karlenburgh, when she fled her Communist-overrun country more than five decades ago. After being forced to witness her husband's brutal execution, she'd escaped with the clothes on her back, her infant daughter in her arms and a fortune in jewels hidden inside the baby's teddy bear.

She'd eventually settled in New York City and become an icon of the social and literary scenes. Few of the duchess's wealthy, erudite friends were aware this stiff-spined aristocrat had pawned her jewels over the years to support herself and the two young granddaughters who'd come to live with her after the tragic death of their parents. Jack knew only because Dev Hunter had hinted that he should tread carefully where Charlotte and her granddaughters' financial situation were concerned.

Very carefully, Jack's one previous encounter with the duchess made it clear her reduced circumstances had not diminished either her haughty air or the fierce protectiveness she exhibited toward her granddaughters. That protectiveness blazed in her face now.

"I just spoke with Gina. She says you're still trying to convince her to marry you."

"Yes, I am."

"Why?"

Jack was tempted to fall back on Gina's excuse and suggest that a wedding reception was hardly the proper place for this discussion. The steely look in the duchess's faded blue eyes killed that craven impulse.

"I think the reason would be obvious, ma'am. Your granddaughter's carrying my child. I want to give her and the baby the protection of my name."

The reply came coated with ice. "The St. Sebastian name

provides more than enough cachet for my granddaughter and her child."

Well, hell! And he called himself a diplomat! Jack was delivering a mental swift kick when the duchess raised her cane and jabbed the tip into his starched shirt front.

"Tell me one thing, Mr. Ambassador. Do you honestly believe the baby is yours?"

He didn't hesitate. "Yes, ma'am, I do."

The cane took another sharp jab at his sternum.

"Why?"

For two reasons, one of which Jack wasn't about to share.

He was still pissed that his father had reacted to the news that he would be a grandfather by hiring a private investigator. With ruthless efficiency the P.I. had dug into every nook and cranny of Gina St. Sebastian's life for the past three months. The report he submitted painted a portrait of a woman who bounced from job to job and man to man with seeming insouciance. Yet despite his best efforts, the detective hadn't been able to turn up a single lover in Gina's recent past except John Harris Mason III.

Furious, Jack had informed his father that he didn't need any damned report. He'd known the baby was his from the moment Gina called from Switzerland, sobbing and nearly incoherent. He now tried to convey that same conviction to the ferocious woman about to skewer him with her cane.

"As I've discovered in our brief time together, Duchess, your granddaughter has her share of faults. So do I. Neither of us have tried to deceive the other about those faults, however."

"What you mean," she countered with withering scorn, "is that neither of you made any protestations of eternal love or devotion before you jumped into bed together."

Jack refused to look away, but damned if he didn't feel heat crawling up the back of his neck. Wisely, he sidestepped the jumping-into-bed issue. "I'll admit I have a lot to learn yet about your granddaughter but my sense is she doesn't

lie. At least not about something this important," he added with more frankness than tact.

To his relief, the duchess lowered the cane and leaned on it with both hands. "You're correct in that assessment. Gina doesn't lie."

She hesitated, and a look that combined both pride and exasperation crossed her aristocratic features. "If anything, the girl is too honest. She tends to let her feelings just pour out, along with whatever she happens to be thinking at the time."

"So I noticed," Jack said, straight-faced.

Actually, Gina's exuberance and utter lack of pretense had delighted him almost as much as her luscious body during their weekend together. Looking back, Jack could admit he'd shucked a half-dozen layers of his sober, responsible self during that brief interlude. They hadn't stayed shucked, of course. Once he'd returned to Washington, he'd been engulfed in one crisis after another. Right up until that call from Switzerland.

The duchess reclaimed his attention with a regal toss of her head. "I will say this once, young man, and I suggest you take heed. My granddaughter's happiness is my first—my *only*—concern. Whatever Eugenia decides regarding you and the baby, she has my complete support."

"I wouldn't expect anything less, ma'am."

"Hrrmph." She studied him with pursed lips for a moment before delivering an abrupt non sequitur. "I knew your grandfather."

"You did?"

"He was a member of President Kennedy's cabinet at the time. Rather stiff and pompous, as I recall."

Jack had to grin. "That sounds like him."

"I invited him and your grandmother to a reception I hosted for the Sultan of Oman right here, in these very rooms. The Kennedys attended. So did the Rockefellers."

A distant look came into her eyes. A smile hovered at the corners of her mouth.

"I wore my pearls," she murmured, as much to herself as to her listener. "They roped around my neck three times before draping almost to my waist. Jackie was quite envious."

He bet she was. Watching the duchess's face, listening to her cultured speech with its faint trace of an accent, Jack nursed the hope that marriage to her younger granddaughter might not be such a disaster, after all.

With time and a little guidance on his part, Gina could learn to curb some of her impulsiveness. Maybe even learn to think before she blurted out whatever came into her mind. Not that he wanted to dim her sparkling personality. Just rein it in a bit so she'd feel comfortable in the restrained diplomatic circles she'd be marrying into.

Then, of course, there was the sex.

Jack kept his expression politely attentive. His diplomatic training and years of field experience wouldn't allow him to do otherwise. Yet every muscle in his body went taut as all-too-vivid images from his weekend with Gina once again grabbed him.

He hadn't been a saint since his wife died, but neither had he tomcatted around. Five women in six years didn't exactly constitute a world record. Yet the hours he'd spent in that Beverly Hills penthouse suite with Gina St. Sebastian made him come alive in ways he hadn't felt since...

Since Catherine.

Shaking off the twinge of guilt that thought brought, Jack addressed the woman just coming out of her reverie of presidents and pearls.

"Please believe me, Duchess. I want very much to do right by both your granddaughter and our child."

Those shrewd, pale eyes measured him for long, uncomfortable moments. Jack had faced cold-blooded dictators whose stares didn't slice anywhere as close to the bone as this white-haired, seemingly frail woman's did.

"You may as well call me Charlotte," she said finally. "I

suspect we may be seeing a good deal of each other in the weeks ahead."

"I suspect we may."

"Now, if you'll excuse me, I must help Sarah prepare to depart for her honeymoon."

Two

After Sarah changed and left for the airport with Dev, Gina escorted her grandmother and Maria down to the limo she'd ordered for them.

"I'll be a while," she warned as the elevator opened onto the Plaza's elegant lobby. "I want to make sure Dev's family is set for their trip home tomorrow."

"I should think that clever, clever man Dev employs as his executive assistant has the family's travel arrangements well in hand."

"He does. He's also going to take care of shipping the wedding gifts back to L.A., thank goodness. But I need to verify the final head count and see he has a complete list of the bills to expect."

The duchess stiffened, and Gina gave herself a swift mental kick. Dang it! She shouldn't have mentioned those bills. As she and Sarah knew all too well, covering the cost of the wedding had come dangerously close to a major point of contention between Dev and the duchess. Charlotte had insisted on taking care of the expenses traditionally paid by the bride's family. It was a real tribute to Dev's negotiating skills that he and Grandmama had reached an agreement that didn't totally destroy her pride.

And now Gina had to bring up the sensitive subject again! It was Jack's fault, she thought in disgust. Their confrontation had thrown her off stride. Was still throwing her off. Why the heck had she agreed to meet him for lunch tomorrow?

She was still trying to figure that one out when the limo pulled up to the Plaza's stately front entrance. The driver got out to open the door but before his two passengers slid into the backseat, the duchess issued a stern warning.

"Don't overtax yourself, Eugenia. Pregnancy saps a woman's strength, especially during the first few months. You'll find you're more fatigued than usual."

"Fatigue hasn't been a problem yet. Or morning sickness, knock on..."

She glanced around for some wood to rap. She settled for wiggling a branch of one of the massive topiary trees guarding the front entrance.

"My breasts are swollen up like water balloons, though. And my nipples ache like you wouldn't believe." Grimacing, she rolled her shoulders to ease the constriction of her tight bodice. "They want *out* of this gown."

"For pity's sake, Eugenia!" The duchess shot a glance at the stony-faced limo driver. "Let's continue this discussion tomorrow, shall we?"

Nodding, Gina bent to kiss her grandmother's cheek and breathed in the faint, oh-so-familiar scent of lavender and lace. "Make sure you take your medicine before you go to bed."

"I'm not senile, young lady. I think I can manage to remember to take two little pills."

"Yes, ma'am."

Trying to look properly chastised, she helped the duchess into the limo and turned to the Honduran native who'd become a second mother to her and Sarah. "You'll stay with her, Maria? I shouldn't be more than another hour or two. I'll have a car take you home."

"Take as long as you need. *La duquesa* and I, we'll put our feet up and talk about what a fine job you did organizing such a beautiful wedding."

"It did come off well, didn't it?"

Maria beamed a wide smile. "*Sí, chica,* it did."

Buoyed by the compliment, Gina returned to the reception room. Most of the guests had departed. Including, she saw after a quick sweep, a certain obnoxious ambassador who'd shown up unexpectedly. She should have had him escorted out when he first walked in. Being summarily ejected from the wedding would have put a dent in the man's ego. Or maybe not. For a career diplomat, he seemed as impervious to Gina's snubs as to her adamant refusal to marry him. He didn't understand why she wouldn't even consider it for their baby's sake. Neither did the duchess. Although Grandmama and Sarah both supported Gina's decision to go it alone, she knew they wondered at her vehemence. On the surface, John Harris Mason III certainly made excellent husband material. He was rich, handsome and charming as the devil when he wanted to be.

It was what lurked below the surface that held Gina back. Every story, every bio printed about the charismatic diplomat, hinted that Jack had buried his heart with the young wife he'd first dated in high school and married the day they both graduated from Harvard. From all reports, Catherine Mason had been every bit as smart, athletic and politically involved as her husband.

Gina knew in her heart she couldn't compete with the ghost of his lost love. Not because she lacked her own set of credentials. The Duchy of Karlenburgh might now be little more than an obscure footnote in history books, but Grandmama could still hold her own with presidents and kings. What's more, she'd insisted her granddaughters be educated in accordance with their heritage. Gina had actually graduated from Barnard with a semi-decent grade point average.

She'd pretty much majored in partying, though, and to this day had zero interest in politics.

She might have cultivated an interest for Jack. Had actually toyed with the idea during that crazy weekend. For all her seemingly casual approach to life and love, she'd never met anyone as fascinating and entertaining and just plain hot as Jack Mason.

Any thoughts of fitting into the mold of a diplomat's wife went poof when Gina discovered she was pregnant. There was no way she could dive into politics *and* marriage *and* motherhood at the same time. She already felt as though she were on an emotional roller coaster. All she could think about right now, all she would *allow* herself to think about, was proving she could take care of herself and her baby.

"You put on a helluva party, lady."

Smiling, she turned to Dev's gravel-voiced buddy from his air force days. Patrick Donovan now served as Dev's executive assistant and pretty much ruled his vast empire with an iron fist.

"Thanks, Pat."

Tall and lanky and looking completely at home in his Armani tux, Donovan winked at her. "You decide you want to come back to L.A., you let me know. We could use someone with your organizational skills in our protocol office. Seems like we're hosting some bigwig industrialists from China or Germany or Australia every other week."

"I appreciate the offer but I'm going to try to break into the event-planning business here in New York. Plus, I'm thinking about moving in with Grandmama for the next eight months or so."

If the duchess would have her. They'd all been so busy these past few weeks with Sarah's wedding, Gina hadn't found the right time to broach the subject. Her sister heartily endorsed the plan, though. Both she and Gina hated the thought of the duchess living alone now that Sarah was moving out.

Okay! All right! So Gina needed a place to stay until she landed a job and became self-supporting. Despite her determination to prove herself, she had to have a base to build on. Grandmama wouldn't object to letting her move in. Probably.

"I've got some pretty good contacts in New York," Patrick was saying. "You want me to make a few calls? Grease the skids a little?"

"I need to do this on my own, Pat. But thanks for the offer."

"It stays on the table," he said with a shrug as he wrapped an arm around her shoulders and gave her a squeeze. "Call me if you change your mind. Or better yet, let your new brother-in-law know. Dev is complete mush right now. He'd set you up with your own agency if you so much as hint that's what you want. And let me know if you want me to close up your apartment in L.A. and have your things shipped here."

"I will. Thanks again."

Gina climbed out of a cab some two hours later. The Dakota's red sandstone turrets poked against the darkening night sky, welcoming her to the castlelike apartment complex that was one of New York City's most prestigious addresses. The duchess had bought an apartment here shortly after arriving in New York City. The purchase had put a serious dent in her cache of jewels, but careful investments during those first years, along with the discreet sale of a diamond bracelet here, a ruby necklace there, had allowed Charlotte to maintain the apartment and an elegant lifestyle over the decades.

Keeping up the facade had become much tougher in recent years. The jewels were gone. So were most of the haute couture gowns and designer suits that once filled her grandmother's closet. With her love of the classic retro look, Sarah had salvaged a number of the outfits and saved money by not splurging on new clothes for herself, but she'd had to struggle to cover the bills from her own salary.

Dev, bless him, wanted to make things easier for his wife's grandmother. But like the wedding expenses, taking over the duchess's financial affairs involved delicate negotiations that had yet to reach a satisfactory conclusion. Which put the burden on Gina's shoulders. She couldn't just move in and expect her grandmother to support her. She had to pay her own way.

On that determined note, she thanked Maria for staying so late and told her to sleep in the next morning. "I'll make breakfast for Grandmama."

The Honduran looked dubious. "Are you sure, *chica? La duquesa*, she likes her egg poached just so."

"I know. It has to sit for exactly four minutes after the heat's turned off."

"And her tea. It must be..."

"The Twinings English Black. I've got it covered. The car's waiting for you. Go home and get some rest."

Maria obviously had her doubts but gathered her suitcase-sized purse. "I'll see you tomorrow."

Gina was up and waiting when her grandmother walked into the kitchen just after eight-thirty the next morning. The duchess was impeccably dressed as always in a calf-length black skirt and lavender silk overblouse. Her hair formed its usual, neat snowy crown atop her head, but Gina saw with a quick dart of concern that she was leaning more heavily than she normally did on her cane.

"Good morning," she said, masking her worry behind a cheerful smile. "I got a text from Sarah a while ago. She says it's balmy and beautiful in Majorca."

"I expect it is. Are you doing breakfast?"

"I am. Sit, and I'll bring your tea."

Surprised and just a little wary, the duchess seated herself in the sunny breakfast room off the kitchen. Its ivy-sprigged wallpaper, green seat cushions and windows overlooking

Central Park seemed to bring the bright May spring right into the room.

Gina poured hot water over the leaves she'd measured into her grandmother's favorite Wedgwood teapot and placed the pot on the table. While the Twinings Black steeped, she popped some wheat bread in the toaster and brought a saucepan of water back to a boil before easing two raw eggs out of their shells. The sight of the yolks gave her a moment's qualm, but it passed. Still no twinge of morning nausea, thank God! With any luck, she'd escape that scourge altogether.

"Here we are."

She hadn't kept the yolks from breaking and going all runny, but the duchess thanked her with a smile and buttered her toast. Sensing there was something behind this special effort, she munched delicately on a corner of toast and waited patiently.

Gina pulled in a deep breath and took the plunge. "I was wondering, Grandmama..."

Dang! Admitting she was a screwup and needed to come live with her grandmother until she got her life in order was harder than she'd anticipated.

"I thought perhaps I might stay with you until I get a job. If you don't mind, that is."

"Oh, Eugenia!" Charlotte's reaction came swift and straight from the heart. "Of course I don't mind, my darling girl. This is your home. You must stay for as long as you wish. You and the baby."

Gina wasn't crying. She really wasn't. The tears just sort of leaked through her smile. "Thanks, Grandmama."

Her own lips a little wobbly, the duchess reached for her granddaughter's hand. "I admit I wasn't looking forward to rattling around this place by myself now that Sarah's moving out. I'm delighted you want to stay here. Will you need to fly back to L.A. to pack up your things?"

"Dev's assistant, Patrick, said he would take care of that if I decided to stay in New York."

"Good!" Charlotte gave her hand a quick squeeze and picked up her fork. "Now, what's this Sarah told me about you wanting to go into the catering business?"

"Not catering. Event planning. I did a little of it in L.A. Just enough to know I'm better at organizing and throwing parties than..." She managed a watery chuckle. "Than everything else I've tried."

"Well, you certainly did an excellent job with the wedding."

The praise sent Gina's spirits winging. "I did, didn't I?" She preened for a moment, her tears forgotten. "And the photographer from Sarah's magazine shot some amazing video and stills. He gave me a disk with enough material to put together a portfolio. I just emailed it to the woman I'm interviewing with this afternoon."

Her grandmother paused with her fork halfway to her lips. "You have an interview this afternoon?"

"I do. With Nicole Tremayne, head of the Tremayne Group. TTG operates a dozen different event venues, three right here in the city."

"Hmm. I knew a Nicholas Tremayne some years ago. Quite well, actually." Her thoughts seemed to go inward for a moment. Shaking them off, she lowered her fork. "This Nicole must be his daughter. If so, I'll call him and..."

"No, Grandmama, please don't."

The urgent plea brought a look of surprise. "Why ever not?"

"I want to do this on my own."

"That sentiment does you justice, Eugenia, but..."

"You don't have to say it. I know my track record doesn't suggest I'll make a very reliable employee. When you add the fact that I'm pregnant, it'll be a miracle if I land any job. I want to try, though, Grandmama. I really do."

"Very well. I'll refrain from interfering."

"Thank you. Dev and Patrick made the same promise. And I'll get Jack to do the same when I meet him for lunch today."

The duchess tilted her head. Sudden interest gleamed in her faded blue eyes. "You're having lunch with Jack? Why? I thought you'd said all you have to say to him."

"I did. Several times! The man won't take no for an answer."

"So again I ask, why are you having lunch with him?"

"He badgered me into it," Gina admitted in disgust. "You can see why I don't want to marry him."

The duchess took her time replying. When she did, she chose her words carefully.

"Are you sure, Eugenia? I treasure every moment I had with your mother and with you and Sarah, but I speak from experience when I say raising a child on your own can be quite terrifying at times."

"Oh, Grandmama!"

Her eyes misted again. Blinking furiously, Gina bared her soul. "I'm scared out my gourd. I admit it! The only thing that makes me even think I can do this is you, and the love you lavished on Sarah and me. You filled our lives with such joy, such grand adventures. You still do. I can give that to my child. I know I can."

A smile started in her grandmother's eyes and spread to Gina's heart.

"I know you can, too."

Gina had intended to spend the rest of the morning prepping for her interview with Nicole Tremayne. To her annoyance, her thoughts kept slipping away from party planning and instead landed on Jack Mason.

Her irritation increased even more when she found herself scowling at the few outfits she'd brought to New York with her. They were all flashy, all playful. Thigh-skimming skirts in bold prints. Tights in eye-popping colors. Spangled,

midriff-baring T-shirts. Reflective of her personality, maybe, but not the image she wanted to project to Ms. Tremayne. Or to a certain ambassador-at-large.

Abandoning the meager offering, she went next door to Sarah's room and rummaged through the designer classics her sister had salvaged from their grandmother's closet. After much debate and a pile of discards strewn across the bed, Gina decided on wide-legged black slacks. She topped them with a summer silk Valentino jacket in pearl gray that boasted a flower in the same fabric on one lapel. The jacket strained a bit at the bust but gave her the mature, responsible air she was aiming for. A wad of cotton stuffed into the toes of a pair of sensible black pumps added to the look. As a final touch, she went light on the makeup and wrestled her waterfall of platinum-blond curls into a French twist. When she studied the final result in the mirror, she gulped.

"Oh, God. I look like Grandmama."

If the duchess recognized herself, she mercifully refrained from saying so. But Gina caught the slightly stunned look she exchanged with Maria as her new, subdued granddaughter departed for her lunch meeting.

If Gina had needed further evidence of her transformation, she got it mere moments after walking into the Boathouse. A favorite gathering place of tourists and locals alike, the restaurant's floor-to-ceiling windows gave unimpeded views of the rowboats and gondolas gliding across Central Park's Reservoir Lake. Both the lake and the trees surrounding it were showcased against the dramatic backdrop of the Manhattan skyline.

The Boathouse's casual bar and restaurant buzzed with a crowd dressed in everything from business to smart casual to just plain comfortable. Despite the logjam, Gina spotted Jack immediately. As promised, he'd secured a table tucked in a quiet corner that still gave an unobstructed view of the lake. She stood for a moment at the top of the short flight of

steps leading down to the dining area and put a hand on the railing to steady herself.

Oh, Lord! Her hormones must be cartwheeling again. Why else would her knees get all wobbly at the way the sunlight streaked his tawny hair? Or her lungs wheeze like an old accordion at the sight of his strong, tanned hands holding up a menu? In the tux he'd worn to the wedding yesterday, Jack had wreaked havoc on her emotions. In a crisply starched pale blue shirt with the cuffs rolled up on muscled forearms lightly sprinkled with gold fuzz, he almost opened the floodgates.

She was still clinging to the wooden rail when he glanced up. His gaze swept the entrance area from left to right. Passed over her. Jerked back. He was too polished a diplomat to reveal more than a flash of surprise, but that brief glimpse gave Gina the shot in the arm she needed. Channeling the duchess at her most regal, she smiled at the head waiter, who hurried over to assist her.

"May I show you to a table?"

"Thank you, but I see the party I'm meeting."

She tipped her chin toward Jack, now rising from his chair. The waiter followed her gaze and offered a hand.

"Yes, of course. Please, watch your step."

Jack had recovered from his momentary surprise. Gina wasn't sure she liked the amusement that replaced it.

"I almost didn't recognize you," he admitted. "Are you going for a new look?"

"As a matter of fact, I am."

She took the seat next to him and considered how much to share of her plans. After a swift internal debate, she decided it might be good to let him know that she did, in fact, have plans.

"I'm also going for a new career. I have a job interview this afternoon with the head of the Tremayne Group. TTG is one of the biggest event-coordinating companies in the business, with venues in New York, Washington and Chicago."

The change in Jack was so subtle she almost missed it. Just a slight stiffening of his shoulders. She bristled, thinking he was going to object to her making a foray into the professional party world while carrying his child. Instead, he responded quietly, calmly.

"TTG also has a venue in Boston. My wife used them to coordinate our wedding."

Three

"Oh, Jack!"

Gina's soft heart turned instantly to mush. She didn't want to marry this man but neither did she want to hurt him. Ignoring the obvious inconsistency in that thought, she dug in her purse for her cell phone.

"I'm sorry. I didn't know you had that connection to TTG. I'll call and cancel my interview."

"Wait." Frowning, he put a hand on her arm. "I'll admit I would prefer not to see you pursue a career here in New York. Or anywhere else, for that matter. But…"

"But?"

Still frowning, he searched her face. "Are you really dead set against marriage, Gina?"

Her gaze dropped to his hand, so strong and tan against the paler skin of her forearm. The stress and confusion of the past weeks made a jumble of her reply.

"Sort of."

"What does that mean?"

She looked up and met his serious brown eyes. "I like you, Jack. When you're not coming on all huffy and autocratic, that is. And God knows we were fantastic together in bed."

So fantastic she had to slam the door on the images that thought conjured up.

"But I think…I know we both want more in a marriage."

He was silent, and Gina gathered her courage.

"Tell me about your wife. What was she like?"

He sat back, withdrawing his hand in the process. Withdrawing himself, as well. His glance shifted to the rowboats circling the lake. The ripples from their oars distorted the reflected images of the high-rises peeking above Central Park's leafy green tree line. The buildings seemed to sway on the lake's blue-green surface.

"Catherine was funny and smart and had a killer serve," he said finally, turning back to Gina. "She cleaned my clock every time we got on a tennis court. She might have turned pro if she hadn't lived, breathed and slept politics."

The waiter appeared at that moment. Gina ordered decaffeinated mango tea, Jack a refill of his coffee. They listened to the specials and let the menus sit on the table after the waiter withdrew. She was afraid the interruption had broken the thread of a conversation she knew had to be painful, but Jack picked it up again.

"Catherine and another campaign worker were going door-to-door to canvas unregistered voters for the presidential campaign. She suffered a brain aneurysm and collapsed. The docs say she was dead before she hit the sidewalk."

"I'm so sorry."

"We didn't learn until after the autopsy that she had Ehlers-Danlos syndrome. It's a rare, inherited condition that can cause the walls of your blood vessels to rupture. Which," he said as he eased a leather portfolio out from under his menu, "is why I prepared this."

"This" turned out to be a set of stapled papers. For a wild moment Gina thought they might be a prenup. Or a copy of a will, naming the baby as his heir if he should die as unexpectedly as Catherine had. Or…

"Your obstetrician will want a complete medical history

of both parents," he said calmly. "As far as I know, I haven't inherited any rare diseases but my father and grandfather both suffer from chronic high blood pressure and my mother is a breast cancer survivor. Who's your doctor, by the way?"

"I don't have one yet."

The frown came back. "Why the delay? You should've had your first prenatal checkup by now."

"It's on my list, right after getting resettled in New York and finding a job."

"Move the obstetrician to the top of the list," he ordered, switching into his usual take-charge mode. "I'll cover your medical expenses until you land a job."

"No, Mr. Ambassador, you won't."

"Oh, for…!"

He dropped the papers, closed his eyes for a moment and adopted a calm, soothing tone that made Gina want to hiss.

"Let's just talk this through. You're currently unemployed. I assume you have no health insurance. Few obstetricians will take you on as a patient unless there's some guarantee you can pay for their services."

"I. Will. Find. A. Job."

"Okay, okay." He held up a placating hand. "Even if you do land a job in the next few days or weeks, health benefits probably won't kick in for at least six months. And then they may not cover preexisting conditions."

Well, crap! Gina hadn't considered that. Her throat closed as her carefully constructed house of cards seemed to teeter and topple right before her eyes.

No! No, dammit! Hormones or no hormones, she would not break down and bawl in front of Jack.

He must have sensed her fierce struggle for control. His expression softened, and he dropped the grating, let's-be-reasonable tone. "This is my baby, too, Gina. Let me help however I can."

She could handle autocratic and obnoxious. Nice was

harder to manager. Shoving back her chair, she pushed away from the table.

"I have to go to the bathroom."

After some serious soul-searching, she returned from the ladies' room to find the waiter had delivered their drinks. Gina dumped artificial sweetener in her tea and took a fortifying sip before acknowledging the unpalatable truth.

"I guess I didn't think this whole insurance thing through. If it turns out I can't get medical benefits in time to cover my appointments with an obstetrician, I would appreciate your help."

"You've got it." He hesitated a moment before extending another offer. "Finding a good doctor isn't easy, especially with everything else you have going on right now. Why don't I call my chief of staff and have him email you a list of the top OB docs in the city? He can also verify that they're accepting new patients."

And coordinate the payment process, Gina guessed. Swallowing her pride, she nodded. "I'd appreciate that."

"Just call me when you decide on a doctor. Or call Dale Vickers, my chief of staff. He'll make sure your appointments get on my schedule."

"Your schedule?"

"I'll fly up from D.C. to go with you, of course. Assuming I'm in the country."

"Oh. Of course."

The sense that she could do this on her own was rapidly slipping away. Trying desperately to hang on to her composure, Gina picked up her menu.

"We'd better order. My appointment at the Tremayne Group is at two-thirty."

Jack's hand hovered over his menu. "This might sound a little crass but between Catherine's family and mine, we spent an obscene amount of money on our wedding. I could make a call and…"

"No!"

Gina gritted her teeth. Was she the only person in the whole friggin' universe who didn't have an inside connection at TTG? And the only fool who refused to exploit that connection? Sheer stubbornness had her shaking her head.

"No calls. No pulling strings. No playing the big ambassadorial cheese. I have to do this myself."

He lifted a tawny brow but didn't press the point. After signaling the waiter over to take their orders, he steered the conversation into more neutral channels.

The awkwardness of the situation eased, and Gina's spirits took an upward swing. Jack soon had her laughing at some of his more humorous exploits in the field and realizing once again how charming he could be when he wanted to.

And sexy. So damned sexy. She savored the lump crab cake she'd ordered for lunch and couldn't help admiring the way the tanned skin at the corners of his eyes crinkled when he smiled. And how the light reflecting off the lake added glints to the sun-streaked gold of his hair. When he leaned forward, Gina caught the ripple of muscle under his starched shirt. She found herself remembering how she'd run her palms over all that hard muscle. That tight butt. Those iron thighs. The bunched biceps and...

"Gina?"

She almost choked on a lump of crab. "Sorry. What were you saying?"

"I was asking if you'd consider coming down to D.C. for a short visit. I'd like to show you my home and introduce you to my parents."

The request was reasonable. Naturally Jack's parents would want to meet the mother of their grandchild. From the little he'd let drop about his staunchly conservative father, though, Gina suspected John Harris Mason II probably wouldn't greet her with open arms.

"Let's talk about that later," she hedged. "After I get settled and find a job."

They finished lunch and lingered a few minutes over tea and coffee refills. Gina's nerves had started to get jittery by the time they exited the Boathouse. Jack walked with her through the park now filled with bicyclers and in-line skaters and sun worshippers sprawled on benches with eyes closed and faces tilted to the sky.

A group of Japanese tourists had congregated at Bethesda Fountain and were busy snapping photos of each other with the bronze statue of the *Angel of the Waters* towering over them. At the shy request of one of the younger members of the group, Jack obligingly stopped to take a picture of the whole party. Everyone wanted a copy on their own camera so Gina ended up acting as a runner, passing him ten or twelve cameras before they were done. By the time they reached Fifth Avenue and Jack hailed a cab to take her to her interview, she was feeling the pressure of time.

"Keep your fingers crossed," she said without thinking as the cab pulled over to the curb.

Only as he reached to open the door for her did she remember that he would prefer she didn't land this—or any job—in New York. He made no secret of the fact that he wanted to put a ring on her finger and take care of her and their child. To his credit, he buried those feelings behind an easy smile.

"I'll do better than that. Here's a kiss for luck."

He kept it light. Just a brush of his lips over hers. On the first pass, at least.

Afterward Gina could never say for sure who initiated the second pass. All she knew was that Jack hooked a hand behind her nape, she went up on tiptoe and what had started as a friendly good-luck token got real deep and real hungry.

When he finally raised his head, she saw herself reflected in his eyes. "I…I have to go!"

He stepped back and gave her room to make an escape. She slid into the cab and spent the short drive to the Tremayne Group's headquarters trying desperately to remember all the reasons why she wanted—no, needed!—this job.

* * *

At three-ten, she was reiterating that same grim list. She'd been sitting in Nicole Tremayne's ultramodern outer office for more than half an hour while a harried receptionist fielded phone calls and a succession of subordinates rushed in and out of the boss's office. Any other time Gina would have walked out after the first fifteen or twenty minutes. She didn't have that luxury now.

Instead, she'd used the time to reread the information she'd found on Google about the Tremayne Group. She also studied every page in the slick, glossy brochure given out to prospective clients. Even then she had to unlock her jaw and force a smile when the receptionist finally ushered her into the inner sanctum.

Stunned, Gina stopped dead. This dark cavern was the command center of a company that hosted more than two thousand events a year at a dozen different venues? And this tiny whirlwind erupting from behind her marble slab of a desk was the famed Nicole Tremayne?

She couldn't have been more than five-one, and she owed at least four of those inches to her needle-heeled ankle boots. Gina was still trying to marry the bloodred ankle boots to her salt-and-pepper corkscrew curls when Nicole thrust out a hand.

"Sorry to keep you waiting. You're Eugenia, right? Eugenia St. Sebastian?"

"Yes, I…"

"My father had a thing for your grandmother. I was just a kid at the time, but I remember he talked about leaving my mother for her."

"Oh. Well, uh…"

"He should have. My mother was a world-class ballbreaker." Swooping a thick book of fabric swatches off one of the chairs in front of her desk, Tremayne dumped it on the floor. "Sit, sit."

Still slightly stunned, Gina sat. Nicole cleared the chair

next to hers and perched on its edge with the nervous energy of a hummingbird.

"I looked at the digital portfolio of your sister's wedding. Classy job. You did all the arrangements?"

"With some help."

"Who from?"

"Andrew, at the Plaza. And Patrick Donovan. He's..."

"Dev Hunter's right-hand man. I know. We coordinated a major charity event for Hunter's corporation last year. Three thousand attendees at two thousand a pop. So when can you start?"

"Excuse me?"

"One of the assistant event planners at our midtown venue just got busted for possession. She's out on bail, but I can't have a user working for TTG." Her bird-bright eyes narrowed on Gina. "You don't do dope, do you?"

"No."

"I'd better not find out otherwise."

"You won't."

Tremayne nodded. "Here's the thing. You have a lousy work record but a terrific pedigree. If you inherited half your grandmother's class and a quarter of her smarts, you should be able to handle this job."

Gina wasn't sure whether she'd just been complimented or insulted. She was still trying to decide when her prospective boss continued briskly.

"You also grew up here in the city. You know your way around and you know how to interact with the kind of customers we attract. Plus, the classy digital portfolio you sent me shows you've got a flair for design and know computers. Whether you can handle vendors and show yourself as a team player remains to be seen, but I'm willing to give you a shot. When can you start?"

Tomorrow!

The joyous reply was almost out before Gina caught it. Gulping, she throttled back her exhilaration.

"I can start anytime but there's something I need to tell you before we go any further."

"What's that?"

"I'm pregnant."

"And I'm Episcopalian. So?"

Could it really be this easy? Gina didn't think so. Suspicion wormed through her elation.

"Did my grandmother call you?" she asked. "Or Pat Donovan?"

"No."

Her jaw locked. Dammit! It had to have been Jack.

"Then I assume you talked to the ambassador," she said stiffly.

"What ambassador?"

"Jack Mason."

"Jack Mason." Tremayne tapped her chin with a nail shellacked the same red as her ankle boots. "Why do I know that name?"

Gina didn't mention that TTG had coordinated Jack's wedding. For reasons she would have to sort out later, that cut too close to the bone.

"Who is he," Tremayne asked, "and why would he call me?"

"He's a friend." That was the best she could come up with. "I told him about our interview and…and thought he might have called to weigh in."

"Well, it certainly never hurts to have an ambassador in your corner, but no, he didn't call me. So what's the deal here? Do you want the job or not?"

There were probably a dozen different questions she should ask before jumping into the fray. Like how much the job paid, for one. And what her hours would be. And whether the position came with benefits. At the moment, though, Gina was too jazzed to voice any of the questions buzzing around in her head.

"Yes, ma'am, I do."

"Good. Have my assistant direct you to the woman who handles our personnel matters. You can fill out all the necessary forms there. And call me Nikki," she added as her new employee sprang out of her chair to shake on the deal.

Gina left the Tremayne Group's personnel office thirty or forty forms later. The salary was less than she'd hoped for but the description of her duties made her grin. As assistant events coordinator she would be involved in all phases of operation for TTG's midtown venue. Scheduling parties and banquets and trade shows. Devising themes to fit the clients' desires. Creating menus. Contracting with vendors to supply food and decorations and bar stock. Arranging for limos, for security, for parking.

Even better, the personnel officer had stressed that there was plenty of room for advancement within TTG. The tantalizing prospect of a promotion danced before Gina's eyes as she exited the high-rise housing the company's headquarters. When she hit the still glorious May sunshine, she had to tell someone her news. Her first, almost instinctive, impulse was to call Jack. She actually had her iPhone in hand before she stopped to wonder why.

Simple answer. She wanted to crow a little.

Not so simple answer. She wanted to prove she wasn't all fun and fluff.

With a wry grimace, she acknowledged that she should probably wait until she'd actually performed in her new position for a few weeks or months before she made that claim. She decided to text Sarah instead. The message was short and sweet.

I'm now a working mom-to-be. Call when you and Dev come up for air.

She took a cab back to the Upper West Side and popped out at a deli a few blocks from the Dakota. Osterman's had

occupied the same choice corner location since the Great Depression. Gina and Sarah had developed their passion for corned beef at the deli's tiny, six-table eating area. The sisters still indulged whenever they were in the city, but Gina's target tonight was the case displaying Osterman's world famous cheesecakes. With unerring accuracy, she went for a selection that included her own, her grandmother's and Maria's favorites.

"One slice each of the white chocolate raspberry truffle, the key lime and the Dutch apple caramel, please. And one pineapple upside down," she added on an afterthought.

The boxed cheesecake wedges in hand, she plucked a bottle of chilled champagne from the cooler in the wine corner. She had to search for a nonalcoholic counterpart but finally found it in with the fruit juices. Driven by the urge to celebrate, she added a wedge of aged brie and a loaf of crusty bread to her basket. On her way to check out she passed a shelf containing the deli's selection of caviars.

The sticker price of a four-ounce jar of Caspian Sea Osetra made her gasp. Drawing in a steadying breath, she reminded herself it was Grandmama's caviar of choice. The duchess considered Beluga too salty and Sevruga too fishy. Gina made a quick calculation and decided her credit card would cover the cost of one jar. Maybe.

"Oh, what the hell."

To her relief, she got out of Osterman's without having the credit card confiscated. A block and a half later she approached the Dakota with all her purchases.

"Let me help you with those!"

The doorman who'd held his post for as long as she could remember leaped forward. Although she would never say so to his face, Gina suspected Jerome assumed his present duties about the same time Osterman's opened its doors.

"You should have called a cab, Lady Eugenia."

Sarah and Gina had spent most of their adult years try-

ing to get Jerome to drop their empty titles. They'd finally agreed it was a wasted effort.

"I'm okay," Gina protested as he tried to relieve her of her burdens. "Except for this."

She sorted through her purchases and fished out a wedge-shaped box. Jerome peeked inside and broke into a grin.

"Pineapple upside down! Trust you to remember my favorite."

Gina's emotions jumped on the roller coaster again as she thought about his devoted loyalty to her and Grandmama over the years.

"How could I forget?" she said with a suspicious catch to her voice. "You slipped me an extra few dollars every time I said I was going to Osterman's."

For a moment she thought the embarrassed doorman would pat her on the head as he'd done so many times when she was a child. He controlled the impulse and commented instead on the bottles poking out of her bag.

"Still celebrating Lady Sarah's wedding?"

"Nope. This celebration is in my honor."

Riding her emotional roller coaster to its gravity-defying apex, she poured out her news.

"I'm moving back to New York, Jerome."

"Lady Eugenia! That's wonderful news. I admit I was a bit worried about the duchess."

"There's more. I've got a job."

"Good for you."

"Oh," she added over her shoulder as she made for the lobby. "I'm also pregnant."

Four

Gina walked into the Tremayne Group's midtown venue at 9:30 a.m. the next morning. She didn't drag out again until well past midnight.

Her first impression was *wow!* What had once been a crumbling brick warehouse overlooking the East River was now a glass-fronted, ultra-high-rent complex of offices, restaurants and entertainment venues. TTG occupied a slightly recessed four-story suite smack in the center of the complex. The primo location allowed into a private ground-floor courtyard with bubbling fountains and a top-floor terrace that had to offer magnificent views of the river.

A young woman with wings of blue in her otherwise lipstick-red hair sat at a curved glass reception desk and fielded phone calls. Gina waited until she finished with one caller and put two others on hold to introduce herself.

"I'm Gina St. Sebastian. I'm the new…"

"Assistant coordinator. Thank God you're here! I'm Kallie. Samuel's in the banquet hall. He said to send you right up. Third floor. The elevators are to your right."

Gina used the ride to do a quick check in mirrored panels. She'd left her hair down today but confined the silky curls behind a wide fuchsia headband studded with crystals. A

belt in the same hot pink circled the waist of her apple-green
J. Crew tunic. Since this was her first day on the job she'd
gone with sedate black tights instead of the colorful prints
she preferred. She made a quick swipe with her lip gloss and
drew in a deep, steadying breath. Then the elevator door
glided open and she stepped out into a vortex of sound and
fury.

What looked like a small army of workers in blue overalls
was yanking folded chairs from metal-sided carrier racks,
popping them open and thumping them around a room full
of circluar tables. Another crew, this one in black pants and
white shirts, scurried after the first. They draped each chair
in shimmering green, the tables in cloth of gold. Right behind
them came yet another crew rattling down place settings of
china and crystal. The *rat-tat-tat* of staple guns fired by intent set designers erecting a fantastic Emerald City added
to the barrage of noise, while the heady scent of magnolias
wafted from dozens of tall topiaries stacked on carts waiting to be rolled to the tables.

Soaking up the energy like a sponge, Gina wove her way
through the tables to a wild-haired broomstick with a clipboard in one hand, a walkie-talkie in the other and a Bluetooth headset hooked over one ear. "Not *The Wizard of Oz,*"
he was shouting into the headset. "Christ, who does Judy
Garland anymore? This is the new movie. *Oz the... Oz the...*"

Scowling, he snapped his fingers at Gina.

"Oz the Great and Powerful," she dutifully asserted.

"Right. *Oz the Great and Powerful.* It's a Disney flick
starring Rachel Weisz and..."

More finger snaps.

"Mila Kunis."

"Right. Mila Kunis. That's the music the clients requested." The scowl deepened. "Hell, no, I don't! Hold on."

He whipped his head around and barked at Gina. "You
the new AC?"

"Yes."

"I'm Samuel DeGrange."

"Nice to…"

He brushed aside the pleasantries with an impatient hand. "Go upstairs and tell the DJ to pull his head out of his ass. The clients don't want Dorothy and Toto, for God's sake! Then make sure the bar supervisor knows how to mix the fizzy green juice concoction that's supposed to make the kids think they're dancing down a new, improved Yellow Brick Road."

Eight and a half hours later Gina was zipped into the Glinda the Good Witch costume that had been rented for her predecessor and making frantic last-minute changes to seating charts. Kallie the receptionist—now garbed as a munchkin—wielded a calligraphy pen to scribble out place cards for the twenty additional guests the honoree's mother had somehow forgotten she'd invited until she was in the limo and on her way from Temple with the newly bat mitz-vahed Rachel.

Another six hours later, Gina collapsed into a green-draped chair and gazed at the rubble. Iridescent streamers in green and gold littered the dance floor. Scattered among them was a forgotten emerald tiara here, an empty party-favors box there. The booths where the seventy-five kids invited to celebrate Rachel's coming of age had fired green lasers and demolished video villains were being dismantled. Only a few crumbs remained of the fourteen-layer cake with its glittering towers and turrets. The kids invited to the party had devoured it with almost as much gusto as the more than two hundred parents, grandparents, aunts, uncles, cousins and family friends had drained the open bar upstairs.

Gina stretched out her feet in their glittery silver slippers and aimed a grin at the toothpick-thin Tin Man who flopped into the chair beside her.

"This party business is fun."

"You think?" Samuel shoved back his tin hat and gave her a jaundiced smile. "Talk to me again after you've had an inebriated best man puke all over you. Or spent two hours sifting through piles of garbage to find a guest's diamond-and-sapphire earrings. Which, incidentally, she calls to tell you she found in her purse."

"At least she let you know she found it," Gina replied, laughing.

"She's one of the few. Seems like our insurance rates take another jump after every event." He slanted her a sideways glance. "You did good tonight, St. Sebastian. Better than I expected when I read your resumé."

"Thanks. I think."

"You need to keep a closer finger on the pulse of the party, though. The natives got a little restless before the cake was brought out."

Gina bit her lip. No need to remind her new boss that he'd sent her out to the terrace to shepherd some underage smokers back inside right when the cake was supposed to have been presented.

"I'll watch the timing," she promised.

"So go home now. I'll do the final bar count and leave this mess to the cleaning crew."

She wasn't about to argue. "I'll see you tomorrow."

"Nine sharp," he warned. "We've got a preliminary wedding consult. I'll talk, you listen and learn."

She popped a salute. "Yes, sir."

"Christ! You got enough energy left for that?" He didn't wait for an answer, just shooed her away. "Get out of here."

The *Oz the Great and Powerful* bat mitzvah set the stage for the dozens of events that followed during the busy, busy month of May. Almost before she knew it Gina was caught up in a whirl of wedding and engagement and anniversary and graduation and coming-of-age parties. She gained both experience and confidence with each event.

So much so that Samuel soon delegated full responsibility for computing and placing orders with the subs for everything from decorations to bar stock. He also tapped her for fresh ideas for themes and settings. In rapid succession she helped plan a white-on-white wedding, a red-and-black "Puttin' on the Ritz" debutante ball and a barefoot-on-the-beach engagement party at a private Hamptons estate. And then there was her grand coup—snaring Justin Bieber for a brief appearance at the national Girl Scout banquet to be held in the fall. He was in town for another event and Gina played shamelessly on his agent's heartstrings until every teen's favorite heartthrob agreed.

Not all events went smoothly. Frantically working her cell phone and walkie-talkie, Gina learned to cope with minor crises like a forgotten kosher meal for the rabbi, a groom caught frolicking in the fourth-floor bridal suite shower with the maid of honor and a drunken guest held hostage by an irate limo driver demanding payment for damage done to the vehicle's leather seats.

In the midst of all the craziness she unpacked the boxes Dev's assistant had shipped back from L.A. and welcomed her sister and her new brother-in-law home from their honeymoon. Gina and Sarah and the duchess were all teary-eyed when the newlyweds departed again, this time to look at homes for sale close to Dev's corporate headquarters in California.

Miracle of miracles, Gina also managed to snag an appointment with the top OB doc on the short list of three Jack had emailed. She suspected he'd used his influence or family clout to make sure she got in to see one of them. She didn't object to outside help in this instance. The health of her baby took precedence over pride.

As promised, she called Jack's office to let him know about the appointment. A secretary routed her to his chief of staff.

"This is Dale Vickers, Ms. St. Sebastian. The ambassador is in conference. May I help you?"

"Jack asked me to let him know the date and time of my prenatal appointment. It's Thursday of next week, at three-fifteen, with Dr. Sondra Martinson."

"I'm looking at his calendar now. The ambassador is unavailable next Thursday. Please reschedule the appointment and call me back."

The reply was as curt as it was officious. Gina held out the phone and looked at it in surprise for a moment before putting it to her ear again.

"Tell you what," she said, oozing sweetness and light, "just tell Jack to call me. We'll take it from there."

The man must have realized his mistake. Softening his tone, he tried to regain lost ground.

"I'm sorry if I sounded abrupt, Ms. St. Sebastian. It's just that the ambassador is participating all next week in a conference with senior State Department officials. They're assessing U.S. embassy security in light of recent terrorist attacks. I can't overstate the importance of this conference to the safety and security of our consular personnel abroad."

Properly put in her place, Gina was about to concede the point when he made a suggestion.

"Why don't I call Dr. Martinson's office and arrange an appointment that fits with the ambassador's schedule?"

"That won't work. We need to work around my schedule, too."

"I'm sure you can squeeze something in between parties for twelve-year-olds."

The barely disguised put-down dropped Gina's jaw. What was with this character? Sheer obstinacy had her oozing even more saccharine.

"I'm sure I can. After all, the tab for our last twelve-year-old's party only ran to sixty-five thousand dollars and change. Just have Jack call me. We'll work something out."

"Really, Ms. St. Sebastian, we don't have to trouble the ambassador with such a trivial matter."

Heat shot to every one of Gina's extremities. Given her normally sunny and fun-loving disposition, she'd never believed that old cliché about seeing red. She did now.

"Listen, asshole, you may consider the ambassador's baby a trivial matter. I'm pretty sure he won't agree. The appointment is for three-fifteen next Thursday. End of discussion."

As instructed, she arrived at Dr. Martinson's office a half hour prior to her scheduled appointment. The time was required for a final review and signature on the forms she'd downloaded from the office website. She hadn't heard from Jack or from his stick-up-the-butt chief of staff. So when she walked into the reception area and didn't spot a familiar face, she wasn't surprised.

What did surprise her was how deep the disappointment went. She'd been so busy she hadn't had time to dwell on the confused feelings Jack Mason stirred in her. Except at night, when she dropped into bed exhausted and exhilarated and wishing she had someone to share the moments of her day with. Or when her body reminded her that she wasn't its sole inhabitant anymore. Or when she happened to spot a tall, tanned male across the room or on the street or in the subway.

"Don't be stupid," she muttered as she signed form after form. "He's making the world safer for our embassy people. That has to take precedence."

She was concentrating so fiercely on the clipboard in her hand that she didn't hear the door to the reception area open.

"Good, I'm not late."

The relieved exclamation brought her head up with a jerk.

"Jack! I thought… Vickers said…"

Of all the idiotic times to get teary-eyed! How could she handle every crisis at work with a cheerful smile and turn into such a weepy wimp around this man? She had to jump off this emotional roller coaster.

"Vickers told me what he said." Grinning, he dropped into the chair beside hers. "He also told me what you said."

"Yes, well, you shouldn't piss off a preggo. The results aren't pretty."

"I'll remember that."

Guilt wormed through the simple, hedonistic pleasure of looking at his handsome face. She let the clipboard drop to her lap and made a wry face.

"You shouldn't have come. Vickers said you had a top-level conference going on all week."

"We wrapped up the last of the key issues this morning. All that's left is to approve the report once it gets drafted. I can do that by secure email. Which means," he said as he took the clipboard and flipped through the forms, "I don't have to fly back to D.C. right away. Here, you forgot to sign this one."

She scribbled her signature and tried not to read too much into his casual comment about extending his trip up from D.C. Didn't work. When he tacked on an equally casual invitation, her heart gave a little bump.

"If you don't have plans, I thought I might take you and the duchess to dinner tonight."

"Oh, I can't. I'm working a fiftieth anniversary party. I had to sneak out for this appointment."

"How about tomorrow?"

The bump was bigger this time. "Are you staying over that long?"

"Actually, I told Dale to clear the entire weekend."

"Ha! Bet he loved that."

"He's not so bad, Gina. You two just got off on the wrong foot."

"Wrong foot, wrong knee, wrong hip and elbow. How long has he worked for you, anyway?"

"Five years."

"And no one's ever told you he's officious or condescending?"

"No."

"It has to be me, then." Grimacing, she rolled out the reason she suspected might be behind his aide's less-than-enthusiastic response to her call. "Or the fact that the paparazzi will have a field day when they hear you knocked me up."

"They probably will," he replied, not quite suppressing a wince. "But when they do, you might want to use a different phrase to describe the circumstances."

"Really? What phrase do you suggest I use, Mr. Ambassador?"

He must have seen the chasm yawning at his feet. "Sorry. I didn't mean to come across as such a pompous jerk."

The apology soothed Gina's ruffled feathers enough for her to acknowledge his point. "I'm sorry, too. I know the pregnancy will cause you some embarrassment. I'll try not to add to it."

"The only embarrassing aspect to this whole situation is that I can't convince the beautiful and very stubborn mother of my child to marry me."

She wanted to believe him, but she wasn't that naive. She chewed on her lower lip for a moment before voicing the worry that had nagged her since Switzerland.

"Tell me the truth, Jack. Is this going to impact your career?"

"No."

"Maybe not at the State Department, but what about afterward? I read somewhere that certain powerful PACs think you have a good shot at the presidency in the not-too-distant future."

"Gina, listen to me." He curled a knuckle under her chin and tipped her face to make sure he had her complete attention. "We met, we were attracted to each other, we spent some time together. Since neither of us were then, or are now, otherwise committed, the only ones impacted by the result of that meeting are you, me and our baby."

"Wow," she breathed. "That was some speech, Mr. Ambassador. Those PACs may be right. You should make a bid for the Oval Office. You'd get my vote."

He feathered the side of her jaw with his thumb. "I'd rather get your signature on a marriage license."

Maybe…maybe she was being blind and pigheaded and all wrong about this marriage thing. So he didn't love her? He wanted her, and God knew she wanted him. Couldn't their child be the bridge to something more?

The thought made her cringe inside. What kind of mother would pile her hopes and dreams on a baby's tiny shoulders?

"We've had this discussion." Shrugging, she pulled away from his touch. "Let's not get into it again."

Surprise darkened his brown eyes, followed by a touch of what could have been either disappointment or irritation. Before Gina could decide which, a nurse in pink-and-blue scrubs decorated with storks delivering bundles of joy popped into the waiting room.

"Ms. St. Sebastian?"

"Right here."

"If you'll come with me, I'll get your height and weight and show you to an exam room."

Gina pushed out her chair. Jack rose with her. The nurse stopped him with a friendly smile. "Please wait here, Mr. St. Sebastian. I'll come get you in a few minutes."

The look on his face was more than enough to disperse Gina's glum thoughts. Choking back a laugh, she floated after the nurse. When Jack joined her in the exam room five minutes later, she was wearing a blue paper gown tied loosely in the front and a fat grin.

"I set her straight on the names."

"Uh-huh."

"Come on," she teased. "You have to admit it was funny."

The only thing in Jack's mind at the moment was not something he could admit. How could he have forgotten how full and lush and ripe her breasts were? Or had her pregnancy

enhanced the creamy slopes he glimpsed through the front opening of her gown?

Whatever! That one glimpse was more than enough to put him in a sweat. Thoroughly disgusted, he was calling himself all kinds of a pig when the doctor walked in.

"Hello, Ms. St. Sebastian. I'm Dr. Martinson."

Petite and gray-haired, she shook hands with her patient before turning to Jack. "And you're Ambassador Mason, the baby's father?"

"That's right."

"I read through your medical and family histories. I'm so pleased neither of you smoke, use drugs, or drink to excess. That makes my job so much easier."

She included Jack in her approving smile before addressing Gina.

"I'm going to order lab tests to confirm your blood type and Rh status. We'll also check for anemia, syphilis, hepatitis B and the HIV virus, as well as your immunity to rubella and chicken pox. I want you to give a urine sample, as well."

Her down-to-earth manner put her patient instantly at ease…right up until the moment she extracted a pair of rubber gloves from a dispenser mounted on the wall.

"Let's get the pelvic exam out of the way, then we'll talk about what to expect in the next few weeks and months."

She must have caught the consternation that flooded into Gina's china blue eyes. Without missing a beat, the doc snapped on the gloves and issued a casual order.

"Why don't you wait outside, Ambassador Mason? This will only take a few moments."

Five

When Jack accompanied Gina out of the medical plaza complex and into the early throes of the Thursday evening rush hour, he was feeling a little shell-shocked.

The news that he would be a father had surprised the hell out of him initially. Once he'd recovered, he'd progressed in quick order from consternation to excitement to focusing his formidable energy on hustling the mother of his child to the altar. Now, with a copy of *A Father's Guide to Pregnancy* tucked in the pocket of his suit coat and the first prenatal behind him, he was beginning to appreciate both the reality and the enormity of the road ahead.

Gina, amazingly, seemed to be taking her pregnancy in stride. Like a gloriously painted butterfly, she'd gone through an almost complete metamorphosis. Not that she'd had much choice. With motherhood staring her in the face, she appeared to have shed her fun-loving, party-girl persona. The hysterical female who'd called Jack from Switzerland had also disappeared. Or maybe those personas had combined to produce this new Gina. Still bubbling with life, still gorgeous beyond words, but surprisingly responsible.

She'd listened attentively to everything the doctor said, asked obviously well-thought-out questions and made care-

ful notes of the answers. She also worked the calendar on her iPhone with flying fingers to fit a visit to the lab for the required blood tests and future appointments with Dr. Martinson into her schedule.

In between, she fielded a series of what had sounded like frantic calls from work with assurances that yes, she'd confirmed delivery of the ice sculpture; no, their clients hadn't requested special permission from the New York City Department of Corrections for their grandson currently serving time at Rikers to attend their fiftieth wedding anniversary celebration; and yes, she'd just left the doctor's office and was about to jump in a cab.

Jack waited on the sidewalk beside her while she finished that last call. The sky was gray and overcast but the lack of sunshine didn't dim the luster of her hair. The tumble of shining curls and the buttercup-yellow tunic she wore over patterned yellow-and-turquoise tights made her a beacon of bright cheer in the dismal day.

Jack stood beside her, feeling a kick to the gut as he remembered exploring the lush curves under that bright tunic. Remembering, too, the kiss they'd shared the last time he put her in a cab. He'd spent more time trying to analyze his reaction to that kiss than he wanted to admit. It was hot and heavy on his mind when Gina finished her call.

"I have to run," she told him. "If you still want to take Grandmama and me to dinner, I could do tomorrow evening."

"That works."

"I'll check with her to make sure tomorrow's okay and give you a call."

He stepped to the curb and flagged a cab. She started to duck inside and hesitated.

Was she remembering the last time he'd put her in a cab, too? Jack's stomach went tight with the anticipation of taking her in his arms again. He'd actually taken a step forward when she issued a tentative invitation.

"Would you like to see where I work?"

The intensity of his disappointment surprised him, but he disguised it behind an easy smile. "Yeah, I would."

"It'll have to be a brief tour," she warned when they got in the cab. "We're in the final throes of an anniversary celebration with two hundred invited guests."

"Not including the grandson at Rikers."

She made a face. "Keep your fingers crossed he doesn't break out! I have visions of NYPD crashing through the doors just when we parade the cake."

"You parade cakes?"

"Sometimes. And in this instance, we'll do it very carefully! We're talking fifteen layers replicating the Cape Hatteras lighthouse that stands on the spot where our honorees got engaged."

She thumbed her iPhone and showed Jack an image of the iconic black-and-white striped lighthouse still guarding the shores of North Carolina's Outer Banks.

"We're doing an actual working model. The caterer and I had several sticky sessions before we figured out how to bury the battery pack in the cake base and power up the strobe light at the top without melting all his pretty sugar frosting into a black-and-white blob."

"I'm impressed."

And not just with the ingenuity and creativity she obviously brought to her new job. Enthusiasm sparkled in her blue eyes, and the vibrancy that had first snared his interest bubbled to the surface again.

"Hopefully, our clients will be impressed, too. We're decorating the entire venue in an Outer Banks theme. All sand, seashells and old boats, with enough fishnet and colorful buoys to supply the Atlantic fleet."

Unbidden and unwanted, a comparison surfaced between the woman beside him and the woman he'd loved with every atom of his being. The vivid images of Catherine were starting to fade, though, despite Jack's every effort to hang on

to them. He had to dig deep to remember the sound of her laughter. Strain to hear an echo of her chuckle. She'd been so socially and politically involved. So serious about the issues that mattered to her. She had fun, certainly, but she hadn't regarded life as a frothy adventure the way Gina seemed to. Nor would she have rebounded so quickly from the emotional wringer of Switzerland.

As his companion continued her lighthearted description of tonight's event, Jack's memories of his wife retreated to the shadows once again. Even the shadows got blasted away when he and Gina exited the elevators onto the third floor of the Tremayne Group's midtown venue.

They could be on the Outer Banks, right at the edge of the Atlantic. Bemused, Jack took in the rolling sand dunes, the upended rowboat, the electronic waves splashing across a wall studded with LED lights.

"Wow. Is this all your doing?" he asked Gina.

"Not hardly. Mostly my boss, Samuel, and...uh-oh! There's Samuel now. He's with our big boss. 'Scuse me a minute. I'd better find out what's up."

Jack recognized the diminutive woman with the salt-and-pepper corkscrew curls at first look. Nicole Tremayne hadn't changed much in the past eight years. One of the underlings in her Boston operation had handled most of the planning for Jack's wedding to Catherine, but Nicole had approved the final plans herself and flown up from New York to personally oversee the lavish affair.

He saw the moment she recognized him, too. The casual glance she threw his way suddenly sharpened into a narrow-eyed stare. Frowning, she exchanged a few words with Gina, then crossed the floor.

"John Harris Mason." She thrust out a hand. "I should have made the connection when Gina demanded to know if Jack Mason had contacted me."

"I hope you told her no. She almost bit off my head when I offered to call and put in a word for her."

"She did? Interesting."

Chin cocked, Tremayne studied him through bird-bright eyes. She wasn't so crass as to come out and ask if he were the father of Gina's baby but Jack could see the speculation rife in her face.

"I was sorry to hear about your wife," she said after a moment.

"Thank you."

God, what a useless response. But Jack had uttered it so many times now that the words didn't taste quite as bitter in his mouth.

"Are you still in Boston?" she asked.

"No, I'm with the State Department now. Right now I'm assigned to D.C."

"Hmm." She tapped a bloodred nail against her chin. "Good to know."

With that enigmatic comment she excused herself and returned to her underlings. Gina rushed over a few moments later.

"I'm so sorry, Jack. We'll have to postpone the tour. I've got to take care of an ice-sculpture crisis."

"No problem. Just let me know if tomorrow evening's a go for the duchess."

"I will."

The following evening was not only a go, but the duchess's acceptance also came with an invitation for drinks at the Dakota prior to dinner.

Jack spent all that day at the NYPD Counterterrorism Bureau established after 9/11. While coordination between federal, state and local agencies had increased exponentially since that horrific day, there was always room for improvement. The NYPD agents were particularly interested in Jack's recent up-close-and-personal encounter with a rabidly anti-U.S. terrorist cell in Mali. They soaked up every detail of the terrorists' weaponry and tactics and poured over

the backgrounds of two Americans recently ID'd as part of the group. Since the parents of one of the expatriates lived in Brooklyn, NYPD was justifiably worried that the son might try to slip back into the country.

Jack in turn received in-depth briefings on the Counterterrorism Bureau's Lower Manhattan Security Initiative. Designed to protect the nation's financial capital, the LMSI combined increased police presence and the latest surveillance technology with a public-private partnership. Individuals from both government and the business world manned LMSI's operations center to detect and neutralize potential threats. Jack left grimly hopeful that this unique public-private cooperative effort would prove a model for other high-risk targets.

He rushed back to his hotel and had his driver wait while he hurried upstairs to change his shirt and eliminate his five-o'clock shadow. A half hour later he identified himself to a uniformed doorman at the castlelike Dakota. The security at the famed apartment complex had stepped up considerably after one of its most famous tenants, John Lennon, was gunned down just steps away from the entrance years ago. Jack had no problem providing identification, being closely scrutinized and waiting patiently while the doorman called upstairs.

"The duchess is expecting you, sir. You know the apartment number?"

"I do."

"Very good." He keyed a remote to unlock the inner door. "The elevators are to your left."

A dark-haired, generously endowed woman Jack remembered from the wedding reception answered the doorbell. She wore a polite expression but he sensed disapproval lurking just below the surface.

"*Hola.* I am Maria, housekeeper to *la duquesa* and auntie to Sarah and Gina."

Auntie, huh? That explained the disapproval. She obvi-

ously considered him solely responsible for the failure of the box of condoms he and Gina had gone through during their sexual extravaganza.

"Good evening, Maria. I saw you at Sarah's wedding but didn't get a chance to introduce myself. I'm Jack Mason."

"*Sí,* I know. Please come with me. *La duquesa* waits for you in the *salón.*"

He followed her down a hall tiled in pale pink Carrara marble. The delicate scent of orange blossoms wafted from a Waterford crystal bowl set on a rococo side table. The elegant accessories gave no hint of how close the duchess had come to financial disaster. Jack picked up faint traces of it, however, when Maria showed him into the high-ceilinged salon.

The room's inlaid parquet floor was a work of art but cried for a hand-knotted Turkish carpet to soften its hard surface. Likewise, the watered silk wallpaper showed several barely discernible lighter rectangles where paintings must have once hung. The furniture was a skillful blend of fine antiques and modern comfort, though, and the floor-to-ceiling windows curtained in pale blue velvet gave glorious views of Central Park. Those swift impressions faded into insignificance when Jack spotted the woman sitting ramrod-straight in a leather-backed armchair, her cane within easy reach. Thin and frail though she was, Charlotte St. Sebastian nevertheless dominated the salon with her regal air.

"Good evening, Jack."

She held out a veined hand. He shook it gently and remembered her suggestion at the wedding that he use her name instead of her title.

"Good evening, Charlotte."

"Gina called a few moments ago. She's been detained at work but should be here shortly."

She waved him to the chair beside hers and smiled a request at Maria. "Would you bring in the appetizer tray before you leave?"

When the housekeeper bustled out, the duchess gestured

to a side table holding a dew-streaked bucket and an impressive array of crystal decanters.

"May I offer you an aperitif?"

"You may."

"I'm afraid I must ask you to serve yourself. The wine is a particularly fine French white, although some people find the Aligoté grape a bit too light for their tastes. Or…"

She lifted the tiny liqueur glass sitting on the table next to her and swirled its amber liquid.

"You may want to try *žuta osa*. It's produced in the mountains that at one time were part of the Duchy of Karlenburgh."

The bland comment didn't fool Jack for a second. He'd responded to too many toasts by foreign dignitaries and downed too many potent local brews to trust this one. He poured a glass of wine instead.

Maria returned with a silver tray containing a selection of cheeses, olives and prosciutto ham slices wrapped around pale green melon slices. She placed the tray on a massive marble-topped coffee table within easy reach of the duchess and her guest.

"Thank you." Charlotte gave her a smile composed of equal parts gratitude and affection. "You'd better leave now. You don't want to miss your bus."

"I'll take a later one."

Her quick glance in Jack's direction said she wasn't about to leave her friend and employer in his clutches. The duchess didn't miss the suspicion in her dark eyes.

"We're fine," she assured the woman. "Go ahead and catch your bus."

Maria looked as though she wanted to dig in her heels but yielded to her employer's wishes. The kitchen door swished shut behind her. Several moments later, her heavy footsteps sounded in the hall.

"Actually," Jack said when he resumed his seat beside the duchess, "I'm glad we have some time alone."

"Indeed?"

"As you know, Gina and I didn't spend all that much time together before our lives became so inextricably linked."

"I am aware of that fact."

Deciding he'd be wise to ignore the pained expression on Charlotte's face, Jack pressed ahead. "I'm just beginning to appreciate the woman behind your granddaughter's dazzlingly beautiful exterior. I'm hoping you'll help me add to that portrait by telling me a little more about her."

One aristocratic brow lifted. "Surely you don't expect me to provide ammunition for your campaign to convince Gina to marry you?"

"As a matter of fact, that's exactly what I'm hoping you'll provide."

"Well!" The brow shot up another notch. "For a career diplomat, you're very frank."

"I've found being frank works better than tiptoeing around tough issues."

"And that's how you categorize my granddaughter?" the duchess said haughtily. "A tough issue?"

"Ha!" Jack didn't bother to disguise his feelings. "Tough doesn't even begin to describe her. To put it bluntly, your granddaughter is the toughest, stubbornest, most irritating issue I've ever dealt with."

Oh, hell. The frozen look on his hostess's face said clearer than words that he'd overshot his mark. He was just about to apologize profusely when the facade cracked and the duchess broke into somewhat less than regal snorts of laughter.

"You do know," she responded some moments later, "that Gina says exactly the same thing about you?"

"Yes, ma'am, I do."

Still chuckling, she lifted her glass and tossed back the remainder of the amber liquid.

"Shall I pour you another?" Jack asked.

"Thank you, no. My doctor insists I limit myself to one a day. He's a fussy old woman, but he's kept me alive this

long so I suppose I can't complain. Now, what do you want to know about Gina?"

Feeling as though he'd managed to negotiate a particularly dangerous minefield, Jack relaxed. "Whatever you feel comfortable sharing. Maybe you could start when she was a child. What kind of mischief did she get into?"

"Good heavens! What kind didn't she get into?" A fond smile lit the duchess's clouded blue eyes. "I remember one incident in particular. She couldn't have been more than seven or eight at the time. Maria had taken her and Sarah to the park. Gina wandered off and threw us all into a state of complete panic. The police were searching for her when she showed up several hours later with a lice-infested bag-lady in tow. She'd found the woman asleep under a bush and simply couldn't leave her on the cold, hard ground. I believe the woman stayed with us for almost a week before Gina was satisfied with the arrangements we worked out for her."

Charlotte's wry tale added another piece to the mosaic that was Gina St. Sebastian. Jack was trying to assemble the varied and very different sections into a coherent whole when the front door slammed.

"It's me, Grandmama. Is Jack here yet?"

The question was accompanied by the thud of something heavy hitting the table in the hall. Wincing, the duchess called out an answer.

"He is. We're in the salon."

With a kick in his pulse, Jack rose to greet her. His welcoming smile faltered and came close to falling off his face when she waltzed into the salon.

"Sorry I'm late."

"Eugenia!" the duchess gasped. "Your hair!"

"Pretty, isn't it?" Gina patted her ruler-straight, bright purple locks and shot her grandmother a mischievous grin. "We're doing a manga-themed birthday party tomorrow afternoon. I'm Yuu Nomiya."

"I don't have the faintest idea who manga or Yuu are, but I sincerely hope that color isn't permanent."

"It'll come out after a few washings." With that blithe assurance, she gave Jack an apologetic smile. "I'm sorry I kept you waiting. We haven't missed our dinner reservation, have we?"

"We've plenty of time." He struggled to keep his eyes on her face and off the neon purple framing it. "Would you like something to drink? I'm doing the honors."

"God, yes!"

She dropped onto the sofa in an untidy sprawl and caught the suddenly disapproving expressions on the two faces turned in her direction.

"What? Oh! I don't want anything alcoholic. Just tonic, with lots of ice."

Jack delivered the tonic and listened while Gina tried to explain the concept of Japanese manga comics to her grandmother. In the process, she devoured most of the contents of the appetizer tray.

To her credit, the duchess appeared genuinely curious about the phenomenon now taking the world by storm. Or perhaps she just displayed an interest for her granddaughter's sake. Whatever the reason, she asked a series of very intelligent questions. Gina answered them with enthusiasm…at first. Gradually, her answers grew shorter and more muddled. At the same time she slipped lower against the sofa cushions. When her lids drooped and she lost her train of thought in midsentence, the duchess sighed.

"Eugenia, my darling. You're exhausted. Go to bed."

The order fell on deaf ears. Her granddaughter was out like a light.

"I warned her," Charlotte said with affectionate exasperation. "The first few months especially sap a woman's strength."

"Dr. Martinson said the same thing."

"We'll have to forego dinner, Jack. She needs to rest."

"Of course."

When the duchess grasped her cane and aimed the tip at her sleeping granddaughter, he pushed out of his chair.

"Don't wake her."

Bending, he eased her into his arms. She muttered something unintelligible and snuggled against his chest. The scent and the feel of her tantalized Jack's senses. His throat tightening, he growled out a request for directions.

"Which way is her bedroom?"

Six

Gina was having the best dream. She was cradled in strong arms, held against a warm, hard chest. She felt so safe, so secure. So treasured. Like something precious and fragile, which even in her dream she knew she wasn't. Savoring the sensation of being sheltered and protected, she ignored a pesky pressure low in her belly and nuzzled her nose into something soft and squeezy.

The soft and squeezy, her hazy mind determined a moment later, was her pillow. And that irritating pressure was her bladder demanding relief. She pried up an eyelid and made out the dim outlines of her bedroom. The faint glow of the night-light always left on showed she was tucked under the satin throw she normally kept folded at the foot of the bed. She was also fully dressed.

Grunting, she got an elbow under her and sat up. Her slept-in clothes felt scratchy and twisted and tight. Long strands of purple hair fell across her eyes. She brushed them back and tossed aside the throw. Still groggy, she made her way to the bathroom. Once back in the bedroom she shed her clothes and slid into bed, between the sheets this time.

Sleep tugged at her. She drifted toward it on the vague

remnants of her dream. Those strong arms… That steady pulse of a heartbeat under her cheek…

"Jack?"

She sat up again, suddenly and fully awake, and flipped onto her other hip. The covers on the other side of the bed lay smooth and flat. Intense and totally absurd disappointment made her scrunch her face in disgust.

"Idiot! Like the man's going to crawl into bed with you? Right here, in the apartment? And Grandmama only a snore away?"

She flopped back down and yanked the sheet up to her chin. In almost the next breath, her disappointment took a sharp right turn into thigh-clenching need. The hunger shot straight from her breasts to her belly. From there it surged to every extremity, until even her fingernails itched with it.

She stared at the ceiling, her breath coming hot and fast. Images fast-forwarded in her mind. Jack leaning over her, his muscles slick and taunt. Jack laughing as she rolled him onto his back and straddled him. Jack's hands splayed on her naked hips and his jaw tight while he rose up to meet her downward thrust.

Oh, man! She should have expected this. One of the pamphlets Dr. Martinson had provided specifically addressed the issue of heightened sex drive during pregnancy. The rampaging hormones, the supersensitive breasts, the increased blood supply to the vulva— Taken together they could brew up a perfect storm of insatiable physical hunger.

Gina was there. Smack in the eye of the storm. She ached for Jack. She wanted him on her and in her and…

"Oh, for Pete's sake!"

Throwing off the sheet, she stalked to the antique dressing table with its tri-fold mirror, marble top and dozens of tiny drawers. She couldn't begin to count the number of hours she'd spent at this table. First as a youngster playing dress-up in Grandmama's pearls and Sarah's lacy peignoir. Then as a preteen, giggling with her girlfriends while they pirou-

etted in panties and training bras to show off their budding figures. After that came the high school years of mascara and eye shadow and love notes and trinkets from a steady stream of boys drooling over her nicely filled-out curves.

The notes and trinkets were long gone but her trusty vibrator was tucked in its usual drawer. She didn't have to resort to it often, but this…this gnawing hunger constituted a medical emergency.

So much of an emergency that the relief was almost instantaneous. And too damned short-lived! Gina tried to go from limp and languid into sleep. Jack kept getting in the way. Had he been bummed about dinner? Did he and Grandmama go without her? Would he try to see her again before he flew back to Washington?

She was forced to wait for the answers to those questions. With the manga birthday party set to kick off at 11:00 a.m., she had to leave for work before the duchess emerged from her bedroom. Maria came in at midmorning on Saturdays so Gina got no help from that quarter, either.

She toyed with the idea of calling Jack during the short subway ride to midtown, but all-too-vivid memories of last night's searing hunger kept her cell phone in her purse. The memories raised heat in her cheeks. She suspected that hearing his voice, all deep and rich, would produce even more graphic effects. She wasn't showing up for work with her nipples threatening to poke through bra and blouse.

That didn't stop said nipples from sitting up and taking notice, however, when Jack contacted her just after nine-thirty.

"How are you doing, sleepyhead?"

"Better this morning than last night." Jamming the phone between her chin and shoulder, she initialed the final seating plan and handed it to Kallie to add table numbers to name tags. "Sorry I zonked out on you."

"No problem. The duchess didn't want to leave you, so we ordered in."

"Corned beef on rye from Osterman's, right?"

"How did you know?"

"That's what we usually order in."

"We had a nice, long talk while we ate, by the way."

"Uh-oh! Did she leave any stones from my misspent youth unturned?"

"One or two. She said you'll have to turn over the rest yourself. She also said she was meeting with her opera club this evening. So that leaves just us. We can do a make-up dinner. Unless you have to work…"

He'd left her an easy out. It said much for Gina's state of mind that she didn't even consider taking it.

"I'm doing the party kickoff but Samuel's taking cleanup. I should be done here by three."

"I'll pick you up then."

"Kind of early for dinner," she commented.

"We'll find something to do."

His breezy confidence took a hit when she slid into the cab he drove up in. Groaning, she let her purpled head drop onto the seat back.

"Next time I tell you I'm helping with a birthday party for a slew of eight- and nine-year-olds, be kind. Just shoot me right between the eyes."

"That bad, huh?"

"Worse."

"Guess that means you're not up for a stroll down Fifth Avenue."

"Do I look like I'm up for a stroll?"

"Well…"

She angled her head and studied him through a thick screen of purple-tipped lashes. "You, bastard that you are, appear relaxed and refreshed and disgustingly up for anything."

Jack laughed and decided not to bore her with the details of his day, which had kicked off at 4:32 a.m. with a call from the State Department's twenty-four-hour crisis monitoring desk. They reported that an angry crowd had gathered at the U.S. Embassy in Islamabad, and a debate was raging within the department over whether to reinforce the marine guard by flying in a fleet antiterrorist security team. Thankfully, the crowd dispersed with no shots fired and no FAST team required, but Jack had spent the rest of the morning and early afternoon reading the message traffic and analyzing the flash points that had precipitated the seemingly spontaneous mob.

Although the crisis had been averted, Jack knew he should have jumped a shuttle and flown back to D.C. His decision to remain in New York another night had surprised him almost as it had his chief of staff, Dale Vickers.

Jack had first met Dale at Harvard, when they both were enrolled in the Kennedy School of Government. Like Jack, Dale had also gone into the Foreign Service and had spent almost a decade in the field as a Foreign Service Officer until increasingly severe bouts of asthma chained him to a desk at State Department headquarters. *Chained* being the operative word. Unmarried and fiercely dedicated, Vickers spent fourteen to sixteen hours a day, every day, at his desk.

Jack appreciated his second-in-command's devotion. He didn't appreciate the disdain that crept into Vickers's voice after learning his boss intended to stay another night in New York.

"We've kept your relationship with Ms. St. Sebastian out of the press so far, Ambassador. I'm not sure how much longer we can continue to do so."

"Don't worry about it. I don't."

"Easy for you to say," Dale sniffed, displaying the prissy side he didn't even suspect he possessed. "Media relations is my job."

"I repeat, don't worry about it. If and when the story breaks, Ms. St. Sebastian and I will handle it."

That was met with a short, charged silence. Jack had worked with Vickers long enough now to know there was more to come. It came slowly, with seeming reluctance.

"You might want to discuss the slant we should give Ms. Sebastian's pregnancy with your father, Ambassador. He expressed some rather strong views on the matter when he called here and I told him you were in New York."

"First," Jack said coldly, "I don't want you discussing my personal affairs with anyone, including my father. Second, there is no slant. Gina St. Sebastian is pregnant with my child. What happens next is our business. Not the media's. Not the State Department's. Not my father's. Not yours. Got that?"

"Yes, sir."

"Good. I'll let you know when I book the return shuttle to D.C."

Fragments of that conversation played in Jack's mind now as he studied the purple-tipped lashes framing Gina's eyes. When his gaze drifted from those purple tips to her hair, he found himself repressing an inner qualm at the prospect of bumping into some member of the paparazzi. Jack could only imagine his father's reaction to seeing Gina splashed across the tabloids in her manga persona.

John Harris II still mourned Catherine's death but in recent years he'd turned his energy to finding a suitable replacement. Preferably someone with his daughter-in-law's family wealth and political connections. He would accept an outsider if pushed to the edge. But Gina...?

"What are you thinking?" she asked, yanking Jack back to the present.

Everything fell away except the woman next to him. He relaxed into a lazy sprawl, his thighs and hips matched with hers. "I'm thinking I skipped lunch. How about you? Did you scarf down whatever you ordered up for that slew of eight- and nine-year-olds?"

"Puh-leez." Her shoulders quivered in an exaggerated shudder. "My system can only take so much sugar."

Her system, and her baby.

Only now did Gina appreciate the 180-degree turn her diet had taken. She'd cut out all forms of alcohol the moment she'd suspected she was pregnant. After her initial appointment with Dr. Martinson, she'd also cut out caffeine and started tossing down neonatal vitamins brimming with iron and folic acid. She hadn't experienced any middle-of-the-night cravings yet but suddenly, inexplicably, she had to have a foot-long smothered in sauerkraut.

"How does a picnic sound?" she asked. "One of my favorite street vendors works a corner close to Bryant Park. We could grab a couple of fat, juicy hot dogs and do some serious people watching."

"I'm game."

Bryant Park encapsulated everything Gina loved about New York. Located between 5th and 6th Avenues and bounded on the eastern side by the New York Public Library, it formed an island of leafy green amid an ocean of skyscrapers. On weekdays office workers crowded the park's benches or stretched out on the lawn during their lunch hours. If they had the time and the ambition, they could also sign up for a Ping-Pong game or backgammon or a chess match. Out-of-towners, too, were drawn to the park's gaily painted carousel, the free concerts, the movies under the stars and, glory of glory, the superclean public restrooms. Chattering in a dozen different languages, tourists wandered the glassed-in kiosks or collapsed at tables in the outdoor restaurant to take a breather from determined sightseeing.

This late in the afternoon Gina and Jack could have snagged a table at the Bryant Park Grill or the more informal café. She was a woman on a mission, however. Leaning forward, she instructed the cab driver to cruise a little way

past the park and kept her eyes peeled for an aluminum-sided cart topped by a bright yellow umbrella.

"There he is. Pull over."

Mere moments later she and Jack carried their soft drinks and foil-wrapped treasures into the park. Gina had ordered hers doused with a double helping of sauerkraut. Jack had gone the more conservative mustard-and-relish route. The scent had her salivating until they snagged an empty bench.

"Oh, God," Gina moaned after the first bite. "This is almost better than sex."

Jack cocked a brow and paused with his dog halfway to his mouth.

"I said 'almost.'"

If she'd had a grain of common sense, she would have left it there. But, no. Like an idiot, she had to let her mouth run away with her.

"Not that I've had anything to compare it to in the past couple of months," she mumbled around another bite.

"We can fix that."

Jack tossed the words out so easily, so casually, that it took a second or two for his meaning to register. When it did, Gina choked on the bite she'd just taken.

"I've been doing my assigned reading," he said as he gave her a helpful thump on the back. "*A Father's Guide to Pregnancy* says it's not uncommon for a woman's libido to shoot into the stratosphere, particularly during the first trimester. It also warned me not to feel inadequate if I don't satisfy what could turn into an insatiable appetite."

He didn't look all that concerned about the possibility. Just the opposite. The wicked glint in his brown eyes positively challenged Gina to give him a shot.

She wanted to. God, she wanted to! Just looking at his beautiful mouth with a tiny smear of mustard at the corner made her ache to lean in and lick it off. She had to gulp down a long slug of Sprite Zero to keep from giving in to the impulse.

"I appreciate the offer," she said with what she hoped was a cheeky smile. "I'll keep it in mind if I run out of batteries."

"Ouch."

He put on a good show of being wounded, but when the laughter faded from his eyes she saw the utter seriousness in their depths.

"I know you want a relationship based on more than just sex, Gina. I'm hoping we can build that partnership."

"I know you are."

"We're not there yet," he admitted with brutal honesty, "but we're getting closer."

Ha! He could speak for himself. She was standing right on the edge, and every moment she spent with this man cut more ground from under her feet. All it would take was one gentle push. She'd fall for him so fast he wouldn't know what hit him.

Unfortunately, everything else would fall with her. Her fledgling career. Her self-respect. Her pride. She was just starting to feel good about herself. Just beginning to believe she could be the responsible parent she wanted so desperately to become.

Oh, hell! Who was she kidding? She would dump it all in a heartbeat if Jack loved her.

But he didn't. Yet.

So she wouldn't. Yet.

Consoled by the possibilities embedded in that little three-letter word, she tried to keep it light. "Too bad this isn't horseshoes. We would score points for close. Let's just…let's just press on the way we have been and hope for a ringer."

Stupid metaphor but the best she could come up with at the moment. Jack looked as if he wanted to say more but let it go. They sat knee-to-knee in the sunshine and devoured their hot dogs. Or more correctly, Gina devoured hers. Jack had set his on the unwrapped foil to pop the top of his soft drink. He took a long swig and rested the can on his knee while he watched two twentysomethings duking it out at

the Ping-Pong table. The crack of their paddles smacking the ball formed a sharp counterpoint to the carousel's merry tune and the traffic humming along 6th Avenue.

"This is nice," Jack commented. "I don't get to just sit and bask in the sun much anymore."

"Uh-huh."

He stretched an arm along the back of the bench. "Did you come here often when you were growing up?"

"Yep."

Her abbreviated responses brought his gaze swinging back to her just in time to catch the covetous looks she was giving his not-yet-consumed weenie. She didn't bother to plead innocence.

"Are you going to eat that?"

"It's all yours. Or shall I go get you another one doused with sauerkraut?"

She gave the question serious consideration before shaking her head. "This will do me."

The remains disappeared in two bites. Semi-satisfied, Gina leaned against the bench and stretched out her legs. His arm formed a comfortable backrest as she replied to his earlier query.

"I couldn't even hazard a guess how many times I've been to Bryant Park. Maria used to bring Sarah and me to ride the merry-go-round or ice-skate on Citi Pond. Grandmama would come, too, after shopping on Fifth Avenue or to wait while we girls hit the library."

"Your grandmother's a remarkable woman."

"Yes, she is."

"Are she and Sarah the only family you have left?"

"There are some distant cousins in Slovenia. Or maybe it's Hungary. Or Austria. To tell the truth, I'm not real sure which countries got which parts of Karlenburgh after the duchy was broken up."

"Has Charlotte ever gone back?"

"No, never. She doesn't say so, but I know it would be too painful for her."

"What about you?" He toyed with the ends of her hair, still straight, still purple. "Have you ever visited your ancestral lands?"

"Not yet. I'd like to, though. One of these days…"

She could sit here for hours, she thought lazily. Listening to the crack of the Ping-Pong paddles, watching the tourists nose through the kiosks, nestling her head on the solid heat of Jack's arm. She didn't realize her eyelids had fluttered shut until his amused voice drifted down to her.

"You going to sleep on me again?"

"Maybe."

"Before you zone out completely, let's set a date for you to make a visit to D.C. My folks are anxious to meet you."

That woke her up. The little she knew about Jack's family suggested they probably wouldn't welcome her with open arms. Not his father, anyway. But she'd promised. Digging into her purse, she checked the calendar on her iPhone.

"I can't do next weekend. Does the second weekend in June work for you?"

"I'll make it work. Go back to sleep now."

Seven

Gina ended up making the jaunt down to Washington a week earlier than expected. Her change of plans kicked off the following Thursday morning with a summons to Samuel's office, where her boss relayed a request from the head office.

"Nicole just called. She needs you to fly down to D.C. You've got a reservation on the two-twenty shuttle."

"Today?"

"Yes, today. TTG's coordinating a black-tie reception and private, prerelease movie showing for two hundred tomorrow evening."

"And Elaine needs help?"

Elaine Patterson managed the TTG's Washington venue. Gina had met the trim, elegant brunette once when she'd flown to New York for a meeting with Samuel.

"Elaine's father had a heart attack. She's in Oregon and her assistant just checked into the ICU with a bad case of pancreatitis, whatever the hell that is. The rest of the staff is too junior to handle a function this large. Nicole wants you to take charge."

Samuel shoved a folder across his desk. "Here are faxed copies of the timetable, menu, floor plans, proposed setup,

list of suppliers and contact phone numbers. I had them also email copies so you'll be able pull 'em on your iPad in case you need to make changes on the fly. You can stay in the venue's bridal suite. It's fully equipped and stocked."

"But…"

"I'll cover the consult you have scheduled for this afternoon."

"What about the Hanrahan retirement party on Saturday? I'm lead on that."

"I scanned the file. From the looks of the checklist, you've got everything in good shape. I'll take care of the last few prep tasks and get Kallie to pull floor duty with me."

Gina thought fast. She'd have to call Maria to see whether she could come in Sunday and check on Grandmama. If she could, Gina might extend her stay in D.C. for another day, possibly two.

The prospect of spending those days with Jack made her heart do its own version of a happy dance. She could feel it skittering and skipping as she let drop a casual comment.

"My calendar's pretty light on Monday. I don't have anything scheduled that can't be moved. I may take some comp time and stay over in Washington."

"Fine by me." He flapped a hand. "Just get your butt in gear."

She got her butt in gear!

A call made while the cab whisked her uptown confirmed Maria would be happy to check on *la duquesa* Sunday afternoon. When Gina dashed in and explained the arrangement, Grandmama issued an indignant protest.

"I'm neither crippled nor incapacitated, Eugenia. There's no need for Maria to come all the way in to check on me."

"She's not doing it for you, she's doing it for me."

"Really," the duchess huffed. "It's not necessary."

"I know. Just humor me, okay? The thing is, I may stay

over in D.C. a day or two. Jack wants me to meet his parents. If they're available, I'll try to cram in a visit."

"Indeed?"

That bit of news stifled any further objections from her grandmother. Her faded blue eyes lingered thoughtfully on Gina's face for a moment before she commented dryly, "How fortunate the purple washed out of your hair."

Extremely fortunate, Gina thought as she rushed into the bedroom. She hurried out again after stuffing toiletries, a sequined tuxedo jacket she appropriated from Sarah's closet, black satin palazzo pants and some casual clothes into a weekender.

"I'll call you," she promised, dropping a kiss on her grandmother's cheek.

She hit the lobby and had Jerome flag her a cab to La-Guardia. Collapsing in the backseat, she fished out her phone and called Jack. His cell phone went to voice mail, so she left a quick message. For added insurance, she called his office and got shuffled to his chief of staff. Her nose wrinkling, she asked Vickers to advise his boss that she was flying down to Washington.

"Certainly, Ms. St. Sebastian."

He sounded a little more polite but about a mile and half from friendly. Gina wanted to ask him what his problem was but she suspected she already knew the answer.

She made her flight with all of five minutes to spare. When the adrenaline rush subsided and the plane lifted off, she rested her head against the seat back. The next thing she knew, the flight attendant was announcing their imminent arrival at Ronald Reagan National Airport. Gina blinked the sleep out of her eyes and enjoyed her view through the window of the capital's marble monuments.

The short nap left her energized and eager to plunge into the task ahead. She wheeled her weekender through the airport with a spring in her step and exited into a beautiful June

day only slightly tainted by the exhaust pluming out of the cars and taxis and shuttles lined up outside the terminal.

Gina didn't have to dig deep to know why she was so jazzed. The idea that Nicole trusted her enough to step in at the last minute and take charge of a major event had given her self-confidence a shot in the arm.

Then there was the chance she might cram in some time with Jack. That possibility prodded her to whip out her cell phone and take it off airplane mode. The flashing icon indicating a text from Jack put a smile on her lips.

Just heard you're en route to D.C. Call when you arrive.

She crossed the street to the parking garage and aimed for the rental car area while she tried his private number. He answered on the second ring.

"You're here?"

The sound of his voice moved the smile from her lips to her heart. "I'm here. Just got in."

"This is a surprise. What brought you to D.C.?"

For once she managed to catch herself before blurting out the truth. He didn't need to know the possibility of spending some time with him was one of the reasons—the main reason—she'd jumped at this job.

"I'm a last-minute stand-in to coordinate an event tomorrow night."

"Which event?"

"A fancy-schmancy cocktail party and prerelease showing of the new action flick starring Dirk West."

Gina wasn't a real fan of the shoot-'em-up, blow-'em-up type movies West had been making for several decades but she knew every new release pulled in millions.

"The event's being hosted by Global Protective Services," she told Jack. "According to their company propaganda, they're—"

"One of the largest private security contractors in the

world," he interrupted. "They have more boots on the ground in Afghanistan right now than the U.S. military. Rumor is they put up most of the money for the movie. Probably because the script makes a very unsubtle case for decreasing the size of our standing armies and increasing the use of private mercenaries."

Holding the phone to her ear, Gina skimmed the Hertz reservation board to find the parking slot for the car Kallie said would be waiting for her.

"Sounds like this shindig would be right up your alley," she commented as she started down the long row of parked vehicles, "but I didn't see your name on the attendee list."

"That's because I declined the invitation. I might have to rethink that, though, if you're going to be working the event."

"Oh, sure," she said with a laugh. "Screw up the head count, why don't you?"

"I won't eat much," he promised solemnly.

"Well…" She found her car and tossed her briefcase onto the passenger seat. "I guess I can add you to the list."

"That takes care of tomorrow, then. What's on your agenda tonight?"

"I've got what's left of the TTG crew standing by." She slid into the driver's seat but waited to key the ignition. "We're going to go over the final task list and walk through the venue."

"How long will that take?"

"I have no idea."

She hesitated a moment before laying the possibility of an extended stay on him. Would she really be up to meeting his parents after working this event? Yes, dammit, she would.

"I told Samuel I might take a couple extra days in D.C. If it fits with your schedule and theirs, maybe we could work in a visit with your folks."

"We'll make it fit. I'll give them a call and arrange a time. Where are you staying?"

"At TTG's L'Enfant Plaza venue. We have a full bridal suite on the top floor."

"A bridal suite, huh?" His voice dropped to a slow, warm caress. "Want some company?"

God, yes! She gripped the phone, almost groaning at the idea of rolling around with Jack on the Tremayne Group's signature chocolate-brown sheets. Instant, erotic images of their bodies all sweaty and naked buzzed in her head like a swarm of pesky flies.

"Thanks for the offer," she said, making a valiant attempt to bat away the flies, "but I'd better pass."

Somewhat to her disappointment Jack didn't press the issue.

"You sure you can't sneak away for an hour or two and have dinner with me?" he asked instead.

Desire waged a fierce, no-holds-barred, free-for-all with duty. The old, fun-loving Gina would have yielded without a second thought. The new, still fun-loving but not quite as irresponsible Gina sighed.

"Sorry, Jack. I really need to spend this afternoon and evening prepping for the event."

He conceded with his usual easy charm. "I understand. I'll see you tomorrow."

Jack disconnected, swung his desk chair around and settled his gaze on the slice of Washington visible from his third-floor office. Since he held ambassadorial rank, he rated a full suite at the State Department's main headquarters on C Street.

The thirties-era building was originally designed to house the War Department, but the war planners outgrew it before it was completed. When they moved into the Pentagon in 1941, State inherited this massive structure constructed of buff-colored sandstone. It and its more modern annexes were located in the area of D.C. known as Foggy Bottom, so named because this section of the city was once a dismal,

gray-misted swamp. Many of the talking heads who filled today's airwaves with their dubious wisdom liked to suggest the decisions coming out State were still pretty foggy and swampy.

The windows in Jack's office gave a narrow view down 21st Street to the National Mall, with the Lincoln Memorial at one end and the Washington Monument at the other. On good days he could almost catch the glitter of sunlight bouncing off the reflecting pool. The view didn't hold a particle of interest at the moment.

All his thoughts centered on Gina. The news that she was coming to Washington had proved the only bright spark in an otherwise grim morning spent reviewing casualty reports and incident analyses from twenty years of attacks on U.S. diplomatic outposts. Just the sound of her voice and merry laugh lightened his mood.

Thoughtfully, Jack tipped back his chair. Simply knowing that Gina was here, on his home turf, sparked a need that dug into him with sharp, fierce claws. Her image was etched in his mind. Those bright blue eyes. That luscious mouth. The tumble of white-blond curls.

The image shifted, and he pictured her manga'ed mane. God, what if she was still sporting that look? He could only imagine his father's reaction. The thought produced a wry grin as he swung his chair around and dialed his parents' number.

Jack brought his tux in to the office with him the next morning and changed before leaving work that evening. Anxious to see Gina, he arrived at L'Enfant Plaza early.

The plaza was named for Pierre Charles L'Enfant, the French-born architect recruited by General LaFayette to serve as an engineer with George Washington's Continental army. A long rectangle, the plaza was bordered on three sides by an amalgamation of office buildings, government agencies, retail shops and hotels. One of I. M. Pei's iconic

glass pyramids dominated the center. A sister to the pyramid in front of the Louvre, it rose from a lower level with gleaming majesty.

The spot was a good choice for evening events. Foot and vehicle traffic died out when the surrounding offices emptied, leaving plenty of underground parking for guests. Or they could hop off the Metro and let the escalators whisk them up to the plaza. Jack had opted for plan B and emerged from the Metro's subterranean levels into a balmy June evening. Tiny white lights illuminated the trees lining two sides of the plaza. Centered between those sparkling rows, the lighted pyramid formed a dramatic backdrop for lavishly filled buffet tables and strategically placed carving stations.

Two dozen or so other early arrivals grazed the tables or clumped together in small groups with drinks in hand. Jack took advantage of the sparse crowd and lack of lines to hit one of the S-shaped bars set up close to the pyramid. He kept an eye out for Gina as he crossed the plaza but didn't spot either her blond curls or a waterfall of purple. Nor did he find a bartender behind the ebony-and-glass counter. He angled around to check the other bars and saw an attendant at only one. Flipping and tipping bottles, the harried attendant splashed booze and mixers into an array of glasses and shoved them at the tuxedoed waitstaff standing in line at his station.

The fact that three of the four bars weren't ready for action surprised Jack until he spotted Gina, a male in a white shirt and black vest and a plump female with a radio clipped to her waist hurrying out onto the plaza. The man peeled off in the direction of one unattended bar, the woman aimed for another. Gina herself edged behind the ebony S where Jack stood.

"Shorthanded?" he asked as she whipped bottles of champagne out of a refrigerated case and lined them up on the bar.

She rolled her eyes. "Just a tad."

When she started to attack the foil caps, he moved be-

hind the bar to help. She flashed him a grateful look and set him to popping corks while she extracted champagne flutes from a rack beneath the counter.

"I should be in the media center making a last check of the seating," she told him, "but I've been on the phone with the bar subcontractor for twenty friggin' minutes. He's supposed to be sending replacements for their no-shows. You can bet this is the last time the jerk will do business with TTG."

The fire in her eyes told Jack that was a safe bet.

"Keep your fingers crossed the replacements get here before the real hordes descend," she muttered as she began pouring champagne into the tall crystal flutes.

He nodded toward the crowd emerging from the bank of elevators. "I think they're descending."

"Crap." She slapped the filled flutes onto a tray and hooked a finger at one of the waitstaff. "You're over twenty-one, right?"

"Right."

"Take this and start circulating."

"I'm a food server," he protested.

"Not for the next half hour, you're not. Take it! I've cleared it with your boss."

Champagne sloshing, she thrust the tray at him and reached under the counter for more flutes.

"Good thing the subcontractors aren't union," she said fervently. "My ass would be grass if I got TTG crosswise of the culinary workers and bartenders local."

Jack eyed the racks of glasses, bottles and nozzles behind the counter. Everything appeared to be clearly labeled.

"I've fixed a few martinis and Manhattans in my time. I'll pull bar duty until your replacements arrive. You go do your thing in the media center."

"No way! I can't let you sling booze. You're a guest."

"I won't tell if you don't. Go. I've got this."

Jack had no trouble interpreting the emotions that flashed across her expressive face. He could tell the instant the idea

of John Harris Mason III dishing up drinks at Global Protective Service's big bash struck her as too irresistible to pass up.

"All right," she conceded, laughter sparkling in her eyes. "But let's hope Nicole doesn't hear about this. My ass won't just be grass. It'll be mowed and mulched."

"And it's such a nice ass." He couldn't help it. He had to reach behind her and caress the body part under discussion. "Trust me, sweetheart, I won't let anyone mow or mulch it."

She backed away and tried to look stern, but the light still danced in her eyes. "I can't believe you just did that."

Jack couldn't believe it, either. He'd do it again, though, in a heartbeat. Or better yet, drag her upstairs to that bridal suite she'd mentioned and caress a whole lot more than her ass. Sanity intruded in the form of the gray-haired senior senator from Virginia.

Thomas Dillon broke away from the group he was with and strolled over to the bar. "Jack?"

The senator looked from him to Gina and back again. Clearly he didn't understand what an ambassador-at-large was doing behind the drinks counter, but he contained his confusion behind a broad smile.

"I thought I recognized you, son. How's your father?"

"He's still kicking butt and taking names, Senator. What can I get you to drink?"

"Pardon me?"

"I'm pulling special duty tonight. What would you like?"

Despite the near-disastrous start, the remainder of the event went off without a hitch. Most of the invitees were jaded Washingtonians who had attended too many black-tie functions to do more than guzzle down the free booze and food, but Jack heard more than one guest comment on the quality of both.

His replacement arrived before he'd had to mix up more than a dozen drinks. He surrendered his post with some re-

luctance and mingled with the other guests. Jaded they might be, but the arrival of the movie's star started a low buzz. Gina had returned to the plaza and stood next to Jack while Dirk West graciously made the rounds.

"Wow," she murmured, eyeing his shaved head and six-feet-plus of tuxedo-covered muscle. "He looks tougher in real life than he does on the screen."

Tough, and extremely savvy. West worked the crowd like a pro and seemed to sense instinctively the real power brokers and potential backers. He might have been aided in that by the CEO of Global Protective Services, who stuck to the star's side like a barnacle and made a point of steering him over to Jack.

"This is Ambassador John Harris Mason," he said by way of introduction. "He's the man who faced down a cell of armed insurgents in Mali a few years ago."

"I read about that." West crunched Jack's hand in his. "Sounded like a pretty hairy situation. I might have to send a script writer to ferret out the details that didn't get into print."

Jack could have told him not to bother since most of the details were still classified but West had already turned his attention to Gina.

"And who's this?"

The bronze-edged name tag pinned to her lapel should have given him a clue. He ignored it, concentrating all his star power on her face.

"Gina St. Sebastian." She held out her hand and had it enfolded. "I'm with the Tremayne Group. We're coordinating this event."

West's appreciative gaze made a quick trip south, edged back up. "You ever considered taking a shot at acting, Ms. St. Sebastian?"

"I've toyed with the idea once or twice."

"If you decide to do more than toy, you give me a call."

Global's CEO was more interested in Jack's connections

at the State Department than the acting aspirations of the hired hands.

"I hear you've got a meeting with the Senate Intelligence Committee next week regarding embassy security, Ambassador. I've got some ideas in that regard."

"I'm sure you do."

"I'd like to discuss them with you. I'll have my people call and set up an appointment."

His mission accomplished, he steered West to the next group. Jack waited until they were out of earshot to fill Gina in on his conversation with his parents.

"I got ahold of my folks. They're anxious to meet you, but mother's chairing a charity auction tomorrow evening so I told them we'd drive down for Sunday brunch."

"Sunday brunch works for me."

"Good. That leaves tomorrow for just you and me."

She started to comment, but spotted the plump brunette with the radio clipped to her waist signaling from across the plaza.

"Gotta go. It's almost showtime."

She turned, spun back and flashed one of her megawatt smiles.

"Thanks for helping out earlier. Remind me to pay you for services rendered."

"I will," he murmured to her retreating back. "I most certainly will."

Jack carried fantasies of the various forms that payment might take with him into the plush media hall. They teased his thoughts all through Dirk West's explosive attempts to single-handedly save the world from evil. But not even his wildest imaginings could compete with reality when a tired but triumphant Gina invited him up to the bridal suite several hours later.

<u>Eight</u>

Gina had tried to convince Jack he didn't need to hang around while she signed off on the final tally sheets and supervised the breakdown. She'd honestly tried. Yet she couldn't suppress a little thrill of pleasure when he insisted on waiting for her to finish up.

So she'd extended the invitation to join her upstairs. When they entered the lushly appointed suite, though, all she wanted to do was plop down on the sofa, kick off her shoes and plunk her feet on the coffee table. Which was exactly what she did. And all she would have done if Jack hadn't plopped down beside her!

"That's some view," he commented lazily, his eyes on the dramatic vista of the floodlit capital dome framed by the suite's windows.

"Mmm."

She only half heard him. Her mind was still decompressing after the pressure-packed night. He responded by tugging loose his bow tie and popping the top button of his dress shirt before patting his lap.

"Here."

She blinked, suddenly very much in the present. She didn't trust either his simple gesture or her body's instant

response to it. He read the sudden wariness in her face and patted his thighs again.

"I've been told I give a pretty good foot massage. Swing your feet up and see if you agree."

Oooooh, yeah! Gina most definitely agreed. Ten seconds after he went to work on her toes and arch, she was approaching nirvana. Groaning with pleasure, she wedged deeper into the corner of the sofa.

"If you ever decide to give up ambassadoring, you could make a bundle plying the foot trade."

"I'll keep that in mind."

Curious, she eyed him through the screen of her lashes. "What *are* you going to do when you give up ambassadoring?"

"Good question."

His clever, clever fingers worked magic on the balls of her right foot before moving to the left.

"What about those PACs I read about?" she asked. "The ones that think you've got the makings of a future president?"

"*Future* being the operative word. There are a few steps I'd have to take in between."

"Such as?"

"Running for public office, to start with. I've been just a career bureaucrat up to this point."

"Su-u-ure you have. I wonder how many career bureaucrats go toe-to-toe with armed terrorists."

"Too many, unfortunately. Still, elected office is almost a required stepping stone to anything higher. Except for the war heroes like Washington and Eisenhower, almost all of our presidents served as either governors or members of Congress."

"So run for governor. Or Congress. You'd make a great senator or representative. More to the point, someone's got to get in there and straighten out that mess."

"Am I hearing right?" Ginning, he pulled on her toes.

"This enthusiastic endorsement can't be coming from the same woman who's called me obnoxious and uptight and a few other adjectives I won't repeat."

"You are obnoxious and uptight at times. Other times…" She circled a hand in the air, trying to pluck out one or two of his less irritating traits. "Other times you surprise me, Mr. Ambassador. Like tonight, for instance, when you got behind the bar. You went above and beyond the call of duty there."

"I'm a man of many talents," he said smugly. "And that reminds me. I was promised payment for services rendered."

"So you were. Have you given any thought to what form that payment should take?"

"Oh, sweetheart, I haven't thought of anything else all evening."

Red flags went up instantly. Gina knew she was playing with fire. Knew the last thing she should do was slide her feet off his lap and curl them under her, rising to her knees in the process.

All she had to do was look at him. The tanned skin, the white squint lines at the corners of his eyes, the square chin and the strong, sure column of his throat. Like a vampire hit with a ravenous hunger, her weariness disappeared in a red flash. She had to taste him. Had to lean forward and press her mouth to the warm skin in the V of his shirt. Had to nip the tendons in his neck, the prickly underside of his chin, the corner of his mouth.

And of course, he had to turn his head and capture her lips with his. There was nothing gentle about the kiss. Nothing tentative. It went from zero to white-hot in less than a heartbeat. Mouths, teeth, tongues all engaged. Hips shifted. Hands fumbled. Muscles went tight.

Jack moved then, tipping her back onto the cushions. He came down with her, one leg between hers, one hand brushing her hair off her face. Careful not to put all his weight on her middle but taut and coiled and hungry.

She could feel him get hard against her hip. The sensa-

tion shot a hot, fierce rush through her veins. Shoving his jacket lapels aside, she tugged his starched shirt free of the satin cummerbund and tore at the buttons. When she got to the shoulder muscle underneath, she ran her palm over the smooth curve, then felt it bunch under her fingers as Jack's hand went to her waist. The two buttons on her borrowed sequin jacket proved a flimsy barrier. Jack peeled back the lapels and came to a dead stop. Every muscle and tendon in his body seemed to freeze.

"God."

It was half prayer, half groan. His brown eyes hot with desire, he brushed a finger along the lace trimming her demi-bra.

"Good thing I didn't know this was all you had on under those sequins. It was hard enough making it through the movie."

Gina tucked her chin and surveyed her chest with something less than enthusiasm. The underwired half cup of black silk and lace mounded her breasts almost obscenely.

"I've gone up another whole size," she muttered in disgust. "I had to buy all new bras."

Jack picked up on her tone and wisely didn't comment. Good thing, because she probably wouldn't have heard him. All it took was one brush of his thumb over her sensitized nipple and she was arching her back. And when he tugged down the lace and caught the aching tip between his teeth, every part of her screamed with instant, erotic delight.

She arched again, and he took what she offered. His hands and mouth and tongue drove her higher and higher. The knee he wedged between her thighs and pressed against her center almost sent her over the edge.

"Wait!" Gasping, she wiggled away from the tormenting knee. "Wait, Jack!"

He raised his head, a shudder rippling across his face. Disgust followed a moment later.

"Sorry. That was a little more than you probably expected to pay for my bartending services."

When he started to sit up, Gina grabbed his lapels and kept him in place. "Hold on, Ambassador. That little tussle doesn't even constitute minimum wage. I just…I just thought we should shed a few more layers."

Jack stared down at her, eyes narrowed. He knew as well as she did they wouldn't stop at a few layers. He was damned if he'd give her a chance to change her mind, though. Getting the stubborn Gina St. Sebastian into bed ranked almost as high up there as getting her to the altar.

"Shedding is good," he said with a crooked grin that masked his sudden iron determination. "I'll start."

His tux jacket hit the floor. The cummerbund and shirt followed a moment later. He held out a hand and helped her to her feet, taking intense satisfaction from the play of her greedy hands over his bare chest.

Once he'd disposed of the sequined jacket, he helped her shimmy out of her black satin pants. His self-control took a severe hit when he got a look at the hipsters that matched her black lace bra. They dipped to a low V on her still-flat belly and barely covered her bottom cheeks.

He cupped his hand over those sweet, tantalizing curves and brought her against him. He saw her eyes flare when she felt him against her hip, rock-hard and rampant. Her head tipped. Red singed her cheeks.

"Okay," she exhaled in a low, choked voice. "I really, really need to make payment in full. But the two of us going to bed together doesn't change anything."

The hell it didn't.

Jack kept that thought to himself as he scooped her into his arms and strode toward the bedroom.

The Tremayne Group had done their guest suite up right. A king-size bed sat on a raised dais, its chocolate-brown comforter draping almost to the floor. Mounds of brown,

aqua and silver-trimmed pillows piled high against the padded headboard. Floor lamps gave the corners of the room a subdued glow, while a crystal dish filled with creamy wax pebbles emitted a faint scent of vanilla.

Jack absorbed the details with the situational awareness that was as much instinct as training. That alertness had kept him alive in Mali and served him well in so many other tense situations. But it shut down completely when he stretched Gina out on the soft, fluffy ocean of brown. Her hair spilled across the comforter in a river of pale gold. Her eyes were hot blue and heavy. Her long, lush body drove every thought from his mind but one.

Aching for her, he yanked down the zipper of his pleated black slacks. He discarded them along with his socks and jockey shorts, joined her on the bed and ran his hand over the flat planes of her belly.

"You are so incredibly gorgeous."

Her stomach hollowed under his palm even as she gave a breathless, delighted chuckle.

"Flattery will get you everywhere, Ambassador."

He slid his hand under the lace panties and found the wet heat at her center. Her head went back. Her lips parted. As Jack leaned down to cover her mouth with his, he realized he didn't want to be anywhere but here, with this woman, tasting her, touching her, loving her.

He was rougher than he'd intended when he stripped off her underwear. More urgent than he ever remembered being when he pried her knees apart and positioned himself between her thighs. And when she hooked her calves around his and canted her hips to fit his, he lost it.

Driven by a need that would shock the hell out of him when he analyzed it later, he thrust into her. It was a primal urge. An atavistic instinct to claim his mate. To brand her as his. Leave his scent on her. Plant his seed in her belly.

Except he'd already done that.

The thought fought its way through the red haze of Jack's

mind. He went stiff, his member buried in the hot satin that was Gina. Hell! What kind of an animal was he? He levered up on his elbows, blinking away the sexual mists that clouded his vision. When they cleared, he saw Gina glaring up at him.

"What?" she demanded.

"I didn't mean to be so rough. The baby…"

"Is fine! I, however, am not."

To emphasize her point, she hooked her calves higher on his and clenched her vaginal muscles. Jack got the message. Hard not to, since it damned near blew off the top of his head. He slammed his hips into hers again. And again. And again.

They could only spend so many hours in bed. Theoretically, anyway. Jack would have kept Gina there all day Saturday but even he had to come up for air. Since they wouldn't drive down to his parents' house in Richmond until the following day, he offered to show her his favorite spots in D.C. She approved the proposed agenda, with two quick amendments.

"I'd like to see where you live. And where you work."

Jack had no problem with either. Gina had packed clothes for the weekend but he had to get rid of his tux before he could appear in public again. That naturally lent itself to a first stop at his town house.

It was classic Georgetown. Three narrow stories, all brick. Black shutters. Solid brass door knocker in the shape of a horse's head. Gina's nose wrinkled when Jack mentioned that the detached garage at the back had once been slave quarters, but she was gracious enough to acknowledge he'd taken occupancy of the ivy-covered premises long after those tragic days.

The framed photo of Catherine still occupying a place of honor on the entryway table gave her pause, though. Almost as much as it gave Jack. He stood next to Gina as she gazed at the black-and-white photo.

It was one of his favorite shots. He'd taken it after losing

yet another tennis match to his hypercompetitive wife. She laughed at the camera, her racquet resting on her shoulder. Her dark hair was caught back in a ponytail. A sweatband circled her forehead. All her energy, all her pulsing life, shone in her eyes.

"I bet she kept you jumping," Gina murmured.

"She did."

Almost too much.

The thought darted into Jack's mind before he could block it. That energy, that formidable legal mind, the all-consuming passion for politics. He'd had to march double time to keep up with her. More than once he'd wished she'd just relax and drift for a while.

The thought generated a sharp jab of guilt. Jack had to work to shrug it off as he left Gina to explore the town house's main floor and went upstairs to change. He came back down a half hour later, showered and shaved and feeling comfortable in jeans and his favorite University of Virginia crewneck.

"You sure you want to swing by my office? There's not a whole lot to see but we can make a quick visit if you want."

Gina forced a smile. The pictures of his wife scattered around the town house had gotten to her more than she would admit. She'd spotted several shots of Catherine alone. Several more of Catherine with Jack. The perfect marriage of smarts and ambition.

And here Gina was, trying desperately to anchor herself after years of flitting from job to job, man to man. Her life to this point seemed so frivolous, so self-centered. How could Jack have any respect for her?

She buried her crushing doubts behind a bright smile. "I've never been to the State Department. I'd like to see it."

"Okay, but don't say I didn't warn you."

Gina took Jack's disclaimer with a grain of salt. It should have been a teaspoon, she decided when he escorted her

through State's echoing marble halls and into his impressive suite of offices.

The first thing she noticed was the view from the windows of the outer office. It cut straight down 21st Street to the Lincoln Memorial Reflecting Pool and presented a narrow, if spectacular, slice of Washington.

The second item that caught her attention was the individual in jeans, a button-down yellow shirt and round eyeglasses hunched over a computer. She shouldn't have been surprised that Jack's people were dedicated enough to come in on weekends. And when he introduced her to his chief of staff, she tried hard to bury her antipathy behind a friendly smile.

"I'm glad to finally meet you, Dale."

That was true enough. She'd been curious about this man. More than curious. She wasn't usually into stereotypes, but her first glimpse of Dale Vickers pegged him immediately as a very short, very insecure male suffering from a rampaging Napoleon complex. He kept his desk between him and his boss. Also between him and Gina. She had to reach across it to shake his hand. He acknowledged her greeting with a condescending nod and turned to his boss.

"I didn't know you were coming in this morning."

What a prick! Gina couldn't see why Jack put up with him until she spotted the framed 4x6 snapshot on the man's workstation. Catherine *and* Jack *and* Dale Vickers with their arms looped over each other's shoulders. All smiling. All wearing crimson sweatshirts emblazoned with the Harvard logo.

Images of Catherine Mason hovered at the back of Gina's mind for the rest of the day. She managed to suppress them while Jack gave her a private tour of the State Department's hallowed halls. Ditto when they took advantage of the glorious June afternoon to stroll the banks of the Potomac and cheer the scullers pushing against the vicious current.

After browsing the upscale shops in Georgetown Mall,

Jack took Gina to his favorite Thai restaurant later that evening. The owner greeted him with a delighted hand pump.

"Mr. Ambassador! Long time since we see you."

"Too long, Mr. Preecha."

The slender Asian whipped around, checked his tables and beamed. "You want by the window, yes? You and...?"

He made a heroic effort to conceal his curiosity when Jack introduced Gina. She felt it, though, and as soon as they were seated and their drink order taken, the question tumbled out.

"Did you and Catherine come here often?"

"Not often. We'd only lived in D.C. four or five months before she died. Do you like shumai? They serve them here with steamed rice and a peanut ginger sauce that'll make you swear you were in Bangkok."

The change of subject was too deliberate to ignore. Gina followed the lead.

"Since I have no idea what shumai are and have never been to Bangkok, I'll take your word on both."

Shumai turned out to be an assortment of steamed dumplings filled with diced pork, chicken or shrimp. She followed Jack's lead and dipped each morsel in ginger or soy sauce before gobbling it down. Between the dumplings, steamed rice, golden fried tofu triangles, some kind of root vegetable Gina couldn't begin to pronounce and endless cups of tea, she rolled out of the restaurant feeling like a python just fed its monthly meal. Too stuffed for any more wandering through Georgetown. Almost too stuffed for sex. When she tried to convince Jack of that sad state of affairs, though, he just laughed and promised to do all the work.

He followed through on his promise. The chocolate-brown sheets were a tangled mess and Gina was boneless with pleasure when he finally collapsed beside her.

For the second night in a row she fell asleep in his arms. And for the second morning in a row, she greeted the day cradled in the same warm cocoon.

She came awake slowly, breathing in Jack's scent, twitching her nose when his springy chest hair tickled her nose. It felt right to cuddle against his side. Safe and warm and right.

Slowly, without Gina willing them, the images she'd glimpsed of Jack's wife yesterday took form and shape in her mind. For an uneasy moment, she almost sensed Catherine's presence. Not hostile, not heartbroken at seeing her husband in bed with another woman, but not real happy, either.

"We'd better get up and get moving."

Jack's voice rumbled up from the chest wall her ear was pressed against. "Sunday brunch is a long-standing family tradition," he warned, stroking her hair with a lazy touch. "Hopefully, it'll just be us and my parents today but you should be prepared for the worst."

"Great! Now he tells me."

She could do this, Gina told herself as she showered and blow-dried her hair and did her makeup. She could run the gauntlet of Jack's family, all of whom had known and no doubt adored his wife. She wasn't looking forward to it, though.

And damned if she couldn't almost hear Catherine snickering in the steamy air of the bathroom.

Nine

Light Sunday–morning traffic was one of the few joys of driving in Washington. Jack's Range Rover whizzed through near deserted streets and crossed the 14th Street Bridge. The Jefferson Memorial rose in graceful symmetry on the D.C. side of the bridge. The gray granite bulk of the Pentagon dominated the Virginia side. From there they shot south on 395.

Once south of the Beltway, though, Jack exited the interstate and opted instead to drive a stretch of the old U.S. Highway 1. Gina understood why when he pulled into the parking lot of the Gas Pump Café just outside Woodbridge.

"We won't sit down for brunch until one or two. And this place," he said with a sweeping gesture toward the tin-roofed cafe, "serves the best biscuits and gravy this side of the Mason-Dixon line."

Gina hid her doubts as she eyed the ramshackle structure. It boasted a rusting, thirties-era gas pump out front. Equally rusty signs covered every square inch of the front of the building. The colorful barrage advertised everything from Nehi grape soda to Red Coon chewing tobacco to Gargoyle motor oil. The scents of sizzling bacon and smoked

sausage that emanated from the café, though, banished any doubts the place would live up to Jack's hype.

It didn't occur to Gina that he'd made the stop for her sake until they were seated at one of the wooden picnic tables. He obviously didn't consider the slice of toast and half glass of orange juice she'd downed while getting dressed adequate sustenance for mother and child. She agreed but limited her intake to one biscuit smothered in gravy, two eggs, a slab of sugar-cured ham and another glass of juice. Since it was just a little past nine when they rolled out of the café, Gina felt confident she would be able to do justice to brunch at one or two o'clock.

She also felt a lot more confident about meeting Jack's family. Strapped into the Range Rover's bucket seat, she patted her tummy. "Hope you enjoyed that, baby. I sure did."

Jack followed the gesture and smiled. "Have you started thinking about names?"

She didn't hesitate. "Charlotte, if it's a girl."

"What if it's a boy?"

She slanted him a sideways glance. He'd left his window cracked to allow in the warm June morning. The breeze lifted the ends of his dark gold hair and rippled the collar of his pale blue Oxford shirt. He'd rolled the cuffs up on his forearms and they, too, glinted with a sprinkling of gold.

She guessed what was behind his too-casual question. If Jack won his on-going marriage campaign, he no doubt envisioned hanging a numeral after his son's name. John Harris Mason IV. Not for the first time, Gina wondered if she was being a total bitch for putting her needs before Jack's. Why did she have to prove that she could stand on her own two feet, anyway? This handsome, sophisticated, wealthy man wanted to take care of her and the baby. Why not let him?

She sighed, acknowledging the answers almost before she'd formulated the questions. She would hate herself for giving up now. That had been her modus operandi her en-

tire adult life. Whenever she got bored or developed a taste for something new, she would indulge the whim.

But she couldn't quit being a mother. Nor did she want to give up a job she'd discovered she was good at. Really good. Then again, who said she had to quit? The Tremayne Group's Washington venue had plenty of business.

All of which was just a smoke screen. The sticking point—the real, honest-to-goodness sticking point—was that Jack didn't love her. He'd been completely honest about that. Although…the past two nights had made Gina begin to wonder if what they did feel for each other might be enough. Uneasy with that thought, she dodged the issue of boys' names.

"I haven't gotten that far," she said lightly. "Tell me about your parents. Where they met, how long they've been married, what they like to do."

Jack filled the rest of the trip with a light-handed sketch of a family steeped in tradition and dedicated to serving others. His mother had been as active in volunteerism over the years as his father had in his work for a series of presidents.

Gina might have been just the tiniest bit intimidated if she hadn't grown up on stories of the literary and social giants Grandmama had hobnobbed with in her heyday. Then, of course, there was her title. Lady Eugenia Amalia Therése St. Sebastian, granddaughter to the last Duchess of Karlenburgh. That and five bucks might get her a cup of coffee at Starbucks but it still seemed to impress some people. Hopefully, she wouldn't have to resort to such obvious measures to impress Jack's folks.

She didn't. Fifteen minutes after meeting John II, Gina knew no title would dent the man's rigid sense of propriety. He did not approve of her refusal to marry his only son and give his grandson the Mason name.

"Now, John," his wife admonished gently. She was a soft-spoken Southern belle with a core of tempered steel be-

neath her Donna Karan slacks and jewel-toned Versace tunic. "That's a matter for Gina and Jack to decide."

"I disagree."

"So noted," Ellen Mason said dryly. "Would you care for more iced tea, Gina?"

There were only the four of them, thank goodness. They were sitting in a glass-enclosed solarium with fans turning overhead. A glorious sweep of green lawn shaded by the monster oaks that gave the place its name filled the windows. The Masons' white-pillared, three-story home had once been the heart of a thriving tobacco plantation. The outlying acres had been sold off over the decades, but the current owner of Five Oaks had his lord-of-the-manner air down pat.

"I'd better not," Gina replied in response to Ellen's question. "I'm trying to cut out caffeine. Water with lemon would be great."

Jack's mother tipped ice water from a frosted carafe and used silver tongs to spear a lemon wedge. "We didn't worry about caffeine all those years ago when I was pregnant. That might explain some of my son's inexhaustible energy."

Her guest kept a straight face, but it took some doing. Ellen's son was inexhaustible, all right. Gina had the whisker burns on her thighs to prove it.

"I know you must have questions about this side of your baby's family tree," the older woman was saying with a smile in her warm brown eyes. "We have a portrait gallery in the upper hall. Shall I give you a tour while Jack and his father catch up on the latest political gossip?"

"I'd love that."

The duchess had taken Gina and Sarah to all the great museums, both at home and abroad. The Louvre. The Uffizi. The Hermitage. The National Gallery of Art in Washington. As a result Sarah had developed both an interest in and an appreciation for all forms of art. Gina's knowledge wasn't anywhere near as refined but she recognized the touch of a master when she saw it. None of the portraits hanging in

the oak-paneled upstairs hall had that feel. Still, the collection offered a truly fascinating glimpse of costumes and hairstyles from the 17th century right down to the present.

Gina paused before the oil of Jack's grandfather. He wore the full dress uniform of an army colonel, complete with gold shoulder epaulets and saber. "My grandmother knew him," she told Ellen. "She said he and your mother-in-law attended a reception she once gave for some sultan or another."

"I've read about your grandmother," her hostess commented as they moved to the next portrait, this one of Ellen and her husband in elegant formal dress. "She sounds like an extraordinary woman."

"She is." Lips pursed, Gina surveyed the empty space at the end of the row. "No portrait of Jack and Catherine?"

"No, unfortunately. We could never get them to sit still long enough for a formal portrait. And…" She stopped, drew in a breath. "And of course, we all thought there was plenty of time."

She turned and held out both hands. Gina placed hers in the soft, firm fold.

"That's why I wanted this moment alone with you, dear. Life is so short, and so full of uncertainties. I admire you for doing what your heart tells you is right. Don't let Jack or his father or anyone else bully you into doing otherwise."

The brief interlude with Ellen made her husband a little easier to bear. John II didn't alter his attitude of stiff disapproval toward Gina but there was no disguising his deep affection for his son. He not only loved Jack. He was also inordinately proud of his son's accomplishments to date.

"Did he tell you he's the youngest man ever appointed as an ambassador-at-large?" he asked during a leisurely brunch that included twice-baked cheese grits, green beans almondine and the most delicious crab cakes Gina had ever sampled.

"No, he didn't," she replied, silently wishing she could

sop up the béchamel sauce from the crab cakes with the crust of her flaky croissant.

"Then he probably also didn't tell you some very powerful PACs have been suggesting he run for the U.S. Senate as a first step toward the White House."

"Dad…"

"Actually," Gina interrupted, "I read about that. I know those PACs love Jack. And he and I talked about his running for office the other night."

John II paused with his knife and fork poised above his food. "You did?"

"Yep. I told him he should go for it."

"Dad…"

Once again the father ignored the son's low warning. His lip curled, and a heavy sarcasm colored his voice. "I'm sure our conservative base will turn out by the thousands to support a candidate with an illegitimate child."

"That's enough!"

Jack shoved away from the table and tossed down his napkin. Anger radiated from him in waves. "We agreed not to discuss this, Dad. If you can't stick to the agreement, Gina and I will leave now."

"I'm sorry." The apology was stiff but it was an apology. "Sit down, son. Please, sit down."

Ellen interceded, as Gina suspected she had countless times in the past. "Jack, why don't you take our guest for a stroll in the rose garden while I clear the table and bring in dessert?"

Gina jumped up, eager for something to do. "Please, let me help."

"Thank you, dear."

A decadent praline cheesecake smoothed things over. Everyone got back to being polite and civilized, and Ellen deftly steered the conversation in less sensitive channels.

Gina thought they might make it through the rest of the

visit with no further fireworks. She nursed that futile hope right up until moments before she and Jack left to drive back to Washington. At his mother's request, he accompanied her into her study to pick up a flyer about an organization offering aid to abused children overseas she wanted him to look at.

That left Gina and John II standing side by side in the foyer for a few moments. An uncomfortable silence stretched between them, broken when he made an abrupt announcement.

"I had you investigated."

"What?"

"I hired a private investigator."

Gina's brows snapped together, and her chin tipped in a way that anyone familiar with the duchess would have recognized immediately as a warning signal.

"Did you?"

"I wanted him to chase down rumors about the other men you might have been involved with."

Her hand fluttered to her stomach in a protective gesture as old as time. "The other men I might have screwed, you mean."

He blinked at the blunt reply, but made no apology. "Yes."

The thought of a private investigator talking to her friends, asking questions, dropping insinuations, fired twin bolts of anger and mortification. Gina's chin came up another inch. Her eyes flashed dangerously.

"Why go to the expense of a private investigator? A simple DNA test would have been much cheaper."

"You were in that clinic in Switzerland. Jack flew over right after you called him. I told him to insist on a paternity test, but…" He broke off, grimacing. "Well, no need to go into all that now. What I want to say is I accept that you're carrying my grandchild."

"How very magnanimous of you."

The icy response took him aback. He looked as though

he wanted to say more, but the sound of footsteps stilled him. Both Jack and his mother sensed the tension instantly. Ellen sighed and shook her head. Her son demanded an explanation.

"What's wrong?"

"Nothing," Gina said before his father could respond. "Nothing at all. Thank you for a lovely lunch, Ellen."

She kissed the older woman's cheek before offering a cool glance and a lukewarm handshake to Jack's father.

"Perhaps I'll see you again."

He stiffened, correctly interpreting the threat buried in that polite "perhaps."

"I certainly hope so."

"All right," Jack said as the Range Rover cut through the tunnel of oaks shading the drive. "What was that all about?"

Gina wanted to be cool about it, wanted to take the high road and shrug off the investigation as inconsequential, but her roiling emotions got the better of her. She slewed around as much as the seat belt would allow. Anger, hurt and suspicion put a razor's edge in her words.

"Did you know your father hired a P.I. to investigate me?"

"Yes, I…"

"With or without your approval?"

"Christ, Gina." His glance sliced into her. "What do you think?"

She was still angry, still hurt, but somewhat mollified by his indignation. Slumping against the seat back, she crossed her arms. "Your father's a piece of work, Ambassador."

Which was true, but probably not the smartest comment to make. Jack could criticize his father. He wouldn't appreciate an outsider doing so, however, any more than Gina would tolerate someone making a snide comment about the duchess. The tight line to Jack's jaw underscored that point.

"I'm sorry," she muttered. "I shouldn't have said that."

He accepted the apology with a curt nod and offered one

of his own. "I'm sorry, too. I should have told you about the investigation. The truth is I didn't know about it until after we got back from Switzerland and then it just didn't matter."

Her anger dissipated, leaving only an urgent question. "Why not, Jack? Didn't you…? Don't you have any doubts?"

"No. Not one." The rigid set to his shoulders eased. His reply was quiet and carried the ring of absolute truth. "We may disagree on a number of important issues, marriage included, but we've always been honest with each other."

Her eyes start to burn. She refused to cry, she flatly refused, but she suddenly felt miserable and weary beyond words. "Look," she said tiredly, "this has been a busy few days. I may have overdone it a bit. I think…I think I'd better fly back to New York this evening."

He knifed her a quick look. "Is it the baby?"

"No! The baby's fine."

"Then it's my father." Another sharp glance. "Or is it us?"

"Mostly us." She forced a smile. "You have to admit we didn't get much sleep the past two nights. I need to go home and rack out."

"Is that what you really want?"

"It's what I really want."

The drive back to D.C. took considerably less time than the drive down to Richmond. No cutting off to ramble along Route 1. No stops at picturesque cafés. Jack stuck to the interstate, and Gina used the time to check airline schedules. She confirmed a seat on a 7:20 p.m. flight to New York. It was a tight fit, but she could make it if she threw her things in her weekender and went straight to the airport.

"You don't have to wait," she told Jack as he pulled into the parking garage at L'Enfant Plaza. "I can grab a cab."

"I'll drive you."

She was in and out of TTG's guest suite in less than twenty minutes. A quick call ensured the cleaning crew would come in the following day. The key cards she sealed

in an envelope and slid under the door to the main office. Elaine Patterson, manager of the Washington venue, was due back tomorrow. Gina would coordinate the after-event report with her and tie up any other loose ends by email.

Her emotions were flip-flopping all over the place again when Jack pulled up at the airport terminal. Part of her insisted she was doing the right thing. That she needed to pull back, assess the damage to her heart done by the nights she'd spent in his arms. The rest of her ached for another night. Or two. Or three.

If Jack were experiencing the same disquiet, it didn't show. He left the Range Rover in idle and came around to lift out her weekender. His expression was calm, his hand steady as he buried it in her hair and tilted her face to his.

"Call me when you get home."

"I will."

"And get some rest."

"Yes, sir."

"I'll see you at our next doctor's appointment, if not before."

Before would be good, she thought as she closed her eyes for his kiss. Before would be very good.

When she climbed out of a cab outside the Dakota almost seven hours later, her ass was well and truly dragging. Her flight had been delayed due to mechanical problems before being canceled completely. The passengers had sat for well over an hour on the plane before being shuffled off and onto another. She'd called Jack once she was aboard the alternate aircraft so he wouldn't worry, and again when she landed at LaGuardia.

Since they'd touched down at almost midnight, she didn't call her grandmother. The duchess would have gone to bed hours ago and Gina didn't want to wake her. Feeling dopey with exhaustion, she took a cab into the city. Jerome wasn't on duty and she didn't know the new night doorman except to

nod and say hello. Wheeling her suitcase to the elevator, she slumped against the mirrored wall as it whisked her upward.

The delicate scent of orange blossoms telegraphed a welcome to her weary mind. She dropped her purse and key next to the Waterford crystal bowl filled with potpourri. Her weekender's hard rubber wheels made barely a squeak as she rolled it over the marble tiles.

She'd crossed the sitting room and was almost to the hall leading to the bedrooms when she caught the sound of a muffled clink in the kitchen. She left the suitcase in the hall and retraced her steps. Light feathered around edges of the swinging door between the dining room and kitchen. Another clink sounded just beyond it.

"Grandmama?"

Gina put out a hand to push on the door and snatched it back as the oak panel swung toward her. The next second she was staring at broad expanse of black T-shirt. Her shocked glance flew up and registered a chin shadowed with bristles, a mouth set in a straight line and dark, dangerous eyes topped by slashing black brows.

Ten

Everything Gina had ever learned or heard or read about self-defense coalesced into a single, instinctive act. Whipping her purse off her shoulder, she swung it with everything she had in her.

"Hé!" The intruder flung up his arm and blocked the savage blow. *"Várj!"*

"Várj yourself, you bastard!"

Gina swung again. This time his arm whipped out and caught the purse strap. One swift tug yanked it out of her hands.

"If you've hurt my grandmother..."

She lunged past him into the kitchen. Her fingers wrapped around the hilt of the largest knife in the upright butcher-block stand.

"Jézus, Mária és József!" The stranger chopped his hand down on her wrist, pinning it to the counter. "Stop, Eugenia. Stop."

The terse command pierced her red haze of fear but her heart still slammed against her chest as the questions tumbled out. "How do you know my name? What are you doing here? Where's my grandmother?"

"The duchess is in her bedroom, asleep, I presume. I am

here because she invited my sister and me to stay. And I know your name because we're cousins, you and I."

"Cousins?"

"Of a sort."

When she tugged her wrist, he released his brutal grip. A smile softened the stark angles of his face. "I'm Dominic. Dominic St. Sebastian. I live in Budapest, but my parents came from Prádzec. Your grandmother's home," he added when she looked at him blankly.

It took her a moment to recognize the name of the town on the border between Austria and Hungary, in the heart of what was once the Duchy of Karlenburgh.

"I don't understand. When did you get here?"

"This afternoon." He gestured behind him to the coffee-maker just starting to bubble and brew on the counter. "It's midnight in New York, but morning in Hungary. My body has yet to adjust to the time change and craves its usual dose of caffeine. Will you join me for coffee and I'll explain how Anastazia and I come to be here, in your home."

"No coffee," Gina murmured, her hand fluttering to her stomach as she tried to absorb the presence of this dangerous-looking man in her grandmother's kitchen.

He was as sleek and as dark as a panther. Black hair, black shirt, black jeans slung low on his hips. The T-shirt stretched taut across a whipcord-lean torso. The hair was thick and razored to a ragged edge, as though he didn't have time or couldn't be bothered with having it styled.

"Tea, then?" he asked.

"Tea would be good." Slowly getting her wind back, Gina nodded to the cabinet behind his head. "The tea caddy is in there."

"Yes, I know." His smile reached his eyes. "The duchess told me to make myself to home. I took her at her word and explored the cupboards."

Whoa! This man's face cast in hard angles and tight lines was one thing. The same face relaxing into a lazy grin was

something else again. Gina had a feeling Dominic St. Sebastian could have his pick of any woman in Budapest. Or pretty much anywhere else in the world.

The fact that he knew his way around a tea caddy only added to the enigma. While the fresh-made coffee dripped into the carafe, he brewed a pot of soothing chamomile. Moments later he and Gina were sitting across from each other with steaming mugs in hand.

"So," he said, slanting her a curious look. "The duchess never spoke to you of me or my family?"

His speech held only a trace of an accent. A slight emphasis on different syllables that made it sound intriguing and sexy as all hell. Wondering where he'd learned to speak such excellent English, Gina shrugged.

"Grandmama told my sister and me that we had some cousins, four or five times removed."

"At least that many times. So we could marry if we wished to, yes?"

The tea sloshed in her mug. "Excuse me?"

"We're well outside the degree of kinship forbidden by either the church or the law. So we could marry, you and I."

A sudden suspicion darted into Gina's consciousness. Despite the duchess's seeming acceptance of her granddaughter's single-and-pregnant status, was she resorting to some Machiavellian scheming?

"Just when did my grandmother invite you and your sister to New York?"

"She didn't. I had to come on business and since Anastazia had never been to the States, she decided to accompany me. When we phoned the duchess to arrange a visit, she invited us for tea. She was so charmed by my sister that she insisted we stay here."

Charmed by his sister? Gina didn't think so.

"How long will you be in New York?"

"That depends on how swiftly I conclude my business. But not, I hope, before I get a chance to know you and the

duchess. I've heard many tales of her desperate flight after the duke's execution."

"She doesn't speak of those days. I think the memories still haunt her."

"Is that why she's never returned to Austria, or traveled to any part of what is now Hungary?"

"I think so."

"That's certainly understandable, but perhaps some day she will visit and allow Anastazia and me to return her gracious hospitality. She would find everything much changed."

"I'm sure she would."

"You must come, too. I would enjoy showing you my country, Eugenia."

"Gina, please. Grandmama's the only one who calls me Eugenia, and then it's generally because I've screwed up."

"And does that happen often?"

She made a face. "Far more often than either of us would like."

The tea and the European rhythm of Dominic's speech had combined to bring Gina the rest of the way down from the adrenaline spike of her scare. When she reached bottom, weariness hit like a baseball bat.

Her jaw cracked on a monster yawn. She barely got a hand up in time to cover it and gave Dominic a laughing apology.

"Sorry 'bout that. It's been a long day."

"For me, also." His mesmerizing onyx eyes held hers. "Shall we go to bed?"

Okay, she had to stop attaching sexual innuendo to every word that came out of the man's mouth.

They took their mugs to the sink. Dominic rinsed them while Gina emptied the coffeemaker. He flicked off the kitchen light as they passed through the swinging door, plunging them both into temporary blindness.

Gina had grown up in this apartment and was intimately familiar with every piece of furniture a mischievous girl could crawl under or hide behind. She also knew which sharp

edges to avoid, blind or not. Instinctively, she angled to the left to skirt the corner of a marble-topped table.

The move brought her into contact with Dominic's thigh, and his hand shot out to save her from what he must have assumed was a near fall.

"Careful."

For the second time that night he'd captured her arm. Gina wasn't quite as quick to shake off his hold this time.

"Thanks. I assume Grandmama put Anastazia in my sister's room and you in the study?"

"Is the study the baronial hall with the oak paneling and crown molding?" he asked dryly.

"It is." They stopped outside the double sliding doors. "Here you go. I guess I'll see you in the morning. Correction. Make that later in the morning."

His fingers slid from her forearm to her elbow to her wrist. Raising her hand, he bowed and dropped a kiss on it with old-world charm right out of the movies.

"*Aludj jól,* Gina."

"And that means?"

"Sleep well."

"*Aludj jól,* Dominic."

She left him standing by the sliding doors and reclaimed her suitcase. No light shone from under the door to her grandmother's room, so Gina slipped quietly into her own. She was asleep almost before her head hit the pillow.

She woke mere hours later. Grunting at what felt like a bowling ball resting atop her bladder, she rolled out of bed and headed for the bathroom.

When she snuggled between the sheets again, sleep didn't descend as swiftly. And when it did, it brought confusing dreams of a shadowy figure whose hair morphed from black to gold to black again.

Since Samuel wasn't expecting her back from Washington for another day, possibly two, Gina didn't feel compelled

to go in to the office the next morning. Good thing, because she didn't wake up a second time until almost nine.

She took her time in the shower, wondering if she'd dreamed that kitchen encounter last night. It was so surreal, and so unlike her grandmother to invite complete strangers to stay in their home. Maybe she was more tied to the land of her birth than she let on.

Gina followed the scent of coffee and cinnamon toast to the kitchen, where Maria was turning fresh toast onto a plate.

"There you are. Dominic told us, *la duquesa* and me, that you came in late last night."

"I just about jumped out of my skin when I came in last night and bumped into him." Dying for a cup of coffee, Gina poured a glass of apple juice instead. "I'm surprised Grandmama invited him and his sister to stay here."

"Me, as well. But they are very nice and have made your grandmother smile. You will see," Maria said, flipping the last of the toast onto the platter.

"Here, I'll take that."

The scene in the sunny, green-and-white breakfast room certainly seemed to give credence to Maria's comment. The duchess was holding court, her snowy hair in a crown of braids, her chin feathered by the high lace collar of her favorite lavender silk blouse. Her smile was far from regal, though. Wide and lively, it transformed her face as she carried on an animated conversation with her guests in their native language.

But it was those guests who stopped Gina in her tracks. In the bright light of day, Dominic appeared every bit as dangerous as he had last night. Must be that European, unshaved whisker thing. Or his preference for black shirts. This one was starched cotton and open-collared, showing just a hint of a silver chain at his throat.

The woman seated across from him was almost as riveting. Her hair fell well past her shoulders, as lustrous and raven-black as her brother's. Her cheekbones were high and

sharp, her mouth a glistening red. Thick lashes framed dark eyes with just the hint of a slant. If the rest of her was as striking as that sculpted face, the woman could walk into any modeling agency in New York and sign a high six-figure contract within minutes.

All of a sudden Gina felt fat and dumpy and just a tad jealous of the way these two outsiders seemed to have glommed on to her grandmother. That lasted only until the duchess spotted her. Her lined face lit up with love.

"You're awake at last. Come and join us, dearest."

Dominic pushed back his chair and took the platter of toast so Gina could bend to give her grandmother a kiss. The look he gave her banished any lingering nasty thoughts. Fat and dumpy wouldn't have put such an admiring gleam in his eyes.

"Good morning, cousin. Did you sleep well?"

"Very."

"You must let me introduce my sister. Anastazia, this is…"

"Eugenia Amalia Therése," the brunette said in an accent noticeably heavier than her brother's.

She, too, pushed back her chair and came around the table. Holding out both hands, she kissed Gina's cheeks. "I have been so eager to meet you, cousin. I, too, was named for the Archduchess Maria Amalia of Parma." She wrinkled her perfect nose. "I am Anastazia Amalia Julianna. Such long names we have, yes?"

Despite her cover-model looks, she was open and friendly and engaging. Gina couldn't help but smile back.

"We do indeed."

"You must call me Zia. And I will call you Gina."

That thorny matter settled, they joined the others at the table. Gina helped herself to two slices of cinnamon toast while her grandmother gave them all a rare glimpse into the family archives.

"Poor Archduchess Maria Amalia," she said with a wry

smile. "Married against her will to a mere duke while two of her sisters became queens. Marie Antoinette of France and Marie Caroline of Naples and Sicily."

Charlotte took a sip of her tea and shared another historical tidbit.

"The three sisters were reportedly very close. They often exchanged letters and portraits and gifts. One of the last letters Marie Antoinette smuggled out of her prison was to Amalia."

"I'm told there's a miniature of their mother, the Empress Marie Therese of Austria, in your Metropolitan Museum of Art," Zia said eagerly. "It is one of the places I hope to visit while I am here."

"You must get Eugenia to take you. She spent many hours at the Met as a child."

"Oh, but I must not impose." The brunette turned her brilliant smile on Gina. "From what your grandmother has told us, you're very busy with your work."

"Actually, I'm off today. We can go this afternoon, if you like."

"I would! And you, Dom. You must come, too, to see this long-dead ancestor of ours."

His gaze met and held Gina's. His mouth curled in a slow smile. "I'll have to see if I can reschedule my afternoon appointment."

Gina didn't get a chance to corner her grandmother until midmorning. Zia had gone out onto the terrace to check her phone for voice messages and emails. Dominic retreated to the study to make some calls. As soon as he was out of the room, Gina pounced.

"Okay, Grandmama, 'fess up. What's behind this sudden spurt of hospitality to distant relatives you've never met."

"Really, Eugenia! I should hope I'm not so lacking in generosity as to let two young and very charming relations stay in a hotel when we have plenty of room here."

"But you don't know anything about them."

"That's what Dominic said when I extended the invitation. He tried to refuse, but I insisted."

"Did either of them tell you what they do for a living?"

"Dominic does some kind of security work. Anastazia just got her MD degree from Semmelweis University in Budapest."

Gorgeous and smart and a doc. Another nasty little worm of jealousy poked its head up. Gina might have started feeling dumpy and fat again if Dominic hadn't come back into the room.

"I'm yours for the afternoon, if you're sure you wish to…"

He broke off and pivoted on the balls of his feet in the direction of the hall. Startled, Gina strained to hear in the sudden silence and picked up a faint buzz.

"Oh, that's my phone. I left it in my purse on the hall table last night. Excuse me."

The call had already gone to voice mail when she fished the phone out of her jam-packed bag. She saw the name on caller ID and stabbed the talk button just in time.

"Hello, Jack."

"Hi, Gina. I just wanted to check and see how you're feeling after your long odyssey last night."

The sound of his voice stirred the usual welter of confused emotions. Despite her abrupt departure yesterday, she couldn't believe how much she missed him. How much she ached for him.

"I'm good," she said, "although I decided not to go in to work since I had the day off, anyway."

"So you're going to put your feet up and rest, right?"

"Pretty much. Although I did agree to take my cousins to the Met this afternoon."

"Cousins?"

"Two of them. Dominic and his sister, Anastazia. Their parents came from Prádzec, which was once part of the Duchy of Karlenburgh."

"And is now in Hungary."

Trust an ambassador-at-large to know that. The phone to her ear, Gina wandered toward the end of the hall. Dom sat next to her grandmother's chair and appeared to be amusing her with some anecdote.

"Did the duchess know they were coming?" Jack asked.

"They surprised her. Me, too! I thought Dom was a burglar when I came chest-to-chest with him last night."

"They were there, in the apartment when you got home?"

"They're staying here."

That was met with a short silence.

"What did you say their names were again?"

"Dominic and Anastazia St. Sebastian. She's just finished med school and he does something in security. Grandmama didn't get the specifics."

She caught a flash of sunlight as the terrace doors opened and Zia rejoined the group.

"Oh, there's Anastazia. I'd better go, Jack."

"Gina…"

"Yes?"

"About this weekend—"

"It was just me," she interrupted quickly. She hadn't had time to sort through everything that had happened during their days together. And the nights! Dear God, the nights.

"Chalk it up to hormones run amok. I'll talk to you soon, okay?"

"Okay."

She blew out a breath and hit the end button, but some of the emotions Jack had stirred must have shown in her face when she walked into the sitting room. She couldn't hide them from the duchess. Her faded blue eyes locked onto to Gina's.

"Who was that, dearest?"

"Jack."

"Hmm."

The odd inflection in that murmur snared the interest of

both guests. They were too polite to ask, however, and the duchess left it to Gina to elaborate.

"Jack Mason. He's an ambassador-at-large with the U.S. State Department in Washington."

Dominic's expression of casual interest didn't change but just for a second she thought she saw something flicker in his dark eyes. Like the duchess, he must have sensed there was more to the call than she wanted to reveal.

Oh, hell. Might as well let it all hang out.

"He's the father of my baby."

After Gina disconnected, Jack spent several long moments staring at the slice of the Mall viewable through his office windows. Their brief conversation ricocheted around in his mind.

Two of them. From Hungary. They surprised her. Chest-to-chest.

He wanted to believe it was his recent showdown with the Russian Mafia thugs who'd spilled across the borders of Eastern and Central Europe that prompted him to reach for the phone. Yet he couldn't get that chest business out of his head.

His chief of staff answered the intercom. "What's up, boss?"

"I need you to run a check on a pair from Hungary. They say they're siblings and are going by the names Dominic and Anastazia St. Sebastian."

Eleven

The next few days flew by. Gina got caught up at work. During her spare hours she showed Zia and Dominic the best of New York. She also delighted in the slow unfurling of her grandmother's memories. Prompted by her guests' presence and their gentle probing, the duchess shared some of her past.

She'd kept it locked inside her for so long that each anecdote was a revelation. Even now she would only share those memories that gave glimpses of a girl born into a wealthy, aristocratic family, one who'd grown up with all Europe as her playground. A fascinated Gina learned for the first time that her grandmother might have qualified as an Olympic equestrian at the age of fifteen had her family allowed her to compete. She'd retaliated for their adamant refusal by insisting she be allowed to study Greek and Roman history at Charles University in Prague.

"Prague is such a romantic city," the duchess mused to her audience of three over a dinner of Hungarian dishes prepared by Zia and Dominic as a small thank-you to their hostess.

Candles flickered in tall silver holders. The remains of the meal had been cleared away but no one was in a hurry to leave the table. A Bohemian crystal decanter of *pálinka* sat within easy reach. Double-distilled and explosively po-

tent, the apricot-flavored brandy had been a gift from Zia and Dom. The duchess and her guests sipped sparingly from balloon-shaped snifters. Gina was more than content with a goblet of diet cranberry juice and the dreamy expression on her grandmother's face.

"That's where I first met the duke," the duchess related with smile. "In Prague. There'd been talk off and on about a possible liaison between our families but nothing had come of it at that point."

"So what was he doing in Prague?" Gina asked.

"He'd evidently decided it was time to take a wife, and came to find out if I was scandalously modern as the rumors said."

She took a sip of brandy and a faraway look came into her eyes.

"When he walked into the café where my friends and I were having dinner, I didn't know who he was at first. All I saw was this tall, impossibly handsome man with jet-black hair and the swarthy skin of his Magyar ancestors. Even then, he had such a presence. Every head in the café turned when he walked over to my table," she murmured. "Then he bowed, introduced himself, and I was lost."

The duchess paused, drifting on her memories, and Gina's gaze drifted to Dominic. His olive-toned skin and dark eyes indicted Magyar blood ran in his veins, too.

A nomadic, cattle-herding tribe that swept into Europe from the Steppes, the Magyars were often depicted in art and literature as the early Hungarian equivalent of America's Wild West cowboys. Gina was back in the 8th or 9th century, picturing Dominic riding fast and low in the saddle, when the intercom sounded.

She returned to the present with a start. The buzz brought the duchess out of her reverie, as well. A small frown of annoyance creased her forehead.

"I'll get it," Gina said.

She crossed to the intercom's wall unit and saw the flashing light signaling a call from the lobby. "Yes?"

"It's Jerome, Lady Eugenia. There's a gentleman to see you. Mr. John Mason."

Jack! Surprise and pure, undiluted delight flooded her veins.

"Send him up! Excuse me," she said to the three interested parties at the table. "I need to get the door."

She rushed to the entryway and out into the hall, wishing she'd spiffed up a little more for this evening at home. Oh, well, at least she still fit into her skinny jeans. And her crab-apple-green stretchy T-shirt did accent her almost-nursing-mother boobs.

When Jack stepped out of the elevator, Gina forgot all about her appearance and devoured his. Ohmanohman-ohman! Hungarian cowboys had nothing on tall, tanned Virginians.

The sight of him erased last weekend's awkward moments. Her hurt and indignation over learning that his father had hired a P.I. evaporated. Ditto the poisonous little barbs planted by his obnoxious chief of staff. Double ditto the ache in her heart when she'd spotted the pictures of Catherine at his home. Like the duchess had so many years ago, all Gina needed to do was look at this man and know she was lost.

"What are you doing here?"

"Two reasons. One, I didn't like the way our weekend ended. I'm still kicking myself for letting you leave with little more than a peck on the cheek."

"Oh. Well. I suppose we can correct that."

"You suppose right."

When he hooked her waist, she went into his arms eagerly, joyfully. He buried a hand in her hair and more than made up for any deficiencies in their parting.

Gina could have stayed there forever. The feel and the taste and the scent of him wrapped around her like warm

silk. She felt his heart beating under her spread palms, breathed in the heady mix of aftershave and male.

When he raised his head, her heart was in her smile. "You said there were two reasons. What's the second?"

The pause was brief, hardly more than half a breath, but still noticeable.

"I missed you."

"Was it that hard to say?" she teased.

"You try it."

"I missed you." It came so easily she added a little embellishment. "Bunches."

The murmur of voices inside the apartment snagged Jack's attention. "Did I catch you at a bad time?"

"No, we finished dinner a while ago and are just sitting around the table talking. Come meet my cousins."

She led him to the dining room and had time to note widely varied reactions before she made the introductions. Zia's first glimpse of the newcomer brought her elbows off the table and a look of instant interest to her face. As her eyes raked Jack over, a slow, feline smile curved her lips.

Gina couldn't help herself. She was bristling like a barnyard cat when she noticed Dominic's expression. It was as shuttered as his sister's was open. The duchess's, on the other hand, was warm and welcoming.

"Good evening, Ambassador. It's good to see you again."

The title sent Zia's brows soaring. Her gaze whipped from Jack to Gina and back again, while Dominic slowly pushed his chair back from the table and stood.

"It's good to see you, too, Duchess." Jack crossed the dining room to take her hand. "I'm sorry to barge in like this."

"No need to apologize. Allow me to introduce my guests. They're visiting from Hungary."

"So Gina told me."

"Anastazia, may I present Ambassador Jack Mason."

He was at his most urbane with the sultry brunette. A smile, a lift of her hand, a light kiss on the fingers.

"You must call me Zia," she purred. "And I will call you Jack, yes?"

"Igen."

"How wonderful! You speak our language."

"Only enough to order a drink in a bar."

"In Hungary," she laughed, "that is more than enough. This is my brother, Dominic."

Jack rounded the table and extended his hand. It was a simple courtesy, a universal gesture recognized the world over. Yet there was something about the look accompanying it that made Gina pause. The message was subtle. Almost *too* subtle. She caught a hint of it, though, or thought she did.

So did Dominic. His smile took on a sardonic edge, his eyes a sudden glint as he shook Jack's hand.

"We've met before, Ambassador, although I doubt you'll remember."

"I remember. I also remember you were using another name at the time."

The two men ignored the surprise that produced among the women. Their gazes locked, they seemed to be engaged in a private and very personal duel.

"I was, indeed," Dominic drawled. "And you, as I recall, had not yet acquired your so very impressive diplomatic credentials."

The duchess's notions of propriety didn't include what was fast assuming the air of an Old West showdown in her dining room. With a touch of irritation, she thumped her hand on the table to get the combatant's attention.

"Do sit down, both of you. Jack, would you care to try this very excellent cognac? Or there's coffee if you prefer."

"Cognac, please."

"Gina, if you'll get another snifter perhaps Jack or Dominic will condescend to tell us where or when they met before."

The acidic comment found its mark. While Gina retrieved a cut crystal snifter from the graceful Louis XV china cabi-

net that took up almost an entire wall, the tension between
the two men eased by imperceptible degrees. She brought
the snifter to the table and splashed in the aromatic brandy
as Dom yielded the floor to Jack with upturned palms.

"It's more your story than mine, Ambassador."

Jack accepted the snifter with a murmured thanks and
addressed himself to the duchess. "Dominic and I met a
number of years ago in Malta. I was on a UN fact-finding
mission investigating the transshipment of young women
kidnapped from Eastern Europe and sold to wealthy pur-
chasers in the Arab world."

"Dear Lord!" The duchess shot her guest a sharp, questioning look, but he merely gestured for Jack to continue.

"While the UN team was in Malta, we heard rumors of a
shipment coming in from Albania. We worked with Interpol
and the Maltese authorities to intercept the trawler transporting the merchandise. There were six girls aboard, all between
the ages of fifteen and twenty, all drugged to the gills."

Jack lifted the balloon goblet and swirled its contents.
His gaze shifted from the duchess to the man sitting across
of him.

"The captain of the trawler was killed in the cross fire.
That's the word that was put out, anyway."

"What do you mean?" Gina demanded. "Was the captain
killed or wasn't he?"

She didn't like where this was going. Had she and her
grandmother been too trusting? Had they accepted too readily that Dom and Zia were who they said they were? With
a sinking sensation, she remembered how dangerous Dom
had seemed that first night, when she'd come home and surprised him in the kitchen.

"The captain went down," Jack confirmed, "but not in
a cross fire. Evidently he spotted the intercept boats on his
radar and started dragging the girls to the rail. He was going
to throw them overboard and get rid of the incriminating

evidence before we closed in. That's when he took a shot point-blank to the forehead."

Dom lifted a shoulder. "The bastard had one of those kids shoved against the rail. There was no time to negotiate."

"I don't understand." Gina frowned at her cousin. "Were you on one of the intercept boats?"

"I was on the trawler."

"What?"

He leaned forward, acknowledging her shock. "I was undercover, Gina. I'd been working to take down the head of that particular white slavery ring for months, but I couldn't allow the captain to murder those girls."

"Or blow your cover," Jack murmured in the stunned silence that followed.

Dom's glance slewed back to him. "Or blow my cover."

"Funny thing about that." Jack swirled his cognac again, his eyes never leaving Dom's face. "Interpol put out the word that the second crewman on the trawler escaped after being taken into custody. Yet there was never any record made of the arrest. And the officer who supposedly took the man into custody disappeared two days later."

Dom's smile didn't quite make it to his eyes. "The Albanians play rough."

Gina couldn't believe they were sitting in this elegant dining room, sipping brandy and cranberry juice from Baccarat crystal while calmly discussing kidnapped fifteen-year-olds and death on the high seas. She glanced at her grandmother and found the same incredulity on the duchess's face. Even Zia looked stunned. Evidently her brother's undercover persona was news to her, too.

"I'm curious," Jack said. "Where did you go from Malta, St. Sebastian?"

"I had several assignments. As did you, Mason."

"You're no longer with Interpol."

It was a statement, not a question, but Dominic responded

with a quick, slashing grin. "Not anymore. I'm now what you might term an independent entrepreneur."

And just like that, the ominous spell was broken. He was Gina's cousin again. Handsome, charming, exotic and more intriguing than she'd ever imagined.

She made the fatal mistake of saying so when she walked Jack to the door an hour later.

"I had no idea my cousin was an undercover agent."

"Isn't that the whole point of 'undercover'?"

The acerbic comment raised Gina's brows.

"I suppose," she replied. "But still, you have to admit it's all pretty James Bondish."

"If you say so. Are you tired?"

The abrupt change of subject made her blink. It also made her realize she wasn't the least tired. Probably because the hour was still relatively early. Either that, or the extraordinary conversation at the dinner table had stimulated her. Or just standing here, so close to Jack, set every one of her nerves to dancing.

"Not really. Why?"

"I'm staying at the Excelsior. It's only a few blocks from here. Do you feel like getting out for a little while? We still need to talk about last weekend."

Cold, hard logic dictated a negative. She still hadn't completely sorted through the confused feelings left over from their weekend together. Luckily, Gina had never been particularly concerned with logic. At that moment, looking up into Jack's brown eyes, all she knew was that she craved an hour or two or six alone with him.

She'd never been the kind to play games, much less hide her feelings. Coyness didn't factor anywhere into her makeup. A smile of eager anticipation slid into her eyes as she tipped her head toward the dining room.

"Hang loose. I'll tell Grandmama and the others not to wait up for me."

* * *

They opted to walk to the Excelsior. The June night was too balmy and the city lights too enticing to take a cab for a few short blocks. When they reached the lobby of the Dakota, she steered him away from the main entrance on West 72nd toward the inner courtyard.

"This way. It's shorter."

They exited on 73rd and cut back to Central Park West. Somehow Gina's hand found her way into Jack's as they strolled past the imposing bulk of the Museum of Natural History. And somehow, when they were in the elevator shooting up to his suite, his lips found hers.

She couldn't blame the heat that raced through her on hormones. It was Jack. All Jack. Only Jack. He stoked her senses. Fired her blood. She made herself wait until he keyed the door to his room before she pounced. Then there were no holds barred.

"I hope this is what you had in mind when you asked if I wanted to get out for a while," she muttered as she tore feverishly at his shirt buttons.

"Pretty much."

His voice was low and rough. So were his hands. Dragging up the hem of Gina's T-shirt, he cupped her aching breasts. All it took was one flick of his thumbs over her supersensitive nipples to have her moaning. On fire for him, she locked her mouth and her body with his. They were both half-naked when she threw a glance around the luxurious sitting room.

"There's a bed here somewhere, right?"

"Oh, yeah."

The bedroom was as palatial as the rest of the suite. All crown molding and watered silk wallpaper. Not that either of them noticed. The bed was the center of their focus. Four ornately carved posts. Champagne-colored gauze dripping from each corner. A silk duvet in the same color just begging to be yanked back.

Jack did the honors before tumbling Gina onto the cool sateen sheets. Standing beside the bed, he stripped off the rest of his clothes. Her greedy eyes feasted on his muscled chest. His washboard ribs and flat stomach. His rampant sex.

Gina had to cup him. Had to taste him. Rolling onto her knees, she scooted to the edge of the mattress and wrapped her hand around him. He was hot to her touch. Hot and ridged and already oozing. The milky bead at the tip of his erection stirred a deep, feminine thrill. The idea that she could bring her man to this point with just a kiss, just a stroke, set a torch to her own wild desire. Dipping her head, Gina took him in her mouth.

Jack stood it as long as he could. Then the atavistic need that had been building in him since the moment he'd walked into the duchess's apartment swept everything else aside. He wanted to claim this woman. Mark her as his.

Driven by that primal instinct, he pushed her onto the pillows and followed her down. She spread her legs for him willingly, eagerly, and Jack sank into her. Her hips rose, rammed into his. Once. Twice. Again. Then she opened her eyes and the red mist that had obscured Jack's mind cleared.

This was Gina of the bright, contagious smile.

Gina, who enticed and excited him.

Gina, who'd erased everything and everyone else from his mind.

Jack came out of a deep sleep with his customary, instant awareness. The hotel room was still dark, the silence deep, although a faint gray light was just beginning to show at the edge of the drapes blanketing the window.

Gina lay sprawled at his side. Soft puffs of air escaped her lips with each breath. Not quite snores but close enough to make him smile. With slow, careful moves he nudged down the knee digging into his hip and eased out of bed.

His slacks and shorts lay where he'd dropped them. He

pulled them on but left his belt unbuckled and shirt lying where it was as he crossed to the window. Lifting the drape a crack, he saw the city hadn't yet roared to life. Like Jack, it was enjoying the final quiet moments before the rush of the day.

He stared at the shadowy bulk of the Museum of Natural History across the street and tried to remember the last time he'd felt so relaxed. More important, the last time his world had felt so right. Not since Catherine, certainly.

Or even before.

The traitorous thought slipped in before he could block it. Only here, in the dim stillness, with Gina just a few feet away, could he admit the painful truth.

Catherine had been all brilliant energy. Athletic, competitive, totally committed to the causes she believed in. Loving and living with her had demanded the same high level output from Jack.

Would he have burned out? Would they?

Or would they have found what he'd somehow found so swiftly and so unexpectedly with Gina? Jack struggled to find the right word for it. It wasn't peace. Or contentment. Or certainty. God knew, there was nothing certain or predictable about Eugenia Amalia Thérése St. Sebastian!

Nor was what he felt for her wrapped up in the baby. The fact she was carrying his child played, of course. No way it couldn't. But what had Jack by the throat right now was Gina. Just Gina.

Christ! Why didn't he just admit it? He was in love with her. Everything about her. Okay, she pissed him off royally at times. And yes, she was one of the most stubbornly hardheaded females he'd ever encountered. Yet everything inside him warmed at the thought of waking up next to her for the next…the next…

His jaw locked. Whirling, he strode back to the bed and sat on the edge.

"Gina. Wake up."

She grunted and tried to burrow into her pillow.

"Wake up."

"Wha…?" She raised a face half-obscured by a tangle of hair and blinked owlishly. "What?"

"Sit up a moment."

Grumbling, she rolled onto a hip and wiggled up against the headboard. The sheet came with her in a waterfall of Egyptian cotton.

"This better be good," she muttered.

She shoved her hair out of her face and tucked the sheet around her breasts, scowling at him through still sleepy eyes. He figured that was as good as he would get.

"Okay, here's the deal. I love you. I want to wake up beside you every morning for as long as we have together. The problem is, neither of us knows how long that might be."

He gripped her upper arms. His fingers dug into soft flesh as he pressed his point.

"I learned the hard way there are no guarantees. You… we have to grab whatever chance at happiness we have now, today. I understand you're still trying to sort through all the changes going on in your life right, but…"

"Wait! Just hold on!"

She pulled away from him, and Jack smothered a curse. He'd overplayed it. Pushed her too hard. He was falling back to regroup when she scrambled off the bed, sheet and all, and pointed a finger at him.

"You stay right where you are. I have to pee. And wash my face. And brush my teeth. Afterward, I'm going to come back to bed and you're going to repeat part of your speech."

"Which part?"

She looked over her shoulder on her way to the bathroom. The smile she sent him lit up the entire room.

"The I-love-you part."

Jack sat there, grinning like an idiot.

* * *

He was still grinning when he heard a faint click coming from the sitting room. A second later, the outer door thudded back against the wall and three men rushed in.

Jack reacted instantly. His one thought, his only thought, was to direct them away from Gina. Springing to the far side of the bed, he grabbed the only available weapon. He had his arm back to hurl the nightstand lamp when the bald giant leading the pack leveled a silenced semiautomatic. The beam of his laser sight painted a red eye dead-center in Jack's naked chest.

"Don't be foolish, Ambassador."

He recognized the voice even before Dominic St. Sebastian stepped from behind baldy's hulking frame.

Twelve

"Now," Gina said gleefully as she yanked open the bathroom door, "let's pick up where we…"

She stopped dead. Clutching the towel she'd wrapped around her like a sarong, she gaped in stunned disbelief at the frozen tableau that greeted her. Jack, gripping a table lamp like a baseball bat. A monster with a shaved head aiming a gun at his chest. Another stranger eying her half-naked body with a leer. And Dom, his dark eyes flashing an urgent message she couldn't even begin to interpret.

"Wh…?" She backed up an involuntary step, two, hit the bathroom door frame. "What…?"

"Very nice, Ambassador." The leering stranger's accent was so thick Gina's shocked mind could barely understand him. "Your woman would bring a good price, yes?"

"Jack! Dom!" Her frantic gaze whipped from one to the other. "What's going on?"

Dom stepped toward her, still telegraphing a signal that refused to penetrate her frantic brain.

"Listen to me, Gina. These men and I have some unfinished business to take care of, business that involves Jack. When you wake, you will understand."

"When I…when I wake?"

A small, apologetic smile altered his grim expression for a moment. Just long enough to distract Gina from the blow that clipped her chin and snapped her head back. She felt Dom catch her as she crumpled. Heard Jack snarl out a curse. Sensed some sort of violent movement on the other side of the room, followed by a low pop.

Then everything faded to black.

She came to slowly, dazed and disoriented. As the gray mist cleared, she discovered she was stretched on the unmade bed. Alone. With the towel draped over her naked body.

She also discovered that her jaw hurt like nobody's business. The ache cut through her lingering haze. A montage of images leaped into her head, sharp and cold and terrifying. The men. Dom. The gun with its ugly silencer.

"Jack!"

Terror engulfing her, Gina shoved off the bed. The violent lunge brought a dark, dizzying wave. She had to reach out a hand to steady herself for a moment, as the towel puddled around her ankles. As soon as the wave receded enough to reclaim her scant body covering, she rushed into the sitting room.

Nothing. No one. Not a table out of place. No overturned chairs. No Jack, or any strangers.

Or Dom.

She hadn't fully processed those moments right before her cousin clipped her, hadn't really understood the vivid images that had popped into her head. She strung them together now, and the pattern they formed made her want to retch.

Dom! Dear God, Dom! What was he involved in? Why had he led those men to Jack? What did they want?

Five exhausting hours later, Gina still didn't have an answer to any of those questions. Neither did the small army of city, state and federal officials who'd descended on the Excelsior in response to her 911 call.

Two uniformed NYPD officers arrived hard on the heels of hotel security. They were followed in a bewildering succession by two plainclothes detectives; a CSI team to scour the suite for fingerprints and other evidence; a grim-faced individual who identified himself as being with the city's counterterrorism unit; two agents from the regional FBI office; a liaison from the governor's office in Albany; a Department of Homeland Security rep and a tall, angular woman from the State Department's New York Office of Foreign Missions, who'd been sent at the urgent request of her boss to find out what the hell happened to Ambassador-At-Large Mason.

Senior FBI Agent Pamela Driskell assumed charge of the hastily assembled task force. It was done with tact and a smooth finesse that told Gina the agent had considerable prior experience dealing with prickly jurisdictional issues.

"Section 1114 of Title 18 U.S. Code assigns the FBI the responsibility for protecting officers and employees of the United States," she explained in a peaches-and-cream Southern drawl at odds with her short, no-nonsense hair and stocky frame. "Now tell me everything you know about this cousin of yours."

Gina started with the surprise visit by Dom and his sister and ended with last night's startling revelations.

"I didn't get all the details. Just that he and Jack—Ambassador Mason—crossed paths some years ago during a UN mission investigating white slavery."

Driskell shot a look at the State Department rep. "You know anything about that?"

"No, but I'll check it out."

Whipping out her BlackBerry, the woman turned away. Driskell swung back to Gina.

"What else?"

"Dom—my cousin—was an undercover agent at the time. Working for Interpol."

"That right? Well, we'll check that out, too. Now I think it's time we talk to your cousin's sister."

She flapped a hand to get the attention of everyone else in the suite.

"Y'all have any further questions for Ms. St. Sebastian? No? Okay, I'm taking her home. Kowalski and I will interview Anastazia St. Sebastian."

When Gina and her escort arrived, Jerome was at his station. Concern etched deep grooves in his seamed face, and his shocked gaze went to the bruise that had blossomed on her chin.

"It's not as bad as it looks," she assured the doorman.

Actually, it was worse but Jerome didn't need to know that.

"Two police officers arrived earlier," he reported.

Gina nodded. Driskell had requested NYPD dispatch the officers. Just in case Dom made an appearance.

"One officer's waiting in the lobby," Jerome said with a worried frown. "The other went up to the duchess's apartment. Can you tell me what's going on, Lady Eugenia?"

Special Agent Driskell started to intervene but Gina held up a palm. "It's okay. I've known this man all my life. I feel safer with him on the door than any five FBI agents."

Driskell hiked a brow but didn't argue the point. "We're investigating the suspected kidnapping of Ambassador Jack Mason," she said instead. "We have reason to believe Dominic St. Sebastian may be involved."

"No!" Jerome reeled back a step. "I don't believe it!"

"Why not?"

He had to stop and think about his instinctive denial. "I've seen Mr. St. Sebastian and his sister with the duchess," he said after a moment. "They're so good with her. So caring and solicitous."

Driskell's curled lip said what she thought of caring and solicitous. "What time did you come on duty this morning?"

"Nine o'clock."

Too late for the events that happened at the Excelsior hours earlier, but Driskell tried, anyway.

"Have you seen two men loitering anywhere in the vicinity? One big and bald? The other smaller, with a heavy accent?"

Jerome drew himself up, all wounded dignity under his summer uniform. "If I'd seen anyone loitering in the vicinity of the Dakota, you may rest assured I would have seen they were attended to."

"I'll take that as a no," Driskell said in her deceptively soft, magnolia-petal drawl.

The uniformed cop in the lobby reported no sighting of Dominic St. Sebastian, his suspected accomplices, or Ambassador Mason. The cop who'd been assigned to wait in the duchess's apartment gave the same report.

Gina only half heard him. Her attention went straight to her grandmother. The duchess sat as straight-spined as ever in her high-backed chair. Maria huddled with shoulders hunched in the chair beside hers. Both women showed worried, strained faces. And both jerked their heads up when Gina walked in.

"Eugenia!"

Relief flooded the duchess's face. Then she seemed to fold into herself, like someone who'd been granted a reprieve from her worst fears.

Gina rushed across the room and dropped to her knees beside the woman who'd always been her anchor. The terror she'd been holding at bay rose up again but she choked it back. She wasn't about to aggravate her grandmother's heart condition by indulging in a fit of hysterics like she really, really wanted to.

"I'm okay, Grandmama."

"What happened to your face?"

She hesitated but couldn't find any way around the truth. "Dom knocked me unconscious."

"No!"

The single syllable arced through the air like summer lightning. Sudden. Tense. Electrifying. Gina jerked her head around and saw Zia leap off the sofa. Her face was ablaze, her eyes feral.

"My brother would not strike a woman!"

"Guess again," Gina snapped.

"I don't believe you!"

The savage denial pulled her up short. Jerome and Anastazia. That made two people in less than five minutes who refused to accept Dom's role in the morning's events.

Her grandmother made a third.

"I can't believe it, either," the duchess said in a more shaky voice than Gina had ever heard coming from her. "Please, Eugenia. Introduce me to these people. Then for heaven's sake sit down and tell us what happened. Zia and Maria and I have been imagining every sort of horrible disaster."

The introductions didn't take much time. The telling took only a little longer. What could Gina add to the stark facts? She'd emerged from the bathroom. Found Dom and two strange men in Jack's suite. Dom stepped forward, knocked her out. She woke alone.

"I cannot understand any of this," Zia said fiercely. "But whatever happened, Dom had some reason for his actions."

Agent Driskell chose to exert her authority at that point. "We'd like to talk to you about your brother, Ms. St. Sebastian."

"It's Dr. St. Sebastian," Zia interrupted acidly.

"Right." The agent turned to the duchess. "Is there some place my partner and I can speak privately with Dr. St. Sebastian?"

"Yes, of course. Maria, will you show them to the breakfast room?"

The kitchen door swished behind them, leaving Gina and her grandmother alone for a few precious moments.

"Eugenia, for God's sake, be honest with me." The duch-

ess held out a trembling hand. "Did you fall? Hurt yourself or the baby?"

"No." She took her grandmother's hand and sank into the chair Maria had just vacated. "Dom caught me before I hit the floor."

"He knocked you unconscious but didn't let you fall? This…none of this makes any sense."

"I know."

She was no closer to understanding when Agent Driskell and her partner departed some time later. Before leaving, Driskell gave Gina a business card imprinted with her office and cell phone numbers.

"There's a chance your cousin or whoever's he's working with may try to reach you. If they do, call me at once."

"I will," Gina promised, slipping the card into the pocket of her jeans. "And you'll call me immediately if they contact someone in Jack's office?"

Driskell nodded. "In the meantime, we'll pull the police officer here in the apartment but keep one in the lobby just in case."

With the agents' departure, an uneasy silence gripped the four women. Maria broke it by pushing heavily to her feet.

"You must eat, *Duquesa.* All of us must. I will make a frittata."

She swished through the swinging door to the kitchen, leaving Gina and the duchess to face a clearly worried Zia.

"I knew my brother had worked with Interpol," the Hungarian said with a deep crease between her brows, "but I was not aware he was…he was…." She waved a hand, as though trying to pull down the right word.

"An undercover agent?" Gina supplied.

"*Igen!* An undercover agent." Her accent reflected her agitation. The Eastern European rhythm grew more marked with each word. "Dominic never spoke of such things to me. Nor to our parents."

Gina wanted to believe her. Her aching chin dictated otherwise.

"He said last night he's no longer with Interpol," she reminded Zia coolly. "As I recall, he mentioned that he's now an independent entrepreneur. What, exactly, does that mean?"

Her cousin's eyes flashed. "I don't know. He has business all over. Many parts of the world. Something to do with security. But…I don't know."

She raked a hand through her silky black hair. She was dressed casually today in navy leggings and a belted, cream-colored tunic with a scoop neckline that dipped off one shoulder. Tall and slender and impossibly elegant, she stirred Gina's frumpy, dumpy feelings again.

Of course, it didn't help that she'd been in such a hurry to jump back into bed with Jack this morning that all she'd done in the bathroom was pee, splash her face with cold water and brush her teeth. Nor was her appearance uppermost in her mind when she'd come to. After her panicked 911 call, she'd scrambled into the same jeans and crab-apple stretchy T-shirt she'd worn last night. If she'd dragged a comb through her hair, she couldn't remember it. Makeup had never entered her mind. Aside from the ice pack Agent Driskell's partner had thrown together with a towel and minicubes from the wet bar to keep her jaw from swelling, Gina had given zero thought to how she looked.

She was feeling that omission now. She wanted a shower, a hairbrush, a change of clothes and another ice pack in the worst way. She hated to take the time for even a quick scrub, though. What if Agent Driskell called? Or Dom? Or Jack?

She was still debating the issue when Zia addressed the duchess. "This is very awkward for you," she said stiffly. "And for me. I think perhaps I should pack my things and… and Dom's…and go to a hotel."

The duchess frowned but before she could reply the cord-

less phone on the table beside her chair rang. Gina dived for it, praying fervently. Jack! Please, God, let it please be Jack!

"Hello?" Stabbing the talk button, she fumbled the receiver to her ear. "Hello?"

"Gina! Thank God!"

She had to strain to hear her sister's voice over the roar of some kind of engine.

"Grandmama called us early hours and hours ago," Sarah shouted above the noise. "She said you'd been in some kind of an incident. Are you okay?"

"I'm fine."

"The baby?"

Gina laid a hand over her still-flat stomach. Dom had caught her just as her knees crumpled. She hadn't hit the floor. Hadn't bruised anything but her chin. Which, she realized belatedly, must have been his intent.

"Also fine," she assured Sarah. "What's that noise? Where are you?"

"Just about to touch down at the 34th Street Heliport."

"You're here? In New York?"

"Dev ordered his private jet two minutes after Grandmama called. We'll be at the Dakota shortly. Gina, you're not hurt? You swear you're not hurt?"

"I swear."

"Okay, see you in a bit."

Gina cut the connection, battling the almost overwhelming urge to burst into tears. Dammit! These kamikaze hormones were killing her! But just knowing that the sister who always was and always would be her closest friend had rushed to New York on the basis of a single phone call made her want to bawl.

She fought back the tears and sent the duchess a tremulous smile. "That was Sarah."

"So I gathered. They're in New York?"

"They're about to touch down at the 34th Street Heliport."

Her grandmother's paper-thin eyelids fluttered down, as though in prayer. "Thank heavens."

When her lids lifted again, relief was stamped all across her face. "If anyone can get to the bottom of all this, Dev can."

Gina wasn't sure what her brother-in-law could do that two dozen assorted city, state and federal law officials couldn't. She'd put her money on Dev, though. He didn't have to play by the same rules those officials did.

"Now I must leave," Zia said, returning to the topic she'd introduced before the phone call. "Your other granddaughter comes, yes? You will need the bedroom for her."

"Why don't we wait until Sarah and Dev arrive before we decide that?" the duchess suggested.

Zia wasn't fooled. Neither was Gina. They both knew the duchess intended to keep their only connection to Dom on a short leash until Dev had a chance to talk to her.

Her cousin acknowledged as much with a curt nod. "Very well."

Then the stiffness went out of her spine. Like an elegant doll that suddenly lost its stuffing, Zia collapsed onto the sofa and put her head in her hands.

"Dominic is the best of all brothers," she said on a small moan. "I don't understand this. I don't understand any of this."

Her distress was so genuine, so obviously unfeigned. If Zia loved her brother even half as much as Gina loved Sarah, this crazy situation had to be tearing her apart.

The realization gave Gina more of a sense of kinship with her cousin than she'd felt at any point before. It brought her out of her chair and halfway across the sitting room before the buzz of the intercom sent her spinning toward the wall unit. The flashing number on the panel signaled a call from the lobby.

"It's Gina, Jerome."

"There's a gentleman to see you, Lady Eugenia. Mr. John Mason says…"

"Send him up!"

Thank God, thank God, thank God! Jack had returned from wherever he'd disappeared to.

She raced to the front door and flung it open. She was dancing from foot to foot in wild impatience when the elevator doors pinged open. Like a stork hit by lightning, she froze with one foot lifted in the air.

Jack's father stalked out of the elevator, his face red with suppressed fury. "What the hell have you involved my son in?"

Thirteen

She fell back a step, stunned by the vicious accusation. Before she could respond, before she could even think of a response, Zia came running down the hall.

"Come quickly! Special Agent Driskell's on the phone. She thinks they have a link to the kidnappers."

Gina spun on one heel and raced for the sitting room. Footsteps pounded behind her but she had no thought for Jack's father at the moment. Her heart pounding, she snatched up the phone the duchess held out and jammed it to her ear.

"This is Gina St. Sebastian. What's happening?"

"We just got a tip from Interpol," Pam Driskell said with barely suppressed excitement. "Antonio Cordi disappeared from their radar three days ago and may have entered the U.S. under a fake passport."

Like that told Gina anything!

"Who's Antonio Cordi?"

"He's the suspected capo of a vicious crime family operating out of southern Italy. Unfortunately, no one's been able to penetrate the family or get close enough to pin anything on him."

"You're kidding!" She gripped the phone with a white-

knuckled fist. "What connection does Jack—Ambassador Mason—have to a Mafia don?"

A grim, white-faced John Harris Mason II surged into her field of view. "I can answer that."

Gina had the phone plastered against her ear, trying to assimilate John II's startling announcement, when she heard a commotion in the foyer. Her heart jumped into her throat.

Jack! Dom! Please God, let it be one of them!

She was hit with alternating waves of crushing disappointment and heartfelt joy when Sarah and Dev appeared. Waving a frantic hello, she relayed the latest development to Special Agent Driskell.

"Ambassador Mason's father is here at our apartment. He says he's got information about this Antonio Cordi."

"Keep him there! My partner and I are only a few blocks away. We'll return immediately."

Her thoughts whirling, Gina inserted the phone into its base. "Agent Driskell wants you to hang loose. She's on her way back here."

The thump of a cane against the parquet floor commanded her attention. "I believe introductions are in order, Eugenia."

"Oh. Right. Grandmama, Sarah, Dev, Zia…this is Jack's father, John Mason. John, this is my grandmother, sister, brother-in-law and…and cousin."

She hadn't intended the stumble over that last part. In her heart of hearts, Gina refused to believe Dom had gone over to the dark side. She still hadn't been able to come up with an explanation for his role in this morning's extraordinary events, though. Neither had his sister. Their unanswered questions hung over the room like a black cloud.

Zia acknowledged as much with a terse nod in the general direction of the newcomers. Which left Gina to pray the duchess hadn't heard the accusation flung at her by Jack's father in the hall a few moments ago. If Charlotte had, blood might yet be spilled.

Mason skated on that one, thank God. The duchess rose

from her chair with the aid of her ebony cane and held out a blue-veined hand.

"I'm sorry we have to meet under such unhappy circumstances, John. I may call you John, mightn't I?"

He gave a curt nod, his thoughts obviously spinning more on his son than on social niceties.

"Good, and you may call me Charlotte. Now, please, sit down and tell us what connection your son has to a Mafia don."

Mason a dismissive gesture with one hand. "I'll wait for the FBI."

Gina chalked the rudeness up to the worry that had to be gnawing at him but cringed at the expression his brush-off put on her grandmother's face.

"Gina says this FBI agent is on the way to take my statement. I'll wait and…"

"No, sir, you will not."

The duchess's cane whipped up and took aim at his chest.

"Look at that bruise on my granddaughter's chin," she commanded with icy hauteur. "If you have an explanation for why her cousin felt compelled to strike her and disappear into thin air with your son, I want to hear it. Now."

Gina guessed John II rarely, if ever, tucked his tail between his legs and backed off. He didn't exactly do either at that point, but he offered a stiff reply.

"I can't tell you why this…this cousin of Gina's struck her or how *he's* involved in this situation. I have my suspicions," he said, his jaw tight, "but nothing solid to base them on. All I can tell you is that I once headed a delegation chartered to examine international banking practices that shielded money laundering, both in the U.S. and abroad. We spent months in South America, more months in Europe digging into accounts reputedly owned by an Italian crime organization called the 'Ndrangheta."

"Go on," the duchess instructed as she resumed her seat. "And for heaven's sake, do sit down."

The demand for at least a semblance of normality drained the last of John II's hostility. He sank into a chair, looking suddenly haggard and far older than his years.

Gina and Sarah and Zia huddled together on the sofa. Dev took the straight-backed chair at the duchess's gilt-edged escritoire. Every pair of eyes was locked on Jack's father as he reduced what had to be a dramatic tale of international crime and intrigue to a few, stark sentences.

"We were in Rome. With the help of the Italian authorities, we'd actually begun to decipher the labyrinthine flow of third- and fourth-tier transactions. One of those tiers led to a member of the 'Ndrangheta named Francesco Cordi."

"I thought his name was Antonio," Gina said, frowning.

"Francesco is—was—Antonio's brother.

"Was?"

"Francesco's dead."

John scrubbed a hand over his face. It was evident to everyone in the room he still carried vivid memories of those days in Rome.

"He didn't like us nosing around in his business and decided to let us know about it. Two of my associates were incinerated when their vehicle was firebombed. We found out later I was next on the hit list. Fortunately—or unfortunately as it now turns out—Jack flew over to Rome at the first sign of trouble. He was with me when Francesco made his move." A fleeting smile creased the retired diplomat's face. "There wasn't a whole lot left of him to send home to his brother Antonio."

"Who's now here, in the States," Gina explained for Sarah and Dev. "The FBI says they got a tip that…"

The buzz of the intercom had her springing her off the sofa.

"That must be Agent Driskell and her partner now."

It wasn't. Her stomach sank like a stone when Jerome announced another visitor.

"I'm sorry to bother you, Lady Eugenia, but there's a Mr. Dale Vickers in the lobby."

Jack's obnoxious chief of staff. That's all she needed! Squeezing her eyes shut, Gina pressed her forehead against the wall.

"He wishes to speak with you. Shall I send him up?"

Hell, no! She knew darn well the officious little turd possessed no vital information relating to his boss's kidnapping. If he had, he would have taken it straight to the FBI. She would also bet he'd already used the weight of his office to extract every detail he could from them. Now he wanted to hear it straight from the horse's mouth.

She guessed she couldn't blame him. Vickers and Jack went back a long way. He had to be as shaken as everyone in the room. Sighing, Gina raised her head.

"Send him up."

Mere moments after the short, tightly wired Vickers said hello to Jack's father and was introduced to others, he confirmed Gina's cynical guess. The man had spoken to just about every local, state and federal official involved into the case.

"They can't tell me a damned thing beyond the basics. All they could confirm was that you and the ambassador were screwing around when he got snatched and…"

"Stop right there, young man!"

Incensed, the duchess tilted her chin to a dangerous angle.

"You will address Lady Eugenia with courtesy and respect or you will leave this apartment immediately."

"I…"

"Do we understand each other?"

"I just…"

"A simple 'yes, ma'am' will do."

"Yes, ma'am."

Despite the tension engulfing the room, Gina and Sarah exchanged a small smile. The sisters had seen their grand-

mother reduce bigger and stronger men than Dale Vickers to quivering blobs of sorry.

Vickers's next comment erased any inclination to smile, however. Too wired to accept the duchess's icily polite invitation to have a seat, he paced the sitting room.

"I know it was clutching at straws, but I even thought this might have something to do with the face-to-face between the ambassador and the CEO of Global Protective Services at that little soiree TTG put on last weekend."

Little soiree? Gina swallowed an indignant huff. She had to work hard to refrain from suggesting Vickers take a short leap off a tall building.

Unaware he'd ignited her fuse, the staffer proceeded to send her straight into orbit. "If Global's power structure thought the ambassador was going to undercut them on the fat embassy security contract they're trying to land, they might want him out of the picture. When I called Nikki, though, she assured me…"

"Whoa! Back up a minute. Did you just say you called Nikki?" Gina asked incredulously. "Nicole Tremayne? My boss?"

"Of course I called her. She appreciates the business we've sent TTG's way since you and the ambassador…uh…" He caught the duchess's warning glance. "Since you and the ambassador started seeing each other. But I knew she didn't understand the awkward position you put him in by enticing him to attend an event sponsored by Global."

Gina barely heard the last, insulting remark. She was still dealing with the shock of learning that Jack and his staff had funneled business to TTG.

Her pride crumbled. Like an old, rotted rowboat, it just fell apart right before her eyes. What a fool she was! All these weeks she'd thought, she'd actually believed, she was making her own mark at TTG.

She struggled to her feet. She refused to burst into tears in front of Vickers, but her throat was thick when she re-

minded the assembled group that Special Agent Driskell and her partner were expected at any moment.

"Sarah, would you show them in when they get here? I need to… I need to…"

She didn't trust herself to finish. With a vague gesture toward the arched hallway leading to the rear of the apartment, she turned on her heel. Her eyes were burning by the time she made it the bath linking her bedroom with Sarah's old room. She dropped the lid to the stool and sank down sideways, crossing both arms on the counter beside it.

Strangely, the tears didn't gush. Gina stared at the wall, her pride in shreds, and waited for the usual flood to burst through the dam. It took a moment for her to understand why the tsunami didn't happen.

None of it mattered. Not her job or TTG or Vickers's snide comments. The *only* thing that mattered right now was Jack's safety. She would eat crow or humble pie or black, slimy worms if that would bring him back to her.

She was still staring blankly at the wall when Sarah tapped on the bathroom door.

"Gina? Are you okay?"

"Mostly."

"May I come in?"

She mumbled an assent and almost lost it when her sister eased down onto her knees beside the stool. Gina had counted on Sarah to bail her out of so many of life's little catastrophes. Turned to her, too, to soothe the ruffled feathers of the men she'd fallen for, then dropped with such careless abandon.

"It'll be okay," Sarah murmured, stroking her hair. "It'll be okay. Judging by everything I've heard in the past few minutes, Jack's been in tight spots before. He'll find a way out of this one, too."

Halfway across town Jack was was hungry, hurting and totally pissed.

He'd been sitting on his ass for hours now in a wobbly

chair with one leg shorter than the other. His arms were twisted behind his back. Plastic restraints cut into his wrists. The wound from the bullet that had grazed his upper arm had scabbed over, but the trail of dried blood it left itched like the devil under the shirt and suit coat he'd been told to pull on before they'd departed his hotel suite.

Jack had complied with the order. Hell, with Dominic St. Sebastian cradling an unconscious Gina in his arms, Jack would have jumped out the eighth-story window if so ordered to prevent the bastard from hurting her any worse.

He'd had time these past hours to think about that, though. How fast St. Sebastian had put himself between Gina and his two pals with guns. How quickly he'd clipped her, then caught her before she hit the floor. As though he wanted to neutralize her and get her out of the picture immediately, before the other goons turned their weapons in her direction.

If so, he hadn't bothered to communicate his strategy to Jack. Or anything else, for that matter. St. Sebastian and the shorter of his two pals had disappeared right after they'd dumped Jack in this abandoned warehouse.

They'd left the shaved-head Goliath to stand guard. The giant had heaved his bulk up twice in the past six hours, both times to take a leak. He'd sprayed the grimy brick wall like a fire hose, adding his contribution to the stench of vomit, urine and rat feces littering what was obviously a hangout for homeless druggies. He'd also grunted into a cell phone a few times in a heavy dialect Jack couldn't understand but otherwise refused to say a word.

Shifting in his chair to ease the ache in his shoulder joints, Jack decided to take another shot at him. "Hey! Num nuts! I know you won't respond to English."

He tried Spanish again, then French, then his limited Russian. All he got was a sneer and a shake of the thug's massive head.

Okay. All right. Jack couldn't wait any longer. If the nine or ten layers of local, state and federal officials he knew had

to be looking for him hadn't closed in on the warehouse by now, odds were pretty damned good they wouldn't. If Jack were going to get out of this mess, he had to do it on his own.

For the fifth or sixth time he did a visual sweep of the warehouse. Rat droppings weren't the only objects littering its dim, cavernous interior. A stained mattress, some moldy fast-food sacks and a scatter of rusted tin cans gave ample evidence of prior occupation. So did the syringes dropped on the concrete floor.

His glance lingered on the syringes. He'd considered those earlier but the damned things were plastic, not glass. Even if he could toe one within reach, somehow get it into his hands and break the barrel before the gorilla noticed, the plastic shard wouldn't cut through the restraints.

He'd have to go with a rusted can. The closest was about four feet away. Its lid was jagged and bent back, as though someone had used an old-fashioned can opener to get at the contents, then tossed it aside.

He couldn't wiggle the rickety chair that far without getting Goliath all excited. He had to take a dive. Probably more than one. He just hoped to hell he didn't knock himself unconscious when he hit the cement floor.

"Hey! You!"

Goliath slewed a disinterested glance Jack's way.

"I need to take a leak, too."

Hard to pantomime without the use of your arms. He tipped his chin toward his fly. When that didn't produce results, he nodded toward the urine-splashed wall, arced his arms behind him to clear the chair and started to push to his feet.

His guard grunted a warning. Jack ignored it. He was almost upright when the giant lunged out of his own chair and swung the beefy fist gripping his silenced semiautomatic.

The blow knocked Jack sideways. He crashed to the cement. The rickety chair went with him. Goliath said something that was obviously a warning and hooked a paw under

Jack's arm. Of course, he had to grab the one grazed by the bullet.

When Jack grimaced in pain, amusement lit Goliath's broad, flat face. He muttered a few words that no doubt translated to "serves you right, asshole" and righted the overturned chair. He shoved Jack into it and headed back to his own.

"I have to piss."

His jaw set, Jack started to rise again. And again, Goliath let fly with a backhanded blow. And this time, he couldn't be bothered to right the chair or haul his hostage up into it.

Jack's lips curled in a snarl. His eyes never left the gorilla's. Muttering profanities that only seemed to increase the big man's amusement, he got a grip on the rusted can he'd landed almost on top of. He maneuvered it with his fingertips until he turned the jagged lid inward. As he surreptitiously sawed at the plastic restraints, he wondered fleetingly how long it had been since his last tetanus shot. No matter. Lockjaw was the least of his worries right now. His gut told him Dominic St. Sebastian's pals played for keeps.

He got confirmation of that just moments after the giant's cell phone buzzed. Goliath picked up the instrument, glanced at the number displayed on the screen and hit Talk. Two grunts later, he set the phone down. A few moments after that, a door at the far end of the warehouse opened.

Still lying on his side, Jack curved his body so his front faced the door and his wrists were hidden behind his back. The damned can lid was slippery with blood from slicing into his skin, but the grim realization that it was now or never kept him razoring at the restraints.

He also kept his eyes on the three men who came through the door. One he recognized from the hotel. The second was a stranger. The third was Dominic St. Sebastian. His features seemed to freeze when he spotted the body sprawled

on the concrete. Then his eyes caught Jack's. He flashed a swift, silent message, but before Jack could interpret that damned thing, the stranger took a wide-legged stance a few yards away. He was dressed in a sleek gray suit and white wing tips. A distant corner of Jack's mind was wondering who the hell wore wing tips anymore when a vicious smile cut across the man's swarthy face.

"I have waited a long time for this, Ambassador."

"That right?"

"I thought to take you in Washington, but security there is too tight. How convenient that you have a woman here in New York."

The jagged lid took another slice out of Jack's thumb. He couldn't work the lid too hard with the stranger's eyes on him, but he didn't give up.

"Convenient for you, maybe," he drawled. "Not so much for me. Who the hell are you, anyway?"

"I am Antonio Cordi, the brother of Francesco Cordi. Perhaps you remember him?"

"Yeah, I remember him. Hard to forget the man who tried to gun down my father."

"And failed, unfortunately. We don't often miss our targets."

"'We' being you and the other scumbags who comprise 'Ndrangheta."

Jack was all too familiar with the confederation of Italian families that rose to power after the Cosa Nostra's decline in the 1990s. By forming alliances with Central and South American drug cartels, 'Ndrangheta had gone global and was now one of the world's most powerful criminal organizations. Its members were up to their hairy armpits in drug trafficking, prostitution, extortion, weapons smuggling and kidnappings for ransom. One U.S. State Department white paper estimated that their illegal activities accounted for more than $43 billion in 2007 alone—or approximately three percent of Italy's total gross domestic product.

Jack had gotten up close and personal with only one member of the clan, when his dad had been tapped to lead a delegation exploring the extent to which the 'Ndrangheta's money laundering had infiltrated the international banking system. The delegation followed one of the links to Francesco Cordi. When they dug a little too deep, Cordi retaliated by going after the high-ranking members of the delegation. Two died when their car was firebombed. Jack flew to Rome as soon as he heard about it and was with his father when Cordi came after him.

He had no regrets about taking Cordi down. Not then, not now. Even though he'd been advised by several concerned Italian officials that every member of the 'Ndrangheta swore a blood oath to always, *always* avenge the death of one of their own.

So he wasn't surprised when Cordi's brother slid a hand inside the jacket of his pearl-gray suit. Or that the hand emerged holding a blue steel Beretta.

Fourteen

Gina had never been inside a military command post but she suspected they couldn't be any more crowded or more tense than the apartment once Special Agent Driskell and her partner arrived.

With the duchess's permission, the FBI agents commandeered the study to interview Jack's father in private. That left Gina, her grandmother, Sarah, Dev, Zia and the obnoxious Dale Vickers to pick at the buffet lunch Maria had miraculously managed to augment with the arrival of each new wave of visitors.

Gina re-ee-eally wanted to tell Vickers to find somewhere else to squat, but the man was so worried about his friend and boss she didn't have the heart to kick him out of their unofficial command center. Besides, he and Dev seemed to have formed an unlikely partnership.

She tried to set aside her animosity for Vickers and study the two men objectively as they sat across from her, with the remains of the buffet lunch still littering the table. Jack's chief of staff was in an expensive-looking suit with his tie loosened and the top button of his shirt popped. Dev wore jeans and a faded, light blue denim shirt with the sleeves rolled up. With his broad shoulders, close-cropped black hair

and tanned skin, he looked as if he spent more time on his parents' New Mexico ranch than in boardrooms all around the globe. Yet anyone looking at the two men could easily pick out the power broker. Dev Hunter exuded the utter confidence that came with having built a multinational aerospace corporation from the ground up.

"Are you sure Jack had his cell phone on him when he left Washington?" he asked Vickers.

"I'm sure."

Frowning, Dev worked the buttons of his handheld device. "It's not emitting a signal."

"I could have told you that," Gina said. "Someone…"

She scrunched her forehead and ran through a mental litany of officials who'd responded to her 911 call. The NYPD detectives? The guy from the counterterrorism office? Pam Driskell? Aside from the short, stocky FBI agent, they were all pretty much a nameless, faceless blur now.

"I can't remember who, but someone ran a trace on Jack's cell phone within moments of showing up at the Excelsior. Maybe several someones. They said any recently manufactured cell phone has a built-in tracking device that allows eavesdroppers to pinpoint its location to within just a few feet."

"Unless the battery is removed," Dev muttered, playing with his gizmo. "Which must be the case here, or the ultra high frequency cargo container signal receptor we're developing for MilSatCom would pick it up."

"The what for the who?"

"I can't speak to the 'what,'" Sarah said as Dev continued to scowl at the instrument in his hand, "but the 'who' is the Military Satellite Communications System."

When both the duchess and Gina turned to stare at her, she smiled at their look of astonishment. "Don't be so surprised. I've been receiving a crash course on all things military since we got back from our honeymoon."

"You're serious?"

"As serious as the self-contained, bolt-on/bolt-off special operations surveillance system mounted in the belly of a C-130," she said solemnly.

Gina tried, she really tried, to picture her oh-so-elegant sister in one of the retro designer classic outfits she loved clambering around the belly of a C-130. Not that Gina knew what a C-130 was, exactly.

"What about your brother?" Dev asked Zia, cutting into Gina's wild imaginings. "Do you know Dom's cell phone number?"

"Of course," she said wearily. "But the police ran a trace on that, too, with no results."

"With all due respect to our various law enforcement agencies, they don't yet have access to the kind of technology I'm talking about here. It's still in the developmental stage and... Well, damn! That's it!"

Dev's exclamation shot up the tension level among the others in the room. The women all sat up in their chairs. Vickers hunched closer as Dev whipped out his own cell phone.

"That's what?" Vickers asked.

Shaking his head in obvious self-disgust, Dev tapped a number on his speed dial. "Why the hell didn't I think of it before?"

"Think of what?"

"Hold on." He put the phone to his ear. "Pat, I need the MilSat access code for the gamma version of CSR-II. I've been trying to get on using the beta version but... Yeah, I know. I know. Just get me the damned code."

"Ooooh," Sarah murmured, her green eyes dancing, "that's going to cost him."

"Pat Donovan is Dev's right-hand man," Gina explained to a bewildered Zia. "He's a wizard. Really, I think the man has magical powers. He can move mountains with a single phone call."

"If not mountains, at least the occupants of an entire Pa-

risian hotel," Sarah recalled. "I don't know what kind of a bonus Dev paid him for that particular trick but I have a feeling it ran to big bucks."

"Say again," Dev barked into the phone, his brows knit. "Right. Right. Okay, got it. What? Yeah, we'll talk about that later."

He disconnected and switched to his handheld device. The thing looked so innocuous. Just a small, wafer-thin box with a greenish-colored digital screen and a set of icons that appeared with the tap of a finger. It fit in the palm of Dev's hand and could easily be mistaken for a smart phone, except this little gadget could evidently bounce signals off the moon or something.

He was entering a long involved code when the sliding doors to the study slammed back. Every head turned in surprise as Driskell's partner raced out and made a beeline for the foyer. Driskell herself was right on his heels, with Jack's dad staggering white-faced behind them.

The FBI agent paused only long enough to throw out a terse explanation. "We've got a report of shots fired. Initial indications are the situation may involve the ambassador."

"Involve *how?*" Gina jumped up. The violent movement sent her chair crashing to the floor. "Agent Driskell, wait! Is Jack hurt?"

"Or my brother?" Zia demanded as she, too, surged to her feet.

"I don't know," the FBI agent replied on the run. "I'll contact y'all as soon as I do."

"I'm coming with you!"

Gina shouted to an empty space. Driskell was already out the front door, leaving a frozen tableau of tension and fear in her wake. Dev shattered the silence with an abrupt command.

"Gina, do you have Driskell's cell phone number?"

She could hardly speak past the terror lodged like a spiked ball in her throat. "Yes."

Wedging a hand into the pocket of her jeans, she extracted

the business card Driskell had given her earlier. Dev snatched it from her fingers and entered the number on his device. Mere seconds later, his blue eyes lit with fierce satisfaction.

"Okay, I've got her." He swung toward the foyer. "Let's go."

Gina, Zia, Jack's dad and Dale Vickers all wheeled in a swift formation that would have done a platoon of marines proud. Their syncopated turn didn't impress Dev.

"Whoa! We can't all—"

"Do not say it!" Zia interrupted. Her dark eyes blazed and her accent went thick with passion. "I am a doctor. If Dom... If anyone is hurt, I can help."

"I'm going, too," Jack's dad growled.

Dale Vickers didn't say a thing but his pugnacious expression dared anyone, Dev included, to try and stop him.

Sarah was the only who exhibited any restraint. "I'll stay with Grandmama." Her gaze drilled into her husband. "But please, please, be careful."

"I will." Dev strode for the foyer. "We'll have to take two cabs."

"Sarah!" Gina called over her shoulder. "Buzz down and tell Jerome to get on his whistle. We need two taxis, like pronto!"

The doorman had them lined up and waiting at the curb when they all poured out of the elevators. Dev aimed for the lead vehicle and issued orders in a voice that said he wasn't allowing vetoes this time.

"Gina, you and Zia with me. Vickers, you follow with Mr. Mason."

They scrambled into their assigned cabs. Gina and Zia took the backseat of the first, Dev folded his tall frame into the front.

"Hey, mon," the cabbie said in a lilting Caribbean accent that matched his shoulder-length dreadlocks and colorful orange, green, yellow and black knit cap. "Where ya goin'?"

"Straight down Central Park West until I tell you to turn."

The cabbie shrugged and activated his meter. As the leafy green of the park zipped by, Dev kept his narrowed gaze on the street grid filling his screen.

Gina edged forward on her seat and looked over his shoulder. All she could see was a tiny red dot racing along the grid.

"Is that Driskell?"

"It is."

"What happens if she gets or makes a call? You won't lose the track, will you?"

"Heads in my R-and-D division will roll if I do."

Not quite reassured by that grim prediction, Gina groped for her cousin's hand. Zia threw her a glance filled with equal parts hope and determination.

"They will be okay, your man and my brother. But to make sure…" She squeezed Gina's fingers. "I shall say a special prayer to Saint Stephen. He is the patron saint of your grandmother's homeland, you know."

No, Gina didn't know. At this point, though, she would pray to any celestial being who might intercede on Jack and Dom's behalf.

As if sensing how close her cousin was to a total meltdown, Zia tried to distract her with details about the saint. "He is Istvan in our language. He was born in 965 or '67 or '75. No one knows for sure. His father was Grand Prince Géza of Hungary. His mother, the daughter of Gylua of Transylvania."

The mention of Transylvania diverted Gina long enough for all-too-vivid images of werewolves springing out of coffins to flash into her mind. Or was it vampires who rose from the dead? For God's sake! Who cared?

Zia refused to let her cousin's wildly careening thoughts and emotions overwhelm her. Speaking calmly, slowly, soothingly, she related how the eventual Saint Istvan married Giselle of Bavaria and ascended to the throne of the Magyars on the death of his father. How he discouraged pagan

customs and strengthened Christianity by a series of strict laws. How he was devastated by the death of his oldest son, Emeric, in a hunting accident, after which his cousin, Duke Vazul, took part in an assassination conspiracy.

"The attempt failed," Zia related as Dev issued a sharp order to the cabbie to cut across town. "Vazul had his eyes gouged out and molten lead poured in his ears."

"Umm," Gina murmured.

Her eyes were on that blinking red dot, her thoughts anywhere but with some long dead saint.

"Without a living heir, King St. Istvan asked the Blessed Virgin Mary to take the Hungarian people as her subjects and become their queen. He died on the same feast day that commemorates the assumption into heaven of the Blessed Virgin Mary, yes?"

"What? Oh. Right."

Gina had no idea what her cousin had been talking about. Her focus was on the bridge ahead. As a native New Yorker, she understood why the cabbie balked.

"I don't do runs to that part of Brooklyn," he said with a head shake that set his dreadlocks swinging.

"There's an extra five hundred in it for you," Dev countered.

"Say no more, mon."

As they cruised onto the bridge, Gina twisted around. The second cab was still following. She dropped back in her seat, wondering how much Jack's dad had offered his driver.

Once across the bridge they entered a twilight zone of abandoned warehouses and crumbling industrial facilities. The area had formerly been home to the Brooklyn Navy Yard and had died a painful death in the '60s or '70s. Gina knew a comeback was planned, but it was still a ways off.

Artists and commercial activities rented space in the cavernous building that hadn't collapsed under the weight of time and disuse. She saw a bright pink neon sign indicating

a movie studio. Another, slightly less attention-grabbing billboard advertised Brooklyn Grange Farm. The farm supposedly utilized 45,000 square feet on the roof of Building 3, wherever that was. Sadly, all too many of the structures showed an endless vista of graffiti-covered walls, trash-strewn yards fenced off with razor wire, and row after row of broken windows.

With every deserted block the cab skimmed past, Gina's hopes dipped lower and lower. They hit rock-bottom when the taxi turned a corner and she spotted what looked like twenty or more emergency vehicles dead ahead.

The cabbie screeched to a halt a half block away. "Hey, mon, I can't cruise close to no cop cars. They might have dogs with 'em."

"Christ," Dev muttered, "what are you hauling in... Oh, hell, never mind."

He shoved a wad of bills at the driver and shouldered open the door. Gina and Zia scrambled out at the same time.

"Stay here until I scope out the situation," Dev ordered brusquely.

"No way," Gina said, her frantic gaze locked on the two ambulances parked side by side amid the other vehicles.

She took off after Zia, who'd already broken into a dead run. All Dev could do at that point was curse and charge after her. If shots were fired from any of the broken windows staring sightlessly down at them, he'd damned well better get in front of Gina and shield her body with his. Sarah would never forgive him if her sister got hurt. Zia would just have to take her chances.

The cabbie barely waited for them to clear his vehicle before screeching into a three-point turn. He almost swiped the second cab's fender when he peeled off. Dev heard the shriek of brakes, the thud of doors slamming, the slam of footsteps on pavement as Vickers and Jack's father raced down the street.

Luckily, they all reached the protective screen of emer-

gency vehicles without shots erupting from the warehouse. The uniformed officer on the perimeter looked as if he might draw his weapon, though, when the two women leading the charge ignored his command to stop. Parting like the proverbial Red Sea, they started to go around him.

"Hey! Hold it right there."

He made a grab for the closest, which happened to be Zia, and got a face full of raging female.

"*Vagyok orvos!* Ach! I am doctor! Doctor!"

Her unleashed emotions made her accent so heavy that the English was almost indistinguishable from the Hungarian. Neither made an impression on the uniformed officer.

"Look, lady, you…all of you…better not take another friggin' step until I see some ID, log you in and get clearance to…"

"*Ide,* Anastazia!"

The shout came from an unmarked vehicle parked inside the cordon. Zia whirled and gave a glad cry. The rest of the group spun around, as well. Gina registered a half-dozen wildly careening thoughts as she watched Dominic stride toward them.

Blood seeped from a slash high on one cheek. One eye was swollen shut. He wasn't in handcuffs. And he was alone.

Dear God! He was alone.

With a sob of sheer terror, she dodged the uniformed officer and broke into another run. He gave a shout, but interpreted a short air-chop from Dominic as a signal that his duty lay in keeping the rest of the crowd corralled.

Ten steps later, Gina flung herself at Dominic. Her fists hammered a frantic drumbeat on his chest. "Where's Jack? What did you do with him? If you or those thugs you were with hurt him, I'll carve out your heart and shove it down your throat."

Dom's eyes widened, and Gina shocked even herself with the viciousness of the threat. A distant corner of her mind registered a flicker of surprise that she hadn't burst into her

by-now-usual flood of tears. Her otherwise volatile hormones seemed to have narrowed to a single, deadly and completely primal urge.

If this man—if any man—had harmed her mate, she'd make that Italian crime organization Jack's dad mentioned seem like a bunch of playful kindergarteners.

"Tell me, dammit. Where's Jack?"

Dom caught her pounding fists before they did serious damage to his chest wall. "He's there, Gina." Keeping a careful grip on her wrists, he angled her around. "Talking with some agents from the FBI."

She spotted him the same moment he followed Agent Driskell's nod and glanced over his shoulder. In the ten seconds it took for Gina to wrestle out of Dom's hold and Jack to sprint the fifty or so yards separating them, she saw that he was as bruised as her cousin.

But it was his eyes that lit her heart up like the Fourth of July. His fierce, unguarded expression. The raw, male pheromones shooting off him like live sparks when he caught her in his arms. Her blood singing with joy, she returned his kiss with every ounce of relief, of desire, of love that was in her.

Swift, frightening sanity came in the form of a sticky residue that transferred from the sleeve of his dark charcoal suit coat to Gina's palm. In her mad rush to his arms, she hadn't noticed the stain.

She couldn't miss it now. It left her palm a rusty red and a lump of dismay the size of a basketball bouncing around in her stomach. Gently, gingerly, she tried to ease away from the injured arm.

"You're hurt."

"So are you."

He curled a knuckle under her chin and angled her chin to survey the ugly bruise.

"I thought slamming my fist into your cousin's eye made up for this," he said, murder in his voice. "Looks like he still has some payment coming."

"You gave Dom his black eye?" Gina couldn't make sense of any of this. "If he was part of the plot to kidnap you, why isn't he under arrest?"

"Long story. Why don't we…?" He broke off, his gaze going to the men who now approached. "Hello, Dad. Dale."

Jack didn't seem the least surprised to see his father or chief of staff. Gina backed away to give them access to the man they all loved. She could share him with his family. With his obnoxious assistant. With his memories of Catherine.

And with the child they would welcome to the world in just a few short months. Lost in a love undiminished by the past or constrained by the present, Gina acknowledged there was more than enough of Jack Mason to go around.

Fifteen

Once again the duchess's spacious apartment served as command central. Most of the key players in the day's drama sat elbow-to-elbow at the dining table, relieving their tension with their choice of coffee, iced tea, fruit juice, *žuta osa* or the last of the double-distilled *pálinka*.

The duchess and Jack's father had opted for the brandy. Jack, Dev, Zia and Dom braved the throat-searing kick of the liqueur. Dale Vickers went with coffee, while Gina and Sarah chose juice. The duchess insisted Maria fill her own glass rather than trying to keep everyone's topped off and just sit down.

Pam Driskell put in a brief appearance, as did Jerome. The doorman had delegated his post to a subordinate to accompany the FBI agent upstairs. He'd abandoned his dignity long enough to wrap Gina in a fierce hug. He then shook Jack's hand, told him how happy he was to see him safe and went back to work.

The only major players who failed to put in an appearance were Antonio Cordi and his two thugs. Cordi because he was dead, shot through the heart during the violence that erupted inside the warehouse just moments before the police arrived. One of his hired hands was also deceased, the big

one Jack bitingly referred to as Goliath. He'd had his jugular sliced by the lid of a rusty tin can and had bled out before the EMTs arrived. The second thug was now a guest of the U.S. government and likely to remain so for a long, long time.

Even now, huddled at the table that could seat twenty comfortably with the leaves in, Gina felt sick at the thought of how close both Jack and Dom had been to being on the receiving end of a bullet.

"Cordi must have wondered if my well-publicized departure from Interpol was a blind," Dom related after tossing back another restorative shot of *pálinka.* "He allowed me into the outer fringe of 'Ndrangheta but never let me get close enough to gather the evidence we needed to nail him."

"So to get close to the capo," Jack drawled, "you suggested using your kinship to Gina as a means to get to me."

"Cordi had sworn a blood oath to avenge his brother," Dom said with an unrepentant shrug. "He would have gotten to you eventually. I merely proved my loyalty by offering to set up the hit."

Gina still couldn't believe the tangled web of lies and deceit Dom had lived for almost a year. Danger had stalked him with every breath, every step.

Zia was even more appalled. She'd had no idea her brother had infiltrated one of Europe's most vicious crime organizations. Or that he'd arranged this "business" trip to New York City for a specific, and very deadly, purpose.

"No wonder you balked at my decision to accompany you," she said, scowling.

"You would not have accompanied me, had I not been sure I could keep you safe from danger."

"Not to mention," Dev guessed shrewdly, "the fact that she added to your credibility with the duchess."

"Yes, there was that consideration." A wry smile curved Dom's lips. "You don't know my sister very well, however, if you think my objections carried any weight with her. If I hadn't been certain I could keep her safe, I would have been

forced to chain her to a wall in the dungeon of the crumbling castle the Duchess Charlotte once called home."

Jack's voice cut across the table like a serrated knife blade. "Too bad you couldn't offer the same guarantees for Gina."

"Ah, yes."

Dom's glance went to the bruise on Gina's chin. His one eye was still swollen shut, but the other showed real chagrin. "I very much regret having to hurt you, cousin. My associates had become impatient, you see, and I had to act or risk blowing my cover."

His glance slewed to Jack, then back to Gina. A rakish glint replaced the regret in his good eye. "If you would but let me," he murmured, "I would kiss away the hurt."

Jack answered that. This time his tone was slow and lazy but even more lethal. "You really do like living on the edge, don't you, St. Sebastian?"

"That's enough!"

The sharp reprimand turned every head to the duchess. Her chin had tilted to a degree that both Gina and Sarah recognized instantly, and her faded blue eyes shot daggers at the two combatants.

"May I remind you that you're guests in my home? Dominic, you will cease making such deliberately provocative comments. Jack, you will stop responding like a Neanderthal ready to club all rivals. Gina…"

When her gimlet gaze zinged to her youngest granddaughter, Gina jerked upright in her chair. She'd been on the receiving end of that stare too many times to take it lightly.

"What did I do?"

"It's what you haven't done," the duchess informed her. "For pity's sake, tell Jack you love him as much as he so obviously loves you and get on with planning your wedding."

A few moments of stark silence greeted the acerbic pronouncement. Jack broke it with a cool reply. "With all due respect, Duchess, that's something Gina and I should discuss in private."

His father joined the fray with a sudden and explosive exclamation. "Bull hockey!"

"Dad…"

John II ignored his son's warning glance. The face he turned to Gina wore a mix of regret and resolution. "I know I acted like an ass when you came to visit us at Five Oaks."

"Pretty much," she agreed politely.

"I need to apologize for that. And for the ugly name I called you earlier this morning," he added with a wince.

"Christ, Dad, what the hell did you…?"

"Be quiet, Jack. This is between Gina and me."

John Harris Mason II hadn't lost his bite. His son matched him glower for glower but yielded the floor. Once again, the older man addressed Gina.

"That was unforgivable. I hope you'll chalk it up to a father sick to death with worry over his son."

"Consider it chalked," she said with a shaky smile.

Oh, boy! Her emotions were starting one of their wild swings. Now that the danger to Jack had passed and she was surrounded by everyone she loved most in the world, she wasn't sure how long she could hold out before dissolving into wet, sloppy tears.

Jack's father didn't help matters. He leaned forward, his gaze holding hers. "I've never seen anyone turn Jack on his head the way you have, Gina."

"Is that…?" She gulped. "Is that good?"

"Oh, yes. More than I can say. You've shaken him out of the mold I tried… We all tried," he said with a glance at Dale Vickers, "to force him into."

He paused. His throat worked, sending his Adam's apple up and down a few times. When he could speak again, his voice was raw with emotion.

"Jack's mother would be proud to call you daughter. So would I."

That did it. Gina could feel her face getting all blotchy with the effort of holding back tears. "I…I…"

Shoving back her chair, she resorted to her most trust-worthy excuse for beating an instant retreat.

"I have to pee."

Sarah had followed her when she'd retreated to the bath-room earlier in the afternoon. This time it was Jack. Except he didn't knock, as her sister had. Nor did he ask for per-mission to enter. He just barged in and kicked the door shut behind him.

Luckily, Gina hadn't really needed to go. Her panties weren't around her ankles. The skinny jeans she'd been wear-ing for what now felt like two lifetimes were still zipped up. She was on the pot, though, and the tears she'd tried so hard to stem streamed down her cheeks. Like Sarah, Jack sank to his knees beside the stool. Unlike Sarah, he didn't hesitate to drag Gina off the throne and into his arms.

"Don't cry, sweetheart. Please, don't cry."

He held her, rocking back and forth, while the residual stress and tension and fear poured out via her tear ducts.

"It's…it's the hormones," she said through hiccuping sobs. "I never cry. Never! Ask Sarah. Ask…ask Grandmama. They'll tell you."

"It's okay."

"Noooo," she wailed, "it's not."

She grabbed the front of his shirt. His bloodied shirt. He hadn't had time to change, either.

"I didn't get a chance to tell you this morning, Jack. I…I didn't think I'd ever get a chance to tell you. I love you."

"I know, darling."

"No, you don't!"

The tears evaporated, replaced by an urgency that reached deep into her core.

"I think…" She shook her head. "Scratch that! I know I fell a little bit in love with you our first weekend together. I'm not sure when I tumbled all the rest of the way, but I'm all the way there."

"Me, too, my darling."

His smile was all Jack. Charming, roguish and so damned sexy Gina could feel her tears drying and another part of her starting to get wet.

"So what do you think?" he said, dropping a kiss on her nose. "Want get off the floor, go back into the dining room and tell your grandmother to start planning a wedding?"

"No."

His confidence took a hit, but he recovered fast. Shaking his head, he acknowledged his gaffe. "I'm such a jackass. How could I forget you're the world's greatest event coordinator?"

"Yeah, right."

Those damned hormones! Gina could for the sneer curled her lip and the sulky response she couldn't hold back.

"I can't be that great if you had to send Washington business TTG's way."

"What are you talking about?"

"Dale told me you steered business to TTG." She made a heroic effort to keep the hurt out of her voice. "I appreciate it, Jack. I really do. It's just that I wanted to… I was trying to… Oh, crap!"

The hand that took her chin and tilted it up was anything but gentle.

"Listen to me, Eugenia Amalia Thérése St. Sebastian. I'm going to say this once, and once only. If Dale Vickers or anyone else in my office steered business to TTG, they did it without my knowledge or consent. You got that?"

The fire in his blue eyes convinced her as much as the uncomfortable grip on her still sore chin.

"I've got it."

"You'd better," he said, the anger still hot. "Now, do you want to work the wedding arrangements yourself or not?"

"Not."

"Dammit all to hell! I'm past being civilized and modern and reasonable about this. If I have to lock you in those

chains your cousin talked about and drag you to the altar, I will. One way or another, you're going to marry me."

"Oooooh."

Gina batted her eyes and thought about leading him on a little longer. She decided against it, primarily because she wasn't quite sure he wouldn't follow through with that bit about the chains.

"As much as I might enjoy the kinky aspects of your proposal," she breathed, "I think we should go for something a little more traditional."

"Then for God's sake," he bellowed, "tell me what the hell you want."

Whoa! What happened to the smooth, polished diplomat who'd seduced her with his charm and sophisticated wit? This glimpse of the angry male under Jack's urbane shell thrilled and made her just a tad nervous. Yielding to the age-old feminine instinct to soothe and soften and placate her mate, Gina stroked his cheek.

"What I want," she said, "is for us to get off the bathroom floor. Then we'll make a call to your mom and get her up here on the next flight. After which, we'll haul ass to a lab and have our blood drawn so we can stand up before the nearest justice of the peace."

Jack agreed with the last portion of her agenda, if not the first. Instead of pushing to his feet and pulling her up with him, he kept her anchored to the fluffy bath mat. The fire went out of his eyes, the irritation out of his voice.

"Are you sure that's what you want?" he asked in a much subdued tone.

"That's what I want."

"No big fancy wedding? No exotic theme?"

"No big fancy wedding." With silent apologies to Nikki and Samuel and Kallie, she lied her heart out. "No exotic theme. Just you and me and our immediate families in front of a JP."

* * *

Gina should have known that plan wouldn't hold up against the combined assault of her sister, her grandmother and Jack's mom, Ellen. All right, maybe she didn't really want it to. She'd given too much of herself and her energy to the party-planning business. In her heart of hearts, she secretly wished for at least a little splash.

Still, she had to work to overcome her irritation when her boss called less than an hour after Gina and Jack had emerged from the bathroom and announced their intentions to the assembled entourage. Vickers, Gina thought immediately. The little toad probably had TTG on his speed dial.

"Gina," Nikki gushed in her rapid-fire way, "I just heard! You've finally come to your senses."

"I…"

"I'm so, so glad you've agreed to marry your sexy ambassador."

"I have, but…"

"Listen, kiddo, I know Jack is hot to get you to the altar before you change your mind. I also know you want to keep the wedding small and intimate, but the midtown venue's available Thursday evening."

"Nikki…"

"My office, ten tomorrow morning. We'll hammer out the details. Oh, and bring your grandmother. I've been wanting to meet her since the day my father announced he was leaving my mother for her. God, I wish he had! Might have saved me thousands of dollars in shrink fees. *Ciao,* my darling. And don't worry. TTG will send you off in grand style."

Send you off in grand style.

The blithe promise had been intended to reassure. It acted instead like a bucket of frigid water. Every spark of Gina's newfound joy got a thorough dousing.

Grandmama, she thought on a wave of dismay. How could she move to D.C. and live with Jack? Not that he'd remain in

D.C. much longer. Vickers had hinted he was being considered for a major diplomatic posting. London was a definite possibility. So was Athens.

Heartsick, she caught Sarah's eye and telegraphed a silent signal. Her sister's hidden antenna were obviously in full receive mode. She nodded and moments later pushed through the swinging door to the kitchen. As soon as she saw Gina's face, concern clouded her green eyes.

"What's the matter?"

"Nothing out of the ordinary," Gina said bitterly. "I'm just being my usual, selfish self."

"Selfish how?"

"I didn't even think about Grandmama when I agreed to marry Jack. She's so looking forward to the baby. She's already talking about converting the study to a nursery. How can I just flit off and leave her alone?"

"She wants you to be happy. She wants both of us to be happy. You know she does."

Gina might have believed her if not for the guilt clouding Sarah's forest-green eyes. She'd experienced the same wrenching pangs before her wedding to Dev. They hadn't eased until Gina posed the possibility of moving back into the Dakota.

"Dev said he could set up a temporary headquarters here in New York," Sarah reminded her sister. "We could still do that. Or..."

The swish of the swinging door cut off whatever alternate Sarah had intended to propose. She and Gina both turned to face Zia.

"I'm sorry to intrude," she said. "But I wished to speak to you both, and this may be my only chance before Dom and I move to a hotel."

The heavy, stress-induced accent had disappeared. Zia was once again their gorgeous, self-assured cousin.

Or a third sister. One demanding to be included in this

girls-only enclave. The thought struck Gina all of two seconds before Zia gave it flesh and blood.

"As Gina knows," she said to Sarah, "I've just finished my last year of medical school at Semmelweis University in Budapest. It's a very prestigious institution and…well…"

She shrugged, as if to downplay what both sisters knew had to be a major accomplishment. "I've been offered a number of residencies in pediatric medicine," she continued after a moment. "One of them is at Kravis Children's Hospital. That's why I insisted on accompanying Dom on this visit. I…I have an interview with the head of the residency program tomorrow," she finished on a note of uncharacteristic hesitation.

"That's wonderful," Sarah said with unfeigned delight. "You and Grandmama will be able to visit and get to know each other better."

"Yes, well…" Zia's glance shifted from one sister to the other. "The duchess has invited me to live with her, should I do my three-year residency here in New York City. I'm overwhelmed by her generosity but I don't wish to impose on her. If the idea concerns you…either of you…or in any way makes you think I'm taking advantage of her, please tell me."

Gina wished she were a better person. She really did! Here she was, wracked with guilt one moment at the prospect of leaving her grandmother alone. In the next, she was battling a toxic niggle of jealousy at the idea of this ultra-smart, ultra-achieving woman taking her place in the duchess's heart.

And of course, because Zia *was* so damned smart, she read every emotion that flitted across Gina's face.

"I will not live here if you don't wish it," she said quietly. "Or you, Sarah. I know how much you love the duchess. How much she loves you. If it will cause you or her heartache, I'll turn down the offer from Kravis. None of you will ever hear from me again."

Gina knew the speech came straight from the heart. But it was the mist that sheened her cousin's dark eyes that oblit-

erated any and every doubt. Somehow, someway, the knowledge that brilliant, self-assured Anastazia St. Sebastian was susceptible to human emotion made everything all right.

The jealousy fell away, leaving only a profound thankfulness. Smiling, she reached out and squeezed Zia's hand.

"I think it would be wonderful for Grandmama to have your company."

Sixteen

Nicole Tremayne came through as promised. TTG sent
Gina and Jack off in grand style.

The balmy June evening was perfect for an outdoor ceremony. Thousands of tiny white lights gleamed in the topiary
trees outlining the terrace of TTG's midtown venue. More
lights sheathed in filmy white netting were hung in graceful loops to form an archway from the reception room to the
dais. The platform itself was framed by antique wrought-
iron. The intricate iron work was painted pearl-white and
intertwined with netting, lights, ivy and fragrant yellow hon-
eysuckle.

Gina and Jack had kept the guest list small. Relatively
small, that is, compared to the hundreds who usually attended TTG's functions. Still, the attendees filled eight rows
of white chairs arranged in a semicircle on the terrace overlooking the East River.

Gina's coworkers at TTG came as guests for a change instead of employees. Jerome and his wife had been invited,
of course, and Maria beamed from her seat in the front row.
Dominic sat beside her, his black eye still noticeable but
considerably reduced in size and discoloration.

Jack's guests filled the seats on the other side of the aisle.

Following her son's wishes, Ellen had been ruthless. She'd axed every one of the political cronies her husband had tried to add to the list. Only Jack's family, close personal friends and associates survived the hatchet. In his case, though, "close" included the Secretary of State, the current U.S. Ambassador to the U.N. and Virginia's lieutenant governor.

"You ready, Gina?"

Kallie was the only of her fellow employees not seated out front. She'd volunteered to get the major players in place and cue the music. The wings in her red hair were yellow tonight in keeping with the yellow roses that wreathed the hair of the bride and her attendants.

The event coordinator in Gina had her taking a quick peek through the gauze curtains to make sure everyone was where they were supposed to be. Sure enough, Jack waited under the wrought-iron arch with his groomsmen. Dev stood tall and handsome beside him. Dale Vickers was arranged next to Dev. Gina grimaced inwardly but reminded herself of her resolution to *try* to build a better relationship with the little toad.

She let the curtain drop and sent a smile to the other three women clustered with her in the small anteroom. Her grandmother, regal in royal blue silk and lace, looked like the grand duchess she was. Gina had asked Zia to be one of her attendants. And Sarah, of course. They were each wearing the dress of her choice. Zia had hit the shops on 5th Avenue and found a body-hugging gold silk sheath that dipped to her waist in the back. With her black hair piled loosely on top of her head, the rear view was sure to drop most of the male jaws in the house when she glided down the aisle.

Sarah's dress was one of the retro classics she still favored despite Dev's repeated attempts to get her to buy out Rodeo Drive. This one was a Balenciaga that fell in soft, shimmering folds in the same vivid green hue as the Russian emerald Dev had slipped on her finger when they'd become engaged.

Gina's choice of rings was more traditional, if you could

call a three-carat marquise traditional. Particularly since Jack had upped the weight from her original choice and had the stone set in a band studded with another three carats of baguettes.

The diamonds' glitter didn't compare to the sparkle in Gina's smile as she gave Kallie the go-ahead. "I am so ready."

She wasn't sure, but she thought Sarah and the duchess let out a collective sigh of relief. Even Zia perked up as the music swelled and she led the way down the aisle. Sarah gave her sister a quick kiss and went next. Then Gina slipped her arm through her grandmother's.

As they made their slow progress under the arch of netting and tiny white lights, Gina couldn't believe how her world had changed so drastically in such a short time. Was it only two months since Grandmama had made this same, slow walk with Sarah? Two and a half months since Gina had peed on a little purple stick and felt her world tilt off its axis? Those frantic days might have happened in another life, to another person. Everything in Gina's world now was right and bright and perfect.

The duchess seemed to agree. When she and her youngest granddaughter reached the dais, her faded blue eyes shone with love. "My dearest Eugenia. I'm so very proud of you."

Gina wouldn't cry! She wouldn't! She wanted to, though. Big, fat, wet, sloppy tears that would streak her entire face with mascara.

Uh-oh! Jack must have sensed how close she was to a meltdown. He took a hasty step forward, smiling as he relieved the duchess of escort duty.

"I'll take it from here."

Bending, he dropped a kiss on his soon-to-be-grandmother-in-law's cheek. She murmured something for his ears only. Probably the same death threat she'd issued to Dev, Gina guessed, threatening him with unspeakable agony if he hurt so much as a single hair on her head.

Jack acknowledged the warning with a solemn nod. Then

his eyes were on Gina. Only on Gina. Her glorious smile, her tumble of silvery blond curls, her laughing blue eyes. He tucked her arm in his, amazed and humbled by the fact he'd been given the precious gift of love twice in one lifetime.

In all the excitement of the past week, he and Gina had almost missed their second appointment with their OB doc. They'd gone in yesterday and had the first ultrasound done. Jack carried a copy of the scan in his tux pocket now, right next to his heart. As far as his parents knew, he and Gina would welcome the Mason family's first set of twins.

First things first, though! Jack's number one priority at the moment was getting a wedding band on Gina St. Sebastian's finger. He practically dragged her into position on the dais and issued a swift instruction to the senior judge of the U.S. Court of Appeals for the Second Circuit, who also happened to be his former college roommate.

"Let's do this!"

Epilogue

What an exciting, frightening, wonderful week this has been! Eugenia, my darling Eugenia, finally admitted what I've known since the day she returned from Switzerland. She's in love, so very much in love, with the father of her babies. Babies! I can't wait to cradle them in my arms, as I once held Gina.

Then there's Sarah, my lovely Sarah. It makes my heart sing to see her so happy, too. I suspect it won't be long before she and Dev start their family, as well.

I thought my life's work would be complete when I escorted those two precious girls down the aisle. How odd, and how wonderful, that another young and vibrant twosome has helped fill the void of losing them. Dominic goes back to Hungary in a few days and is pressing me to return to my homeland for a visit. I shall have to think about that. In the meantime, I'll share Anastazia's trials and tribulations as she begins what I know will be a grueling residency.

Who would have imagined my plate would be so full at this late stage in my life?

From the diary of Charlotte,
Grand Duchess of Karlenburgh

* * * * *

HER
UNFORGETTABLE
ROYAL LOVER

BY
MERLINE LOVELACE

To Neta and Dave, friends, traveling buds and the source of all kinds of fodder for my books. Thanks for the info on research grants and nasty bugs, Neta!

Prologue

Who would have imagined my days would become this rich and full, and at such a late point in my life! My darling granddaughter Sarah and her husband, Dev, have skillfully blended marriage with their various enterprises, their charitable work and their travels to all parts of the world. Yet Sarah still finds time to involve me in the book she's writing on lost treasures of the art world. My input has been limited, to be sure, but I've very much enjoyed being part of such an ambitious undertaking.

And Eugenia, my carefree, high-spirited Eugenia, has surprised herself by becoming the most amazing wife and mother. Her twins are very much like she was at that age. Bright-eyed and lively, with very distinct personalities. And best of all, her husband, Jack, is being considered for appointment as US Ambassador to the United Nations. If he's confirmed, he and Gina and the babies would live only a few blocks away.

Until that happens, I have the company of my longtime friend and companion, Maria. And Anastazia, my lovely, so serious Anastazia. Zia's in her second year of a residency in pediatric medicine and I played shamelessly on our somewhat tenuous kinship to convince her to live with me for the three-year program. She wears herself to the bone, poor dear, but Maria and I see that she eats well and gets at least some rest.

It's her brother, Dominic, I fret about. Dom insists he's not ready to settle down, and why should he with all the women who throw themselves at him? His job worries me, however. It's too dangerous, too high-risk. I do wish he would quit working undercover, and may have found just the enticement to encourage him to do so. How surprised he'll be when I tell him about the document Sarah's clever research assistant has discovered!

From the diary of Charlotte,
Grand Duchess of Karlenburgh

One

August was slamming New York City when Dominic St. Sebastian climbed out of a cab outside the castle-like Dakota. Heat waves danced like demented demons above the sidewalks. Across the street, moisture-starved leaves drifted like yellowed confetti from the trees in Central Park. Even the usual snarl of cabs and limos and sightseeing buses cruising the Upper West Side seemed lethargic and sluggish.

The same couldn't be said for the Dakota's doorman. As dignified as ever in his lightweight summer uniform, Jerome abandoned his desk to hold the door for the new arrival.

"Thanks," Dom said with the faint accent that marked him as European despite the fact that English came as naturally to him as his native Hungarian. Shifting his carryall to his right hand, he clapped the older man's shoulder with his left. "How's the duchess?"

"As strong-willed as ever. She wouldn't listen to the rest of us, but Zia finally convinced her to forego her daily constitutional during this blistering heat."

Dom wasn't surprised his sister had succeeded where others failed. Anastazia Amalia Julianna St. Sebastian combined the slashing cheekbones, exotic eyes and stunning beauty of a supermodel with the tenacity of a bulldog.

And now his beautiful, tenacious sister was living with

Grand Duchess Charlotte. Zia and Dom had met their long-lost relative for the first time only last year and formed an instant bond. So close a bond that Charlotte had invited Zia to live at the Dakota during her pediatric residency at Mt. Sinai.

"Has my sister started her new rotation?" Dom asked while he and Jerome waited for the elevator.

He didn't doubt the doorman would know. He had the inside track on most of the Dakota's residents but kept a close eye on his list of favorites. Topping that list were Charlotte St. Sebastian and her two granddaughters, Sarah and Gina. Zia had recently been added to the select roster.

"She started last week," Jerome advised. "She doesn't say so, but I can see oncology is hard on her. Would be on anyone, diagnosing and treating all those sick children. And the hospital works the residents to the bone, which doesn't help." He shook his head, but brightened a moment later. "Zia wrangled this afternoon off, though, when she heard you were flying in. Oh, and Lady Eugenia is here, too. She arrived last night with the twins."

"I haven't seen Gina and the twins since the duchess's birthday celebration. The girls must be, what? Six or seven months old now?"

"Eight." Jerome's seamed face folded into a grin. Like everyone else, he'd fallen hard for an identical pair of rosebud mouths, lake-blue eyes and heads topped with their mother's spun-sugar, silvery-blond curls.

"Lady Eugenia says they're crawling now," he warned. "Better watch where you step and what you step in."

"I will," Dom promised with a grin.

As the elevator whisked him to the fifth floor, he remembered the twins as he'd last seen them. Cooing and blowing bubbles and waving dimpled fists, they'd already developed into world-class heartbreakers.

They'd since developed two powerful sets of lungs,

Dom discovered when a flushed and flustered stranger yanked open the door.

"It's about time! We've been…"

She stopped, blinking owlishly behind her glasses, while a chorus of wails rolled down the marble-tiled foyer.

"You're not from Osterman's," she said accusingly.

"The deli? No, I'm not."

"Then who…? Oh! You're Zia's brother." Her nostrils quivered, as if she'd suddenly caught a whiff of something unpleasant. "The one who goes through women like a hot knife through butter."

Dom hooked a brow but couldn't dispute the charge. He enjoyed the company of women. Particularly the generously curved, pouty-lipped, out-for-a-good-time variety.

The one facing him now certainly didn't fall into the first two of those categories. Not that he could see more than a suggestion of a figure inside her shapeless linen dress and boxy jacket. Her lips were anything but pouty, however. Pretty much straight-lined, as a matter of fact, with barely disguised disapproval.

"Igen," Dom agreed lazily in his native Hungarian. "I'm Dominic. And you are?"

"Natalie," she bit out, wincing as the howls behind her rose to high-pitched shrieks. "Natalie Clark. Come in, come in."

Dom had spent almost seven years now as an Interpol agent. During that time, he'd helped take down his share of drug traffickers, black marketeers and the scum who sold young girls and boys to the highest bidders. Just last year he'd helped foil a kidnapping and murder plot against Gina's husband right here in New York City. But the scene that greeted him as he paused at the entrance to the duchess's elegant sitting room almost made him turn tail and run.

A frazzled Gina was struggling to hang on to a red-

faced, furiously squirming infant in a frilly dress and a lacy headband with a big pink bow. Zia had her arms full with the second, equally enraged and similarly attired baby. The duchess sat straight-backed and scowling in regal disapproval, while the comfortably endowed Honduran who served as her housekeeper and companion stood at the entrance to the kitchen, her face screwed into a grimace as the twins howled their displeasure.

Thankfully, the duchess reached her limit before Dom was forced to beat a hasty retreat. Her eyes snapping, she gripped the ivory handle of her cane in a blue-veined, white-knuckled fist.

"Charlotte!" The cane thumped the floor. Once. Twice. "Amalia! You will kindly cease that noise at once."

Dom didn't know whether it was the loud banging or the imperious command that did the trick, but the howls cut off like a faucet and surprise leaped into four tear-drenched eyes. Blessed silence reigned except for the babies' gulping hiccups.

"Thank you," the duchess said coolly. "Gina, why don't you and Zia take the girls to the nursery? Maria will bring their bottles as soon as Osterman's delivers the milk."

"It should be here any moment, *Duquesa*." Using her ample hips, the housekeeper backed through the swinging door to the kitchen. "I'll get the bottles ready."

Gina was headed for the hall leading to the bedrooms when she spotted her cousin four or five times removed. "Dom!" She blew him an air kiss. "I'll talk to you when I get the girls down."

"I, as well," his sister said with a smile in her dark eyes.

He set down his carryall and crossed the elegant sitting room to kiss the duchess's cheeks. Her paper-thin skin carried the faint scent of gardenias, and her eyes were cloudy with age but missed little. Including the wince he couldn't quite hide when he straightened.

"Zia told me you'd been knifed. Again."

"Just nicked a rib."

"Yes, well, we need to talk about these nicked ribs and bullet wounds you collect with distressing frequency. But first, pour us a…" She broke off at the buzz of the doorbell. "That must be the delivery. Natalie, dear, would you sign for it and take the milk to Maria?"

"Of course."

Dom watched the stranger head back to the foyer and turned to the duchess. "Who is she?"

"A research assistant Sarah hired to help with her book. Her name's Natalie Clark and she's part of what I want to talk to you about."

Dominic knew Sarah, the duchess's older granddaughter, had quit her job as an editor at a glossy fashion magazine when she married self-made billionaire Devon Hunter. He also knew Sarah had expanded on her degree in art history from the Sorbonne by hitting every museum within taxi distance when she accompanied Dev on his business trips around the world. That—and the fact that hundreds of years of art had been stripped off walls and pedestals when the Soviets overran the Duchy of Karlenburgh decades ago—had spurred Sarah to begin documenting what she learned about the lost treasures of the art world. It also prompted a major New York publisher to offer a fat, six-figure advance if she turned her notes into a book.

What Dom *didn't* know was what Sarah's book had to do with him, much less the female now making her way to the kitchen with an Osterman's delivery sack in hand. Sarah's research assistant couldn't be more than twenty-five or twenty-six but she dressed like a defrocked nun. Mousy-brown hair clipped at her neck. No makeup. Square glasses with thick lenses. Sensible flats and that shapeless linen dress.

When the kitchen door swung behind her, Dom had to

ask. "How is this Natalie Clark involved in what you want to talk to me about?"

The duchess waived an airy hand. "Pour us a *pálinka*, and I'll tell you."

"Should you have brandy? Zia said in her last email that…"

"Pah! Your sister fusses more than Sarah and Gina combined."

"With good reason, yes? She's a doctor. She has a better understanding of your health issues."

"Dominic." The duchess leveled a steely stare. "I've told my granddaughters, I've told your sister, and I'll tell you. The day I can't handle an aperitif before dinner is the day you may bundle me off to a nursing home."

"The day you can't drink us all under the table, you mean." Grinning, Dom went to the sideboard and lined up two cut-crystal snifters.

Ah, but he was a handsome devil, Charlotte thought with a sigh. Those dark, dangerous eyes. The slashing brows and glossy black hair. The lean, rangy body inherited from the wiry horsemen who'd swept down from the Steppes on their sturdy ponies and ravaged Europe. Magyar blood ran in his veins, as it did in hers, combined with but not erased by centuries of intermarriage among the royals of the once-great Austro-Hungarian Empire.

The Duchy of Karlenburgh had been part of that empire. A tiny part, to be sure, but one with a history that had stretched back for seven hundred years. It now existed only in dusty history books, and one of those books was about to change Dominic's life. Hopefully for the better, although Charlotte doubted he would think so. Not at first. But with time…

She glanced up as the instigator of that change returned to the sitting room. "Ah, here you are, Natalie. We're just about to have an aperitif. Will you join us?"

"No, thank you."

Dom paused with his hand on the stopper of the Bohemian crystal decanter he and Zia had brought the duchess as a gift for their first meeting. Thinking to soften the researcher's stiff edges, he gave her a slow smile.

"Are you sure? This apricot brandy is a specialty of my country."

"I'm sure."

Dom blinked. *Mi a fene!* Did her nose just quiver again? As though she'd picked up another bad odor? What the hell kind of tales had Zia and/or Gina fed the woman?

Shrugging, he splashed brandy into two snifters and carried one to the duchess. But if anyone could use a shot of *pálinka*, he thought as he folded his long frame into the chair beside his great-aunt's, the research assistant could. The double-distilled, explosively potent brandy would set more than her nostrils to quivering.

"How long will you be in New York?" the duchess asked after downing a healthy swallow.

"Only tonight. I have a meeting in Washington tomorrow."

"Hmm. I should wait until Zia and Gina return to discuss this with you, but they already know about it."

"About what?"

"The Edict of 1867." She set her brandy aside, excitement kindling in her faded blue eyes. "As you may remember from your history books, war with Prussia forced Emperor Franz Joseph to cede certain concessions to his often rambunctious Hungarian subjects. The Edict of 1867 gave Hungary full internal autonomy as long as it remained part of the empire for purposes of war and foreign affairs."

"Yes, I know this."

"Did you also know Karlenburgh added its own codicil to the agreement?"

"No, I didn't, but then I would have no reason to," Dom

said gently. "Karlenburgh is more your heritage than mine, Duchess. My grandfather—your husband's cousin—left Karlenburgh Castle long before I was born."

And the duchy had ceased to exist soon after that. World War I had carved up the once-mighty Austro-Hungarian Empire. World War II, the brutal repression of the Cold War era, the abrupt dissolution of the Soviet Union and vicious attempts at "ethnic cleansing" had all added their share of upheavals to the violently changing political landscape of Eastern Europe.

"Your grandfather took his name and his bloodline with him when he left Karlenburgh, Dominic." Charlotte leaned closer and gripped his arm with fingers that dug in like talons. "You inherited that bloodline and that name. You're a St. Sebastian. And the present Grand Duke of Karlenburgh."

"What?"

"Natalie found it during her research. The codicil. Emperor Franz Joseph reconfirmed that the St. Sebastians would carry the titles of Grand Duke and Duchess forever and in perpetuity in exchange for holding the borders of the empire. The empire doesn't exist anymore, but despite all the wars and upheavals, that small stretch of border between Austria and Hungary remains intact. So, therefore, does the title."

"On paper, perhaps. But the lands and outlying manors and hunting lodges and farmlands that once comprised the duchy have long since been dispersed and redeeded. It would take a fortune and decades in court to reclaim any of them."

"The lands and manor houses are gone, yes. Not the title. Sarah will become Grand Duchess when I die. Or Gina if, God forbid, something should happen to her sister. But they married commoners. According to the laws of primogeniture, their husbands can't assume the title of

Grand Duke. Until either Sarah or Gina has a son, or their daughters grow up and marry royalty, the only one who can claim it is you, Dom."

Right, he wanted to drawl. That and ten dollars would get him a half-decent espresso at one of New York's over-priced coffee bars.

He swallowed the sarcasm but lobbed a quick glare at the woman wearing an expression of polite interest, as if she hadn't initiated this ridiculous conversation with her research. He'd have a thing or two to say to Ms. Clark later about getting the duchess all stirred up over an issue that was understandably close to her heart but held little relevance to the real world. Particularly the world of an undercover operative.

He allowed none of those thoughts to show in his face as he folded Charlotte's hand between his. "I appreciate the honor you want to bestow on me, Duchess. I do. But in my line of work, I can hardly hang a title around my neck."

"Yes, I want to speak to you about that, too. You've been living on the edge for too many years now. How long can you continue before someone nicks more than a rib?"

"Exactly what I've been asking him," Zia commented as she swept into the sitting room with her long-legged stride.

She'd taken advantage of her few hours away from the hospital to pull on her favorite jeans and a summer tank top in blistering red. The rich color formed a striking contrast to her dark eyes and shoulder-length hair as black and glossy as her brother's. When he stood and opened his arms, she walked into them and hugged him with the same fierce affection he did her.

She was only four years younger than Dom, twenty-seven to his thirty-one, but he'd assumed full responsibility for his teenage sibling when their parents died. He'd been there, too, standing round-the-clock watch beside her hospital bed when she'd almost bled to death after a

uterine cyst ruptured her first year at university. The complications that resulted from the rupture had changed her life in so many ways.

What hadn't changed was Dom's bone-deep protectiveness. No matter where his job took him or what dangerous enterprise he was engaged in, Zia had only to send a coded text and he would contact her within hours, if not minutes. Although he always shrugged off the grimmer aspects of his work, she'd wormed enough detail out of him over the years to add her urging to that of the duchess.

"You don't have to stay undercover. Your boss at Interpol told me he has a section chief job waiting for you whenever you want it."

"You can see me behind a desk, Zia-mia?"

"Yes!"

"What a poor liar you are." He made a fist and delivered a mock punch to her chin. "You wouldn't last five minutes under interrogation."

Gina had returned during their brief exchange. Shoving back her careless tumble of curls, she entered the fray. "Jack says you would make an excellent liaison to the State Department. In fact, he wants to talk to you about that tomorrow, when you're in Washington."

"With all due respect to your husband, Lady Eugenia, I'm not ready to join the ranks of bureaucrats."

His use of her honorific brought out one of Gina's merry, irreverent grins. "Since we're tossing around titles here, has Grandmother told you about the codicil?"

"She has."

"Well then…" Fanning out the skirts of her leafy-green sundress, she sank to the floor in an elegant, if theatrical, curtsy.

Dom muttered something distinctly unroyal under his breath. Fortunately, the Clark woman covered it when she pushed to her feet.

"Excuse me. This is a family matter. I'll leave you to discuss it and go back to my research. You'll call me when it's convenient for us to continue our interview, Duchess?"

"I will. You're in New York until Thursday, is that correct?"

"Yes, ma'am. Then I fly to Paris to compare notes with Sarah."

"We'll get together again before then."

"Thank you." She bent to gather the bulging briefcase that had been resting against the leg of her chair. Straightening, she nudged up her glasses back into place. "It was good to meet you, Dr. St. Sebastian, and to see you again, Lady Eugenia."

Her tone didn't change. Neither did her polite expression. But Dom didn't miss what looked very much like a flicker of disdain in her brown eyes when she dipped her head in his direction.

"Your Grace."

He didn't alter his expression, either, but both his sister and his cousin recognized the sudden, silky note in his voice.

"I'll see you to the door."

"Thank you, but I'll let myself… Oh. Uh, all right."

Natalie blinked owlishly behind her glasses. The smile didn't leave Dominic St. Sebastian's ridiculously handsome face and the hand banding her upper arm certainly wouldn't leave any bruises. That didn't make her feel any less like a suspect being escorted from the scene of a crime, however. Especially when he paused with a hand on the door latch and skewered her with a narrow glance from those dark eyes.

"Where are you staying?"

"I beg your pardon?"

"Where are you staying?"

Good Lord! Was he hitting on her? No, he couldn't

be! She was most definitely not his type. According to Zia's laughing reports, her bachelor brother went for leggy blondes or voluptuous brunettes. A long string of them, judging by the duchess's somewhat more acerbic references to his sowing altogether too many wild oats.

That more than anything had predisposed Natalie to dislike Dominic St. Sebastian sight unseen. She'd fallen for a too-handsome, too-smooth operator like him once and would pay for that stupidity for the rest of her life. Still, she tried, she really tried, to keep disdain from seeping into her voice as she tugged her arm free.

"I don't believe where I'm staying is any of your business."

"You've made it my business with this nonsense about a codicil."

Whoa! He could lock a hand around her arm. He could perp-walk her to the door. He could *not* disparage her research.

Thoroughly indignant, Natalie returned fire. "It's not nonsense, as you would know if you'd displayed any interest in your family's history. I suggest you show a little more respect for your heritage, *Your Grace*, and for the duchess."

He muttered something in Hungarian she suspected was not particularly complimentary and bent an elbow against the doorjamb, leaning close. Too close! She could see herself in his pupils, catch the tang of apricot brandy on his breath.

"My respect for Charlotte is why you and I are going to have a private chat, yes? I ask again, where are you staying?"

His Magyar roots were showing, Natalie noted with a skitter of nerves. The slight thickening of his accent should have warned her. Should have sent her scurrying back into the protective shell she'd lived inside for so long it was now

as much a part of her life as her drab hair and clothes. But some spark of her old self tilted her chin.

"You're supposed to be a big, bad secret agent," she said coolly. "Dig out the information yourself."

He would, Dom vowed as the door closed behind her with a small thud. He most definitely would.

Two

All it took was one call to arm Dom with the essential information. Natalie Elizabeth Clark. Born Farmington, Illinois. Age twenty-nine, height five feet six inches, brown hair, brown eyes. Single. Graduated University of Michigan with a degree in library science, specializing in archives and presentation. Employed as an archivist with Centerville Community College for three years, the State of Illinois Civil Service Board for four. Currently residing in L.A. where she was employed by Sarah St. Sebastian as a personal assistant.

An archivist. Christ!

Dom shook his head as his cab picked its way downtown later that evening. He envisioned a small cubicle, her head bent toward a monitor screen, her eyes staring through those thick lenses at an endless stream of documents to be verified, coded and electronically filed. And she'd done it for seven years! Dom would have committed ritual hara-kiri after a week. No wonder she'd jumped when Sarah put out feelers for an assistant to help research her book.

Ms. Clark was still running endless computer searches. Still digging through archives, some electronic, some paper. But at least now she was traveling the globe to get at the most elusive of those documents. And, Dom guessed as his cab pulled up at the W New York, doing that traveling on a very generous expense account.

He didn't bother to stop at the front desk. His phone call had confirmed that Ms. Clark had checked into room 1304 two days ago. And a tracking program developed for the military and now in use by a number of intelligence agencies confirmed her cell phone was currently emitting signals from this location.

Two minutes later Dom rapped on her door. The darkening of the peephole told him she was as careful in her personal life as she no doubt was in her work. He smiled his approval, then waited for the door to open.

When neither of those events happened, he rapped again. Still no response.

"It's Dominic St. Sebastian, Ms. Clark. I know you're in there. You may as well open the door."

She complied but wasn't happy about it. "It's generally considered polite to call ahead for an appointment instead of just showing up at someone's hotel room."

The August humidity had turned her shapeless linen dress into a roadmap of wrinkles, and her sensible pumps had been traded for hotel flip-flops. She'd freed her hair from the clip, though, and it framed her face in surprisingly thick, soft waves as she tipped Dom a cool look through her glasses.

"May I ask why you felt compelled to come all the way downtown to speak with me?"

Dom had been asking himself the same thing. He'd confirmed this woman was who she said she was and verified her credentials. The truth was he probably wouldn't have given Natalie Clark a second thought if not for those little nose quivers.

He'd told himself the disdain she'd wiped off her face so quickly had triggered his cop's instinct. Most of the scum he'd dealt with over the years expressed varying degrees of contempt for the police, right up until they were cuffed and led away. His sister, however, would probably insist

those small hints of derision had pricked his male ego. It was true that Dom could never resist a challenge. But despite Zia's frequent assertions to the contrary, he didn't try to finesse *every* female who snagged his attention into bed.

Still, he was here and here he intended to remain until he satisfied his curiosity about this particular female. "I'd like more information on this codicil you've uncovered, Ms. Clark."

"I'm sure you would. I'll be happy to email you the documentation I've…"

"I prefer to see what you have now. May I come in, or do we continue our discussion in the hall?"

Her mouth pursing, she stood aside. Her obvious reluctance intrigued Dom. And, all right, stirred his hunting instincts. Too bad he had that meeting at the National Central Bureau—the US branch of Interpol—in Washington tomorrow. It might have been interesting to see what it would take to get those prim, disapproving lips to unpurse and sigh his name.

He skimmed a glance around the room. Two queen beds, one with her open briefcase and neat stacks of files on it. An easy chair angled to get the full benefit of the high-definition flat-screen. A desk with a black ergonomic chair, another stack of files and a seventeen-inch laptop open to a webpage displaying a close-up of an elaborately jeweled egg.

"One of the Fabergé eggs?" he asked, moving closer to admire the sketch of a gem-encrusted egg nested in a two-wheeled gold cart.

"Yes."

"The Cherub with a Chariot," Dom read, "a gift from Tsar Alexander III to his wife, Maria Fyodorovna for Easter, 1888. One of eight Fabergé eggs currently lost."

He glanced at the researcher hovering protectively close to her work, as if to protect it from prying eyes.

"And you're on the hunt for it?"

"I'm documenting its history."

Her hand crept toward the laptop's lid, as if itching to slam it down.

"What have you found so far?"

The lips went tight again, but Dom was too skilled at interrogations to let her off the hook. He merely waited until she gave a grudging nod.

"Documents show it was at Gatchina Palace in 1891, and was one of forty or so eggs sent to the armory at the Kremlin after the 1917 Revolution. Some experts believe it was purchased in the 1930s by Victor and Armand Hammer. But..."

He could see when her fascination with her work overcame her reluctance to discuss it. Excitement snuck into her voice and added a spark to her brown eyes. Her very velvety, very enticing brown eyes, he thought as she tugged off her glasses and twirled them by one stem.

"I found a reference to a similar egg sold at an antiques shop in Paris in 1930. A shop started by a Russian émigré. No one knows how the piece came into his possession, but I've found a source I want to check when I'm in Paris next week. It may..."

She caught herself and brought the commentary to an abrupt halt. The twirling ceased. The glasses whipped up, and wariness replaced the excitement in the doe-brown eyes.

"I'm not trying to pump you for information," Dom assured her. "Interpol has a whole division devoted to lost, stolen or looted cultural treasures, you know."

"Yes, I do."

"Since you're heading over to Paris, I can set up a meeting for you with the division chief, if you like."

The casual offer seemed to throw her off balance. "I... Uh... I have access to their database but..." Her glance

went to the screen, then came back to Dom. "I would appreciate that," she said stiffly. "Thank you."

A grin sketched across his face. "There now. That didn't taste so bad going down, did it?"

Instant alarms went off in Natalie's head. She could almost hear their raucous clanging as she fought to keep her chin high and her expression politely remote. She would *not* let a lazy grin and a pair of glinting, bedroom eyes seduce her. Not again. Never again.

"I'll give you my business card," she said stiffly. "Your associate can reach me anytime at my mobile number or by email."

"So cool, so polite." He didn't look at the embossed card she retrieved from her briefcase, merely slipped it into the pocket of his slacks. "What is it about me you don't like?"

How about everything!

"I don't know you well enough to dislike you." She should have left it there. Would have, if he hadn't been standing so close. "Nor," she added with a shrug, "do I wish to."

She recognized her error at once. Men like Dominic St. Sebastian would take that as a challenge. Hiding a grimace, Natalie attempted some quick damage control.

"You said you wanted more information on the codicil. I have a scanned copy on my computer. I'll pull it up and print out a copy for you."

She pulled out the desk chair. He was forced to step back so she could sit, but any relief she might have gained from the small separation dissipated when he leaned a hand on the desk and bent to peer over her shoulder. His breath stirred the loose tendrils at her temple, moved lower, washed warm and hot against her ear. She managed to keep from hunching her shoulder but it took an iron effort of will.

"So that's it," he said as the scanned image appeared, "the document the duchess thinks makes me a duke?"

"Grand Duke," Natalie corrected. "Excuse me, I need to check the paper feed in the printer."

There was nothing wrong with the paper feed. Her little portable printer had been cheerfully spitting out copies before St. Sebastian so rudely interrupted her work. But it was the best excuse she could devise to get him to stop breathing down her neck!

He took the copy and made himself comfortable in the armchair while he tried to decipher the spidery script. Natalie was tempted to let him suffer through the embellished High German, but relented and printed out a translation.

"I stumbled across the codicil while researching the Canaletto that once hung in the castle at Karlenburgh," she told him. "I'd found an obscure reference to the painting in the Austrian State Archives in Vienna."

She couldn't resist an aside. So many uninformed thought her profession dry and dull. They couldn't imagine the thrill that came with following one fragile thread to another, then another, and another.

"The archives are so vast, it's taken years to digitize them all. But the results are amazing. Really amazing. The oldest document dates back to 816."

He nodded, not appearing particularly interested in this bit of trivia that Natalie found so fascinating. Deflated, she got back to the main point.

"The codicil was included in a massive collection of letters, charters, treaties and proclamations relating to the Austro-Prussian War. Basically, it states what the duchess told you earlier. Emperor Franz Joseph granted the St. Sebastians the honor of Karlenburgh in perpetuity in exchange for defending the borders for the empire. The duchy may not exist anymore and so many national lines have been redrawn. That section of the border between

Austria and Hungary has held steady, however, through all the wars and invasions. So, therefore, has the title."

He made a noise that sounded close to a snort. "You and I both know this document isn't worth the paper you've just printed it on."

Offended on behalf of archivists everywhere, she cocked her chin. "The duchess disagrees."

"Right, and that's what you and I need to talk about."

He stuffed the printout in his pocket and pinned her with a narrow stare. No lazy grin now. No laughter in those dark eyes.

"Charlotte St. Sebastian barely escaped Karlenburgh with her life. She carried her baby in her arms while she marched on foot for some twenty or thirty miles through winter snows. I know the story is that she managed to bring away a fortune in jewels, as well. I'm not confirming the story…"

He didn't have to. Natalie had already pieced it together from her own research and from the comments Sarah had let drop about the personal items the duchess had disposed of over the years to raise her granddaughters in the style she considered commensurate with their rank.

"…but I am warning you not to take advantage of the duchess's very natural desire to see her heritage continue."

"Take advantage?"

It took a moment for that to sink in. When it did, she could barely speak through the anger that spurted hot and sour into her throat.

"Do you think…? Do you think this codicil is part of some convoluted scheme on my part to extract money from the St. Sebastians?"

Furious, she shoved to her feet. He rose as well, as effortlessly as an athlete, and countered her anger with a shrug.

"Not at this point. If I discover differently, however, you and I will most certainly have another chat."

"Get out!"

Maybe after she cooled down Natalie would admit flinging out an arm and stabbing a finger toward the door was overly melodramatic. At the moment, though, she wanted to slam that door so hard it knocked this pompous ass on his butt. Especially when he lifted a sardonic brow.

"Shouldn't that be 'Get out, *Your Grace*'?"

Her back teeth ground together. "Get. Out."

As a cab hauled him back uptown for a last visit with the duchess and his sister, Dom couldn't say his session with Ms. Clark had satisfied his doubts. There was still something he couldn't pin down about the researcher. She dressed like a bag lady in training and seemed content to efface herself in company. Yet when she'd flared up at him, when fury had brought color surging to her cheeks and fire to her eyes, the woman was anything but ignorable.

She reminded him of the mounts his ancestors had ridden when they'd swept down from the Steppes into the Lower Danube region. Their drab, brown-and-dun-colored ponies lacked the size and muscle power of destriers that carried European knights into battle. Yet the Magyars had wreaked havoc for more than half a century throughout Italy, France, Germany and Spain before finally being defeated by the Holy Roman Emperor Otto I.

And like one of those tough little ponies, Dom thought with a slow curl in his belly, Ms. Clark needed taming. She might hide behind those glasses and shapeless dresses, but she had a temper on her when roused. Too bad he didn't have time to gentle her to his hand. The exercise would be a hell of a lot more interesting than the meetings he had lined up in Washington tomorrow. Still, he entertained himself for the rest of the cab ride with various techniques

he might employ should he cross paths with Natalie Elizabeth Clark anytime in the near future.

He'd pretty much decided he would make that happen when Zia let him into the duchess's apartment.

"Back so soon?" she said, her eyes dancing. "Ms. Clark didn't succumb to your manly charms and topple into bed with you?"

The quip was so close to Dom's recent thoughts that he answered more brusquely than he'd intended. *"I didn't go to her hotel to seduce her."*

"No? That must be a first."

"Jézus, Mária és József! The mouth on you, Anastazia Amalia. I should have washed it with soap when I had the chance."

"Ha! You would never have been able to hold me down long enough. But come in, come in! Sarah's on FaceTime with her grandmother. I think you'll be interested in their conversation."

FaceTime? The duchess? Marveling at the willingness of a woman who'd been born in the decades between two great world wars to embrace the latest in technology, Dom followed his sister into the sitting room. One glance at the tableau corrected his impression of Charlotte's geekiness.

She sat upright and unbending in her customary chair, her cane close at hand. An iPad was perched on her knees, but she was obviously not comfortable with the device. Gina sat cross-legged on the floor beside her, holding the screen to the proper angle

Sarah's voice floated through the speaker and her elegant features filled most of the screen. Her husband's filled the rest.

"I'm so sorry, Grandmama. It just slipped out."

"What slipped out?" Dom murmured to Zia.

"You," his sister returned with that mischievous glint in her eyes.

"Me?"

"Shh! Just listen."

Frowning, Dom tuned back into the conversation.

"Alexis called with an offer to hype my book in *Beguile*," Sarah was saying. "She wanted to play up both angles." Her nose wrinkled. "My former job at the magazine and my title. You know how she is."

"Yes," the duchess drawled. "I do."

"I told Alexis the book wasn't ready for hype yet. Unfortunately, I also told her we're getting there much quicker since I'd hired such a clever research assistant. I bragged about the letter Natalie unearthed in the House of Parma archives, the one from Marie Antoinette to her sister describing the miniature of her painted by Le Brun that went missing when the mob sacked Versailles. And…" She heaved a sigh. "I made the fatal mistake of mentioning the codicil Nat had stumbled across while researching the Canaletto."

Although the fact that Dom's cousin had mentioned that damned codicil set his internal antennae to vibrating, it didn't appear to upset the duchess. Mention of the Canaletto had brought a faraway look to her eyes.

"Your grandfather bought me that painting of the Grand Canal," she murmured to Sarah. "Right after I became pregnant with your mother."

She lapsed into a private reverie that neither of her granddaughters dared break. When she emerged a few moments later, she included them both in a sly smile.

"That's where it happened. In Venice. We were supposed to attend a *carnival* ball at Ari Onassis's palazzo. I'd bought the most gorgeous mask studded with pearls and lace. But…how does that rather obnoxious TV commercial go? You never know when the mood will hit you? All I can say is something certainly hit your grandfather that evening."

Gina hooted in delight. "Way to go, Grandmama!"

Sarah laughed, and her husband issued a joking curse. "Damn! My wife suggested we hit the carnival in Venice this spring but I talked her into an African photo safari instead."

"You'll know to listen to her next time," the duchess sniffed, although Dom would bet she knew the moment could strike as hot and heavy in the African savannah as it had in Venice.

"I don't understand," Gina put in from her perch on the floor. "What's the big deal about telling Alexis about the codicil?"

"Well…" Red crept into Sarah's cheeks. "I'm afraid I mentioned Dominic, too."

The subject of the conversation muttered a curse, and Gina let out another whoop. "Ooh, boy! Your barracuda of an editor is gonna latch on to that with both jaws. I foresee another top-ten edition, this one listing the sexiest single royals of the male persuasion."

"I know," her sister said miserably. "It'll be as bad as what Dev went through after he came out on *Beguile*'s top-ten list. When you see Dominic tell him I'm so, so sorry."

"He's right here." Hooking a hand, Gina motioned him over. "Tell him yourself."

When Dominic positioned himself in front of the iPad's camera, Sarah sent him a look of heartfelt apology. "I'm so sorry, Dom. I made Alexis promise she wouldn't go crazy with this, but…"

"But you'd better brace yourself, buddy," her husband put in from behind her shoulder. "Your life's about to get really, really complicated."

"I can handle it," Dom replied with more confidence than he was feeling at the moment.

"You think so, huh?" Dev returned with a snort. "Wait

till women start trying to stuff their phone number in your pants pocket and reporters shove mics and cameras in your face."

The first prospect hadn't sounded all that repulsive to Dom. The second he deemed highly unlikely...right up until he stepped out of a cab for his scheduled meeting at Washington's Interpol office the following afternoon and was blindsided by the pack of reporters, salivating at the scent of fresh blood.

"Your Highness! Over here!"

"Grand Duke!"

"Hey! Your lordship!"

Shaking his head at Americans' fixation on any and all things royal, he shielded his face with his hands like some damned criminal and pushed through the ravenous newshounds.

Three

Two weeks later Dominic was in a vicious mood. He had been since a dozen different American and European tabloids had splashed his face across their front pages, trumpeting the emergence of a long-lost Grand Duke.

When the stories hit, he'd expected the summons to Interpol Headquarters. He'd even anticipated his boss's suggestion that he take some of the unused vacation time he'd piled up over the years and lie low until the hoopla died down. He'd anticipated it, yes, but did *not* like being yanked off undercover duty and sent home to Budapest to twiddle his thumbs. And every time he thought the noise was finally dying down, his face popped up in another rag.

The firestorm of publicity had impacted his personal life, as well. Although Sarah's husband had tried to warn him, Dom had underestimated the reaction to his supposed royalty among the females of his acquaintance. The phone number he gave out to non-Interpol contacts had suddenly become very busy. Some of the callers were friends, some were former lovers. But many were strangers who'd wrangled the number out of *their* friends and weren't shy about wanting to get to know the new duke on a very personal level.

He'd turned most of them off with a laugh, a few of the more obnoxious with a curt suggestion they get a life. But one had sounded so funny and sexy over the phone

that he'd arranged to meet her at a coffee bar. She turned out to be a tall, luscious brunette, as bright and engaging in person as she was over the phone. Dom was more than ready to agree with her suggestion they get a second cup to go and down it at her apartment or his loft. Before he could put in the order, though, she asked the waiter to take their picture with her cell phone. Damned if she hadn't zinged it off by email right there at the table. Just to a few friends, she explained with a smile. One, he discovered when yet another story hit the newsstands, just happened to be a reporter for a local tabloid.

In addition to the attention from strangers, the barrage of unwanted publicity seemed to make even his friends and associates view him through a different prism. To most of them he wasn't Dominic St. Sebastian anymore. He was Dominic, Grand Duke of a duchy that had ceased to exist a half century ago, for God's sake.

So he wasn't real happy when someone hammered on the door of his loft apartment on a cool September evening. Especially when the hammering spurred a chorus of ferocious barking from the hound who'd followed Dom home a year ago and decided to take up residence.

"Quiet!"

A useless command, since the dog considered announcing his presence to any and all visitors a sacred duty. Bred originally to chase down swiftly moving prey like deer and wolves, the Magyar Agár was as lean and fast as a greyhound. Dom had negotiated an agreement with his downstairs neighbors to dog-sit while he was on assignment, but man and beast had rebonded during this enforced vacation. Or at least the hound had. Dom had yet to reconcile himself to sharing his Gold Fassl with the pilsner-guzzling pooch.

"This better not be some damned reporter," he muttered as he kneed the still-barking hound aside and checked the spy hole. The special lens he'd had installed gave a

180-degree view of the landing outside his loft. The small area was occupied by two uniformed police officers and a bedraggled female Dom didn't recognize until he opened the door.

"Mi a fene!" he swore in Hungarian, then switched quickly to English. "Natalie! What happened to you?"

She didn't answer, being too preoccupied at the moment with the dog trying to shove his nose into her crotch. Dom swore again, got a grip on its collar and dislodged the nose, but he still didn't get a reply. She merely stared at him with a frown creasing her forehead and her hair straggling in limp tangles around her face.

"Are you Dominic St. Sebastian?" one of the police officers asked.

"Yes."

"Aka the Grand Duke?"

He made an impatient noise and kept his grip on the dog's collar. "Yes."

The second officer, whose nametag identified him as Gradjnic, glanced down at a newspaper folded to a grainy picture of Dom and the brunette at the coffee shop. "Looks like him," he volunteered.

His partner gestured to Natalie. "And you know this woman?"

"I do." Dom's glance raked the researcher, from her tangled hair to her torn jacket to what looked like a pair of men's sneakers several sizes too large for her. "What the devil happened to you?"

"Maybe we'd better come in," Gradjnic suggested.

"Yes, yes, of course."

The officers escorted Natalie inside, and Dom shut the dog in the bathroom before joining them. The Agár whined and scratched at the door but soon nosed out the giant chew-bones Dom stored in the hamper for emergencies like this.

Aside from the small bathroom, the loft consisted of a single, barn-like attic area that had once stored artifacts belonging to the Ethnological Museum. When the museum moved to new digs, their old building was converted to condos. Zia had just nailed a full scholarship to medical school, so Dom had decided to sink his savings into this loft apartment in the pricy Castle Hill district on the Buda side of the river. He'd then proceeded to sand and varnish the oak-plank floors to a high gloss. He'd also knocked out a section of the sloping roof and opened up a view of the Danube that usually had guests gasping.

Tonight's visitors were no exception. All three gawked at the floodlit spires, towering dome, flying buttresses and stained-glass windows of the Parliament Building across the river. Equally elaborate structures flanked the massive building, while the usual complement of river barges and brightly lit tour boats cruised by almost at its steps.

Ruthlessly, Dom cut into their viewing time. "Please sit down, all of you, then someone needs to tell me what this is all about."

"It's about this woman," Gradjnic said in heavily accented English when everyone had found a place to perch. He tugged a small black notebook from his shirt pocket. "What did you say her name was?"

Dom's glance shot to Natalie. "You didn't tell them your name?"

"I...I don't remember it."

"What?"

Her frown deepened. "I don't remember anything."

"Except the Grand Duke," Officer Gradjnic put in drily.

"Wait," Dom ordered. "Back up and start at the beginning."

Nodding, the policeman flipped through his notebook. "The beginning for us was 10:32 a.m. today, when dispatch called to report bystanders had fished a woman out of the

Danube. We responded, found this young lady sitting on the bank with her rescuers. She had no shoes, no purse, no cell phone, no ID of any kind and no memory of how she ended up in the river. When we asked her name or the name of a friend or relative here in Budapest, all she could tell us was 'the Grand Duke.'"

"Jesus!"

"She has a lump the size of a goose egg at the base of her skull, under her hair."

When Dom's gaze shot to Natalie again, she raised a tentative hand to the back of her neck. "More like a pigeon's egg," she corrected with a frown.

"Yes, well, the lump suggests she may have fallen off a bridge or a tour boat and hit her head on the way down, although none of the tour companies have reported a missing passenger. We had the EMTs take her to the hospital. The doctors found no sign of serious injury or concussion."

"No blurred vision?" Dom asked sharply. He'd taken— and delivered—enough blows to the head to know the warning signs. "No nausea or vomiting or balance problems?"

"Only the memory loss. The doctor said it's not all that unusual with that kind of trauma. Since we had no other place to take her, it was either leave her at the hospital or bring her to the only person she seems to know in Budapest—the Grand Duke."

Hit by a wicked sense of irony, Dom remembered those quivering nostrils and flickers of disdain. He suspected Ms. Clark would rather have been left at a dog pound than delivered to him.

"I'll take care of her," he promised, "but she must have a hotel room somewhere in the city."

"If she does, we'll let you know." Gradjnic flipped to an empty page and poised his pen. "Now what did you say her name was?"

"Natalie. Natalie Clark."

"American, we guessed from her accent."

"That's right."

"And she works for your cousin?"

"Yes, as research assistant." Angling around, Dom tried a tentative probe. "Natalie, you were supposed to meet with Sarah sometime this week. In Paris, right?"

"Sarah?"

"My cousin. Sarah St. Sebastian Hunter."

Her first response was a blank stare. Her second startled all three men.

"My head hurts." Scowling, she pushed out of her chair. "I'm tired. And these clothes stink."

With that terse announcement, she headed for the unmade bed at the far end of the loft. She kicked off the sneakers as she went. Dom lurched to his feet as she peeled out of the torn jacket.

"Hold on a minute!"

"I'm tired," she repeated. "I need sleep."

Shaking off his restraining hand, she flopped facedown across the bed. The three men watched with varying expressions of surprise and resignation as she buried her face in the pillow.

Gradjnic broke the small silence that followed. "Well, I guess that does it for us here. Now that we have her name, we'll trace Ms. Clark's entry into the country and her movements in Hungary as best we can. We'll also find out if she's registered at a hotel. And you'll call us when and if she remembers why she took that dive into the Danube, right?"

"Right."

The sound of their departure diverted the Agár's attention from the chew-bone he'd dug out of the hamper. To quiet his whining, Dom let him out of the bathroom but kept a close watch while he sniffed out the stranger

sprawled sideways across the bed. Apparently deciding she posed no threat, the dog padded back to the living area and stretched out in front of the window to watch the brightly lit boats cruising up and down the river.

Dom had his phone in hand before the hound's speckled pink belly hit the planks. Five rings later, his sleepy-sounding cousin answered.

"Hullowhozzis?"

"It's Dom, Sarah."

"Dom?"

"Where are you?"

"We're in…uh…Dalian. China," she added, sounding more awake…and suddenly alarmed by a call in what had to be the middle of the night on the other side of the globe. "Is everyone okay? Grandmama? Gina? Zia? Oh, God! Is it one of the twins?"

"They're all fine, Sarah. But I can't say the same for your research assistant."

He heard a swift rustle of sheets. A headboard creaking.

"Dev! Wake up! Dom says something's happened to Natalie!"

"I'm awake."

"Tell me," Sarah demanded.

"The best guess is she fell off a bridge or a cruise boat. They fished her out of the river early this morning."

"Is she…? Is she dead?"

"No, but she's got a good-size lump at the base of her skull and she doesn't remember anything. Not even her name."

"Good Lord!" The sheets rustled again. "Natalie's been hurt, Dev. Would you contact your crew and have them prep the Gulfstream? I need to fly back to Paris right away."

"She's not in Paris," Dom interjected. "She's with me, in Budapest."

"In Budapest? But…how? Why?"

"I was hoping you could tell me."

"She didn't say anything about Hungary when we got together in Paris last week. Only that she might drive down to Vienna again, to do more research on the Canaletto." A note of accusation slipped through Sarah's concern. "She was also going to dig a little more on the codicil. Something you said about it seemed to have bothered her."

He'd said a lot about it, none of which he intended to go into at the moment. "So you don't know why she's here in Hungary?"

"I have no clue. Is she there with you now? Let me speak to her."

He flicked a glance at the woman sprawled across his bed. "She's zoned out, Sarah. Said she was tired and just flopped into bed."

"This memory thing? Will she be all right?"

"Like you, I have no clue. But you'd better contact her family just in case."

"She doesn't have any family."

"She's got to have someone. Grandparents? An uncle or aunt stashed away somewhere?"

"She doesn't," Sarah insisted. "Dev ran a detailed background check before I hired her. Natalie doesn't know who her parents are or why she was abandoned as an infant. She lived with a series of foster families until she checked herself out of the system at age eighteen and entered the University of Michigan on full scholarship."

That certainly put a different spin on the basic age-height-DOB info he'd gathered.

"I'll fly to Budapest immediately," Sarah was saying, "and take Natalie home with me until she recovers her memory."

Dom speared another glance at the researcher. His gut

told him he'd live to regret the suggestion he was about to make.

"Why don't you hang loose for now? Could be she'll be fine when she wakes up tomorrow. I'll call you then."

"I don't know…"

"I'll call you, Sarah. As soon as she wakes up."

When she reluctantly agreed, he cut the connection and stood with the phone in hand for several moments. He'd worked undercover too long to take anything at face value…especially a woman fished out of the Danube who had no reason to be in Budapest that anyone knew. Thumbing the phone, he tapped in a number. His contact at Interpol answered on the second ring.

"Oui?"

"It's Dom," he replied in swift, idiomatic French. "Remember the query you ran for me two weeks ago on Natalie Clark?"

"Oui."

"I need you to dig deeper."

"Oui."

The call completed, he contemplated his unexpected houseguest for a few moments. Her rumpled skirt had twisted around her calves and her buttoned-to-the-neck blouse looked as though it was choking her. After a brief inner debate, Dom rolled her over. He had the blouse unfastened and was easing it off when she opened her eyes to a groggy squint and mumbled at him.

"Whatryoudoin?"

"Making you comfortable."

"Mmm."

She was asleep again before he got her out of her blouse and skirt. Her panties were plain, unadorned white cotton but, Dom discovered, covered slender hips and a nice, trim butt. Nobly, he resisted the urge to remove her underwear and merely tucked the sheets around her. That done, he

popped the cap on a bottle of a pilsner for himself, opened another for the hound and settled in for an all-night vigil.

He rolled her over again just after midnight and pried up a lid. She gave a bad-tempered grunt and batted his hand away, but not before he saw her pupil dilate and refract with reassuring swiftness.

He woke her again two hours later. "Natalie. Can you hear me?"

"Go away."

He did a final check just before dawn. Then he stretched out on the leather sofa and watched the dark night shade to gold and pink.

Something wet and cold prodded her elbow. Her shoulder. Her chin. She didn't come awake, though, until a strap of rough leather rasped across her cheek. She blinked fuzzily, registered the hazy thought that she was in bed, and opened her eyes.

"Yikes!"

A glistening pink mouth loomed only inches from her eyes. Its black gums were pulled back and a long tongue dangled through a set of nasty-looking incisors. As if in answer to her startled yip, the gaping mouth emitted a blast of powerful breath and an ear-ringing bark.

She scurried back like a poked crab, heart thumping and sheets tangling. A few feet of separation gave her a better perspective. Enough to see the merry eyes above an elongated muzzle, a broad forehead topped with one brown ear and one white, and a long, lean body with a wildly whipping tail.

Evidently the dog mistook her retreat for the notion that she was making space for him in the bed. With another loud woof, he landed on the mattress. The tongue went

to work again, slathering her cheeks and chin before she could hold him off.

"Whoa! Stop!" His joy was contagious and as impossible to contain as his ecstatically wriggling body. Laughing now, she finally got him by the shoulders. "Okay, okay, I like you, too! But enough with the tongue."

He got in another slurp before he let her roll him onto his back, where he promptly stuck all four legs into the air and begged for a tickle. She complied and raised quivers of ecstasy on his short-haired ribs and speckled pink-and-brown belly.

"You're a handsome fellow," she murmured, admiring his sleek lines as her busy fingers set his legs to pumping. "Wonder what your name is?"

"He doesn't have one."

The response came from behind her. Twisting on the bed, she swept her startled gaze across a huge, sparsely furnished area. A series of overhead beams topped with A-frame wooden trusses suggested it was an attic. A stunningly renovated attic, with gleaming oak floors and modern lighting.

There were no interior walls, only a curved, waist-high counter made of glass blocks that partitioned off a kitchen area. The male behind the counter looked at home there. Dark-haired and dark-eyed, he wore a soccer shirt of brilliant red-and-black stripes with some team logo she didn't recognize emblazoned on one breast. The stretchy fabric molded his broad, muscular shoulders. The wavy glass blocks gave an indistinct view of equally muscular thighs encased in running shorts.

She watched him, her hand now stilled on the dog's belly, while he flicked the switch on a stainless-steel espresso machine. Almost instantly the machine hissed out thick, black liquid. Her eyes never left him as he filled two cups and rounded the glass-block counter.

When he crossed the huge room, the dog scrambled to sit up at his approach. So did she, tugging the sheet up with her. For some reason she couldn't quite grasp, she'd slept in her underwear.

He issued an order in a language she didn't understand. When he repeated it in a firmer voice, the dog jumped off the bed with obvious reluctance.

"How do you feel?"

"I…uh… Okay."

"Head hurt?"

She tried a tentative neck roll. "I don't… Ooh!"

Wincing, she fingered the lump at the base of her skull. "What happened?"

"Best guess is you fell off a bridge or tour boat and hit your head. Want some aspirin?"

"God, yes!"

He handed her one of the cups and crossed to what she guessed was a bathroom tucked under one of the eaves. She used his brief absence to let her gaze sweep the cavernous room again, looking for something, *anything* familiar.

Panic crawled like tiny ants down her spine when she finally accepted that she was sitting cross-legged on an unmade bed. In a strange apartment. With a hound lolling a few feet away, grinning from ear to ear and looking all too ready to jump back in with her.

Her hands shaking, she lifted the china cup. The rim rattled against her teeth and the froth coated her upper lip as she took a tentative sip.

"Ugh!"

Her first impulse was to spit the incredibly strong espresso back into the cup. Politeness—and the cool, watchful eyes of the bearer of aspirin—forced her to swallow.

"Better take these with water."

Gratefully, she traded the cup for a glass. She was

reaching for the two small white pills in his palm when she suddenly froze. Her heart slamming against her chest, she stared down at the pills.

Oh, God! Had she been drugged? Did he intend to knock her out again?

A faint thread of common sense tried to push through her balled-up nerves. If he wanted to drug her, he could just as easily have put something in her coffee. Still, she pulled her hand back.

"I...I better not. I, uh, may be allergic."

"You're not wearing a medical alert bracelet."

"I'm not wearing much of anything."

"True."

He set the pills and her cup on a low bookshelf that doubled as a nightstand. She clutched the water glass, looked at him, at the grinning dog, at the rumpled sheets, back at him. Ants started down her spine again.

"Okay," she said on a low, shaky breath, "who *are* you?

Four

"I'm Dominic. Dominic St. Sebastian. Dom to my friends and family."

He kept his eyes on her, watching for the tiniest flicker of recognition. If she was faking that blank stare, she was damned good at it.

"I'm Sarah's cousin," he added.

Nothing. Not a blink. Not a frown.

"Sarah St. Sebastian Hunter?" He waited a beat, then decided to go for the big guns. "She's the granddaughter of Charlotte, Grand Duchess of Karlenburgh."

"Karlenburgh?"

"You were researching a document pertaining to Karlenburgh. One with a special codicil."

He thought for a moment he'd struck a chord. Her brows drew together, and her lips bunched in an all-too-familiar moue. Then she blew out a breath and scooted to the edge of the bed, pulling the sheet with her.

"I don't know you, or your cousin, or her grandmother. Now, if you don't mind, I'd like to get dressed and be on my way."

"On your way to where?"

That brought her up short.

"I…I don't know." She blinked, obviously coming up empty. "Where…? Where am I?"

"Maybe this will help."

Dom went to the window and drew the drapes. Morning light flooded the loft. With it came the eagle's-eye view of the Danube and the Parliament's iconic red dome and forest of spires.

"Ooooh!" Wrapping the sheet around her like a sari, she stepped to the glass wall. "How glorious!"

"Do you recognize the building?"

"Sort of. Maybe."

She sounded anything but sure. And, Dom noted, she didn't squint or strain as she studied the elaborate structure across the river. Apparently she only needed her glasses for reading or close work. Yet...she'd worn them during both their previous meetings. Almost like a shield.

"I give up." She turned to him, those delicate nostrils quivering and panic clouding her eyes. "Where *am* I?"

"Budapest"

"Hungary?"

He started to ask if there was a city with that same name in another country but the panic had started to spill over into tears. Although she tried valiantly to gulp them back, she looked so frightened and fragile that Dom had to take her in his arms.

The sobs came then. Big, noisy gulps that brought the Agár leaping to all fours. His ears went flat and his long, narrow tail whipped out, as though he sensed an enemy but wasn't sure where to point.

"It's all right," Dom said, as much to the dog as the woman in his arms. She smelled of the river, he thought as he stroked her hair. The river and diesel spill and soft, trembling female still warm from his bed. So different from the stiff, disdainful woman who'd ordered him out of her New York hotel room that his voice dropped to a husky murmur.

"It's all right."

"No, it's not!"

The tears gushed now, soaking through his soccer shirt and making the dog whine nervously. His claws clicked on the oak planking as he circled Dom and the woman clinging to his shirt with one hand and the sheet with her other.

"I don't understand any of this! Why can't I remember where I am? Why can't I remember *you*?" She jerked back against his arm and stared up at him. "Are we...? Are we married?"

"No."

Her glance shot to the bed. "Lovers?"

He let that hang for a few seconds before treating her to a slow smile.

"Not yet."

Guilt pricked at him then. Her eyes were so huge and frightened, her nose red and sniffling. Gentling his voice, he brushed a thumb across her cheek to wipe the tears.

"Do you remember the police bringing you here last night?"

"I...I think so."

"They took you to a hospital first. Remember?"

Her forehead wrinkled. "Now I do."

"A doctor examined you. He told the police that short-term memory loss isn't unusual with a head injury."

She jumped on that. "How short?"

"I don't know, *drágám*."

"Is that my name? *Drágám*?"

"No, that's a nickname. An endearment, like 'sweetheart' or 'darling.' Very casual here in Hungary," he added when her eyes got worried again. "Your name is Natalie. Natalie Elizabeth Clark."

"Natalie." She rolled it around in her head, on her tongue. "Not a name I would pick for myself," she said with a sniffle, "but I guess it'll do."

The brown-and-white hound poked at her knee then, as if demanding reassurance that all was well. Natalie eased

out of Dom's arms and knuckled the dog's broad, intelligent forehead.

"And who's this guy?"

"I call him *kutya*. It means 'dog' in Hungarian."

Her eyes lifted to his, still watery but accusing. "You just call him 'dog'?"

"He followed me home one night and decided to take up residence. I thought it would be a temporary arrangement, so we never got around to a baptismal ceremony."

"So he's a stray," she murmured, her voice thickening. "Like me."

Dom knew he'd better act fast to head off another storm of tears. "Stray or not," he said briskly, "he needs to go out. Why don't you shower and finish your coffee while I take him for his morning run? I'll pick up some apple pancakes for breakfast while I'm out, yes? Then we'll talk about what to do next."

When she hesitated, her mouth trembling, he curled a knuckle under her chin and tipped her face to his. "We'll work this out, Natalie. Let's just take it one step at a time."

She bit her lip and managed a small nod.

"Your clothes are in the bathroom," Dom told her. "I rinsed them out last night, but they're probably still damp." He nodded to the double-doored wardrobe positioned close to the bath. "Help yourself to whatever you can find to fit you."

She nodded again and hitched the sheet higher to keep from tripping over it as she padded to the bathroom. Dom waited until he heard the shower kick on before dropping into a chair to pull on socks and his well-worn running shoes.

He hoped to hell he wasn't making a mistake leaving her alone. Short of locking her in, though, he didn't see how he could confine her here against her will. Besides which, they needed to eat and Dog needed to go out. A

point the hound drove home by retrieving his leash from its hook by the door and waiting with an expression of acute impatience.

Natalie. Natalie Elizabeth Clark.

Why didn't it feel right? Sound right?

She wrapped her freshly shampooed hair in a towel and stared at the steamed-up bathroom mirror. The image it reflected was as foggy as her mind.

She'd stood under the shower's hot, driving needles and tried to figure out what in the world she was doing in Budapest. It couldn't be her home. She didn't know a word of Hungarian. Correction. She knew two. *Kutya* and... What had he called her? *Dragon* or something.

Dominic. His name was Dominic. It fit him, she thought with a grimace, much better than Natalie did her. Those muscled shoulders, the strong arms, the chest she'd sobbed against, all hinted at power and virility and, yes, dominance.

Especially in bed. The thought slipped in, got caught in her mind. He'd said they weren't lovers. Implied she'd slept alone. Yet heat danced in her belly at the thought of lying beneath him and feeling his hands on her breasts, his mouth on her...

Oh, God! The panic came screaming back. She breathed in. Out. In. Then set her jaw and glared at the face in the mirror.

"No more crying! It didn't help before! It won't help now."

She snatched up a dry washcloth and had started to scrub the fogged glass when she caught the echo of her words. Her fist closed around the cloth, and her chest squeezed.

"Crying didn't help before *what*?"

Like the steam still drifting from the shower stall,

the mists in her mind seemed to curl. Shift. Become less opaque. Something was there, just behind the thin gray curtain. She could almost see it. Almost smell it. She spun around and hacked out a sound halfway between a sob and a laugh.

She could smell it, all right. The musty odor emanated from the wrinkled items hanging from hooks on the door. The steam from the hot shower must have released the river stink.

Her nose wrinkling, she fingered the shapeless jacket, the unadorned blouse, the mess that must once have been a skirt. Good grief! Were these really her clothes? They looked like they'd come from a Goodwill grab bag. The bra and panties she'd discarded before getting in the shower were even worse.

He—Dominic—said he'd rinsed her things out. He should have tossed them in a garbage sack and hauled them to a dumpster.

"Well," she said with a shrug, "he told me to help myself."

The helping included using his comb to work the tangles from her wet hair and squirting a length of his toothpaste onto her forefinger to scrub her teeth. It also included poking her head through the bathroom door to make sure he was still gone before she raided his closet.

It was a European-style wardrobe, with mirror double doors and beautiful carving. The modern evolution of the special room in a castle where nobles stored their robes in carved wooden chests. Called an armoire in French, a shrunk in German, this particular wardrobe wasn't as elaborate as some she'd seen but…

Wait! How did she know about castles and nobles and shrunks? What other, more elaborate armoires had she seen? She stared at the hunting scene above the doors,

feeling as though she was straining every brain cell she possessed through a sieve, and came up empty.

"Dammit!"

Angry and more than a little scared, she yanked open the left door. Suits and dress shirts hung haphazardly from the rod, while an assortment of jeans, T-shirts and sporting gear spilled from the shelves below. She plucked out a soccer shirt, this one with royal-blue and white stripes but with the same green-and-gold emblem on the right sleeve. The cool, slick material slithered over her hips. The hem hung almost to her knees.

Curiosity prompted her to open the right door. This side was all drawers. The top drawer contained unmatched socks, tangled belts, loose change and a flashlight.

The middle drawer was locked. Securely locked, with a gleaming steel mechanism that didn't give a hair when she tested it.

She slid the third drawer out and eyed the jumble of jock straps, Speedos and boxers. She thought about appropriating a Speedo but couldn't quite bring herself to climb into his underwear.

"Not the neatest guy in the world, are you?" she commented to the absent Dominic.

She started to close the drawer, intending to go back to the bathroom and give her panties a good scrubbing, when she caught a glimpse of delicate black lace amid boxers.

Oh, Lord! Was he into kink? Cross-dressing? Transgender sex play? Did that locked drawer contain whips and handcuffs and ball gags?

She gulped, remembering her earlier thought about strength and power and dominance, and used the tip of a finger to extract a pair of lace-trimmed silk hipsters. A new and very expensive pair of hipsters judging by the embossed tag still dangling from the band. Natalie's eyes widened when she saw the hand-lettered price.

Good grief! Three hundred pounds? Could that be right?

When she recovered from sticker shock, she found it interesting that the price was displayed in British pounds and not in Hungarian…Hungarian whatever. Also interesting, the light-as-air scrap of silk had evidently been crafted by an "atelier" who described her collection as feminine and ethereal, each piece a limited edition made to measure for the client. The matching garter belt and triangle bra, the tag advised, would put the cost for the complete ensemble at just over a thousand pounds.

Well, she thought with a low whistle, if he was into kink, he certainly did it up right. She was about to stuff the panties back in the drawer when she noticed handwriting on the back of the tag.

I stuck these in your suitcase so you'll know what I won't be wearing next time you're in London.
Kiss, kiss, Arabella.

Oh, yuck! Her lip curling, she started to stuff the hipsters back in the drawer. Common sense and a bare butt made her hesitate several seconds too long. She still had the panties in hand when the front door opened and the hound burst in. Sweat darkened the honey-brown patches on the dog's coat. Similar damp splotches stained Dominic's soccer shirt.

"Find everything you need?" he asked as he dropped a leash and a white paper sack on the kitchen counter.

"Almost everything." She lifted her hand. The scrap of silk and lace dangled from her forefinger. "Do you think Arabella will mind if I borrow her knickers?"

"Who?"

"Arabella. London. Kiss, kiss."

"Oh. Right. That Arabella." He eyed the gossamer silk

with a waggle of his brow. "Very nice. Where'd you find them?"

"In with your socks," she drawled. "There's a note on the back of the tag."

He flipped the tag over and skimmed the handwriting. She could smell the sharp tang of his sweat, see the bristles darkening his cheeks and chin. See, too, the smile that played at the corners of his mouth. He managed to keep it from sliding into a full grin as he handed back the panties.

"I'm sure Arabella wouldn't mind you borrowing them," he said solemnly.

But *he* would. The realization hit Dom even before she whirled and the hem of his soccer shirt flared just high enough to give him a glimpse of her nicely curved butt.

"That might have been a mistake," he told the hound when the bathroom door shut. "Now I'm going to be imagining her in black silk all day."

The Agár cocked his head. The brown ear came up, the white ear folded over, and he looked as though he was giving the matter serious consideration.

"She's fragile," Dom reminded the dog sternly. "Confused and frightened and probably still hurting from her dive into the Danube. So you refrain from slobbering all over her front and I'll keep my mind off her rear."

Easier said than done he discovered when she reemerged. She wore a cool expression, the blue crew shirt and, as Dom could all-too-easily visualize, a band of black silk around her slender hips.

And here he'd thought her nondescript back in New York. She certainly looked different with her face flushed and rosy from the shower and her damp hair showing streaks of rich, dark chestnut. The oversize glasses had dominated her face in New York, distracting from those cinnamon-brown eyes and the short, straight nose. And,

he remembered, her full lips had been set in such thin, disapproving lines for most of their brief acquaintance. They were close to that now but still looked very kissable.

Not that he should be thinking about her eyes or her lips or the length of bare leg visible below the hem of his shirt. She's vulnerable, he had to remember. Confused.

"I bought some apple pancakes from my favorite street seller," he told her, indicating the white sack on the counter. "They're good cold, if you're hungry now, but better when crisped a bit in the oven. Help yourself while I take my turn in the shower."

"I'll warm them up."

Rounding the glass counter, she stooped to study the knobs on the stovetop. The soccer shirt rode up again. Barely an inch. Two at the most. All it showed were the backs of her thighs, but Dom had to swallow a groan as he grabbed a pair of jeans and a clean shirt and hit the bathroom.

He didn't take long. A hot, stinging shower and a quick shampoo. He scraped a palm over his three or four days' worth of bristles, but a shave lost out to the seductive scent of warm apples.

She was perched on one of the counter stools, laughing at the shivering bundle of ecstasy hunkered between her bare legs. "No, you idiot! Don't give me that silly grin. I'm not feeding you another bite."

She glanced up, her face still alight, and spotted Dom. The laughter faded instantly. He felt the loss like a hard right jab to the solar plexus.

Jézus, Mária és József! Did she dislike all men, or just him? He couldn't tell but sure as hell intended to find out.

The woman represented so many mysteries. There was the disdain she'd treated him to in New York. That ridiculous codicil. The memory loss. The yet-to-be-explained

reason she was here in his loft, swathed in his soccer shirt. Dom couldn't remember when a woman had challenged him in so many ways. He was about to tell her so when the cell phone he'd left on the counter buzzed.

"It's Sarah," he said after a quick glance at the face that came up on the screen. "My cousin and your boss. Do you want to talk to her?"

"I…uh… All right."

He accepted the FaceTime call and gave his anxious cousin the promised update. "Natalie's still here with me. Physically she seems okay but no progress yet on recovering her memory. Here, I'll put her on."

He positioned the phone so the screen captured Natalie still seated on the high stool. Both he and Sarah could see the desperate hope and crushing disappointment that chased across the researcher's features as she stared at the face on the screen.

"Oh, Nat," Sarah said with a tremulous smile, "I'm so, so sorry to hear you've been hurt."

Her hand crept to her nape. "Thank you."

"Dev and I will fly to Budapest today and take you home."

Uncertainty flooded her eyes. "Dev?"

Sarah swallowed. "Devon Hunter. My husband."

The name didn't appear to register, which caused Natalie such obvious dismay that Dom intervened. Leaning close, he spoke into the camera.

"Why don't you and Dev hold off for a while, Sarah? We haven't spoken to the police yet this morning. They were going to trace Natalie's movements in Hungary and might have some information for us. Also, they might have found her purse or briefcase. If not, we'll need to go to the American Embassy and get a replacement passport before she can leave the country. That could take a few days."

"But…"

Sarah struggled to mask her concern. Dom guessed she felt personally responsible for her assistant being hurt and stranded in a foreign country.

"Are you good with remaining in Hungary a little while yet, Nat?"

"I…" She looked from the screen to Dom to the hound, who now sat with his head plopped on her knee. "Yes."

"Would you feel better staying at a hotel? I can make a reservation in your name today."

Once again Dom felt compelled to intercede. Natalie was in no condition to be left on her own. Assuming, of course, her memory loss was real. He had no reason to believe otherwise but the cop in him went too deep to take anyone or anything at face value.

"Let's leave that for now, too," he told Sarah. "As I said, we need to talk to the police and start the paperwork for a replacement passport if necessary. While we're working things at this end, you could make some inquiries back in the States. Talk to the duchess and Zia and Gina. Maybe the editor you're working with on your book. Find out if anyone's called inquiring about Natalie or her research. It might help jog her memory if we can discover what brought her to Budapest from Vienna."

"Of course. I'll do that today." She hesitated, clearly distressed for her assistant. "You'll need money, Natalie. I'll arrange a draft… No, we'd better make it cash since you don't have any ID. I'll have it delivered to Dom's address this afternoon. Just an advance on your salary," she added quickly when Natalie looked as though she'd been offered charity.

Dom considered telling his cousin that the money could wait, too. He was more than capable of covering his unexpected guest's expenses. More to the point, it might be better to keep her dependent on him until they sorted out

her situation. On reflection, though, he decided the leash was short enough.

The brief conversation left Natalie silent for several long moments. She scratched the hound's head, obviously dismayed over not recognizing the woman she worked for and with. Dom moved quickly to head off another possible panic attack.

"Okay, here's today's agenda," he said with brisk cheerfulness. "First, we finish breakfast. Second, we hit the shops to buy you some shoes and whatever else you need. Third, we visit police headquarters to find out what, if anything, they've learned. We also get a copy of their incident report and contact the embassy to begin the paperwork for a replacement passport. Finally, and most important, we arrange a follow-up with the doctor you saw yesterday. Or better yet, with a specialist who has some expertise dealing with amnesia cases."

"Sounds good to me," she said, relief at having a concrete plan of action edging aside the dismay. "But do you really think we can swing an appointment with a specialist anytime soon? Or even find one with expertise in amnesia?"

"I've got a friend I can call."

He didn't tell her that his "friend" was the internationally renowned forensic pathologist who'd autopsied the victims of a particularly savage drug cartel last year. Dom had witnessed each autopsy, groaning at the doc's morbid sense of humor as he collected the evidence Interpol needed to take down key members of the cartel.

He made the call while Natalie conducted another raid on his wardrobe. By the time she'd dug out a pair of Dom's flip-flops and running shorts with a drawstring waist, one of Budapest's foremost neurologists had agreed to squeeze her in at 11:20 a.m.

Five

The short-notice appointment with the neurologist necessitated a quick change in the day's agenda. Almost before Natalie had downed her last bite of apple pancake, Dom hustled her to the door of the loft and down five flights of stairs to the underground garage.

It'd been dark when she'd arrived the previous evening, so she'd caught only glimpses of the castle dominating the hill on the Buda of the river. The bright light of morning showed the royal palace in its full glory.

"Oh, look!" Her glance snagged on the bronze warrior atop a muscled warhorse that guarded the entrance to the castle complex. "That's Prince Eugene of Savoy, isn't it?"

Dominic slanted her a quick look. "You know about *Priz Eugen*?"

"Of course." She twisted in her seat to keep the statue in view as they negotiated the narrow, curving streets that would take them down to the Danube. "He was one of the greatest military leaders of the seventeenth century. As I recall, he served three different Holy Roman Emperors and won a decisive victory against the Ottoman Turks in 1697 at…"

She broke off, her eyes rounding. "Why do I know that?"

She sank back against her seat and stared through the windshield at the tree-dappled street ahead. Dom said

nothing while she struggled to jam together the pieces of the puzzle.

"Why do I know the Hapsburgs built this palace on the site of the Gothic castle originally constructed by an earlier Holy Roman Emperor? Why do I know it was reconstructed after being razed to the ground during World War II?" Her fists bunched, drummed her thighs. "Why can I pull those details out of my head and not know who I am or how I ended up in the river?"

"Recalling those details has to be a good sign. Maybe it means you'll start to remember other things, as well."

"God, I hope so!"

Her fists stayed tight through the remainder of the descent from Castle Hill and across the majestic Chain Bridge linking Buda and Pest.

Their first stop was a small boutique, where Natalie traded Dom's drawstring shorts, soccer shirt and flip-flops for sandals, slim designer jeans, a cap-sleeved tank in soft peach and a straw tote. A second stop garnered a few basic toiletries. Promising to shop for other necessities later, Dom hustled her back to the car for her appointment with Dr. Andras Kovacs.

The neurologist's suite of offices occupied the second floor of a gracious nineteenth-century town house in the shadow of St. Stephen's Basilica. The gray-haired receptionist in the outer office confirmed Natalie's short-notice appointment, but showed more interest in her escort than the patient herself.

"I read about you in the paper," she exclaimed to Dom in Hungarian. "Aren't you the Grand Duke of…of…something?"

Swallowing a groan, he nodded. "Of Karlenburgh, but the title is an empty one. The duchy doesn't exist any longer."

"Still, it must be very exciting to suddenly find yourself a duke."

"Yes, very. Is Dr. Kovacs running on time for his appointments?"

"He is." She beamed. "Please have a seat, Your Highness, and I'll let his assistant know you and Ms. Clark are here."

When he led Natalie to a set of tall wingback chairs, she sent him a quick frown. "What was all that about?"

"She was telling me about a story she'd read in the paper."

"I heard her say 'Karlenburgh.'"

He eyed her closely. "Do you recognize that name?"

"You mentioned it this morning. I thought for a moment I knew it." Still frowning, she scrubbed her forehead with the heel of her hand. "It's all here, somewhere in my head. That name. That place. You."

Her eyes lifted to his. She looked so accusing, he had to smile.

"I can think of worse places to be than in your head, *drágám.*"

He wasn't sure whether it was the lazy smile or the casual endearment or the husky note to his voice that brought out the Natalie Clark he'd met in New York. Whatever the reason, she responded with a hint of her old, disapproving self.

"You shouldn't call me that. I'm not your sweetheart."

He couldn't help himself. Lifting a hand, he brushed a knuckle over the curve of her cheek. "Ah, but we can change that, yes?"

She pulled away, and Dom was cursing himself for the mix of wariness and confusion that came back to her face when a slim, thirtysomething woman in a white smock coat emerged from the inner sanctum.

"Ms. Clark? I'm Dr. Kovacs's assistant," she said in Hungarian. "Would you and your husband please follow me?"

"Ms. Clark is American," Dom told her. "She doesn't speak our language. And we're not married."

"Oh, my apologies."

Switching to English, she repeated the invitation and advised Natalie it was her choice whether she wished to have her friend join her for the consult. Dom half expected her to refuse but she surprised him.

"I'd better have someone with me who knows who I am."

The PA showed them to a consultation room lined with mahogany bookshelves displaying leather-bound volumes and marble busts. No desk, just high-backed wing chairs in Moroccan leather arranged around a marble-topped pedestal table. The physician fit his surroundings. Tall and lean, he boasted an aristocratic beak of a nose and kind eyes behind rimless glasses.

"I reviewed the computer results of your examination at the hospital yesterday," he told Natalie in flawless English. "I would have preferred a complete physical exam with diagnostic imaging and cognitive testing before consulting with you, of course. Despite the limited medical data available at this point, however, I doubt your memory loss resulted from an organic issue such as a stroke or brain tumor or dementia. That's the good news."

Natalie's breath hissed softly on the air. The sound made Dom reach for her hand.

"What's the bad?" she asked, her fingers closing around his.

"Despite what you see in movies and on television, Ms. Clark, it's very rare for persons suffering from amnestic syndrome to lose their self-identity. A head injury such as the one you sustained generally leads to confusion and problems remembering *new* information, not old."

"I'm starting to remember things." Her fingers curled tighter, the nails digging into Dom's palm. "Historical dates and facts and such."

"Good, that's good. But for you to have blocked your sense of self…"

Kovacs slid his rimless glasses to the tip of his nose. Dom found himself wondering again about Natalie's glasses, but pushed the thought to the back of his mind as the doctor continued.

"There's another syndrome. It's called psychogenic, or dissociative, amnesia. It can result from emotional shock or trauma, such as being a victim of rape or some other violent crime."

"I don't think…" Her nails gouged deeper, sharper. "I don't remember any…"

"The hospital didn't run a rape kit," Dom said when she stumbled to a halt. "There was no reason to. Natalie—Ms. Clark—doesn't have any defensive wounds or bruises other than the swelling at the base of her skull."

"I'm aware of that. And I'm not suggesting the trauma is necessarily recent. It could have happened weeks or months or years ago." He turned back to Natalie. "The blow to your head may have triggered a memory of some previous painful experience. Perhaps caused you to throw up a defensive shield and block all personal memories."

"Will…" She swiped her tongue over her lower lip. "Will these personal memories come back?"

"They do in most instances. Each case is so different, however, it's impossible to predict a pattern."

Her jaw set. "So how do I pry open Pandora's box? Are there drugs I should take? Mental exercises I can do?"

"For now, I suggest you just give it a little time. You're a visitor to Budapest, yes? Soak in the baths. Enjoy the opera. Stroll in our beautiful parks. Let your mind heal along with the injury to your head."

The neurologist's parting advice didn't sit well with Natalie.

"Hit the opera," she huffed as they exited the town house. "Soak in the baths. Easy for him to say!"

"And easy for us to do."

The drawled comment brought her up short. Coming to a dead stop in the middle of the wide, tree-shaded sidewalk, she cocked her head.

"How can you dawdle around Budapest with me? Don't you have a job? An office or a brickyard or a butcher shop wondering where you are?"

"I wish I worked in a butcher shop," he replied, laughing. "I could keep the hound in bones for the rest of his life."

"Don't dodge the question. Where do you work?"

"Nowhere at the moment, thanks to you."

"Me?" A dozen wild possibilities raced through her head but none of them made any sense. "I don't understand."

"No, I don't suppose you do." He hooked a hand under her elbow and steered her toward a café a short distance away. "Come, let's have a coffee and I'll explain."

If Budapest's many thermal springs and public baths had made it a favorite European spa destination since Roman times, the city owed its centuries-old café culture to the Turks. Suleyman the Magnificent first introduced coffee to Europe when he invaded Hungary in the 1500s.

Taste for the drink grew during the Austro-Hungarian Empire. Meeting friends for coffee or just claiming a table to linger over a book or newspaper became a time-honored tradition. Although Vienna and other European cities developed their own thriving café cultures, Budapest remained its epicenter and at one time boasted more than six hundred *kávébáz*.

Hungarians still loved to gather at cafés. Most were small places with a dozen or so marble-topped tables, serving the inevitable glass of water along with a pitcher of milk and a cup of coffee on a small silver tray. But a few of the more elegant nineteenth-century cafés still remained. The one Dom escorted Natalie to featured chandeliers dripping with Bohemian crystal and a monstrous brass coffeemaker that took up almost one whole wall.

They claimed an outside table shaded by a green-and-white-striped awning. Dom placed the order, and Natalie waited only until they'd both stirred milk and sugar into their cups to pounce.

"All right. Please explain why I'm responsible for you being currently unemployed."

"You uncovered a document in some dusty archives in Vienna. A codicil to the Edict of 1867, which granted certain rights to Hungarian nobles. The codicil specifically confirmed the title of Grand Duke of Karlenburgh to the house of St. Sebastian forever and in perpetuity. Does any of this strike a chord?"

"That name. Karlenburgh. I know I know it."

"It was a small duchy, not much larger than Monaco, that straddled the present-day border between Austria and Hungary. The Alps cut right through it. Even today it's a place of snow-capped peaks, fertile valleys and high mountain passes guarded by crumbling fortresses."

"You've been there?"

"Several times. My grandfather was born at Karlenburgh Castle. It's just a pile of rubble now, but Poppa took my parents, then my sister and me back to see it."

"Your grandfather was the Grand Duke?"

"No, that was Sarah's grandfather. Mine was his cousin." Dom hesitated, thinking about the blood ties that had so recently and dramatically turned his life up-

side down. "I suppose my grandfather could have tried to claim the title when the last Grand Duke was executed."

He stirred his coffee again and tried to imagine those long ago days of terror and chaos.

"From what he told me, that was a brutal time. The Soviet invasion leveled everyone—or elevated them, depending on how you looked at it—to the status of comrade. Wealth and titles became dangerous liabilities and made their holders targets. People tried to flee to the West. Neighbors spied on neighbors. Then, after the 1956 Uprising, the KGB rounded up thousands of nationalists. Charlotte, Sarah's grandmother, was forced to witness her husband's execution, and barely escaped Hungary with her life."

The history resonated somewhere in Natalie's mind. She'd heard this story before. She knew she had. She just didn't know how it connected her and the broad-shouldered man sitting across from her.

"So this dusty document you say I uncovered? It links you to the title?"

"Charlotte thinks it does. So, unfortunately, do the tabloids." His mouth twisted. "They've been hounding me since news of that damned document surfaced."

"Well, excuse me for making you aware of your heritage!"

His brows soared. He stared at her with such an arrested expression that she had to ask.

"What?"

"You said almost the same thing in New York. While you were tearing off a strip of my hide."

The revelation that she'd taken him down a peg or two did wonders for her self-confidence. "I'm sure you deserved it," she said primly.

This time he just laughed.

"What?" she demanded again.

"That's you, *drágám*. So proper. So prissy. That's the Natalie who made me ache to tumble her to the bed or a sofa and kiss the disapproval from those luscious lips. I hurt for an hour after I left you in New York."

Her jaw dropped. She couldn't speak. Could barely breathe. Some distant corner of her mind warned that she would lose, and lose badly, if she engaged Dominic St. Sebastian in an exchange of sexual repartee.

Yet she couldn't seem to stop herself. Forcing a provocative smile, she leaned her elbows on the table and dropped her voice to the same husky murmur Dom had employed in Dr. Kovacs's reception area.

"Ah, but we can fix that, yes?"

His blank astonishment shot her ego up another notch. For the first time since she'd come awake and found herself eye to eye with a grinning canine, Natalie was able to shelve her worry and confusion.

The arrival of a waiter with their lunch allowed her to revel in the sensation awhile longer. Only after she'd forked down several bites of leafy greens and crunchy cucumber did she return to their original topic.

"You still haven't explained how inheriting the title associated with a long-defunct duchy put you on the rolls of the unemployed."

He swept the café with a casual glance. So casual she didn't realize he was making sure no one was close enough to overhear until he delivered another jaw-dropper.

"I'm an undercover agent, Natalie. Or I was until all this Grand Duke business hit."

"Like…?" She tried to get her head around it. "Like James Bond or something?"

"Closer to something. After my face got splashed across the tabloids, my boss encouraged me to take a nice, long vacation."

"So that explains the drawer!"

He leaned back in his chair. Slowly. Too slowly. Although the September sun warmed the cozy space under the awning and the exhaust from the cabs clogging the boulevard shimmered on the afternoon air, Natalie had the eerie sensation that the temperature around their table had dropped at least ten degrees.

"What drawer?"

"The locked one in your wardrobe. You store all your 007-type gadgets in there, don't you? Poison pens and jet-propelled socks and laser-guided minimissiles?"

He didn't answer for several moments. When he did, her brief euphoria at being in control evaporated.

"This isn't about me, Nat. You're the one with the empty spaces that need filling. Let's finish our coffee, yes? Then we'll swing by police headquarters. With any luck, they will have found the answers to at least some of your questions."

Dom called before they left the café to make sure Officer Gradjnic, his partner or their supervisor would be available to speak with them. Natalie didn't say a word during the short drive. Budapest traffic was nerve-racking enough to tie anyone in knots. The possibility that the police might lift a corner of the curtain blanketing her mind only added to her twist of nerves.

The National Police Department occupied a multistory, glass-and-steel high-rise on the Pest side of the Danube. Command and control of nationwide operations filled the upper stories. The Budapest PD claimed the first two floors. Officer Gradjnic's precinct was crammed into a corner of the second floor.

Natalie remembered Gradjnic from yesterday. More or less. Enough to smile when he asked how she was feeling, anyway, and thank him for their help yesterday.

"So, Ms. Clark. Do you remember how you ended up in the Danube?"

"No."

"But you might, yes?"

"The doctor we consulted this morning said that was possible." She swiped her tongue over suddenly dry lips. "What have you discovered?"

"A little."

Computers sat on every desk in the office but Officer Gradjnic tugged out his leather notepad, licked his finger and flipped through the pages.

"We've verified that you flew from Paris to Vienna last week," he reported. "We've also learned that you rented a vehicle from the Europcar agency in Vienna three days ago. We had the car rental company retrieve the GPS data from the vehicle and discovered you crossed into Hungary at Pradzéc."

"Where's Pradzéc?"

"It's a small village at the foot of the Alps, straddling the border between Austria and Hungary."

Her glance shot to Dom. They'd been talking about the border area less than an hour ago. He didn't so much as flick an eyelid but she knew he'd made the connection, just as she had.

"According to the GPS records, you spent several hours in that area, then returned to Vienna. The next day you crossed into Hungary again and stopped in Győr. The vehicle is still there, Ms. Clark, parked at a tour dock on the Danube. We called the tour office and verified that a woman matching your description purchased a ticket for a day cruise to Budapest. Do you recall buying that ticket, Ms. Clark?"

"No."

"Do you remember boarding the tour boat? Watching the scenery as you cruised down the Danube, perhaps?"

"No."

He shrugged and closed his notebook. "Well, that's all I have for you, I'm afraid. You'll have to make arrangements to return the rental car."

Dom nodded. "We'll take care of it. In the meantime, we'd like a copy of your report."

"Of course."

When they walked out into the afternoon sunshine, Natalie couldn't wait to ask. "Was Győr part of the duchy of Karlenburgh?"

"At one time."

"Is Karlenburgh Castle anywhere in that vicinity?"

"It's farther west, guarding a mountain pass. Or was. It's just a pile of ruins now."

"I need to retrace my steps, Dominic. Maybe if I see the ruins or the towns or the countryside I drove through, I'll remember why I was there."

"We'll go tomorrow."

A part of her cringed a bit at being so dependent on this man, who was still almost a stranger to her. Yet she couldn't help feeling relieved he would accompany her.

"We can have someone from Europcar meet us in Győr with a set of master keys," he advised. "That way you can retrieve any luggage you might have left locked in the trunk."

"Assuming it's still there. Rental cars are always such targets."

"True. Now we'd better see about getting you a replacement passport."

He pulled up the necessary information from the US Embassy's consular services on his iPhone. "As I thought. You'll need proof of US citizenship. A birth certificate, driver's license or previous passport."

"None of which I have."

"I can help there. I'll have one my contacts obtain a copy of your driver's license."

"You can do that?"

When he just smiled, she slapped the heel of her hand against her forehead. "Of course you can. You're 007."

They walked to the car and he opened the passenger door for her. Before she slid into the seat, Natalie turned. "You're a man of many different personas, Dominic St. Sebastian. Grand Duke. Secret agent. Rescuer of damsels in distress."

His mouth curved. "Of the three, I enjoy the last most."

"Hmm." He was so close, almost caging her in, that she had to tip her chin to look up at him. "That comes naturally to you, doesn't it?"

"Rescuing damsels in distress?"

"No, that slow, sexy, let's-get-naked grin."

"Is that the message it sends?"

"Yes."

"Is it working?"

She pursed her lips. "No."

"Ah, *drágám*," he said, laughter springing into his eyes, "every time you do that, I want to do this."

She sensed what was coming. Knew she should duck under his arm, drop into her seat and slam the door. Instead she stood there like an idiot while he stooped, placed his mouth over hers and kissed the disapproval off her lips.

Six

It was just a kiss. Nothing to get all jittery about. And certainly no reason for a purr to start deep in Natalie's throat and heat to ball in her belly. She could feel both, though, right along with the sensual movement of Dominic's lips over hers.

She'd thought it would end there. One touch. One pass of his mouth over hers. It *should* have ended there. Traffic was coursing along the busy street, for pity's sake. A streetcar clanged by. Yet Natalie didn't move as his arm went around her waist, drawing her closer, while her pulse pounded in her veins.

She was breathing hard when Dominic raised his head. He was, too, but recovered much quicker than she did.

"There," he teased. "That's better. You don't want to walk around with your mouth all pruned up."

She couldn't think of an appropriate response, so she merely sniffed and ducked into the car.

She struggled to regain her equilibrium as the car negotiated the narrow, winding streets of Castle Hill. Yet with every turn of the wheels she could feel Dominic's mouth on hers, still taste him.

She snuck a sideways glance, wondering if he was experiencing any aftershocks. No, of course not. He was supercool Mr. Secret Agent. Sexy Mr. Grand Duke, who had

women slipping outrageously expensive panties into his carryall. The thought of him cuddling with Kissy Face Arabella struck a sour note in Natalie's mind. Not that it was any of her business *who* he cuddled with, she reminded herself sternly. She certainly had no claim on the man, other than being dropped on his doorstep like an abandoned baby.

That thought, in turn, triggered alternating ripples of worry and fear. She had to battle both emotions as Dom pulled into his parking space in the underground garage and they climbed the five flights of stairs. The enclosed stairwell blocked any glimpse of the river but it did afford a backside view of the uniformed delivery man trudging up ahead of them.

When they caught up with him at the landing outside the loft, Dom gestured to the large envelope in his hand. "Is that for me?"

"It is if you're Dominic St. Sebastian."

He signed for the delivery, noting the address of the sender. "It's from Sarah."

He pulled the tab on the outer envelope and handed Natalie the one inside. She fingered the bulging package before slipping it into her new straw tote. She didn't know the currency or the denomination of the notes her employer had sent but it felt like a fat wad. More than enough, she was sure, to repay Dom for her new clothes and the consult with Dr. Kovacs.

The money provided an unexpected anchor in her drifting world. When Dom unlocked the door to the loft and stood aside for her to enter, the hound provided another. Delirious with joy at their return, he woofed and waggled and whirled in ecstatic circles.

"Okay, Dog, okay." Laughing, Natalie dropped to her knees and fondled his ears. "I missed you, too."

He got in a few quick licks on her cheeks and chin

before she could dodge them. The silly grin on his face tugged at her heart.

"You can't keep calling him 'Dog,'" she scolded Dom. "He needs a proper name."

"What do you suggest?"

She studied the animal's madly whipping tail and white coat with its saddle-brown markings. "He looks a lot like a greyhound, but he's not, is he?"

"There may be some greyhound in him but he's mostly Magyar Agár."

"Magyar Agár." She rolled the words around in her head but drew a blank. "I'm not familiar with that breed."

"They're long-distance-racing and hunting hounds. In the old days, they would run alongside horsemen, often for twenty miles or more, to take down fast game like deer or hare. Anyone could own one, but big fellows like this one normally belonged to royalty."

"Royalty, huh. That settles it." She gave the cropped ears another tug. "You have to call him Duke."

"No."

"It's perfect," she insisted with a wicked glint in her eyes.

"No, Natalie."

"Think of the fun you can have if some pesky reporter wants to interview the duke."

Even better, think of the fun *she* could have whistling and ordering him to heel. "What do you say?" she asked the hound. "Think you could live with a royal title?"

Her answer was an ear-rattling woof.

"There, that settles the matter." She rose and dusted her hands. "What happens to Duke here when you're off doing your James Bond thing?"

"There's a girl in the apartment downstairs who looks after him for me."

Of course there was. Probably another Arabella-From-

London type. Natalie could just imagine what kind of payment she demanded for her dog-sitting services.

The thought was small and nasty and not one she was proud of. She chalked it up to these bizarre circumstances and the fact that she could still feel the imprint of Dom's mouth on her.

"I'd better take his highness out," he said. "Do you want to walk with us?"

She did, but she couldn't get the memory of their kiss out of her head. It didn't help that Dom was leaning against the counter, looking at her with those bedroom eyes.

"You go ahead," she said, needing some time and space. As an excuse she held up the straw tote with its cache of newly purchased toiletries. "Do you mind if I put some of these things in your bathroom?"

"Be my guest, *drágám*."

"I asked you not to call me that."

Nerves and a spark of temper made her sound waspish even to her own ears. He noted the tone but shrugged it off.

"So you did. I'll call you Natushka, then. Little Natalie."

That didn't sound any more dignified but she decided not to argue.

When he left with the dog, she emptied the tote. The toothbrush came out of its protective plastic sleeve first. A good brushing made up for her earlier finger-work, but she grimaced when she tried to find a spot in the bathroom for the rest of her purchases.

The sink area was littered with shaving gear, a hairbrush with a few short hairs that might or might not belong to the dog, dental floss and a dusty bottle of aftershave with the cap crusted on. The rest of the bathroom wasn't much better. Her wrinkled clothes occupied the towel rack. A shampoo bottle lay tipped on its side in the shower. The damp towels from their morning showers were draped over the shower door.

When she swept her skirt, blouse and jacket from the rack, her nose wrinkled at the faint but still-present river smell. They were too far gone to salvage. Not that Natalie wanted to. She couldn't believe she'd traipsed around the capitals of Europe in such a shapeless, ugly suit. Wadding it into a ball, she took it to the kitchen and searched for a wastebasket.

She found one in the cupboard under the sink, right next to some basic cleaning supplies. The suit and blouse went in. A sponge, a bottle of glass cleaner and a spray can of foaming disinfectant came out. Since Dominic was letting her crash at his loft, the least she could do was clean up a little.

The bathroom was small enough that it didn't take her long to get it gleaming and smelling like an Alpine forest. On a roll, she attacked the kitchen next. The coffee mugs and breakfast plates hit the dishwasher. The paper napkins and white bag with its grease stains from the apple pancakes joined her clothes in the trash. The stovetop and oven door got a scrubbing, as did the dog dish in a corner next to a cupboard containing a giant-size bag of dried food. She opened the refrigerator, intending to wipe down the shelves, and jumped back.

"Omig…!"

Gulping, she identified the gory objects in the gallon-size plastic bag as bones. Big bones. Belonging, she guessed, to a cow or boar. The kind of bones a Hungarian hunting dog would gnaw to sharpen his teeth.

The only other objects in the fridge were a to-go carton from an Asian restaurant and a dozen or so bottles of beer with labels touting unfamiliar brands. Curiosity had her opening the cupboards above the sink and stove. She found a few staples, some spices and a half loaf of bread keeping company with a dusty bottle of something called

Tokaji. Dominic St. Sebastian, she decided, was not into cooking at home.

Abandoning the cupboards, she turned her attention to the stainless-steel sink. The scrubbing gave Natalie a sense of fierce satisfaction. She might not be a James Bond type but she knew how to take out sink and shower grunge!

The kitchen done, she attacked the sitting area. Books got straightened, old newspapers stacked. The sleek little laptop nested next to a pair of running shoes on the floor was moved to the drop-down shelf that doubled as a desk. Natalie ran her fingers over the keyboard, gripped by a sudden urge to power up the computer.

She was a research assistant, according to Dom. An archivist. She probably spent most of her waking hours on the computer. What would she find if she went online and researched one Natalie Clark? Or had Dom already done that? She'd have to ask him.

She was dusting the black-and-glass stand of the wide-screen TV when he and the hound returned. The dog burst in first, of course, his claws tattooing on the oak floor. Dominic followed and placed a brown paper sack on the counter. Lifting a brow, he glanced at the now spotless kitchen.

"You've been busy."

"Just straightened up a bit. I hope you don't mind."

"Why would I mind?" Amusement glinted in his eyes. "Although I can think of better ways for both of us to work off excess energy than cleaning and dog walking."

She didn't doubt it for a moment. She was wearing proof of one of his workouts in the form of black silk hipsters. No doubt Kiss Kiss Arabella would supply an enthusiastic endorsement of his abilities in that area.

Not that Natalie required a second opinion. He'd already given her a hint of just how disturbing he could be to her equanimity if she let him. Which she wouldn't. She

couldn't! Her life was in enough turmoil without adding the complication of a wild tumble between the sheets with Dominic St. Sebastian. The mere thought made her so nervous that she flapped the dust cloth like a shield.

"What's in the bag?"

"I stopped by the butcher shop and picked up our supper."

"I hope you've got more than bones in there," she said with a little grimace.

"You found those, did you?"

"They were hard to miss."

"Not to worry. Dog will take care of those, although I'm sure he would much rather share our goulash."

Natalie eyed the tall, round carton he extracted dubiously. "The butcher shop sells goulash?"

"No, but Frau Kemper, the butcher's wife, always makes extra for me when she cooks up a pot."

"Oh?" She caught the prune before it formed but couldn't quite keep the disdain from her tone. "It must be a burden having so many women showering you with gifts."

"It is," he said sadly. "A terrible burden. Especially Frau Kemper. If she keeps forcing stews and cakes on me, I'll soon match her weight of a hundred and fifty kilos or more."

"A hundred and fifty kilos?" Natalie did the math. "Ha! I'd like to see you at three hundred plus pounds."

"No, you would not." He cocked his head. "But you did that calculation very quickly."

"I did, didn't I?" Surprise gave way to panic. "How can I remember metric conversions and not my name? My past? Anything about my family?"

Dom hesitated a fraction of a second too long. He knew something. Something he didn't want to reveal.

"Tell me!" she said fiercely.

"Sarah says you have no family."

"What?" Her fist bunched, crumpling the cloth she'd forgotten she still held. "Everyone has family."

"Let me put the goulash on to simmer, and I'll tell you what I know. But first…" He reached into the bag again and produced a gold-labeled bottle. "I'll open this and we'll drink a glass while we talk, yes?"

A vague memory stirred. Something or someone splashing pale gold liquid into crystal snifter. A man? This man? Desperately, she fought to drag the details to the front of her mind.

"What's in the bottle?"

"A chardonnay from the Badacsony vineyards."

The fragments shifted, realigned, wouldn't fit together. "Not…? Not apple brandy?"

"*Pálinka*? No," he said casually. Too casually. "That's what the duchess and I drank the last time I visited her in New York. You chose not to join us. This is much less potent."

He retrieved two wineglasses and rummaged in a drawer for an opener. She held up a hand before he poured. "None for me, thanks."

"Are you sure? It's light and crisp, one of Hungary's best whites."

"I'm not a drinker." As soon as the words were out, she sensed they were true. "You go ahead. I'm good with water."

"Then I'll have water, also."

With swift efficiency, he poured the goulash into a pot that had seen much better days. Once it was covered and set on low heat, he retrieved a bone for the hound and left him happily gnawing on the mat strategically placed under one of the eaves. Then he added ice to the two wineglasses and filled them with water.

"Let's take them to the balcony."

"Balcony," Natalie discovered when he held aside the

drapes on one side of the windows and opened an access door, was a grandiose term for the narrow platform that jutted out from the steep, sloping roof. Banded by a wrought-iron safety rail, it contained two bar chairs and a bistro-style table. Dominic edged past the table and settled in the farther chair.

Natalie had to drag in a deep breath before feeling her way cautiously to the closer chairs. She hitched up and peered nervously at the sheer drop on the other side of the railing.

"You're sure this is safe?"

"I'm sure. I built it myself."

Another persona. How many was that now? She had to do a mental recap. Grand Duke. Secret agent. Sex object of kissy-faced Englishwomen and full-bodied butcher's wives. General handyman and balcony-builder. All those facets to his personality, and hers was as flat and lifeless as a marble slab. More lifeless than she'd realized.

"You said I don't have any family," she prompted.

His glance strayed to the magnificence across the river. The slowly setting sun was gilding the turrets and spires and towering dome. The sight held him for several seconds. When it came back to her, Natalie braced herself.

"Sarah ran a background check on you before she hired you. According to her sources, there's no record of who your parents were or why they abandoned you as an infant. You were raised in a series of foster homes."

She must have known. On some subconscious level, she must have known. She'd been tossed out like trash. Unwanted. Unwelcome.

"You said a 'series' of foster homes. How many? Three? Five?"

"I don't have a number. I'll get one if you want."

"Never mind." Bitterness layered over the aching emptiness. "The total doesn't really matter, does it? What does

is that in a country with couples desperate to adopt, apparently no one wanted me."

"You don't know that. I'm not familiar with adoption laws in the United States. There may have been some legal impediment."

He played with his glass, his long fingers turning the stem. There was more coming, and she guessed it wouldn't be good. It wasn't.

"We also have to take into account the fact that no one appears to have raised an alarm over your whereabouts. The Budapest police, my contacts at Interpol, Sarah and Dev...none of them have received queries or concerns that you may have gone missing."

"So in addition to no family, I have no friends or acquaintances close enough to worry about me."

She stared unseeing at the stunning vista of shining river and glittering spires. "What a pathetic life I must lead," she murmured.

"Perhaps."

She hadn't been fishing for a shoulder to cry on, but the less-than-sympathetic response rankled...until it occurred to her that he was holding something back.

The thought brought her head up with a snap. She scowled at him, sitting so calm and relaxed on his tiny handkerchief of a balcony. The slanting rays of the late-afternoon sun highlighted the short, glossy black hair, the golden oak of his skin, the strong cheekbones and chin. The speculative look in his dark eyes...

"What do you know that you're not telling me?" she snapped.

"There," he said, tipping his glass toward her in mock salute. "That's what I know."

"Huh?"

"That spark of temper. That flash of spirit. You try so

hard to hide them behind the prim, proper facade you present to the world but every so often they slip out."

"What are you talking about? What facade?"

He parried her questions with one of his own. "Do you see the ironmonger's cast there, right in front of you, stamped into the balcony railing?"

"What?"

"The cast mark. Do you see it?"

Frowning, she surveyed the ornate initial entwined with ivy. The mark was worn almost smooth but still legible. "You mean that *N*?"

He gestured with his glass again, this time at the panorama view across the river. "What about the Liberation Monument, high on that hill?

"Dominic…"

"Do you see it?"

She speared an impatient glance at the bronze statue of a woman holding a palm leaf high aloft. It dominated the hill in the far distance and could obviously be seen from anywhere in the city.

"Yes, I see it." The temper he'd commented on earlier sparked again. "But I'm in no mood for games or quizzes, Mr. Grand Duke. What do you know that I don't?"

"I know you wore glasses in New York," he replied evenly. "Large, square glasses with thick lenses that you apparently don't require for near or distance vision. I know you scraped your hair back most unattractively instead of letting it fall loose to your shoulders, as it does now. I know you chose loose clothes in an attempt to disguise your slender hips and—" his glance drifted south, and an appreciative gleam lit his eyes "—very delightful breasts."

Her mouth had started sagging at the mention of glasses. It dropped farther when he got to her hair, and snapped shut at the mention of her breasts. Fighting the urge to

cross her arms over her chest, she tried to make sense of his observations.

She couldn't refute the part about the clothes. She'd questioned her fashion sense herself before she'd tossed the garments in the trash this morning. But the glasses? The hair?

She scrubbed her palms over her thighs, now encased in the formfitting designer jeans she'd purchased at the boutique. The jeans, the sandals, the short-sleeve T-shirt didn't feel strange or uncomfortable. From what Dom had said, though, they weren't her.

"Maybe what you saw in New York is the real me," she said a little desperately. "Maybe I just don't like drawing attention to myself."

"Maybe," he agreed, his gaze steady on her face. "And maybe there's a reason why you don't."

She could think of several reasons, none of them particularly palatable. Some were so far out she dismissed them instantly. She just couldn't see herself as a terrorist in training or a bank robber on the run. There was another explanation she couldn't shrug off as easily. One Dom brought up slowly, carefully.

"Perhaps your desire to hide the real you relates to a personal trauma, as Dr. Kovacs suggested this morning."

She couldn't deny the possibility. Yet…

She didn't *feel* traumatized. And she'd evidently been doing just fine before her dive into the Danube. She had a job that must have paid very well, judging by the advance on her salary Sarah had sent. She'd traveled to Paris, to Vienna, to Hungary. She must have an apartment back in the States. Books, maybe. Framed prints on the wall or a pen-and-ink sketch or a…

Her thoughts jerked to a stop. Rewound. Focused on a framed print. No, not a print. A painting. A canal scene

with strong, hazy colors and a light so natural it looked as though the sun was shimmering on the water.

She could see it! Every sleek black gondola, every window arch framed by mellow stone, every ripple of the green waters of the lagoon.

"Didn't Sarah tell you I went to Vienna to research a painting?" she asked Dom eagerly.

"She did."

"A Venetian canal scene." She clung to the mental image with a fierce effort of will. "By…by…"

"Canaletto."

"Yes!" She edged off the tall chair and kept a few careful inches away from the iron railing. "Let's go inside. I need to use your laptop."

Seven

The spicy scent of paprika and simmering beef filled the loft when they went inside. Natalie sniffed appreciatively but cut a straight line for the laptop.

"Do I need a password to power up?"

"Just hit the on switch."

"Really?" She dropped into the leather armchair and positioned the laptop on her knees. "I would have thought 007 would employ tighter security."

Dom didn't bother to explain that all electronic and digital communications he received from or sent to Interpol were embedded with so many layers of encryption that no one outside the agency could decipher them. He doubted she would have heard him in any case. She was hunched forward, her fingers hovering over the keys.

"I hope you have Wi-Fi," she muttered as the screen brightened to display a close-up of the hound. All nose and bright eyes and floppy ears, the image won a smile from Natalie. The real thing plopped down on his haunches before Dom and let his tongue loll in eager anticipation of a libation.

Idly, Dom tipped some lager into his dish and watched as Natalie skimmed through site after site relating to the eighteenth-century Italian painter. The cop in him kept returning to their conversation outside on the balcony. He

wasn't buying her quick dismissal of the suggestion she'd tried to downplay her natural beauty.

She most definitely had, and the ploy hadn't worked. Not with Dom, anyway. Despite her disdainful sniffs, daunting glasses and maiden-aunt clothes, she'd stirred his interest from the moment she'd opened the door of the duchess's apartment. And she'd damned near tied him in knots when she'd paraded out of the shower this morning with that crew shirt skimming her thighs.

Now...

His fist tightened on the dew-streaked pilsner bottle. She should see herself through his eyes. The shoulder-length, honey-streaked brown hair. The fierce concentration drawing her brows into a straight line. The lips pooched into a tight rosebud.

Jézus, Mária és József! Those lips!

Swallowing a groan, Dom took another pull of the lager and gave the rest to the ecstatic hound.

"You shouldn't let him have beer."

He glanced over to find her looking all prudish and disapproving again. Maybe it wasn't a disguise, he thought wryly. Maybe there was room in that sexy body for a nun, a shower scrubber and a wanton.

God, he hoped so!

It didn't take her long to find what she was looking for. Dom was still visualizing a steamy shower encounter when she whooped.

"This is it! This is the painting I was researching. I don't know how I know it, but I do."

He crossed the room and peered over her shoulder. Her scent drifted up to him, mingling with that of the goulash to tease his senses. Hair warmed by the sun. Skin dusted from their day in the city. The faint tang of cleaning solutions. Excitement radiated from her as she read him the details she'd pulled up on the laptop.

"It's one of Canaletto's early works. Commissioned by a Venetian doge and seized by Napoleon as part of the spoils of war after he invaded Venice in 1797. It reportedly hung in his study at the Tuileries Palace, then disappeared sometime before or during a fire in 1871."

She scrolled down the page. She was in full research mode now, inhaling every detail with the same eagerness the hound did pilsner.

"The painting disappeared for almost a half a century, until it turned up again in the early '30s in the private collection of a Swiss industrialist. He died in 1953 and his squabbling heirs auctioned off his entire collection. At that point... Look!"

She stabbed a finger at the screen. Dom bent closer.

"At that point," she recited eagerly, "it was purchased by an agent acting for the Grand Duke of Karlenburgh."

She swiveled around, almost tilting the laptop off her knees in her eagerness. Her face was alive, her eyes bright with the thrill of discovery.

"The Grand Duke of Karlenburgh," she repeated. "That was you, several times removed."

"*Many* times removed."

Despite his seeming insouciance, the connection couldn't be denied. It wove around him like a fine, silken thread. Trapping him. Cocooning him.

"The painting was a gift from the duke to his duchess," he related, remembering the mischievous look in Charlotte's eyes. "To commemorate a particularly pleasant visit to Venice."

Natalie's face went blank for a moment, then lit with excitement. "I remember hearing that story! Venice is where she got pregnant, right? With her only child?"

"Right."

They were so close, her mouth just a breath away from

his, that Dom couldn't help himself. He had to drop a kiss on those tantalizing lips.

He kept it light, playful. But when he raised his head confusion and a hint of wariness had replaced the excitement. Kicking himself, he tried to coax it back.

"Charlotte said the painting hung in the Red Salon at Karlenburgh Castle. Is there reference to that?"

"I, uh… Let me look."

She ducked her head and hit the keys again. Her hair feathered against her cheek like a sparrow's wing, shielding her face. He knew he'd lost serious ground when she shook her head and refused to look at him.

"No mention here. All it says is that the painting was lost again in the chaos following the Soviet suppression of the 1956 Hungarian Uprising."

"The same uprising that cost the Grand Duke his life and forced his wife to flee her homeland."

"How sad." With a small sigh, Natalie slumped against the chair back. "Charlotte's husband purchased the painting to celebrate one of the most joyous moments of their lives. And just a little more than a year later, both he and the painting were lost."

Her voice had gone small and quiet. She was drawing parallels, Dom guessed. Empathizing with the duchess's tragic losses. Feeling the emptiness of her own life.

The thought of her being a forgotten, helpless cog in a vast social welfare bureaucracy pulled at something deep inside him. He'd known her for such a short time. Had spoken to her twice in New York. Spent less than twenty-four hours with her here in Budapest. Yet he found himself wanting to erase the empty spaces in her heart. To pull her into his arms and fill the gaps in her mind with new, happy and extremely erotic memories. The urge was so powerful it yanked him up like a puppet on a twisted string.

Christ! He was a cop. Like all cops, he knew that trust

could—and too often did—shift like the sand on a wave-swept shore. Identities had to be validated, backgrounds scrubbed with a wire brush. Until he heard back from his contact at Interpol, he'd damned well better keep his hands to himself.

"The duke was executed," he said briskly, "but Charlotte survived. She made a new life for herself and her baby in New York. Now she has her granddaughters, her great-grandchildren. And you, Ms. Clark, have the finest goulash in all of Budapest to sample."

The abrupt change in direction accomplished precisely what he'd intended. Natalie raised her head. The curtain of soft, shiny hair fell back, and a tentative smile etched across her face.

"I'm ready."

More than ready, she realized. They hadn't eaten since their hurried breakfast and it was now almost seven. The aroma filling the loft had her taste buds dancing in eagerness.

"Ha!" Dom said with a grin. "You may think you're prepared, but Frau Kemper's stew is in a class by itself. Prepare for a culinary tsunami."

While he sniffed and stirred the goulash, Natalie set the counter with the mismatched crockery and cutlery she'd found during her earlier explorations of the kitchen cupboards.

Doing the homey little task made her feel strange. Strange and confused and nervous. Especially when her hip bumped Dominic's in the narrow kitchen area. And when he reached for a paper towel the same time she did. And...

Oh, for pity's sake! Who was she kidding? It wasn't the act of laying out bowls and spoons that had her mind and nerves jumping. It was Dominic. She couldn't look at him without remembering the feel of his mouth on hers.

Couldn't listen to him warning the dog—Duke!—to take himself out of the kitchen without thinking about how he'd called her sweetheart in Hungarian. And not just in Hungarian. In a husky, teasing voice that seemed so intimate, so seductive.

She didn't really know him. Hell, she didn't even know herself! Yet when he went to refill her glass with water she stopped him.

"I'd like to try that wine you brought home."

He looked up from the spigot in surprise. "Are you sure?"

"Yes."

She was. She really was. Natalie had no idea what lay at the root of her aversion to alcohol. A secretive, guilt-ridden tasting as a kid? An ugly drunk as a teen? A degrading experience in college? Whatever had caused it remained shrouded in her past. Right here, though, right now, she felt safe enough enjoy a glass of wine.

Safe?

The word echoed in her mind as Dom worked the cork on the chilled bottle and raised his glass to eye level. *"Egészségére!"*

"I'll drink to that, whatever it means."

"It means 'to your health.' Unless you mispronounce it," he added with a waggle of his brows. "Then it means 'to your arse.'"

She didn't bother to ask which pronunciation he'd used, just took a sip and waited for some unseen ax to fall. When the cool, refreshing white went down smoothly, she started to relax.

The goulash sped that process considerably. The first spoonful had her gasping and reaching desperately for the wineglass. The second, more cautious spoonful went down with less of an assault by the paprika and garlic. By the third, she'd recovered enough to appreciate the subtle

flavors of caraway seed, marjoram and sautéed onions. By the fourth, she was spearing the beef, pork and potatoes with avid enthusiasm and sopping up gravy with chunks of dark bread torn from the loaf Frau Kemper had thoughtfully included with her stew.

She limited her wine intake to a single glass but readily agreed to a second helping of goulash. The Agár sat on his haunches beside her stool as she spooned it down. When she didn't share, his liquid brown eyes filled with such reproach that she was forced to sneak him several dripping morsels. Dom pretended not to notice, although he did mention drily that he'd have to take the hound for an extralong run before bed to flush the spicy stew out of his system.

As casual as it was, the comment started Natalie's nerves jumping again. The loft boasted only one bed. She'd occupied it last night. She felt guilty claiming it again.

"Speaking of bed…"

Dom's spoon paused in midair. "Yes?"

Her cheeks heating, she stirred the last of her stew. He had to be wondering why she hadn't taken Sarah up on her offer of a hotel room. At the moment, she couldn't help wondering the same thing.

"I don't like ousting you out of yours."

"Oh?" His spoon lowered. "Are you suggesting we share?"

She was becoming familiar with that slow, provocative grin.

"I'm suggesting," she said with a disdainful sniff, "I sleep on the sofa tonight and you take the bed."

She hadn't intended her retort as a challenge, but she should have known Dom would view it that way. Laughter leaped into his face, along with something that started Natalie's breath humming in her throat.

"Ah, sweetheart," he murmured, his eyes on her mouth.

"You make it very difficult for me to ignore the instincts bred into me by my wild, marauding ancestors."

Even Duke seemed to sense the sudden tension that arced through her. The dog wedged closer to Natalie and propped his head on her knee. She knuckled his forehead and tried desperately to blank any and all thought of Dom tossing her over his shoulder. Carrying her to his bed. Pillaging her mouth. Ravishing her body. Demanding a surrender she was all too willing to…

"Don't look so worried."

The wry command jolted her back to the here and now. Blinking, she watched Dom push off his stool.

"My blood may run as hot as my ancestors', but I draw the line at seducing a woman who can't remember her name. Come, Dog."

Still racked by the erotic images, Natalie bent her head to avoid looking at Dom as he snapped the Agár's lead to his collar. She couldn't avoid the knuckle he curved under her chin, however, or the real regret in his eyes when he tipped her face to his.

"I'm sorry, Natushka. I shouldn't tease you. I know this is a frightening time for you."

Oh, sure. Like she was going to tell him that fright was *not* what she was feeling right now? Easing her chin from his hold, she slid off her stool and gathered the used utensils.

"I'll wash the dishes while you're gone."

"No need. Just stick them in the dishwasher."

"Go!" She needed to do something with her hands and her overactive, overheated mind. "I'll take care of the kitchen."

She did the dishes. Spritzed the sink and countertop. Drew the drapes. Fussed with paperbacks she'd stacked earlier that afternoon. Curled up in the chair and reached

for the laptop. And grew more annoyed with each passing moment.

Her glance kept darting from the wide sofa with its worn leather cushions to the bed tucked under the eaves at the far end of the loft. She didn't understand why she was so irritated by Dom's assurance that he wouldn't seduce her. Those brief moments of fantasy involving marauding Magyars aside, she didn't really *want* him to. Did she?

Lips compressed, she tried to balance her contradictory emotions. On the one hand, Dominic St. Sebastian constituted the only island in the empty sea of her mind. It was natural that she would cling to him. Not want to antagonize him or turn him away.

Yet what she was feeling now wasn't mental. It was physical, and growing more urgent by the moment. She wanted his hands on her, dammit! His mouth. She wanted that hard, muscled body pinning hers to the wall, the sheets, even the floor.

The intensity of the hunger pumping through her veins surprised her. It also generated an enormous relief. All that talk about a possible past trauma had raised some ugly questions in her mind. In Dom's, too, apparently, judging by his comment about her deliberately trying to downplay her looks. The realization that she could want a man as much as she appeared to want this one was as reassuring as it was frustrating.

Which brought her right back to square one. She threw another thoroughly annoyed look at the bed. She should have taken Sarah up on her offer to arrange a hotel room, she thought sourly. If she had, she wouldn't be sitting here wondering whether she should—or could!—convince Dom to forget about being all noble and considerate.

Shoving out of the chair, she stalked to the wardrobe and reclaimed the shirt she'd slept in last night. She took it into the bathroom to change, and her prickly irritation

ratcheted up another notch when she found the hand towel she'd left folded neatly over the rack tossed in a damp pile atop the counter. Worse, the toiletries she'd carefully arranged to make room for her few purchases were once again scattered haphazardly around the sink.

Muttering, she stripped off her new jeans and top. She didn't think she was obsessive-compulsive. And even if she was, what was so wrong with keeping things neat and orderly?

The sight of her borrowed undies didn't exactly improve her mood. Dom obviously hadn't suffered from an excess of scruples with Kissy Face Arabella. Natalie would have dumped the black silk hipsters in the trash if she'd had another pair to step into. She'd have to do more shopping tomorrow.

Yanking the crew shirt over her head, she scrubbed her face and teeth. Then she carefully refolded *her* towel and scooped up her jeans and top. Just as she exited the bathroom, the front door opened and Duke bounded in. His ecstatic greeting soon had her laughing. Hard to stay in a snit with a cold nose poking her bare thighs and a pink tongue determined to slather her with kisses.

"Okay, enough, stop." She fended off a determined lunge and pointed a stern finger at the floor. "Duke! Sit!"

He looked a little confused by the English command but the gesture got through to him. Ears flopping, he dropped onto his haunches.

"Good boy." She couldn't resist sending his master a smug look. "See, he recognizes his name."

"I think he recognized your tone."

"Whatever." She chewed on her lower lip for a moment. "We didn't resolve the issue of the bed earlier. I don't feel right consigning you to the sofa. I'll sleep there tonight."

"No, you won't."

"Look, I'm very grateful for all you've done for me. I

don't want to inconvenience you any more than I already have."

Dom managed not to snort. If she had any idea of just how badly she was "inconveniencing" him at this moment, she'd shimmy back into her jeans and run like hell. Instead she just stood there while his gaze gobbled up the long, slender legs showing below the hem of his shirt. The mere thought of those legs tangled with his started an ache in his groin.

He damned well better not fantasize about what was *under* the shirt. If he did, neither one of them would make it to the bed. They might not even make it to the sofa.

"I've fallen asleep more nights than I can count in front of the TV," he bit out. "You've got the bed."

He could tell from the way her mouth set that he'd come across more brusque than he'd intended. Tough. After just a little more than twenty-four hours in her company, Ms. Clark had him swinging like a pendulum. One moment his cop's instincts were reminding him that things weren't always what they seemed. The next, he ached to take her in his arms and kiss away the fear she was doing her best to disguise.

Now he just plain ached, and he wasn't happy about the fact that he couldn't—wouldn't!—do anything to ease the hurt. And why was she tormenting him like this, anyway?

"You're not going to bed now, are you?" he asked her.

"It's almost ten."

He managed to keep his jaw from sagging, but it took a heroic effort. He could understand her crashing facedown on the bed last night. She'd been hurt. She'd spent who knew how long in the Danube, and had a lump the size of a softball at the base of the skull.

She'd seemed to recover today, though. Enough for him to make an incautious comment. "At ten o'clock most Hun-

garians are trying to decide where to go for coffee and dessert."

Her chin tilted. "If you want to go out for coffee and dessert, please don't let me stop you."

Whoa! He'd missed something here. When he left to take out the dog twenty minutes ago, Natalie had been all soft and shy and confused. Now she was as stiff and prickly as a horsehair blanket.

Dom wanted to ask what happened in that short time span but he'd learned the hard way to keep his mouth shut. He'd guided his sister through her hormone-driven teen years. He'd also enjoyed the company of his fair share of women. Enough, anyway, to know that any male who attempted to plumb the workings of the female mind had better be wearing a Kevlar vest. Since he wasn't, he quickly backpedaled.

"Probably just as well we make it an early night. We have a full day tomorrow."

She acknowledged his craven retreat with a regal dip of her head. "Yes, we do. Good night."

"Good night."

Dom and the hound both watched as she made her way to the far end of the loft and arranged her jeans and tank top into neat folds before placing them on the table beside the bed. Dom didn't move while she turned back the comforter and slid between the sheets.

The dog didn't exercise the same restraint. His claws scrabbling on the oak floorboards, he scrambled across the open space and made a flying leap. He landed on the bed with paws outstretched and announced his arrival with a happy woof. Natalie laughed and eased to one side to make room for him.

With a muttered curse, Dom turned away from the sight of the Agár sprawled belly-up beside her.

Eight

The next day dawned achingly bright and gloriously cool. The first nip of fall had swept away the exhaust-polluted city air and left Budapest sparkling in the morning light.

Dom woke early after a restless night. Natalie was still hunched under the featherbed when he took the hound for his morning run. Halfway through their usual five miles he received a text message with a copy of her driver's license. He saved the attachment to print out at the loft and thumbed his phone to access the US Embassy website. Once he'd downloaded the application to replace a lost passport, he made a note to himself to call the consular office and set up an appointment.

He was tempted to make another call to his contact at Interpol. When he'd asked Andre to dig deeper, he hadn't expected the excavation to take more than a day. Two at the most. But he knew Andre would get back to him if he uncovered anything of interest.

Dom also knew he belonged in the field! He'd taken down vicious killers, drug traffickers, the remorseless sleaze who sold children to the highest bidders. He didn't claim to be the best at what he did, but he'd done his part. This extended vacation was pure crap.

Or had been, until Natalie had dropped into his life. If Dom hadn't been at such loose ends he might not have been so quick to assume complete responsibility for her.

Now that he had, he felt obligated to keep her close until her memory returned.

It was already trickling back. Bits and pieces had started to pierce the haze. And when the fog dissipated completely, he thought with a sudden tightening of his belly, he intended to do his damnedest to follow up on that one, searing kiss. He'd spent too many uncomfortable hours on the sofa last night, imagining just that eventuality.

A jerk on the leash checked his easy stride. He glanced down to see the hound dragging his rear legs and glaring at him reproachfully.

"Don't look at me like that. You're already in bed with her."

Still the dog wouldn't move.

"Oh, all right. Have at it."

Dom jogged in place while the Agár sniffed the interesting pile just off the track, then majestically lifted a leg to spray it.

As soon as Dom and the hound entered, they were hit with the aroma of sizzling bacon and freshly baked cinnamon bread. The scents were almost as tantalizing as the sight of Natalie at the stove, a spatula in hand and a towel tucked apronlike around her slim hips. Dom tried to remember the last woman who'd made herself at home in his kitchen. None of those who'd come for a drink and stayed for the night, as best he could recall. And certainly not his sister. Even as a child, Anastazia had always been too busy splinting the broken wings of sparrows or feeding baby squirrels with eyedroppers to think about nourishing herself or her brother.

"I went down to the grocery shop on the corner," Natalie said by way of greeting. "I thought we should have breakfast before we took off for Karlenburgh Castle."

"That sounds good. How long before it's ready?"

"Five minutes."

"Make it ten," he begged.

He snagged a cup of coffee and had to hide a grimace. She'd made it American style. Closer to colored water than the real thing. The weak brew provided barely enough punch to get him through a quick shower and shave.

He emerged eager for a taste of the bacon laid out in crisp strips on a paper towel. The fluffy eggs scrambled with mushrooms and topped with fresh-grated Gruyère cheese had his tongue hanging out almost as far as the hound's. But the warm cinnamon rolls tucked in a napkin made him go weak at the knees. Groaning, he sank onto a stool at the counter.

"Do you cook breakfast for yourself every morning?"

She paused with the spatula hovering above the platter of eggs. "I don't know."

"No matter," Dom said fervently. "You're doing fine."

Actually, she was doing great. Her movements concise and confident, she set out his mismatched plates and folded paper napkins into neat, dainty triangles. Amused, he saw that she'd purchased a small bouquet of flowers during her quick trip to the grocers. The purple lupines and pink roses now sprouted from his prized beer stein. He had to admit they added a nice touch of color to the otherwise drab kitchen area.

So did she. She wore the jeans she'd purchased yesterday and had borrowed another of his soccer shirts. The hem of the hunter-green shirt fell well below her hips, unfortunately, but when she leaned across the counter to refill his coffee mug, the deep-V neckline gave him a tantalizing glimpse of creamy slopes.

Promising the hopeful hound he would be fed later, she perched on the stool beside Dom and served them both. The eggs tasted as good as they looked. He was halfway through his when he gave her an update.

"While I was out jogging, I got a text with a copy of your driver's license attached. I also downloaded the application form for a replacement passport. I'll print both after breakfast, then we'll make an appointment with the consular office."

Natalie nodded. The bits and pieces of her life seemed to be falling into place. She just wished they would fall faster. Maybe this excursion to Karlenburgh Castle would help. Suddenly impatient, she hopped off her stool and rinsed her dish in the sink.

"Are you finished?" she asked.

He relinquished his plate but snagged the last cinnamon bun before she could whisk the basket away. She did a quick kitchen cleanup and changed back into her red tank top. Her straw tote hooked over her shoulder, she waited impatiently while Dom extracted a lightweight jacket from his wardrobe.

"You'll need this. It can get cool up in the mountains."

She was disappointed when he decreed the hound wouldn't join them on the expedition…and surprised when he introduced her to the girl in the apartment downstairs who looked after the animal during his frequent absences.

The dog-sitter wasn't the sultry, predatory single Natalie had imagined. Instead she looked to be about nine or ten, with a splash of freckles across her nose and a backpack that indicated she'd been just about to depart for school.

When she dropped to her knees to return the hound's eager kisses, her papa came to the door. Dom introduced Natalie and explained that they might return late. "I would appreciate it if Katya would walk him after school, as per our usual agreement."

The father smiled fondly at his daughter and replied in heavily accented English. "But of course, Dominic. They will both enjoy the exercise. We still have the bones and

bag of food you left last time. If you are late, we'll feed him, yes?"

"We should not call him Dominic anymore, Papa." The girl sent Dom an impish grin. "We should address you as Your Grace, shouldn't we?"

"You do," he retorted, tugging on her ear, "and I won't let you download any more songs from my iTunes account."

Giggling, she pulled away and reminded him of a promise he looked as though he would prefer to forget. "You're coming to my school, aren't you? I want to show off my important neighbor."

"Yes, yes. I will."

"When?"

"Soon."

"When?"

"Katya," her father said in gentle reproof.

"But Dom's on vacation now. He told us so." Her arm looped around the dog's neck, she turned accusing eyes on her upstairs neighbor. "So when will you come?"

Natalie had to bite the inside of her lip to keep from laughing. The kid had him nailed and knew it.

"Next week," he promised reluctantly.

"When next week?"

"Katya, enough!"

"But, Papa, I need to tell my teacher when to expect the Grand Duke of Karlenburgh."

Groaning, Dom committed to Tuesday afternoon if her teacher concurred. Then he grasped Natalie's elbow and steered her toward the garage stairs.

"Let's get out of here before she makes me promise to wear a crown and a purple robe."

"Yes, Your Grace."

"Watch yourself, woman."

"Yes, Your Grace."

She knew him well enough now to laugh off his bad-tempered growl. As they started down the winding streets of Castle Hill, though, she added another facet to his growing list of alter egos. Undercover Agent. Grand Duke. Rescuer of damsels in distress. Loving older brother. Adopter of stray hounds. And now friend to an obviously adoring preteen.

Then there was that other side to him. The hot, sexy marauder whose ancestors had swept down from the Steppes. Sitting right next to her, so close that all she had to do was slide a glance at his profile to remember his taste and his scent and the feel of all those hard muscles pressed against her.

Natalie bit her lip in dismay when she realized she couldn't decide which of Dom's multiple personalities appealed to her most. They were all equally seductive, and she had the scary feeling that she was falling a little bit in love with each one of them.

Lost in those disturbing thoughts, she didn't see they'd emerged onto a broad boulevard running parallel to the Danube until Dom pointed out an impressive complex with an elaborate facade boasting turrets and fanciful wrought-iron balconies.

"That's Gellért Hotel. Their baths are among the best in Budapest. We'll have to follow Dr. Kovacs's advice and go for a soak tomorrow, yes?"

Natalie couldn't remember if she'd been to a communal bath before. Somehow it didn't seem like her kind of thing. "Do the spa-goers wear bathing suits?"

"In the public pools." He tipped her a quick grin. "But we can book a private session, where suits are optional."

Like that was going to happen! Natalie could barely breathe sitting here next to him fully clothed. She refused to think about the two of them slithering into a pool naked.

Hastily, she shoved her thoughts in a different direction. "How far did you say it was to where I left the rental car?"

"Győr's only a little over a hundred kilometers."

"And Pradzéc, where I crossed over from Austria?"

"Another sixty or seventy kilometers. But the going will be slower as we get closer to the border. The road winds as it climbs into the Alps."

"Where it reaches Karlenburgh Castle," she murmured.

She'd been there. She *knew* she'd been there. Dom claimed the castle was nothing but a pile of tumbled rock now but something had pulled Natalie to those ruins. Even now, she could feel the tug. The sensation was so strong, so compelling, that it took her some time to let go of it and pay more attention to the countryside they passed through.

They zipped along the M1 motorway as it cut through the region that Dom told her was called Northern Transdanubia. Despite its bloody history as the traditional battleground between Hungary and the forces invading from the west, the region was one of gentle hills, green valleys and lush forests. The international brown signs designating a significant historic landmark flashed by with astonishing frequency. Each town or village they passed seemed to boast an ancient abbey or spa or fortified stronghold.

The city of Győr was no exception. When Dom pointed out that it was located exactly halfway between Vienna and Budapest, she wondered how many armies had tramped through its ancient, cobbled streets. Natalie caught only a glimpse of Old Town's battlements, however, before they turned north. Short moments later they reached the point where two smaller rivers flowed into the mighty Danube.

A double-decker tour boat was just departing the wharf. Natalie strained every brain cell in an effort to identify with the day-trippers crowding the rails on the upper decks. Nothing clicked. Not even when Dom turned into the park-

ing lot and parked next to the motorized matchbox she'd supposedly rented in Vienna almost two days ago.

Dom had arranged for a rental agency rep to meet them. When the agent popped the trunk with a spare set of keys a tingle began to feather along her nerves. The tingle surged to a hot, excited rush the moment she spotted a bulging leather briefcase.

"That's mine!"

Snatching the case out of the trunk, she cradled it against her breasts like a long-lost baby. She allowed it out of her arms only long enough for Dom to note the initials embossed in gold near the handle…and the fact that it wasn't locked. Her heart pounding, she popped the latch and whooped at the sight of a slim laptop jammed between stacks of fat files.

"This must be yours, too," the rental agency rep said as he lifted out a weekender on wheels.

She didn't experience the same hot rush when the ID tag on the case verified the case was, in fact, hers. Maybe because when she opened it to inspect the contents they looked as though they belonged to an octogenarian. Everything was drab, colorless and eminently sensible. She tried to pump herself up with the realization that she now had several sets of clean undies in her possession. Unfortunately, they were all plain, unadorned undies that Kiss Kiss Arabella wouldn't be caught dead in!

A check of the vehicle's interior produced no purse, passport, ID or credit cards. Nor was there any sign of the glasses Dominic insisted she hadn't really needed. They must have gone into the river with her. Hugging the briefcase, she watched as Dom transferred the weekender to his own car and provided a copy of the police report to the rep from the rental agency. In view of her accident and injury and the fact that there was no apparent damage to the vehicle, the rep agreed to waive the late return charges.

Natalie almost shivered with impatience to delve into the files in the briefcase but Dom wanted to talk to the people at the tour office first on the off-chance they might remember her. They didn't, nor could they provide any more information than the police had already gleaned by tracking her credit card charges.

Natalie stood with Dom next to the ticket booth and stared at the sleek boat now little more than a speck in the distance. "This is so frustrating! Why did I take a river cruise? I don't even like boats."

"How do you know?"

She blinked. "I'm not sure. I just don't."

"Maybe we'll find a clue in your briefcase."

She glanced around the wharf area, itching to get into those fat files, but knew they couldn't spread their contents out on a picnic table where the breeze off the river might snatch them away. Dom sensed her frustration and offered a suggestion.

"We're less than an hour from Karlenburgh Castle. There's an inn in the village below the castle ruins. We can have lunch and ask Frau Dortmann for the use of her parlor to lay everything out."

"Let's go!"

She couldn't resist extracting a few of the files and skimming through them on the way. Each folder was devoted to a lost treasure. A neat table of contents listed everything inside—printed articles from various computer sources, copies of handwritten documents, color photos, black-and-whites, historical chronologies tracing last known ownership, notes Natalie had made to herself on additional sources to check.

"Ooh," she murmured when she flipped to a sketch of jewel-studded egg nested in a gold chariot pulled by a winged cherub. "How beautiful."

Dom glanced at the photo. "Isn't that the Fabergé egg Tsar Alexander gave his wife?"

"I…uh…" She checked her notes and looked up in surprise. "It is. How do you know that?"

"You were researching it in the States. You told me about it when we got together in your hotel room in New York."

"We got together in New York? In my hotel room?"

Dom was tempted, really tempted, but he stuck with the truth. "I thought you might be scheming to rip off the duchess with all that business about the codicil so I came to warn you off. You," he added with a quick grin, "kicked me out on my ass."

The Natalie he knew and was beginning to seriously lust after emerged. "I'm sure you deserved it."

"Ah, Natushka. Don't go all prim and proper on me. We might not make it to the inn."

He said it with a smile but they both knew he was only half kidding. Cheeks flushed, Natalie dug into the file again.

She saw the castle ruins first. She could hardly miss them. The tumbled walls and skeletal remains of a single square tower were set high on a rocky crag and visible from miles away. As they got closer, Natalie could see how the road cut through the narrow pass below—the only pass connecting Austria and Hungary for fifty miles in either direction, Dom informed her.

"No wonder the Habsburgs were so anxious to have your ancestors hold it for the Empire."

Only after they'd topped a steep rise did she see the village at the base of the cliffs. The dozen or so structures were typically Alpine, half-timbered and steep-roofed to slough off snow. A wooden roadside shrine housing a statue of the Virgin Mary greeted them as they approached

the village. In keeping with the mingled heritage of the residents, the few street signs and notices were in both German and Hungarian.

The gasthaus sat at the edge of the village. Its mossy shingles and weathered timbers suggested it had welcomed wayfarers for centuries. Geraniums bloomed in every window box and an ivy-covered beer garden beckoned at one side of the main structure.

When Natalie and Dom went up the steps and entered the knotty-pine lobby, the woman who hustled out to greet them didn't match her rustic surroundings. Dom's casual reference to Frau Dortmann had evoked hazy images of an apron-clad, rosy-cheeked matron.

The fortysomething blonde in leggings and a tiger-striped tunic was as far from matronly as a woman could get. And if there was a Herr Dortmann hanging around anywhere, Natalie was certain he wouldn't appreciate the way his wife flung herself into Dom's arms. Wrapping herself around him like a half-starved boa constrictor, she kissed him. Not on both cheeks like any other polite European, but long and hard and full on the lips.

He was half laughing, half embarrassed when he finally managed to extricate himself. With a rueful glance at Natalie, he interrupted the blonde's spate of rapid Hungarian liberally interspersed with German.

"Lisel, this is Natalie Clark. A friend of mine from America."

"America!" Wide, amethyst eyes turned to Natalie. Eager hands reached out to take both of hers. "*Wilkommen!* You must come in. You'll have a lager, *ja*? And then you will tell me how you come to be in the company of a rogue such as Dominic St. Sebastian." Her laughing glance cut back to Dom. "Or do I address you as 'Your Grace'? *Ja, ja,* I must. The whole village talks of nothing else but the stories about you in the papers."

"You can thank Natalie for that," he drawled.

The blonde's brows soared. "How so?"

"She's an archivist. A researcher who digs around in musty old ledgers. She uncovered a document in Vienna that appears to grant the titles of Grand Duke and Duchess of Karlenburgh to the St. Sebastians until the Alps crumble. As we all know, however, it's an empty honor."

"Ha! Not here. As soon as word gets around that the Grand Duke has returned to his ancestral home, the taproom will be jammed and the beer will flow like a river. Just wait. You will see."

They didn't have to wait long. Dom had barely finished explaining to Frau Dortman that he'd only come to show Natalie the ruins and aid her in her research when the door opened. A bent, craggy-faced gentleman in worn leather pants hobbled in and greeted Dom with the immense dignity of a man who'd lived through good times and bad. This, Natalie soon grasped, was a good time. A very good time, the older man indicated with a wide smile.

He was followed in short order by a big, buff farmer who carried the sharp tang of the barn in with him, two teenagers with curious eyes and earbuds dangling around their necks and a young woman cradling a baby on her hip. Natalie kept waiting for Herr Dortmann to make an appearance. When he didn't show, a casual query revealed Lisel had divorced the lazy good-for-nothing and sent him packing years ago.

Dom tried his best to include Natalie in the conversations that buzzed around them. As more and more people arrived, though, she edged out of the inner circle and enjoyed the show. St. Sebastian might downplay this whole royalty thing, she mused as she settled on a bar stool and placed her briefcase on a counter worn smooth by centuries of use, but he was a natural. It wasn't so much that

he stood two or three inches above the rest of the crowd. Or that he exuded such an easy self-confidence. Or, she thought wryly, that he had already informed Lisel that he would pay for the beer that flowed as freely as the inn-keeper had predicted.

He also, Natalie guessed, paid for the platters piled with sausages and spaetzle and fried potatoes and pickled beets that emerged in successive waves from the kitchen. The feasting and toasts and storytelling lasted through the af-ternoon and into the evening. By then, Dom had downed too much beer to get behind the wheel again.

Lisel had anticipated just such an eventuality. "You will stay here tonight," she announced and drew an old-fashioned iron key from the pocket of her tiger-striped tunic. "The front bedroom has a fine view of the castle," she confided to Natalie. "You and Dominic can see it as you lie in bed."

"It sounds wonderful." She plucked the room key out of the innkeeper's hand. "But Dominic will need other sleeping arrangements."

After Lisel Dortmann's enthusiastic welcome, Nata-lie preferred not to speculate on what those arrangements might be. All she knew was that she wasn't going to share a bed with the man—as much as she wanted to.

Nine

She took the narrow wooden stairs to the second floor and found the front bedroom easily enough. It contained a good-size bath and an alcove tucked under the slanting eaves that housed a small desk and overstuffed easy chair. The beautifully carved wooden headboard and washstand with its porcelain pitcher and bowl provided antique touches, while the flat-screen TV and small placard announcing the inn offered free Wi-Fi were welcome modern conveniences.

As Lisel had promised, the lace-draped windows offered an unimpeded view of the ruins set high atop the rocky promontory. The early evening shadows lent them a dark and brooding aspect. Then the clouds shifted, parted, and the last of the sun's rays cut like a laser. For a few magical moments what remained of Karlenburgh Castle was bathed in bright gold.

She'd seen these ruins before! Natalie knew it! Not all shimmery and ethereal and golden like this but...

A rap on the door interrupted her tumultuous thoughts. Dom stood in the hall with the weekender he'd brought in from the car.

"I thought you might need your case."

"Thanks." She grabbed his arm and hauled him toward the window. "You've got to see this."

He glanced through the windows at the sight she pointed

to but almost immediately his gaze switched back to Natalie. Her eyes were huge, her face alive with excitement. She could hardly contain it as she turned to him.

"Those ruins… That setting… I went up there, Dom."

Her forehead scrunched with such an intense effort to dredge up stubborn memories that it hurt him to watch. Aching for her, he raised his hand and traced his thumb down the deep crease in her brow. He followed the slope of her nose, the line of her tightly folded lips.

"Ah, Natushka." The husky murmur distracted her, as he'd intended. "You're doing it again."

"Doing wh…? Oh."

He couldn't help himself. He had to coax those lips back to lush, ripe fullness. Then, of course, he had to take his fill of them. To his delight, she tilted her head to give him better access.

He wasn't sure when he knew a mere taste wouldn't be enough. Maybe when she gave a little sigh and leaned into him. Or when her hands slid up and over his shoulders. Or when the ache he'd felt when he'd watched her struggling to remember dropped south. Hard and heavy and suddenly hurting, he tried to disentangle.

"No!"

The command was breathy and urgent. She tightened her arms around his neck, dragging him in for another kiss. This time she gave, and Dom took what she offered. The eager mouth, the quick dance of her tongue against his, the kick to his pulse when her breasts flattened against his chest.

He dropped his hands, cupped her bottom and pulled her closer. A serious mistake, he realized the instant her hip gouged into his groin. Biting down a groan, he eased back an inch or two.

"I want you, Natalie. You can see it. Feel it. But…"

"I want you, too."

"But," he continued gruffly, "I'm not going to take advantage of your confusion and uncertainty."

She leaned back in his arms and considered that for several moments while Dom shifted a little to one side to ease the pressure of her hip.

"I think it's the other way around," she said at last. "I'm the one taking advantage. You didn't have to let me stay at the loft. Or go with me to Dr. Kovacs, or get a copy of my driver's license, or come with me today."

"So I was just supposed to set you adrift far from your home with no money and no identity?"

"The point is, you didn't set me adrift." Her voice softened, and her eyes misted. "You're my anchor, Dominic. My lifeline." She leaned in again and brushed his mouth with hers. "Thank you."

The soft whisper sliced into him like a double-bladed ax. Wrapping his hands around her upper arms, he pushed her away. Surprise left her slack-jawed and gaping up at him.

"Is that what this is about, Natalie? You're so grateful you feel you have to respond when I kiss you? Perhaps sleep with me in payment for services rendered?"

"No!" Indignation sent a tide of red to her cheeks. "Of all the arrogant, idiotic…"

She stopped, dragged in a breath and tilted her chin to a dangerous angle.

"I guess you didn't notice, St. Sebastian, but I happen to like kissing you. I suspect I would also like going to bed with you. But I'll be damned if I'll do it with you thinking I'm so pathetic that I should be grateful for any crumbs that you and the hound and Kissy Face Arabella and…" She waved an irate hand. "And all your other friends toss my way."

The huffy speech left Dom swinging from anger to amusement. He didn't trust himself to address her com-

ment about Arabella. Just the thought of Natalie wearing the Londoner's black silk put another kink in his gut. The hound was a different matter.

"This is a first," he admitted. "I've never been lumped in the same category as a dog before."

"You're not in the same category," she retorted. "Duke at least recognizes honest emotions like friendship and loyalty and affection."

"Affection?" His ego dropped another notch. "That's what you feel for me?"

"Oh, for....!" Exasperated, she twisted out of his arms and planted both fists on her hips. "What do you want, *Your Highness*? A written confession that I lay awake last night wishing it was you snuffling beside me instead of Duke? An engraved invitation to take his place?"

He searched her face, her eyes, and read only indignation and frustration. No subliminal fear stemming from a traumatic past event. No prim, old-maidish reluctance to get sweaty and naked. No confusion about what she wanted.

His scruples died an instant death as hunger rushed hot and greedy through his veins. "No engraved invitation required. I'll take this." He reached for her again and found her mouth. "And this," he murmured, nipping at her throat. "And this," he growled as his hand found her breast.

When he scooped her into his arms several long, mind-drugging moments later, his conscience fought through the red haze for a last, desperate battle. She was still lost, dammit! Still vulnerable. Despite her irate speech, he shouldn't carry her to the bed.

Shouldn't, but did. Some contrary corner of his mind said it was her very vulnerability that made him want to strengthen the lifeline she mentioned. Anchor her even more securely.

The last thought shook him. Not enough to stop him,

though. Especially with the moonlight spilling through the windows, bathing her face and now well-kissed lips in a soft glow.

His hunger erupted in a greedy, gnawing need. He stood her on her feet beside the bed and peeled away her clothes with more haste than finesse. Impatience made him clumsy but fired a similar urgency in Natalie. She tugged his shirt over his head and dropped hungry kisses on his chest as she fumbled with the snap of his jeans.

When he dragged back the thick, down-filled feather-bed and tumbled her to the sheets, her body was smooth and warm, a landscape of golden lights and dark shadows. And when she hooked a calf around one of his, he had to fight the primal need to drive into her. He had to get something straight between them first. Thrusting his hands into her hair, he delivered a quick kiss and a wry confession.

"Just so you don't think this is your idea, you should know I was plotting various ways to get you into bed when I came to your hotel room in New York."

Natalie's heart kicked. In a sudden flash, she could see the small hotel room. Two double beds. An open laptop. Herself going nose to nose with Dom about… About…

"You thought I was some kind of schemer, out to fleece the duchess."

He went still. "You remember that?"

"Yes!" She clung to the image, sorting through the emotions that came with it. One proved especially satisfying. "I also remember slamming the door in your face," she said gleefully.

"You do, huh?" He got even for that with a long, hard kiss that left her gasping. "Remember anything else?"

"Not at the moment," she gulped.

He released her hair and slid his hands down her neck, over her shoulders, down her body. "Then I guess we'd better generate a few new memories."

Natalie gasped again as he set to work exploring her body. Nipping her earlobe. Kneading her breasts. Teasing her nipples. Tracing a path down her belly to the apex of her thighs. She was quivering with delight when he used a knee to part her legs.

His hair-roughened thigh rasped against hers. His breathing went fast and harsh. And his hand—his busy, diabolical hand—found her center. She was hot and wet and eager when he slid a finger in. Two. All the while his thumb played over the tight bud at her center and his teeth brought her nipples to taut, aching peaks. As the sensations piled one on top of the other, she arched under him.

"Dom! Dom, I… Ooooooh!"

The cry ripped from deep in her throat. She tried to hold back but the sensations spiraling up from her belly built to a wild, whirling vortex. Shuddering, she rode them to the last, gasping breath.

Minutes, maybe hours later, she pried up eyelids that felt as heavy as lead. Dom had propped his weight on one elbow and was watching her intently. He must be thinking of Dr. Kovacs's hypothesis, she realized. Worrying that some repressed trauma in her past might make her wig out.

"That," she assured him on a ragged sigh, "was wonderful."

His face relaxed into a smile. "Good to hear, but we're not done yet."

Still boneless with pleasure, she stretched like a cat as he rolled to the side of the bed and groped among the clothes they'd left in a pile on the floor. Somehow she wasn't surprised when he turned back with several foil-wrapped condoms. By the time he'd placed them close at hand on the table beside the bed, she was ready for round two.

"My turn," she murmured, pushing up on an elbow to

explore his body with the same attention to detail he'd explored hers.

God, he was beautiful! That wasn't an adjective usually applied to males but Natalie couldn't think of any other to categorize the long, lean torso, the roped muscle at shoulder and thigh, the flat belly and nest of thick, dark hair at his groin. His sex was flaccid but came to instant, eager attention when she stroked a finger along its length.

But it was the scar that caught and held her attention. Healed but still angry in the dim glow of the moon, it cut diagonally along his ribs. Frowning, she traced the tip of her finger along the vicious path.

"What's this?"

"A reminder not to trust a rookie to adequately pat down a seasoned veteran of the Cosa Nostra."

She spotted another scar higher on his chest, this one a tight, round pucker of flesh.

"And this?"

"A parting gift from an Albanian boat captain after Interpol intercepted the cargo of girls he was transporting to Algeria."

He said it with a careless shrug, as if knife wounds and kidnappings were routine occurrences in the career of a secret agent. Which they probably were, Natalie thought with a swallow. Suddenly the whole James Bond thing didn't seem quite so romantic.

"Your employer's brother-in-law took part in that op," Dom was saying. "Gina's husband, Jack Harris."

"He's undercover, too?"

"No, he's a career diplomat. He was part of a UN investigation into child prostitution at the time."

"Have I met him?"

"I don't know."

"Hmm."

It was hard to work up an interest in her employer's

brother-in-law while she was stretched out hip-to-naked-hip with Dominic St. Sebastian. Aching for the insults done to his body, she kissed the puckered scar on his shoulder.

One kiss led to another, then another, as she traced a path down his chest. When she laved her tongue along the scar bisecting his stomach, his belly hollowed and his sex sprang to attention again. Natalie drew a nail lightly along its length and would have explored the smooth satin further but Dom inhaled sharply and jerked away from her touch.

"Sorry! I want you too much."

She started to tell him there was no need for apologies, but he was already reaching for one of the condoms he'd left so conveniently close at hand. Heat coiled low in her belly and then, when he turned back to her, raced through her in quick, electric jolts. On fire for him, she took his weight and welcomed him eagerly into her body.

There was no slow climb to pleasure this time. No delicious heightening of the senses. He drove into her, and all too soon Natalie felt another climax rushing at her. She tried desperately to contain it, then sobbed with relief and sheer, undiluted pleasure when he pushed both her and himself over the edge.

She sprawled in naked abandon while the world slowly stopped spinning. Dom lay next to her, his eyes closed and one arm bent under his head. As she stared at his profile in the dim light of the moon, a dozen different emotions bounced between her heart and her head.

She acknowledged the satisfaction, the worry, the delight and just the tiniest frisson of fear. She hardly knew this man, yet she felt so close to him. *Too* close. How could she tell how much of that was real or the by-product of being too emotionally dependent on him?

As if to underscore her doubts, she glanced over his shoulder at the open window. Silhouetted against a

midnight-blue sky were the ruins that had brought her to Hungary and to Dom.

Somehow.

The need to find the missing pieces of the puzzle put a serious dent in the sensual satisfaction of just lazing next to him. She bit her lip and shifted her attention to the desk tucked in the alcove under the eaves. Her briefcase lay atop the desk, right where she'd placed it. Anticipation tap-danced along her nerves at the thought of attacking those fat files and getting into her laptop.

Dom picked up on her quiver of impatience and opened his eyes. "Are you cold?"

"A little," she admitted but stopped him before he could drag up the down-filled featherbed tangled at their feet. "It's early yet. I'd like to go through my briefcase before we call it a night."

Amusement colored his voice. "Do you think we're done for the night?"

"Aren't we?"

"Ah, Natushka, we've barely begun. But we'll take a break while you look through your files." He rolled out of bed with the controlled grace of a panther and pulled on his clothes. "I'll go down and get us some coffee, yes?"

"Coffee would be good."

While he was gone she made a quick trip to the bathroom, then dug into her suitcase. She scrambled into clean panties but didn't bother with a bra. Or with either of the starched blouses folded atop a beige linen jumper that had all the grace and style of a burlap sack. Frowning, she checked the tag and saw the jumper was two sizes larger than the clothes she'd bought in Budapest.

Was Dom right? Had she deliberately tried to disguise her real self in these awful clothes? Was there something in her past that made her wary of showing her true colors? If so, she might find a clue to whatever it was in the brief-

case. Impatient to get to it, she stuffed the jumper back in the case and slipped on the soccer shirt she'd appropriated from Dom to use as a sleep shirt. It hung below her hips but felt soft and smooth against her thighs.

She lifted the files out of her briefcase and arranged them in neat stacks. She was flipping through one page by page when Dom returned with two mugs of foaming latte.

"Finding anything interesting?" he asked as he set a mug at her elbow.

"Tons of stuff! So far it all relates to missing works of art, like that Fabergé egg and a small Bernini bronze stolen from the Uffizi Gallery in Florence. I haven't found information on the Canaletto painting yet. It's got to be in one of these files, though."

He nodded to the still-closed laptop. "You probably cross-indexed the paper files on your computer. Why don't you check it?"

"I tried." She blew out a frustrated breath. "The laptop's password-protected."

"And you can't remember the password."

"I tried a dozen different combinations, but none worked."

"Do you want me to get into it?"

"How can you…? Oh. Another useful skill you picked up at Interpol, right?"

He merely smiled. "Do you have a USB cord in your briefcase? Good. Let me have it."

He deposited the latte on the table beside the easy chair and settled in with the computer on his lap. It booted up to a smiley face and eight blinking question marks in the password box. Dom plugged one end of the USB cord into the laptop, the other into his cell phone. He tapped a series of numbers on the phone's keypad and waited to connect via a secure remote link to a special program developed by Interpol's Computer Crimes Division for use by agents

in the field. The handy-dandy program whizzed through hundreds of thousands of letter/number/character combinations at the speed of light.

Scant minutes later, the password popped up letter by letter. Dom made a note of it and hit Return. The smiley face on Natalie's laptop dissolved and the home screen came up. The icons were arranged with military precision, he saw with an inner smile. God forbid his fussy archivist should keep a messy electronic filing cabinet. He was about to tell Natalie that he was in when a message painted across the screen.

D—I see you're online. Don't know whose computer you're using. Contact me. I have some info for you. A.

About time! Dom erased the message and de-linked before passing the laptop to Natalie. "You're good to go."

She took it eagerly and wedged it onto the desk between the stacks of paper files. Fingers flying, she conducted a quick search.

"Here's the Canaletto folder!"

A click of the mouse opened the main file. When dozens of subfolders rippled down the screen, Natalie groaned.

"It'll take all night to go through these."

"You don't have all night," Dom warned, dropping a kiss on her nape. "Just till I get back."

"Where are you going?"

"I need to let Katya and her father know we won't be home tonight. I'll get a stronger signal outside."

It wasn't a complete lie. He did need to call his downstairs neighbors. That bit about the stronger signal shaded the truth, but the habit of communicating privately with his contacts at headquarters went too deep to compromise.

He slipped on a jacket and went downstairs. The bar was still open. Lisel waved, inviting him in for another coffee

or a beer, but he shook his head and held up his phone to signal his reason for going outside.

He'd forgotten how sharp and clean and cold the nights could be here in the foothills of the Alps. And how bright the stars were without a haze of smog and city lights to blur them. Hiking up the collar of his jacket, he contacted Andre.

"What have you got for me?"

"Some interesting information about your Natalie Elizabeth Clark."

Dom's stomach tightened. "Interesting" to Andre could mean anything from an unpaid speeding ticket to enrollment in a witness protection program.

"It took a while, but the facial recognition program finally matched to a mug shot."

Hell! His gut had told him Natalie was hiding her real self. He almost didn't want to hear the reason behind the disguise now but forced himself to ask.

"What were the charges?"

"Fraud and related activities in connection with computers."

"When?" he bit out.

"Three years ago. But it looks like the charges were dropped and the arrest record expunged. Someone missed the mug shot, though, when they wiped the slate."

Dom wanted to be fair. The fact that the charges had been dropped could mean the arrest was a mistake, that Natalie hadn't done whatever the authorities thought she had. Unfortunately, he'd seen too many sleazy, high-priced lawyers spring their clients on technicalities.

"Do you want me to contact the feds in the US?" Andre asked. "See what they've got on this?"

Dom hesitated, his gaze going to the brightly illuminated window on the second floor of the gasthaus. Had he just made love to a hacker? Had she tracked him down,

devised a ploy to show up at his loft dripping wet and help-less? Was this whole amnesia scene part of some elabo-rate sting?

Every one of his instincts screamed no. She couldn't have faked the panic and confusion he'd glimpsed in her eyes. Or woven a web of lies and deceit, then flamed in his arms the way she had. The question now was whether he could trust his instincts.

"Dom? What do you want me to do?"

He went with his gut. "Hang loose, Andre. If I need more, I'll get back to you."

He disconnected, hoping to hell he wasn't thinking with the wrong head, and made a quick call to his downstairs neighbors.

Ten

Natalie was still hard at it when Dom went back upstairs. Her operation had spread from the desk to the armchair and the bed, which was now neatly remade. With pillows fluffed and the corners of the counterpane squared, he noted wryly. He also couldn't help noticing how her fingers flew over the laptop's keyboard.

"How's it coming?" he asked.

"So-so. The good news is I'm now remembering many of these details. The bad news is that I went through the Canaletto folder page by page. I also searched its corresponding computer file. I didn't find an entry that would explain why I drove down from Vienna, nor any reference to Győr or Budapest. Nothing to tell me why I hopped on a riverboat and ended up in the Danube." Sighing, she flapped a hand at the stacks now spread throughout the room. "I hope I find something in one of those."

Dom eyed the neat array of files. "How have you separated them?"

"The ones on the chair contain paper copies of documents and reports of lost art from roughly the same period as the Canaletto. The ones on the bed detail the last known locations of various missing pieces from other periods."

"Sorted alphabetically by continent and country, I see."

She looked slightly offended. "Of course. I thought I might have stumbled across something in reports from a

gallery or museum or private collection that gained a new acquisition at approximately the same time the Canaletto disappeared from Karlenburgh Castle."

"What about information unrelated to missing art treasures? Any personal data in the files or on the computer that triggered memories?"

"Plenty," she said with a small sigh. "Apparently I'm as anal about my personal life as I am about professional matters. I've got everything on spreadsheets. The service record for my car. The books I've read and want to read. Checking and savings accounts. A household inventory with purchase dates, cost, serial numbers where appropriate. Restaurants I've tried, sorted by type of food and my rating. In short," she finished glumly, "my entire existence. Precise, well-organized and soulless."

She looked so frustrated, so dejected and lost, that Dom had to fight the urge to take her in his arms. He'd get into the computer later, when she was asleep, and check out the household inventory and bank accounts. Right now he was more interested in her responses to his careful probing.

"How about your email? Find anything there?"

"Other than some innocuous correspondence from people I've tagged in my address book as 'acquaintances,' everything relates to work." Her shoulders slumped. "Is my life pathetic, or what?"

If she was acting, she was the best he'd ever seen. To hell with fighting the urge. She needed comforting. Clearing the armchair, he caught her hand and tugged her into his lap.

"There's more to you than spreadsheets and color-coded files, Ms. Clark."

With another sigh, she laid her head on his shoulder. "You'd think so."

"There are all your little quirks," he said with a smile,

stroking her hair. "The lip thing, the fussiness, the questionable fashion sense."

"Gee, thanks."

"Then there's your rapport with the Agár."

"Ha! I suspect he bonds instantly with everyone."

"And there's tonight," he reminded her. "You, me, this gasthaus."

She tipped her head back to search his face. He supported her head, careful of the still-tender spot at the base of her skull.

"About tonight… You, me, this place…"

"Don't look so worried. We don't have to analyze or dissect what happened here."

"I'm thinking more along the lines of what happens after we leave. Next week. Next month."

"We let them take care of themselves."

As soon as he said it, he knew it was a lie. Despite the mystery surrounding this woman—or maybe because of it—he had no intention of letting her drop out of his life the same way she'd dropped into it. She was under his skin now.

That last thought made him stop. Rewind. Take a breath. Think about the other women he'd been with. The hard, inescapable fact was that none of them had ever stirred this particular mix of lust, tenderness, worry, suspicion and fierce protectiveness.

He might have to change his tactics if and when Natalie's memory fully returned, Dom acknowledged. At the moment she considered him an anchor in a sea of uncertainty. He couldn't add to that uncertainty by demanding more than she was ready to give.

"For now," he said with a lazy smile, "this is good, isn't it?"

"Oh, yes."

She leaned in, brought her mouth to his, gave him a

promise of things to come. He was ready to take her up on that promise when she made a brisk announcement.

"Okay, I'm done wallowing in self-pity. Time to get back to work."

"What do you want me to do?"

She glanced at the files on the bed and caught her lower lip between her teeth. Dom waited, remembering how antsy she'd been about letting him see her research when he'd shown up unannounced at her New York hotel room. He'd chalked that up to a proprietary desire to protect her work. With Andre's call still fresh in his mind, he couldn't help wondering if there was something else in those fat folders she wanted to protect.

"I guess you could start on those," she said with obvious reluctance. "There's an index and a chronology inside each file. The sections are tabbed, the documents in each section numbered. That's how I cross-reference the contents on the computer. So keep everything in order, okay?"

Dom's little bubble of suspicion popped. The woman wasn't nervous about him digging into her private files, just worried that he'd mess them up. Grinning, he pushed out of the chair with her still in his arms and deposited her back at the desk.

"I'll treat every page with care and reverence," he promised solemnly.

She flushed at little at the teasing but stood her ground. "You'd better. We archivists don't take kindly to anyone who desecrates our files."

It didn't take Dom long to realize Natalie could land a job with any investigative agency in the world, including Interpol. She hadn't just researched facts about lost cultural treasures. She'd tracked every rumor, followed every thread. Some threads were so thin they appeared to have no relation to the object of her research. Yet in at least two

of the files he dug through, those seemingly unrelated, unconnected tidbits of information led to a major find.

"Jesus," Dom muttered after following a particularly convoluted trail. "Do you remember this?"

She swiveled around and frowned at a scanned photo depicting a two-inch-long cylinder inscribed with hieroglyphics. "Looks familiar. It's Babylonian, isn't it? About two thousand years old, I'd guess."

"You'd guess right."

"What's the story on it?"

"It went missing in Iraq in 2003, shortly after Saddam Hussein was toppled."

"Oh, I remember now. I found a reference to a similar object in a list of items being offered for sale by a little-known dealer. Best I recall, he claimed he specialized in Babylonian artifacts."

She rubbed her forehead, trying to dredge up more detail. Dom helped her out.

"You sent him a request for a more detailed description of that particular item. When it came in, you matched it to a list the US Army compiled of Iraqi antiquities that were unaccounted for."

"I can't remember...did the army recover the artifact?"

He flipped through several pages of notes and correspondence. "They did. They also arrested the contractor employee who'd lifted it during recovery efforts at the Baghdad Archeological Museum."

"Well! Maybe I'm not so pathetic after all."

She turned back to the laptop with a smug little smile that crushed the last of Dom's doubts. Those two inches of inscribed Babylonian clay were damned near priceless. If Natalie was into shady deals, she wouldn't have alerted the army to her find. The fact that she had convinced Dom. Whatever screwup had led to her arrest, she was no hacker or huckster.

He dug into the next folder and soon found himself absorbed in the search for a thirteenth-century gold chalice studded with emeralds that once graced the altar of an Irish abbey. He was only halfway through the thick file when he glanced up and saw Natalie's shoulders drooping again, this time with fatigue. So much for his anticipation of another lively session under the featherbed. He closed the folder, careful not to dislodge any of its contents, and stretched.

"That's it for me tonight."

She frowned at the remaining files. "We've still got a half dozen to go through."

"Tomorrow. Right now, I need bed, sleep and you. Not necessarily in that order, although you look as whipped as I feel."

"I might be able to summon a few reserves of energy."

"You do that," he said as he headed for the bathroom.

His five-o'clock shadow had morphed into a ten-o'clock bristle. He'd scraped Natalie's tender cheeks enough the first time around. He better shave and go a little more gentle on her this time. But when he reentered the bedroom a scant ten minutes later, she was curled in a tight ball under the featherbed and sawing soft, breathy Z's.

Taking advantage of the opportunity, he settled at the desk. His conscience didn't even ping as he powered up her laptop. Forty minutes later he'd seen everything he needed to. His skills weren't as honed as those of the wizards in Interpol's Computer Crimes Division, but they were good enough for him to feel confident she wasn't hacking into unauthorized databases or shifting money into hidden accounts. Everything he saw indicated she'd lived well within her salary as an archivist for the State of Illinois and was now socking most of the generous salary Sarah paid her into a savings account.

Satisfied and more than a little relieved to have his in-

stincts validated, Dom shed his clothes and slid in beside her lax, warm body. He was tempted to nudge her awake and treat himself to a celebration of his nonfindings. He restrained himself but it required a heroic effort.

Natalie woke to bright morning sunshine, the distant clang of cowbells and a feeling of energy and purpose. She ascribed the last to a solid night's sleep—until she tried to roll over and realized she probably owed it more to the solid wall of male behind her.

God, he felt good! What's more, he made *her* feel good. Just lying nested against his warmth and strength generated all kinds of wild possibilities. Like maybe waking up in the same nest for the next few weeks or months. Or even, her sneaky little subconscious suggested, years.

The thought struck her that Dominic St. Sebastian might be all she needed to feel complete. All she would ever need. Apparently, she had no family. Judging by the dearth of personal emails on her laptop, she didn't have a wide circle of friends. Yet lying here with Dom, she didn't feel the lack of either.

Maybe that's why the details of her personal life were so slow returning. Her life was so empty, so blah, she didn't *want* to remember it. That made her grimace, which must have translated into some small movement because a lazy voice sounded just behind her ear.

"I've been waiting for you to wake up."

Sheets rustling, she angled a look over her shoulder and sighed. "It's not fair."

"What isn't?"

"My eyes feel goopy from sleep, my hair's probably sticking out in all directions and I know my teeth need brushing. You, on the other hand, look fresh and wide-awake and good enough to eat."

Good enough to gobble whole, actually. Those black

eyes and hair, the golden-oak hue of his skin, the square chin and chiseled cheekbones…the whole package added up to something really spectacular to start the day with. Only the nicks and scars of his profession marred the perfection.

"In fact," she announced, "I think I'll have you for breakfast."

She rolled onto her side, trying not to treat him to a blast of morning breath, and wiggled down a few inches. She started with the underside of his jaw and slowly worked her way south. Teasing, tasting, nibbling the cords in his neck, dropping kisses on alternate ribs, circling his belly button with her tongue. By the time she dragged the sheets down to his hips, he was stiff and rampant.

Her own belly tight and quivering now, she circled him with her palm. The skin was hot and satin smooth, the blood throbbing in his veins. She slid her hand up, down, up again, delighted when he grunted and jerked involuntarily.

"Okay," she told him, her voice throaty with desire, "I need a little of that action."

All thought of ratty hair and goopy eyes forgotten, she swung a leg over his thighs and raised her hips. Dom was straining and eager but held her off long enough to tear into another foil package.

"Let me," she said, brushing his hands aside.

She rolled on the condom, then positioned her hips again. Together they rode to an explosive release that had him thrusting upward and her collapsing onto his chest in mindless, mewling pleasure.

Natalie recovered first. Probably because she had to pee really, really bad. She scooped up her jeans and the green-and-white-striped rugby shirt she now claimed as

her own on the way to the bathroom. When she emerged, she found Dom dressed and waiting for his turn.

"Give me five minutes and I'll be ready to go."

Since she wasn't sure whether they would return to the gasthaus, she stuffed the files and laptop back into her briefcase and threw her few miscellaneous items into her weekender. The sight of those plain, sensible, neatly folded blouses made her wrinkle her nose. Whatever happened when—*if*—she regained her memory, she was investing in an entire new wardrobe.

Dom agreed that it was probably better to check out of the gasthaus and head back to Budapest after going up to the castle. "But first, we'll eat. I guarantee you've never tasted anything like Lisel's *bauernfrühstück*."

"Which is?"

"Her version of a German-Austrian-Hungarian farmer's breakfast."

Their hostess gave them a cheerful smile when they appeared in the dining room and waved them to a table. She was serving two other diners, locals by the looks of them, and called across the room.

"Frühstück, ja?"

"Ja," Dom called back as he and Natalie helped themselves to the coffee and fresh juice set out on an elaborately carved hutch.

A short time later Lisel delivered her special. Natalie gaped at the platter-size omelette bursting with fried potatoes, onions, leeks, ham and pungent Munster cheese. The Hungarian input came from the pulpy, stewed tomatoes flavored with red peppers and the inevitable paprika.

When their hostess returned with a basket of freshly baked rolls and a crock of homemade elderberry jam, she lingered long enough to knuckle Dom's shoulder affectionately.

"So you leave us today?"

His mouth full, Dom nodded.

"You must come again soon." The blonde's amethyst eyes twinkled as she included his companion in the invitation. "You, as well. You and Dominic found the bed in my front room comfortable, yes?"

Natalie could feel heat rushing into her cheeks but had to laugh. "Very comfortable."

With a respectable portion of her gargantuan breakfast disposed of and the innkeeper's warm farewells to speed them on their way, Natalie's spirits rose with every twist and turn of the road that snaked up to the mountain pass. Something had drawn her to the ruins dominating the skyline ahead. She felt it in her bones, in the excitement bubbling through her veins. Impatience had her straining against her seat belt as Dom turned off the main road onto the single lane that led to what was left of Karlenburgh Castle.

The lane had once been paved but over the years frost heaves had buckled the asphalt and weeds now sprouted in the cracks. The weedy approach took nothing away from the dramatic aspect of the ruins, however. They rose from a base of solid granite, looking as though they'd been carved from the mountain itself. To the west was a breathstealing vista of the snow-covered Austrian Alps. To the east, a series of stair-stepping terraces that must once have contained gardens, vineyards and orchards. The terraces ended abruptly in a sheer drop to the valley below.

Natalie's heart was pounding by the time Dom pulled up a few yards from the outer wall. The wind slapped her in the face when she got out of the car and knifed through the rugby shirt.

"Here, put this on."

Dom held up the jacket he'd retrieved from the back-

seat. She slid her arms into the sleeves and wrapped its warmth around her gratefully.

"Watch your step," he warned as they approached a gap in the outer ring of rubble. "A massive portcullis used to guard this gate, but the Soviets claimed the iron for scrap—along with everything else of any value. Then," he said, his voice grim, "they set charges and destroyed the castle itself as a warning to other Hungarians foolish enough to join the uprising."

Someone had cleared a path through the rubble of the outer bailey. "My grandfather," Dom explained, "with help from some locals."

Grasping her elbow to guide her over the rough spots, he pointed out the charred timbers and crumpled walls of the dairy, what had been the kitchens in earlier centuries, and the stables-turned-carriage house and garage.

Another gate led to what would have been the inner courtyard. The rubble was too dense here to penetrate but she could see the outline of the original structure in the tumbled walls. The only remaining turret jutted up like a broken tooth, its roof blown and stone staircase exposed to the sky. Natalie hooked her arm through Dom's and let her gaze roam the desolation while he described the castle he himself had seen only in drawings and family photographs.

"Karlenburgh wasn't as large as some border fortresses of the same era. Only thirty-six rooms originally, including the armory, the great hall and the duke and duchess's chambers. Successive generations of St. Sebastians installed modern conveniences like indoor plumbing and electric lights, but for comfort and luxury the family usually wintered in their palazzos on the Italian Riviera or the Dalmatian Coast." A smile lightened his somber expression. "My grandfather had a photo of him and his cousin dunking each other in the Mediterranean. They were very close as children, he and the last Grand Duke."

"Except," Natalie said, squeezing his arm with hers, "he wasn't the last Grand Duke."

For once Dominic didn't grimace or shrug or otherwise downplay his heritage. He couldn't, with its very dramatic remains staring him in the face.

"I've told the duchess she should come back for a visit," he murmured almost to himself. "But seeing it like this…"

They stood with shoulders hunched against the wind, Dom thinking of the duchess and Natalie searching the ruins for something to jog her memory. What had drawn her here? What had she found among the rubble that propelled her from here to Győr and onto that damned boat?

It was there, just behind the veil. She knew it was there! But she was damned if she could pull it out. Disappointment ate into her, doubly sharp and bitter after her earlier excitement.

Dom glanced down and must have read the frustration in her face. "Nothing?" he asked gently.

"Just a sort of vague, prickly sensation," she admitted, "which may or may not be goose bumps raised by the cold."

"Whichever it is, we'd best get you out of the wind."

Dejected and deflated and feeling dangerously close to tears, she picked her way back through the rubble. She'd been so sure Karlenburgh Castle was the key. So certain she'd break through once she stood among the ruins.

Lost in her glum thoughts, her eyes on the treacherous path, it took a moment for a distant, tinny clanging to penetrate her preoccupation. When it did, her head jerked up. That sound! That metallic tinkling! She'd heard it before, and not long ago.

Her heart started pumping. Her mouth went dry. Feeling as though she was teetering on the edge of a precipice, she followed the clanging to a string of goats meandering along the overgrown lane in their direction. A gnarled

gnome of a man trailed the flock. His face was shadowed by the wide brim of his hat and he leaned heavily on a burled wood staff.

"That's old Friedrich," Dom exclaimed. "He helped tend the castle's goats as a small boy and now raises his own. Those are *cou noirs*—black necks—especially noted for their sweet milk. My grandfather always stopped by Friedrich's hut to buy cheese when he brought Zia and me back for a visit."

Natalie stood frozen as Dom forged a path through the goats to greet their herder. She didn't move, couldn't! Even when the lead animals milled inquisitively around her knees. True to their name, their front quarters were black, the rest of their coat a grayish-white. The does were gentle creatures but some instinct told Natalie to keep a wary eye on the buck accompanying them.

A bit of trivia slipped willy-nilly into her mind. She'd read somewhere that Alpine goats were among the earliest domesticated animals. Also that their adaptability made them good candidates for long sea voyages. Early settlers in the Americas had brought this breed with them to supply milk and cheese. And sea captains would often leave a pair on deserted islands along their trade routes to provide fresh milk and meat on return voyages.

Suddenly, the curtains in her mind parted. Not all the way. Just far enough for her to know she hadn't picked up that bit of trivia "somewhere." She'd specifically researched Alpine goats on Google after... After...

Her gaze shot to the herder hobbling alongside Dom, a smile on his wrinkled walnut of a face. Excitement rushed back, so swift and thrilling she was shaking with it when Friedrich smiled and greeted her in a mix of German and heavily accented English.

"*Guten tag, fraülein. Es gut* to see you again."

Eleven

Natalie had spent all those hours soul- and mind- and computer-searching. She'd tried desperately to latch on to something, *anything*, that would trigger her memory. Never in her wildest dreams would she have imagined that trigger would consist of a herd of smelly goats and a wizened little man in a floppy felt hat. Yet the moment Friedrich greeted her in his fractured English, the dam broke.

Images flooded the empty spaces in her mind. Her, standing almost on this same spot. The goatherd, inquiring kindly if she was lost. These same gray-white does butting her knees. The buck giving her the evil eye. A casual chat that sent her off on a wild chase.

"*Guten tag*, Herr Müller." Her voice shook with excitement. "*Es gut* to see you again, too."

Dom had already picked up on the goatherd's greeting to Natalie. Her reply snapped his brows together. "When did you and Friedrich meet?"

"A week ago! Right here, at the castle! I remember him, Dom. I remember the goats and the bells and Herr Müller asking if I was lost. Then…then…"

She was so close to hyperventilating she had to stop and drag in a long, hiccuping breath. Müller looked confused by the rapid-fire exchange, so Natalie forced herself to slow down, space the words, contain the hysterical joy that bubbled to the surface.

"Then we sat there, on that wall, and you told me about the castle before the Soviets came. About the balls and the hunting parties and the tree-lighting ceremony in the great hall. Everyone from the surrounding villages was invited, you said. On Christmas Eve. Uh...*Heiliger Abend*."

"Ja, ja, Heiliger Abend."

"When I mentioned that I'd met the duchess in New York, you told me that you remember when she came to Karlenburgh Castle as a bride. So young and beautiful and gracious to everyone, even the knock-kneed boy who helped tend the goats."

She had to stop and catch her breath again. She could see the scene from last week so clearly now, every detail as though etched in glass. The weeds poking from the cracks in the road. The goats wandering through the rubble. This hunched-shouldered man in his gray felt hat, his gnarled hands folded atop the head of his walking stick, describing Karlenburgh Castle in its glory days.

"Then," she said, the excitement piling up again, "I told you I was searching for a painting that had once hung in the Red Salon. You gave me a very hard look and asked why I, too, should want to know about that particular room after all these years."

Everything was coming at her so fast and furiously and seemingly in reverse, like a DVD rewound at superhigh speed. The encounter with Herr Müller. The drive down from Vienna. A burning curiosity to see the castle ruins. The search for the Canaletto. Sarah and Dev. The duchess and Gina and the twins and Anastazia and meeting Dom for the first time in New York.

The rewind came to a screeching halt, stuck at that meeting with Dom. She could see his laughing eyes. His lazy grin. Hear his casual dismissal of the codicil and the title it conferred on him.

That was one of the reasons she'd returned to Vienna!

Why she'd decided to make a day trip to view the ruins of Karlenburgh Castle, and why she'd been so blasted determined to track the missing Canaletto. She'd wanted to wipe that cynical smile off Dominic St. Sebastian's face. Prove the validity of her research. Rub his nose in it, in fact. And, oh, by the way, possibly determine what happened to a priceless work of art.

And why, when the police tried to determine who she was and what she was doing in Budapest, the only response she could dredge from her confused mind was the Grand Duke of Karlenburgh!

With a fierce effort of will, she sidelined those tumultuous memories and focused on the goatherd. "I asked you who else had enquired about the Red Salon. Remember? You told me someone had come some months ago. And told you his name."

"Ja." His wrinkled face twisting in disgust, Müller aimed a thick wad of spittle at the ground. "Janos Lagy."

Dom had been listening intently without interruption to this point, but the name the goatherd spit out provoked a startled response. "Janos Lagy?"

Natalie threw him a surprised glance but he whipped up a palm and stilled the question he saw quivering on her lips.

"Ja," Müller continued in his thick, accented English. "Janos Lagy, a banker, he tells me, from Budapest. He tells me, too, he is the grandson of a Hungarian who goes to the military academy in Moscow and becomes a *mladshij lejtenant* in the Soviet Army. And I tell him I remember this lieutenant," the goatherd related, his voice shaking with emotion. "He commands the squad sent to destroy Karlenburgh Castle after the Grand Duke is arrested."

Dom mumbled something in Hungarian under his breath. Something short and terse and sounding very unnice to Natalie. She ached to ask him what he knew about

Lagy but Herr Müller was just getting to the crux of the story he'd shared with her less than a week ago.

"When I tell this to the grandson, he shrugs. He shrugs, the grandson of this traitorous lieutenant, as if it's of no matter, and asks me if I am ever in the Red Salon!"

The old man quivered with remembered rage. Raising his walking stick, he shook it in the air.

"I threatened to knock his head. He leaves very quickly then."

"Jézus," Dom muttered. "Janos Lagy."

Natalie couldn't contain herself. "You know him?"

"I know him."

"How!"

"I'll explain in the car, and you can tell me what you did with the information Friedrich gave you. But first…"

He probed for more information but when it was clear the goatherd had shared all he knew, he started to take a gracious leave. To his surprise and acute embarrassment, the old man grabbed his hand and kissed it.

"The Grand Duke and Duchess, they are still missed here," he said with tears swimming in his eyes. "It's good, what I read in the papers, that you are now duke. You'll come back again? Soon?"

"I will," he promised. "And perhaps I can convince the duchess to come, too."

"Ahhhh, I pray that I live to see her again!"

They left him clinging to that hope and picked their way through the weeds back to the car. Natalie was a quivering bundle of nerves but the deep crease between Dom's eyes kept her silent while he keyed the ignition, maneuvered a tight turn and regained the road that snaked up and over the pass. Neither of them spoke until he pulled into a scenic turnout that gave an eagle's-eye view of the valley below.

When Dom swung toward her, his face was still tight. "Start at the beginning. Tell what you remember."

She rewound the DVD again. She focused her growing absorption with both the codicil and Canaletto but glossed over the ignoble desire to rub a certain someone's nose in her research.

"I was there in Vienna, only a little over an hour away. I wanted to see the castle the duchess had told me about during our interviews, perhaps talk to some locals who might remember her."

"Like Friedrich Müller."

"Like Friedrich Müller," she confirmed. "I'd done a review of census records and knew he was one of only a handful of people old enough to have lived through the 1956 Uprising. I intended to go to the address listed as his current residence, but met him by chance there at the ruins instead."

"What a string of coincidences," Dom muttered, shaking his head. "Incredible."

"Not really," she countered, defensive on behalf of her research. "Pretty much everything one needs to know is documented somewhere. You just have to look for it."

He conceded the point. "So you met Friedrich, and he told you about Lagy. What did you do then?"

"I researched him on Google as soon as I got back to my hotel in Vienna. Took me a while to find the right Lagy. It's a fairly common name in Hungary. But I finally tracked him to his office at his bank. His secretary wouldn't put me through until I identified myself as Sarah St. Sebastian Hunter's research assistant and said I was helping with her book dealing with lost works of art. Evidently Janos is something of a collector. He came on the line a few minutes later."

"Did you tell him you were trying to track the Canaletto?"

"Yes, and he asked why I'd contacted him about it. I didn't want to go into detail over the phone, just said I thought I'd

found a possible link through his grandfather that I'd like to pursue with him. He asked if I'd discussed this link with anyone else and I told him no, that I wanted to verify it first. I offered to drive to Budapest but he generously offered to meet me halfway."

"In Györ."

"On the tour boat," she confirmed. "He said cruising the Danube was one of his favorite ways to relax, that if I hadn't taken a day trip on the river before I would most certainly enjoy it. I knew I wouldn't. I hate boats, loathe being on the water. But I was so eager to talk to him I agreed. I drove down to Györ the next day."

"And you met Lagy aboard?"

"No. He called after the damned boat had left the dock and said he'd been unavoidably detained. He apologized profusely and said he would meet me when it docked in Budapest instead."

She made a moue of distaste, remembering the long, queasy hours trying not to fixate on the slap of the current against the hull or the constant engine vibration under her feet.

"We didn't approach Budapest until late afternoon. By then I was huddled at the rail near the back of the boat, praying I wouldn't be sick. I remember getting another call. Remember reaching too fast for my phone and feeling really dizzy. I leaned over the rail, thinking I was going to puke." Frowning, she slid her hand under her hair and fingered the still tender spot at the base of her skull. "I must have banged my head on one of the support poles because there was pain. Nasty, nasty pain. And the next thing I know someone's leaning on my chest, pumping water out of my lungs!"

"You never saw Janos Lagy? Never connected with him?"

"Not unless he was one of the guys who fished me out of the river. Who *is* he, Dom? How do you know him?"

"We went to school together."

"You're friends with him?" she asked incredulously.

"Acquaintances. My grandfather was not one to forgive or forget old wrongs. He knew Jan's grandfather had served in the Soviet Army and didn't want me to have anything to do with the Lagy family. He didn't know the bastard had commanded the squad that leveled Karlenburgh Castle, though. I didn't either, until today."

Natalie had been certain that once she regained her memory, every blank space would fill and every question would have an answer. Instead, all new questions were piling up.

"This is so frustrating." She shook her head. "Like a circle that doesn't quite close. You, me, the duchess, the castle, the painting, this guy Lagy. They're all connected, but I can't see how they come together."

"Nor do I," he said, digging his cell phone out of his jeans pocket, "but I intend to find out."

She watched wide-eyed as he pressed a single key and was instantly connected. She understood just enough of his fluid French to grasp that he was asking someone named Andre to run a check on Janos Lagy.

Their return sent the hound into a paroxysm of delight. When Natalie laughed and bent to accept his joyous adulation, he got several quick, slurpy kisses past her guard before she could dodge them.

As a thank-you to the dog-sitters, Dom gave Katya the green light to purchase the latest Justin Bieber CD on his iTunes account and download it to her iPod—with her father's permission, he added. The indulgent papa received the ten-pound Westphalia ham that Dom had picked up

at the butcher's on the way home. The hound got a bag of bones, which tantalized him all the way up to the loft.

When Dom unlocked the front door and stood aside for Natalie to precede him, she was hit with a sudden attack of nerves. Now that she'd remembered her past, would it overshadow the present? Would the weight of all those months and years in her "real" life smother the brief days she'd spent here, with Dom?

Her heart thumping, she stepped inside and felt instant relief. And instantly at home…despite the dust motes dancing on a stray sunbeam and the rumpled bedcovers she'd straightened so meticulously before the hound had pounced on them. She knew she was just a guest, yet the most ridiculous sense of belonging enveloped her. The big fat question mark now was how long she'd stay camped out here. At least until she and Dom explored this business with Lagy, surely.

Or not. Doubt raised its ugly head when she glanced over her shoulder and saw him standing just inside the still-open door.

"Aren't you coming in?"

He gave himself a little shake, as if dragging his thoughts together, and dredged up a crooked smile.

"We left your case in the car. I'll go get it."

She used his absence to open the drapes and windows to let in the crisp fall air. Conscious of how Dom had teased her about her neat streak, she tried to ignore the rumpled bed but the damned thing pulled her like a magnet. She was guiltily smoothing the cover when he returned.

Propping her roller case next to the wardrobe, he made for the fridge. "I'm going to have a beer. Would you like one? Or wine, or tea?"

"Tea sounds good. Why don't I brew a fresh pitcher while you check with your friend to see what he's turned up on Lagy?"

Dom took the dew-streaked pilsner and cell phone out to the balcony. Not because he wanted privacy to make the call to Andre. He'd decided last night to trust Natalie in spite of that unexplained arrest and nothing had happened since to change his mind. Unless whatever he learned about Lagy was classified "eyes only," he intended to share it with her. No, he just needed a few moments to sort through everything that had happened in the past twenty-four hours.

Oh hell, who was he kidding?

What he needed was, first, a deep gulp of air. Second, a long swallow of Gold Fassl. And third, a little more time to recover from the mule kick that'd slammed into his mid-section when he'd opened the door to the loft and Natalie waltzed in with the Agár frisking around her legs.

He liked having her here. Oddly, she didn't crowd him or shrink his loft to minuscule proportions the way Zia did whenever she blew into Budapest on one of her whirlwind visits, leaving a trail of clothes and scarves and medical books and electronic gadgets in her wake. In fact, Natalie might lean a bit too far in the opposite direction. She would alphabetize and color-code his life if he didn't keep a close eye on her.

He would have to loosen her up. Ratchet her passion for order and neatness down to human levels. He suspected that might take some work but he could manage it. All he had to do was take her to bed often enough—and keep her there long enough—to burn up any surplus energy.

As he gazed at the ornate facades on the Pest side of the river, he could easily envision fall rolling into winter while he lazed under the blankets with Natalie and viewed these same buildings dusted with snow. Or the two of them exercising the hound when the park below was tender and green with spring.

The problem was that he wasn't sure how Natalie felt

about resuming her real life now that she'd remembered it. He suspected she wasn't sure, either. Not yet, anyway. His conscience said he should stick to the suggestion he'd made last night to take things between them slowly, step-by-step. But his conscience couldn't stand up to the homey sounds of Natalie moving around inside the loft, brewing her tea, laughing at the hound's antics.

He wanted her here, with him. Wanted to show her more of the city he loved. Wanted to explore that precise, fascinating mind, hear her breathy gasps and groans when they made love.

And, he thought, his eyes going cold and flat, he wanted to flatten whoever'd hurt her. He didn't believe for a moment she'd hit her head on a support pole and tumbled into the Danube. Janos Lagy had lured her onto that tour boat and Dom was damned well going to find out why.

For once Andre didn't have the inside scoop. Instead, he referred Dom back to the Hungarian agency that conducted internal investigations. The individual Dom spoke to there was cautious and closemouthed and unwilling to share sensitive information with someone she didn't know. She did, however, agree to meet with him and Natalie in the morning.

That made two appointments for tomorrow—one at the US Embassy to obtain a replacement passport and one at the National Tax and Customs Administration.

"Tax and Customs?" Natalie echoed when he told her about the appointments. "Is that like the Internal Revenue Service in the US?"

"More like your IRS and Department of the Treasury combined. The NTCA is our focus for all financial matters, including criminal activities like money laundering and financing terrorist activities."

Her eyes rounded. "And they have something on Lagy?"

"They wouldn't say, but they're interested in talking to you."

"I can't tell them any more than I told you."

"No, but they can tell us what, if anything, Lagy's involved in."

"Well, this has been an amazing day. Two days, actually." Her eyes met his in a smile. "And a pretty amazing night."

The smile clinched it. No way was he letting this woman waltz out of his life the same way she'd waltzed in. Dom thought seriously about plucking the glass out of her hand and carrying her to the bed. Which he would, he promised himself. Later. Right now, he'd initiate a blitz-style campaign to make her develop a passion for all things Hungarian—himself included.

"Did you bring a bathing suit?"

She blinked at the abrupt change of topic. "A bathing suit?"

"Do you have one in your suitcase?"

"I packed for business, not splashing around in hotel pools."

"No matter. We can rent one."

"Rent a bathing suit?" Her fastidious little nose wrinkled. "I don't think so."

"They're sanitized and steam-cleaned. Trust me on this. Stuff a couple of towels in your tote while I feed the hound and we'll go."

"Dom, I don't think public bathing is really my thing."

"You can't leave Budapest without experiencing what gives this city its most distinctive character. Why do you think the Romans called their settlement here Aquincum?"

"Meaning water something?"

"Meaning abundant waters. All they had to do was poke a stick in the ground and a hot spring bubbled up. Get the towels."

* * *

Natalie was even less sure about the whole communal spa thing when they arrived at the elegant Gellért Hotel. The massive complex sat at the base of Gellért Hill, named, Dom informed her, for the unfortunate bishop who came from Venice at the request of King Istivan in 1000 A.D.

"My rebellious Magyar ancestors took exception to the king's conversion to Christianity," Dom related as he escorted her to the columned and colonnaded entrance. "They put the bishop in a barrel, drove long spikes in it and rolled him down the hill."

"Lovely."

"Here we go."

He ushered her into a grand entry hall two or three stories high. A long row of ticket windows lining one side of the hall offered a bewildering smorgasbord of options. Dom translated a menu that included swimming pools, thermal baths with temperatures ranging from a comfortable 86 degrees to a scorching 108 degrees, whirlpools, wave pools, saunas and steam rooms. And massages! Every sort of massage. Natalie gave up trying to pick out options and left the choice to him.

"Don't you need to know what bathing suit size I need?" she asked as they approached a ticket booth.

He cut her an amused glance. "I was with you when you bought those jeans, remember? You're a size forty-two."

Ugh! She hated European sizing. She stood beside him while he purchased their entry and noted that a good number of people passed through the turnstiles with just a flash of a blue card.

"They don't have to pay?"

"They have a medical pass," he explained as he fastened a band around her wrist. "The government operates all spas in Hungary. They're actually part of our health care

system. Doctors regularly send patients here for massage or hot soaks or swimming laps."

Impressed but still a little doubtful, Natalie accompanied him into a gloriously ornate lobby, then to a seemingly mile-long hall with windows offering an unimpeded view of a sparkling swimming pool. Swimmers of all ages, shapes and sizes floated, dog-paddled or cut through the water with serious strokes.

"Here's where we temporarily part ways," Dom told her, extracting one of the towels from her tote. "The men's changing area is on the right, the women's on the left. Just show the attendant your wristband and she'll fix you up with a suit. Then hold the band up to the electronic pad and it'll assign you a changing cabin and locker. Once you've changed, flash the band again to enter the thermal baths. I'll meet you there."

That sounded simple enough—until Natalie walked through the entrance to the women's area. It was huge, with marble everywhere, stairs leading up and down, and seemingly endless rows of massage rooms, saunas, showers and changing rooms. A friendly local helped her locate the alcove containing the suit rental desk.

She still harbored distinct doubts about shimmying into a used bathing suit. But when she slid the chit Dom had given her across the desk, the attendant returned with a sealed package containing what looked like a brand-new one-piece. She held her wristband up to the electronic pad as Dom had instructed and got the number of a changing room. Faced with long, daunting rows of cubicles, she had to ask another local for help locating hers. Once they'd found it, the smiling woman took Natalie's wrist and aimed the band at the electronic lock.

"Here, here. Like this."

The door popped open, and her helpful guide added further instructions.

"It locks behind you, yes? You leave your clothes and towels in the cabin, then go through to the thermal pool."

"Thank you."

"*Szívesen.*"

The room was larger than Natalie had expected, with a bench running along one wall and a locker for her clothes and tote. She was still leery of the rented bathing suit but a close inspection showed it to be clean and fresh-smelling.

And at least one size too small!

Cut high on the thighs and low in the front, the sleek black Spandex revealed far more skin than Natalie wanted to display. She tried yanking up the neck but that only pulled the Spandex into an all-too-suggestive V at her crotch. She tugged it down again, determined not to give Dom a peep show.

Not that he would object. The man was nothing if not appreciative of the opposite sex. Kiss Kiss Arabella and lushly endowed Lisel were proof of that. And, Natalie now remembered, his sister Zia and Sarah's sister Gina had both joked about how women fell all over him. And why not? With that sexy grin and too-handsome face, Dominic St. Sebastian could have his pick of...

She froze, her fingers still tugging at the bottom of the suit, as another handsome face flashed into her mind.

Oh, God!

She dropped onto the bench. Blood drained from her heart and gathered like a cold, dead pool in her belly.

Oh God, oh God, oh God!

Wrapping her arms around her middle, she rocked back and forth on the bench. She remembered now the "traumatic" event she'd tried to desperately to suppress. The ugly incident that had caused her to lose her sense of self.

How could she have forgotten for a day—an hour!—the vicious truth she'd kept buried for more than three years? Tears stung her eyes, raked her throat. Furiously, she

fought them back. She'd cried all the tears she had in her three years ago. She was damned if she'd shed any more for the bastard who destroyed her life then. And would now destroy it again, she acknowledged on a wave of despair.

How could she have let herself believe last night could lead to something more between her and Dominic St. Sebastian? When she told him about her past, he'd be so disappointed, so disgusted. She sat there, aching for what might have been, until the urge to howl like a wounded animal released its death grip on her throat. Then she got off the bench and pushed through the door at the other end of the changing room.

The temperature in the marble hall shot up as she approached the first of the thermal pools. Dom was there, waiting for her as promised. Yesterday, even this morning, she would have drooled at the sight of his tall, muscled torso sporting a scant few inches of electric-blue Speedo. Now all she could do was gulp when he got a look at her face and stiffened.

"What's wrong?"

"I…I…"

"Natalie, what is it? What's happened?"

"I have to tell you something." She threw a wild look around the busy spa. "But not here. I'll…I'll meet you at the car."

Whirling, she fled back to her changing room.

Twelve

Her mind drowning in a cesspool of memories, Natalie scrambled into her clothes and had to ask for directions several times before she emerged from the maze of saunas and massage rooms.

Dom waited at the entrance to the women's changing rooms instead of at the car. His face was tight with concern and unspoken questions when she emerged. He swept a sharp glance around the hall, as though checking to see if anyone lingered nearby or appeared to be waiting or watching for Natalie, then cut his gaze back to her.

"What happened in the changing area to turn your face so pale?"

"I remembered something."

"About Janos Lagy?"

"No." She gnawed on her lower lip. "An incident in my past. I need to tell you about it."

Something flickered in his eyes. Surprise? Caution? Wariness? It came and went so quickly she couldn't have pinned a label on it even if her thoughts weren't skittering all over the place.

"There's a café across the street. We can talk there."

"A café? I don't think… I don't know…"

"We haven't eaten since breakfast. Whatever you have to tell me will go down easier with a bowl of goulash."

Natalie knew nothing could make it go down easier,

but she accompanied him out of the hotel and into the fall dusk. Lights had begun to glow on the Pest side of the Danube. She barely registered the glorious panorama of gold and indigo as Dom took her arm and steered her to the brightly lit café.

Soon—too soon for her mounting dread—they were enclosed in a high-backed booth that afforded both privacy and an unimpeded view of the illuminated majesty across the river. Dom ordered and signaled for her to wait until the server had brought them both coffee and a basket of thick black bread. He cut Natalie's coffee with a generous helping of milk to suit her American taste buds, then nudged the cup across the table.

"Take a drink, take a breath and tell me what has you so upset."

She complied with the first two instructions but couldn't find a way to broach the third. She stirred more milk into her coffee, fiddled with her spoon, gnawed on her lower lip again.

"Natalie. Tell me."

Her eyes lifted to his. "The scum you hunt down? The thieves and con artists and other criminals?" Misery choked her voice. "I'm one of them."

She'd dreaded his reaction. Anticipated his disgust or icy withdrawal. The fact that he didn't even blink at the anguished confession threw her off for a moment. But only a moment.

"Oh, my God! You know?" Shame coursed through her, followed almost immediately by a scorching realization. "Of course you do! You've known all along, haven't you?"

"Not all along, and not the details." His calm, even tone countered the near hysteria in hers. "Only that you were arrested, the charges were later dropped and the record wiped clean."

Her laugh was short and bitter. "Not clean enough, apparently."

The server arrived then with their goulash. The brief interruption didn't give her nearly enough time to swallow the fact that Dom had been privy to her deepest, darkest, most mortifying secret. The server departed, but the steaming soup sat untouched while Natalie related the rest of her sorry tale.

"I'm not sure how much you know about me, but before Sarah hired me I worked for the State of Illinois. Specifically, for the state's Civil Service Board. I was part of an ongoing project to digitize more than a hundred years' worth of paper files and merge them with current electronic records. I enjoyed the work. It was such a challenge putting all those old records into a sortable database."

She really *had* loved her job, she remembered as she plucked a slice of coarse black bread from the basket and played with it. Not just the digitizing and merging and sorting, but the picture those old personnel records painted of previous generations. Their work ethic, their frugal saving habits, their large numbers of dependents and generous contributions to church and charity. For someone like Natalie with no parents or grandparents or any known family, these glimpses into the quintessential American working family were fascinating.

"Then," she said with a long, slow, thoroughly disgusted sigh, "I fell in love."

She tore a thick piece off the bread, squeezed it into a wad, rolled it around and around between her fingers.

"He was so good-looking," she said miserably. "Tall, athletic, blue-eyed, always smiling."

"Always smiling? Sounds like a jerk."

Her lips twisted. "I was the jerk. I bought his line about wanting to settle down and start a family. Actually started weaving fantasies about a nursery, a minivan with car

seats, the whole baby scene. I should've known I wasn't the type to interest someone as smooth and sophisticated as Jason DeWitt for longer than it took for him to hack into my computer."

Dom reached out and put his palm over the fingers still nervously rolling the bread. His grip was strong and warm, his eyes glinting with undisguised anger.

"We'll discuss what type you are later. Right now, I can pretty well guess what came next. Mr. Smooth used your computer to access state records and mine thousands of addresses, dates of birth and social security numbers."

"Try hundreds of thousands."

"Then he sold them, right? I'm guessing to the Russians, although the marketplace is pretty well wide-open these days. And when the crap hit the fan, the feds tracked the breach to you."

"He hadn't sold them yet. They caught him with his hand still in my cookie jar."

Shame and misery engulfed her again. Tears burned as the images from that horrible day played through her head.

"Oh, Dom, it was so awful! The police came to my office! Said they'd been after Jason—the man I *knew* as Jason DeWitt—for over a year. They'd decoded his electronic signature and knew he'd hacked into several major databases. They'd finally penetrated his shields and not only pinpointed his exact location, they kicked in the door to my apartment and nailed him in the act. Then they charged me with being an accomplice to unauthorized access to public records with intent to commit fraud. They arrested me right there in front of all my coworkers and… and…"

She had to stop and gulp back the stinging tears. "Then they hauled me downtown in handcuffs."

"At which point they discovered you weren't a party to the hacking and released you."

Dom's unquestioned acceptance of her innocence should have soothed her raw nerves. Instead, it made it even tougher to finish the sordid tale.

"Not quite."

Writhing inside, she tried to pull her hand away but he kept it caged.

"Jason tried to convince the police it was all my idea. He said I'd teased and taunted him with sex. That would have been laughable," she said, heat surging into her cheeks, "if the police hadn't found a closet full of crotch-high leather skirts, low-cut blouses and peek-a-boo lingerie. Jason kept pestering me to wear that kind of…of slut stuff when we went out. It was enough to make the investigators wring me inside out before they finally released me."

Dom played his thumb over the back of her hand and fought to keep his fury in check. It wasn't enough that the hacker had played on Natalie's lonely childhood and craving for a family. The bastard had also cajoled her into decking herself out like a whore. No wonder she'd swung to the opposite extreme and started dressing like a refugee from a war zone.

Even worse, she'd had no one to turn to for help during what had to be one of the most humiliating moments of her life. No parents to rush downtown and bail her out. No sister to descend like an avenging angel, as Zia would have done. No brother to pulverize the man who'd set her up.

She wasn't alone now, though. Nor would she be alone in the future. Not as long as Dominic had a say in the matter. The absolute certainty of that settled around his heart like a glove as he quietly prompted her to continue.

"What did you do then?"

"I hired a lawyer and got the arrest expunged. Or so I thought," she amended with a frown. "Then I had the lawyer negotiate a deal with my boss. Since the state records hadn't actually been compromised, I said I would quietly

disappear if he agreed that my employment record would contain no reference to the whole sorry mess. After some weeks of wrangling with the state attorney general's office, I packed up and left town. I worked at odd jobs for a while until…"

"Until you went to work for Sarah," he finished when she didn't.

Guilt flooded her face. "I didn't lie to her, Dom. I filled out my employment history truthfully. I knew she would check my references, knew my chances were iffy at best. But my former boss stuck to his end of the deal, and my performance reports before…before that big mess were so glowing and complimentary that Sarah hired me after only one interview."

She turned away, shamefaced.

"I know you think I should have told her. I wanted to. I really did. And I intended to. I just thought…maybe if I tracked down the Canaletto first…helped return it to its rightful owner…Sarah and Dev and the duchess would know I wasn't a thief."

"You're not a thief. Natalie, look at me. You're not a thief or a con artist or a criminal. Trust me, I've been around the breed enough to know. Now I have two questions for you before we eat the soup that's been sitting here for so long."

"Only two?"

Her voice was wobbly, her eyes still tear-bright and drenched with a humiliation that made Dom vow to pulverize the scum who'd put it there.

"Where is this Jason character now?"

"Serving five to ten at the Danville Correctional Facility."

"Well, that takes him off my hit list. For now."

An almost smile worked through her embarrassment. "What's question two?"

"How long are you going to keep mashing that piece of bread?"

She blinked and looked down in surprise at the pulpy glob squishing through her fingers.

"Here." He passed her a napkin. "Eat your soup, *drágám*. Then we'll go home and get back to work on finding your painting."

Home. The word reverberated in Natalie's mind when Dom opened the door to the loft and Duke treated them to an ecstatic welcome. She clung to the sound of it, the thought of it, like a lifeline while man and dog took a quick trip downstairs and she went to unpack the roller suitcase still propped next to the wardrobe.

Her toiletries went into the bathroom, her underwear onto the corner of a shelf in the wardrobe. When she lifted the neatly folded blouses, her mouth twisted.

Natalie knew she'd never been a Princess Kate. She wasn't tall or glamorous or as poised as a supermodel. But she'd possessed her own sense of style. She'd preferred a layered look, she now remembered. Mostly slim slacks or jeans with belted tunics or cardigans over tanks…until Jason.

He'd wanted sexier, flashier. She cringed, remembering how she'd suppressed her inner qualms and let him talk her into those thigh-hugging skirts and lace-up bustiers. She'd burned them. The leather skirts, the bustiers, the stilettos and boob tubes and garter belts and push-up bras. Carted the whole lot down to the incinerator in her building, along with every other item in her apartment that carried even a whiff of Jason's scent or a faint trace of his imprint.

Then she'd gone out and purchased an entire new wardrobe of maiden aunt blouses and shapeless linen dresses. She'd also stopped using makeup and began scraping her hair back in a bun. She'd even resorted to wearing glasses

she didn't need. Paying penance, she now realized, for her sins.

She was still staring at the folded blouses when Dom and the hound returned. When he saw what she was holding, he dropped the dog's lead on the kitchen counter and crossed the room.

"You don't need these anymore." He took the blouses and dumped them back in the case. "You don't need any of this."

When he zipped the case and propped it next to the wardrobe again, Natalie experienced a heady sense of freedom. As though she'd just shed an outer skin that'd felt as unnatural and uncomfortable as the one she'd tried to squeeze into for Jason.

Buoyed by the feeling, she flashed Dom a smile. "If you don't want me to continue raiding your closet, you'll have to take me shopping again."

"You're welcome to wear anything of mine you wish. Although," he confessed with a quick grin, "I must admit I prefer when you wear nothing at all."

The need that splintered through her was swift and clean and joyous. The shame she'd tried to bury for three long years was still there, just below the surface. She suspected traces of it would linger there for a long while. But for now, for this moment, she could give herself completely to Dom and her aching hunger for his touch.

She looped her arms around his neck and let the smile in his eyes begin healing the scars. "I must admit I prefer you that way, too."

"Then I suggest we both shed some clothes."

They made it to the bed. Barely. A stern command prevented Duke from jumping in with them, but Natalie had to force herself not to look at the hound's reproachful face until Dom's mouth and teeth and busy, busy hands made her forget everything but him.

She was boneless with pleasure and half-asleep when he tucked her into the curve of his body and murmured something in Hungarian.

"What does that mean?"

"Sleep well, my darling."

Her heart tripped, but she didn't ask him to expand on that interesting translation. She settled for snuggling closer to his warmth and drifting into a deep, dreamless sleep.

Natalie woke the next morning to the sound of hammering. She pried one eye open and listened for several moments before realizing that was rain pounding against the roof. Burrowing deeper under the featherbed, she resurfaced again only when an amused voice sounded just over her shoulder.

"The dog and I are going for our run. Coffee's on the stove when you're ready for it."

She half rolled over. "You're going out in the rain?"

"That's one of the penalties of being adopted by a racing hound. He needs regular exercise whatever the weather. We both do, actually."

Natalie grunted, profoundly thankful that she wasn't invited to participate in this morning ritual.

"I'll bring back apple pancakes for breakfast," Dom advised as he and the joyously prancing Agár headed for the door. "Then we'll need to leave for the appointments at the embassy and the Tax and Customs Administration."

"And shopping," Natalie called to his back. "I need to shop!"

The prospect of replenishing her wardrobe with bright colors and soft textures erased any further desire to burrow. By the time Dom and Duke returned she'd showered and dressed in her one pair of jeans and tank top. She'd also made the bed, fussed with the folds in the drapes and dust-mopped the loft's wood-plank floors.

Her welcome smile slipped a little when the runners tracked wet foot- and paw-prints across the gleaming floors. She had to laugh, though, and hold up her hands against a flying spray when the hound planted all four paws and shook from his nose to his tail.

She and Dom feasted on the pancakes that he'd somehow protected from the rain. Then he, too, got ready for the morning's appointments. He emerged from the bathroom showered and shaved and looking too scrumptious for words in jeans and a cable-knit fisherman's sweater.

"You'd better bring the Canaletto file," he advised.

"I have it," she said, patting her briefcase. "I made copies of the key documents, just in case."

"Good." He held up the jacket she'd pretty much claimed as her own. "Now put this on and we'll go."

Natalie was glad of its warmth when they went down to the car. The rain had lessened to a misty drizzle but the damp chill carried a bite. Not even the gray weather could obscure the castle ramparts, though, as Dom negotiated the curving streets of Castle Hill and joined the stream of traffic flowing across Chain Bridge.

The US Embassy was housed in what had once been an elegant turn-of-the century palazzo facing a lush park. High metal fencing and concrete blocks had turned it into a modern-day fortress and long lines waited to go through the security checkpoint. As Dom steered Natalie to a side entrance with a much shorter line, she noted a bronze plaque with a raised relief religious figure.

"Who's that?"

"Cardinal József Mindszenty, one of the heroes of modern Hungary. The communists tortured and imprisoned him for speaking out against their brutal regime. He got a temporary reprieve during the 1956 Revolution, but when the Soviets crushed the uprising, the US Embassy granted

him political asylum. He remained here for more than fifteen years.

"Fifteen *years*?"

"Cardinal Mindszenty is one of the reasons Hungary
and the United States enjoy such close ties today."

Dom's Interpol credentials got them into the consular
offices through the side entrance. After passing through
security and X-ray screening, they arrived at their appointment right on time

Replacing Natalie's lost passport took less than a half
hour. She produced the copy of her driver's license Dom's
contact had procured and the forms she'd already completed. After signing the form in front of a consular officer
and having it witnessed by another official, the computer
spit out a copy of her passport's data page.

She winced at the photo, taken when she'd renewed
her passport just over a year ago, but she thanked the official and slipped the passport into her tote with an odd,
unsettled feeling. She should have been relieved to have
both her memory and her identity back. She could leave
Hungary now. Go home to the States, or anywhere else
her research took her. How stupid was she for wishing this
passport business had taken weeks instead of minutes?

Their second appointment didn't go as quickly or as
well. Dom's Interpol credentials seemed to have a negative effect on the two uniformed officers they met with at
the NTCA. One was a spare, thirtysomething woman who
introduced herself as Patrícia Czernek, the other a graying
older man who greeted Natalie with a polite nod before
engaging Dom in a spirited dialogue. It didn't take a genius or a working knowledge of Hungarian to figure out
they were having a bit of a turf war. Natalie kept out of the
line of fire until the female half of the team picked up the
phone and made a call that appeared to settle the matter.

With a speaking glance at her partner, Officer Czernek turned to Natalie. "So Ms. Clark, we understand from Special Agent St. Sebastian that you may have knowledge of a missing painting by a Venetian master. One taken from Karlenburgh Castle during the 1956 Uprising. Will you tell us, please, how you came by this knowledge?"

"Certainly."

Extracting the Canaletto file, she passed each of the officers a copy of the chronology she'd run earlier. "This summarizes my research, step-by-step. As you can see, it began three months ago with a computer search."

The NTCA officers flipped through the four-sheet printout and exchanged looks. Dom merely smiled.

"If you'll turn to page three, line thirty-seven," Natalie continued briskly, "you'll see that I did a search of recently declassified documents from the Soviet era relating to art treasures owned by the state and found an inventory of items removed from Karlenburgh Castle. The inventory listed more than two dozen near priceless works of art, but not the Canaletto. Yet I knew from previous discussions with Grand Duchess Charlotte that the painting *was* hanging in the Red Salon the day the Soviets came to destroy the castle."

She walked them through her search step-by-step. Her decision to drive down from Vienna to interview local residents. Her stop at the ruins and meeting with Friedrich Müller. His reference to an individual who'd inquired previously at the Red Salon.

"Janos Lagy," the older of the two officers murmured. He skimmed down several lines and looked up quickly. "You spoke with him? You spoke with Lagy about this painting?"

"I did."

"And arranged to meet with him on a riverboat?"

"That was his idea, not mine. Unfortunately, he didn't show."

"Do you have a recording of this conversation?" Officer Czernek asked hopefully. "On your cell phone, perhaps?"

"I lost my purse and phone when I went overboard."

"Yes, Special Agent St. Sebastian told us about your accident." A frown etched between her brows. "We also reviewed a copy of the incident report from the metropolitan police. It's very strange that no one saw you fall from the boat or raised an alarm."

"I was at the back of the ship and not feeling very well. Also, this happened in the middle of the week. There weren't many other passengers aboard."

"Still…"

She and her partner engaged in a brief exchange.

"We, too, have a file," she said, turning back to Natalie. "Would you be so kind as to look at some pictures and tell me if you recognize any of the people in them?"

She produced a thin folder and slid out three eight-by-tens. One showed a lone figure in a business suit and tie. The second picture was of the same individual in a tux and smiling down at the svelte beauty on his arm. In the third, he strolled along a city street wearing an overcoat and smart fedora.

"Do you recognize that man?" Czernek asked, her gaze intent on Natalie.

She scrutinized the lean features again. The confident smile, the dark eyes and fringe of brown hair around a head going bald on top. She'd never seen him before. She was sure of it.

"No, I don't recognize him. Is it Lagy?"

The police officer nodded and blew out an obviously disappointed breath. When she reached over to gather the pictures, Natalie had to battle her own crushing disappointment. Lagy's link to the Canaletto had been tenuous

at best but she'd followed thinner threads. Suddenly, she frowned and took another look at the street shot.

"Him!" She stabbed a finger at a figure trailing a little way behind Lagy. "I recognize this man. He was on the boat."

"Are you sure?"

"Very sure. When I got sick, he asked if he could help but I waved him away. I didn't want to puke all over his shoes." She looked up eagerly. "Do you know who he is?"

"He's Janos Lagy's bodyguard."

The air in the small office suddenly simmered with rigidly suppressed excitement. Natalie looked from Czernek to her partner to Dom and back again. All of them, apparently, knew something she didn't.

"Clue me in," she demanded. "What have you got on Janos Lagy?"

The officer hesitated. A cop's natural instinct to hold her cards close to her chest, Natalie guessed. Tough! She wasn't leaving the NTCA until she got some answers.

"Look," she said mutinously, "I've chased all over Europe tracking the Canaletto. I've spent weeks digging through musty records. I whacked my head and took an unplanned swim in the Danube. I didn't know who I was for almost a week. So I think I deserve an answer. What's the story on Lagy?"

After another brief pause, Czernek relented. "We've had him under surveillance for some time now. We suspect he's been trafficking in stolen art and have unsubstantiated reports of a private collection kept in a secret vault in his home."

"You're kidding!"

"No, I am not. Unfortunately, we haven't been able to gather enough evidence to convince a judge to issue a

search warrant." Patrícia Czernek's lips parted in a knife blade of a smile. "Based on what you've told us, we may be able to get that warrant."

Thirteen

After all she'd done, all she'd been through, Natalie considered it a complete and total bummer that she was forced to sit on the sidelines during the final phase of the hunt that had consumed her for so many weeks.

The task force gathered early the morning after Natalie had ID'd the bodyguard. As tenuous as that connection was to Lagy and the missing Canaletto, when combined with other evidence NCTA had compiled on the banker, it proved sufficient for a judge to grant a search warrant. Dom left the loft before dawn to join the team that would hit the banker's villa on the outskirts of Budapest. Natalie was left behind with nothing to do but walk the hound, make another excursion to the butcher shop, scrub the shower stall, dust-mop the floors again and pace.

"This is the pits," she complained to the hound as the morning dragged by.

The Agár cocked his head but didn't look particularly sympathetic.

"Okay, okay! It's true I don't have any official standing that could have allowed them to include me in the task force. And I guess I don't really want to see anyone hauled off in handcuffs. That would cut a little too close to the bone," she admitted with a grimace. "Still," she grumbled, shooting another glance at the kitchen clock, "you'd think

certain people would find a way to let me know what's happening."

Dominic couldn't contact her directly. She knew that. Natalie's phone was at the bottom of the Danube and the loft didn't have a landline. He could've called his downstairs neighbors, though, and asked Katya or her father to relay a message.

Or not. There was probably some rule or protocol that prohibited disseminating information about an ongoing investigation to civilians.

"That better not include me."

The bad-tempered comment produced a nervous whine from the hound. Natalie stooped to scratch behind his ear.

"Sorry, Duke'ums. I'm just a little annoyed with your alter ego."

Annoyed and increasingly worried as morning crawled toward noon, then into the afternoon, she was seriously contemplating going downstairs to ask Katya if she could use her phone when she heard the heavy tread of footsteps on the outside stairs.

"Finally!"

She rushed to the door, startling the dog into a round of excited barking. One look at Dom's mile-wide grin sent all her nasty recriminations back down her throat. She could only laugh when he caught her by the waist and swung her in wide circles. The hound, of course, went nuts. Natalie had to call a halt before they all tripped over each other and tumbled down five flights of stairs.

"Dom, stop! You're making me dizzy."

He complied with a smooth move that shifted her from mostly vertical to horizontal. Still wearing a cheek-splitting grin, he carried her over the threshold and kicked the door shut as soon as the three of them were inside.

"I assume you got your man," she said.

"You assume right. Hold on."

He opened the fridge and dipped her almost vertical again. Squealing, she locked her arms around his neck while he retrieved two frosty bottles from the bottom shelf, then carried her to the sofa. He sank onto the cushions with Natalie in his lap and thumped his boots up on the coffee table.

She managed to keep from pelting him with questions while he offered her one of the dew-streaked bottles of pilsner. When she shook her head, he popped the cap and tilted his head. She watched, fascinated, as he downed half the contents in long, thirsty swallows. He hadn't had time to shave before he'd left. The beginnings of a beard shadowed his cheeks and chin. And his knuckles, she noted with a small gasp, had acquired a nasty set of scrapes and bruises.

"What happened to your knuckles?"

"Lagy's bodyguard ran into them." Something dark and dangerous glinted in his eyes. "Several times."

"What? Why?"

"We had a private discussion about your swim in the Danube. He disavowed any responsibility for it, of course, but I didn't like the way his lip curled when he did."

She gaped at him, her jaw sagging. She'd been alone so long. And so sickened by the way Jason had tried to pin the blame for his illegal activities on her. The idea that Dom had set himself up as her protector and avenger cut deep into her heart. Before she could articulate the chaotic emotions those bruised knuckles roused, however, the hound almost climbed into her lap.

She held him off, but it took some effort. "You'd better give him some of your beer before he grabs the bottle out of your hand, and tell me the rest of the story!"

He tipped the bottle toward the Agár's eager jaws. Natalie barely registered an inward cringe as pale gold lager

slopped in all directions. Duke dropped the empty bottle on the floor and was scooting it across the oak planks to extract the last drops when Dom launched into a detailed account.

"We hit the villa before Lagy had left for the bank. When Czernek showed him the search warrant, he wouldn't let us proceed until his high-priced lawyer arrived on the scene."

"Did Lagy recognize you?"

"Oh, yeah. He made some crack about the newspaper stories, but I could tell the fact that a St. Sebastian had showed up at his door with an armed squad made him nervous. Especially when I flashed my Interpol credentials."

"Then what happened?"

"We cooled our heels until his lawyer showed up. Bastard had the nerve to play lord of the manor and offer us all coffee."

"Which you accepted," she guessed, all too mindful of the Hungarian passion for the brew.

"Which we accepted," he confirmed. "By the time his lawyer arrived, though, we'd all had our fill of acting polite. His attorney tried to posture and bluff, but folded like an accordion when Czernek waved the search warrant under his nose. Apparently he'd gotten crosswise of this particular judge before and knew he couldn't fast-talk his client out of this one. Then," Dom said with savage satisfaction, "we tore the villa apart. Imagine our surprise when infrared imaging detected a vault hidden behind a false wall in Lagy's study."

When he paused to pop the cap on the second bottle, Natalie groaned in sheer frustration.

"Don't you dare drink that before you tell me what was in the vault!"

"See for yourself." Shifting her on his lap, he jammed a hand in the pocket of his jeans and extracted a folded print-

out. "That's just a preliminary inventory. Each piece has to be examined and authenticated by a team of experts."

Her hands shaking with excitement, Natalie unfolded the printout and skimmed the fourteen entries.

"Omigod!"

The list read like a who's who of the art world. Edgar Degas. Josef Grassi. Thomas Gainsborough. And there, close to the bottom, Giovanni Canaletto.

"Did you see the Canaletto?" she asked breathlessly. "Is it the one from Karlenburgh Castle?"

"Looked like it to me."

"I can't believe it!"

"Lagy couldn't, either, when Czernek called for a team to crate up his precious paintings and take them in evidence."

She skimmed the list again, stunned by its variety and richness. "How incredible that he managed to amass such an extensive collection. It must be worth hundreds of millions."

"He may have acquired some of it through legitimate channels. As for the rest…" Dom's jaw hardened. "I'm guessing he inherited many of those paintings from his grandfather. Karlenburgh Castle wasn't the only residence destroyed in retribution for their owners' participation in the '56 Uprising. *Mladshij Lejtenant* Lagy's company of sappers would have been only too eager help take them down. God knows how many treasures the bastards managed to appropriate for themselves in the process."

Natalie slumped against his chest and devoured the brief descriptions of the paintings removed from Lagy's villa. Several she recognized immediately from Interpol's database of lost or stolen art. Others she would need more detail on before she could be sure.

"This," she said, excitement still singing through her veins, "is going make a fantastic final chapter in Sarah's

book. Her editors will eat up the personal angle. A painting purchased for a young duchess, then lost for decades. The hunt by the duchess's granddaughter for the missing masterpiece. The raid that recovered it, which just happened to include the current Grand Duke."

"Let's not forget the part you played in the drama."

"I'm just the research assistant. You St. Sebastians are the star players."

"You're not 'just' anything, Natushka."

To emphasize the point, he tugged on her hair and tilted her head back for a long, hard kiss. Neither of them held back, taking and giving in both a welcome release of tension and celebration.

Natalie was riding high when Dom raised his head. "I can't wait to tell Sarah about this. And the duchess! When do you think her painting will be returned to her?"

"I have no idea. They'll have to authenticate it first, then trace the provenance. If Lagy can prove he purchased it or any of these paintings in good faith from a gallery or another collector, the process could take weeks or months."

"Or longer," she said, scrunching her nose. "Can't you exert some royal influence and hurry the process along?"

"Impatient little thing, aren't you?"

"And then some!" She scooted off his lap and onto the cushion next to him. "Let's contact Sarah via FaceTime. I want to see her reaction when we tell her."

They caught Sarah in midair aboard Dev's private jet. The moment Dom made the connection, her employer fired an anxious query.

"How's Natalie? Has her memory returned?"

"It has."

"Thank God! Where is she now?"

"She's here, with me. Hang on."

He angled the phone to capture Natalie's eager face. "Hello, Sarah."

"Oh, Natalie, we've been so worried. Are you really okay?"

"Better than okay. We've located the Canaletto!"

"What?" Sarah whipped her head to one side. "Dev, you're not going to believe this! Natalie's tracked down Grandmama's Canaletto."

"I didn't do it alone," Natalie protested, aiming a quick smile at Dom. "It was a team effort."

When she glanced back at the screen, Sarah's brows had inched up. "Well," she said after a small pause, "if I was going to team with anyone other than my husband, Dominic would certainly top my list."

A telltale heat rushed into Natalie's cheeks but she didn't respond to the curiosity simmering just below the surface of her employer's reply. Mostly because she wasn't really sure how to define her "teaming" with Dom, much less predict how long it would last. But she couldn't hold back a cheek-to-cheek grin as she related the events of the past few days. Sarah's eyes grew wider with the telling, and at the end of the recital she echoed Natalie's earlier sentiments.

"This is all so incredible. I can't wait to tell Grandmama the Canaletto's been recovered."

Dom leaned over Natalie's shoulder to issue the same warning he had earlier. "They'll have to assemble a team of experts to authenticate each painting and validate its provenance. That could take several months or more."

Dev's face crowded next to his wife's on the small screen. "We'll see what we can do to expedite the process, at least as far as the Canaletto is concerned."

"And I'll ask Gina to get Jack involved," Sarah volunteered. "He can apply some subtle pressure through diplomatic channels."

"I also suggested to the Grand Duke here that he should exercise a little royal muscle," Natalie put in.

"Good for you. With all three of our guys weighing in, I'm sure we can shake Grandmama's painting loose without too long a delay."

The reference to "our" guys deepened the heat in Natalie's cheeks. She floundered for a moment, but before she could think of an appropriate response to the possessive pronoun, Sarah had already jumped ahead.

"We need to update the chapter on the Canaletto, Nat. And if we put our noses to the grindstone, we ought to be able to finish the final draft of the book in two or three weeks. When can you fly back to L.A.?"

"I, uh…"

"Scratch that. Instead of going straight home, let's rendezvous in New York. I'd like you to personally brief my editor. I know she'll want to take advantage of the publicity all this is going to generate. We can fly to L.A. from there."

She could hardly say no. Sarah St. Sebastian Hunter had offered her the job of a lifetime. Not only did Natalie love the work, she appreciated the generous salary and fringe benefits that came with it. She owed her boss loyalty and total dedication until her book hit the shelves.

"No problem. I can meet you in New York whenever it works for you."

"I'll call my editor as soon as we hang up. I'll try to arrange something on Thursday or Friday. Did you get a replacement passport? Great. You should probably fly home tomorrow, then. I'll have a ticket waiting for you at the airport."

She disconnected with a promise to call back as soon as she'd nailed down the time and place of the meeting. Dominic tossed his phone on the coffee table and turned to Natalie.

She couldn't quite meet his eyes. She felt as though

she'd just dropped down an elevator shaft. Mere moments ago she'd been riding a dizzying high. In a few short seconds, she'd plunged back into cold, hard reality. She had a job, responsibilities, a life back in the States, such as it was. And neither she nor Dom had discussed any alternative. Still, the prospect of leaving Hungary drilled a hole in her heart.

"Sarah's been so good to me," she said, breaking the small silence. "I need to help put the final touches on her book."

"Of course you do. I, too, must go back to work. I've been away from it too long."

She plucked at the hem of her borrowed shirt. She should probably ask Dom to take her on a quick shopping run. She could hardly show up for a meeting with Sarah's editor in jeans and a tank top, much less a man's soccer shirt. Yet she hated to spend her last hours in Budapest cruising boutiques.

She tried to hide her misery at the thought of leaving, but Dom had to see it when he curled a knuckle under her chin and tipped her face to his.

"Perhaps this is for the best, *drágám*. You've had so much thrown at you in such a short time. The dive into the Danube. The memory loss. Me," he said with a crooked grin. "You need to step back and take a breath."

"You're probably right," she mumbled.

"I know I am. And when you've helped Sarah put her book to bed, you and I will decide where we go from there, yes?"

She wanted to believe him. Ached all over with the need to throw herself into his arms and make him *swear* this wasn't the end. Unfortunately, all she could think of was Kiss Kiss Arabella's outrageously expensive panties and Lovely Lisel's effusive greeting and Gina's laughing comments about her studly cousin and…

Dominic cut into those lowering thoughts by tugging her up and off the sofa with him. "So! Since this is your last night in Budapest for a while at least, we should make it one to remember."

For a while at least. Natalie clung to the promise of that small phrase as Dom scooped up his phone and stuffed it in his jeans pocket. Taking time only to pull on the red-and-black soccer shirt with its distinctive logo on the sleeve, he insisted she throw on the jacket she'd pretty much claimed as her own before hustling her to the door.

"Where are we going?"

"My very favorite place in all the city."

Since the city boasted spectacular architecture, a world-class opera house, soaring cathedrals, palatial spas and a moonlit, romantic castle perched high on its own hill, Natalie couldn't begin to guess which was Dom's favorite spot. She certainly wouldn't have picked the café/bar he ushered her into on the Pest side of the river. It was tiny, just one odd-shaped room, and noisy and crammed with men decked out in red-and-black-striped shirts. Most were around Dom's age, although Natalie saw a sprinkling of both freckles and gray hair among the men. Many stood with arms looped over the shoulders or around the waists of laughing, chatting women.

They were greeted with hearty welcomes and backslaps and more than one joking "His Grace" or "Grand Duke." Dom made so many introductions Natalie didn't even try to keep names and faces matched. As the beer flowed and his friends graciously switched to English to include her in the lively conversation, she learned she would have a ringside seat—via satellite and high-definition TV—at the World Cup European playoffs. Hungary's team had been eliminated in the quarterfinals, much to the disgust

of everyone in the bar, but they'd grudgingly shifted their allegiance to former rival Slovakia.

With such a large crowd and such limited seating, Natalie watched the game, nestled on Dom's lap. Hoots and boos and foot-stomping thundered after every contested call. Cheers and ear-splitting whistles exploded when Slovakia scored halfway through the first quarter. Or was it the first half? Third? Natalie had no clue.

She was deafened by the noise, jammed knee to knee with strangers, breathing in the tang of beer and healthy male sweat, and she loved every minute of it! The noise, the excitement, the color, the casually possessive arm Dom hooked around her waist. She filed away every sensory impression, every scent and sound and vivid visual image, so she could retrieve them later. When she was back in New York or L.A. or wherever she landed after Sarah's book hit the shelves.

She refused to dwell on the uncertain future during the down-to-the-wire game. Nor while she and Dom took the hound for a romp through the park at the base of the castle. Not even when they returned to the loft and he hooked his arms around her waist as she stood in front of the wall of windows, drinking in her last sight of the Parliament's floodlit dome and spires across the river.

"It's so beautiful," she murmured.

"Like you," he said, nuzzling her ear.

"Ha! Not hardly."

"You don't see what I see."

He turned her, keeping her in the circle of his arms, and cradled her hips against his. His touch was featherlight as he stroked her cheek.

"Your skin is so soft, so smooth. And your eyes reflect your inner self. So intelligent, so brave even when you were so frightened that you would never regain your memory."

"Terrified" was closer to the mark, but she wasn't about to interrupt this interesting inventory.

Smiling, he threaded his fingers through her hair.

"I love how this goes golden-brown in the sunlight. Like thick, rich honey. It's true, your chin hints at a bit of a stubborn streak but your lips... Ah, Natushka, your lips. Have you any idea what that little pout of yours does to me?"

"Children pout," she protested. "Sultry beauties with collagen lips pout. I merely express..."

"Disapproval," he interjected, nipping at her lower lip. "Disdain. Disgust. All of which I saw in your face the first time we met. I wondered then whether I could make these same lips quiver with delight and whisper my name."

The nipping kisses achieved the first of his stated goals. Pleasure rippled across the surface of Natalie's skin even as Dom's husky murmur sent up a warning flag. She'd represented a challenge. She'd sensed that from the beginning. She remembered, too, how his sister and cousins had teased him about his many conquests. But now? Was the slow heat he stirred in her belly, the aching need in her chest, merely the by-product of a skilled seduction? Had she tumbled into love with the wrong man again?

She knew the answer before the question even half formed. Dominic St. Sebastian was most definitely the right man. The *only* man she wanted in her heart. In her life. She couldn't tell him, though. Her one and only previous foray into this love business had left her with too much baggage. Too many doubts and insecurities. And she was leaving in the morning. That more than anything else blocked the words she ached to say.

It didn't keep her from cradling his face in her palms while she kissed him long and hard. Or undressing him slowly, savoring every taut muscle, every hollow and hard plane of his body. Or groaning his name when he drove them both to a shattering climax.

Fourteen

Natalie couldn't classify the next five weeks as totally miserable.

Her first priority when she landed in New York was refurbishing her wardrobe before the meeting with Sarah and her editors. After she'd checked into her hotel she made a quick foray to Macy's. Sarah had smiled her approval at her assistant's conservative but nicely tailored navy suit and buttercup-yellow blouse.

Her smile had morphed to a wide grin when she and Natalie emerged from the meeting at Random House. Her editors were enthusiastic about how close the manuscript was to completion and anxious to get their hands on the final draft.

After a second meeting to discuss advance promo with Sarah's former boss at *Beguile* magazine, the two women flew back to California and hit the ground running. They spent most of their waking hours in Sarah's spacious, glass-walled office on the second floor of the Pacific Palisades mansion she shared with Dev. The glorious ocean view provided no distraction as they revised and edited and polished and proofed.

The final draft contained twenty-two chapters, each dedicated to a specific lost treasure. The Fabergé egg rated one chapter, the Bernini bronze another. The final chapter

was devoted to the Canaletto, with space left for a photograph of the painting being restored to its rightful owner. *If* it was ever restored!

The authentication and provenance process was taking longer than any of the St. Sebastians had hoped. Several big-time insurance companies were now involved, anxious to recoup the hundreds of thousands of dollars they'd paid out over the years.

The Canaletto didn't fall into that category. It *had* been insured, as had many of the valuable objects in Karlenburgh Castle, but the policy contained exclusions for loss due to war and/or acts of God. By categorizing the 1956 Uprising as war, the insurer had wiggled out of compensating the duchess for St. Sebastian heirlooms that had either disappeared or made their way into private collections. Still, with so many conflicting claims to sort out, the team charged with verifying authenticity and rightful ownership had its hands full.

Dominic, Dev Hunter and Jack Harris had done what they could to speed the process. Dev offered to fund part of the effort. Jack helped facilitate coordination between international agencies asserting conflicting claims. Much to his disgust, Dom didn't return to undercover work. Instead, his boss at Interpol detailed him to act as their liaison to the recovery team. He grumbled about that but provided the expertise to link Lagy to several black marketeers and less reputable galleries suspected of dealing in stolen art.

He kept Sarah and Natalie apprised of the team's progress by email and texts. The personal calls came in the evenings, after Natalie had dragged back to her rented one-room condo. They'd spoken every couple of nights when she'd first returned, less frequently as both she and Dom got caught up in their separate tasks. But just the sound

of his voice could make her hurt with a combination of hunger and loneliness.

The doubts crept in after she'd been home for several weeks. Dom seemed distracted when he called. After almost a month, it felt to Natalie as though he was struggling to keep any conversation going that didn't deal directly with the authentication effort.

Sarah seemed to sense her assistant's growing unease. She didn't pry, but she had a good idea what had happened between her cousin and Natalie during their time together in Budapest. She got a far clearer picture when she dropped what she thought was a casual question one rainy afternoon.

"Did Dom give you any glimmer of hope when the team might vet the Canaletto the last time he called?"

Natalie didn't look up from the dual-page layout on her computer screen. "No."

"Damn. We're supposed to fly to New York for another meeting with Random House next week. I hate to keep putting them off. Maybe you can push Dom a little next time you talk to him."

"I'm…I'm not sure when that will be."

From the corner of her eye Natalie saw Sarah's head come up. Swiveling her desk chair, she met her employer's carefully neutral look.

"Dom's been busy… The time difference… It's tough catching each other at home and…"

The facade crumbled without a hint of warning. One minute she was faking a bright smile. Two seconds later she was gulping and swearing silently that she would *not* cry.

"Oh, Natalie." Sympathy flooded Sarah's warm brown eyes. "I'm sure it's just as you say. Dom's busy, you're busy, you're continents apart…"

"And the tabloids have glommed on to him again," Natalie said with a wobbly smile.

"I know," Sarah said with a grimace. "One of these days I'll learn not to trust Alexis."

Her former boss had sworn up and down she didn't leak the story. Once it hit the press, though, *Beguile* followed almost immediately with a four-page color spread featuring Europe's sexiest single royal and his role in the recovery of stolen art worth hundreds of millions. Although the story stopped short of revealing that Dom worked for Interpol, it hinted at a dark and dangerous side to the duke. It even mentioned the Agár and obliquely suggested the hound had been trained by an elite counterterrorist strike force to sniff out potential targets. Natalie might have chuckled at that if the accompanying photo of Dom and Duke running in the park below the castle hadn't knifed right into her heart.

As a consequence, she was feeling anything but celebratory when she joined Sarah and Dev and Dev's extraordinarily efficient chief of operations, Pat Donovan, at a dinner to celebrate the book's completion. She mustered the requisite smiles and lifted her champagne flute for each toast. But she descended into a sputtering blob of incoherence when Sarah broached the possibility of a follow-on book specifically focused on Karlenburgh's colorful, seven-hundred-year history.

"Please, Natalie! Say you'll work with me on the research."

"I, uh…"

"Would you consider a one-year contract, with an option for two more? I'll double what I'm paying you now for the first year, and we can negotiate your salary for the following two."

She almost swallowed her tongue. "You're already paying me twice what the average researcher's services are worth!"

Dev leaned across the table and folded his big hand around Natalie's. "You're not just a researcher, kid. We consider you one of the family."

"Th-Thank you."

She refused to dwell on her nebulous, half-formed thoughts of actually becoming a member of their clan. Those silly hopes had faded in the past month…to the point where she wasn't sure she could remain on the fringe of Sarah's family orbit.

Her outrageously expensive dinner curdled at the thought of bumping into Dom at the launch of Sarah's book six or eight months from now. Or crossing paths with him if she returned to Hungary to research the history of the St. Sebastians. Or seeing the inevitable gossip put out by the tabloids whenever the sexy royal appeared at some gala with a glamorous female looking suspiciously like Natalie's mental image of Kissy Face Arabella.

"I'm overwhelmed by the offer," she told Sarah with a grateful smile. "Can I take a little time to think it over?"

"Of course! But think fast, okay? I'd like to brief my editors on the concept when we meet with them next week."

Before Natalie could even consider accepting Sarah's offer, she had to come clean. The next morning she burned with embarrassment as she related the whole sorry story of her arrest and abrupt departure from her position as an archivist for the State of Illinois. Sarah listened with wide eyes but flatly refused to withdraw her offer.

"Oh, Nat, I'm so sorry you got taken in by such a conniving bastard. All I can say is that he's lucky he's behind

bars. He'd damned well better keep looking over his shoulder when he gets out, though. Dev and Dominic both have long memories."

Relieved by Sarah's unqualified support but racked with doubts about Dom, Natalie was still agonizing over her decision the following Tuesday, when a taxi delivered her and Sarah to the tower of steel and glass housing her publisher. Spanning half a block in downtown Manhattan, the mega-conglomerate's lobby was walled with floor-to-ceiling bookcases displaying the hundreds of books put out each month by Random House's many imprints.

It was Natalie's third time accompanying Sarah to this publishing cathedral but the display of volumes hot off the press still awed her book-lover soul. While Sarah signed them both in and waited for an escort to whisk them up to the thirty-second floor, Natalie devoured the jacket and back-cover copy of a new release detailing the events leading to World War I and its catastrophic impact on Europe. Germany and the Austro-Hungarian Empire were major players in those cataclysmic events.

Karlenburgh sat smack in the juxtaposition of those cultures and epic struggles. Natalie itched to get her hands on the book. She was scrambling for her iPhone to snap a shot of the book jacket when a shrill bark cut through the low-level hum of the busy lobby. She spun around, her jaw dropping as a brown-and-white bullet hurtled straight toward her.

"Duke!" She took two front paws hard in the stomach, staggered back, dropped to her knees. "What…? How…? Whoa! Stop, fella! Stop!"

Laughing, she twisted her head to dodge the Agár's ecstatic kisses. The sight of Dom standing at the lobby entrance, his grin as goofy as the hound's, squeezed the air

from her lungs. The arms fending the dog off collapsed, Duke lunged, and they both went down.

She heard a scramble of footsteps. A frantic voice shouting for someone to call 911 or animal control or whoever. A strangled yelp as a would-be rescuer grabbed Duke's collar and yanked him off her. Sarah protesting the rough handling. Dom charging across the lobby to take control of the situation.

By the time the chaos finally subsided, he'd hauled Natalie to her feet and into his arms. "Ah, Natushka," he said, his eyes alight with laughter, "the hound and I hoped to surprise you, not cause a riot."

"Forget the riot! What are you doing in here?"

"I called Sarah's office to speak with you and was told you'd both flown to New York."

"But…but…" She couldn't get her head and her heart to work in sync. "How did you know we'd be here, at the publisher? Oh! You did your James Bond thing, didn't you?"

"I did."

"I still don't understand. You? Duke? Here?"

"We missed you."

The simple declaration shimmered like a rainbow, breathing color into the hopes and dreams that had shaded to gray.

"I planned to wait until I could bring the Canaletto," he told her, tipping his forehead to hers. "I wanted you with me when we restored the painting and all the memories it holds for the duchess. But every day, every night away from you ate at my patience. I got so restless and bad-tempered even the hound would snarl or slink away from me. The team's infuriatingly slow pace didn't help. You probably didn't notice when I called but…"

"I noticed," she drawled.

"But it all boiled down to frustration," he finished with a rueful smile. "Pure, unadulterated frustration."

She started to tell him he wasn't the only one who'd twisted and turned and tied themself up in knots but he preempted any reply by cradling her face in his palms.

"I wanted to wait before I told you that I love you, *drágám*. I wanted to give you time, let you find your feet again. I was worried, too, about the weeks and months my job would take me away. Your job, as well, if you accept the offer Dev told me about when I called to speak with you. I know your work is important to you, as mine is to me. We can work it out, yes?"

She pretty much stopped listening after the "I love you" part but caught the question in the last few words.

"Yes," she breathed with absolutely no idea what she was agreeing to. "Yes, yes, yes!"

"Then you'll take this?"

She glanced down, a laugh gurgling in her throat as Dom pinned an enameled copy of his soccer club's insignia to the lapel of her suit jacket.

"It will have to do," he told her with a look in those dark eyes that promised the love and home and family she'd always craved, "until we find an engagement ring to suit the fiancée of the Grand Duke of Karlenburgh, yes?"

"Yes!"

As if that weren't enough to keep Natalie dancing on a cloud and completely delight his sister, Sarah and the duchess, Gina and her husband arrived with the twins the next afternoon.

They were house hunting, they informed the assembled family. Jack's appointment as US Ambassador to the UN still needed to be confirmed by the Senate but the chair-

man of the Foreign Affairs Committee had assured him the vote was purely pro forma.

"How wonderful!" Her eyes bright with tears of joy, the duchess thumped her cane and decreed this called for a toast. "Dominic, will you and Jack pour *pálinka* for us all?"

Charlotte's heart swelled with pride as she watched her tall, gold-haired grandson-in-law and darkly handsome young relative move to the sideboard and line up an array of Bohemian cut-crystal snifters. Her gaze roamed the sitting room, lingering on her beautiful granddaughters and the just-crawling twins tended by a radiant Natalie and a laughing, if somewhat tired-looking, Zia. When Maria joined them with a tray of cheese and olives, the only one missing was Dev.

"I've been thinking," Jack said quietly as he and Dom stood shoulder to shoulder, filling delicate crystal aperitif glasses with the potent apricot brandy. "Now that your face has been splashed across half the front pages of Europe, your days as an undercover operative must be numbered."

Dom's mouth twisted. "My boss agrees. He's been trying to convince me to take over management of the organized-crimes division at Interpol Headquarters."

"A desk job in Lyon couldn't be all that bad, but why not put all this hoopla about your title and involvement in the recovery of millions of dollars in stolen art to good use?" Jack's blue eyes held his. "*My* soon-to-be boss at the UN thinks the Grand Duke of Karlenburgh would make a helluva cultural attaché. He and his lovely wife would be accepted everywhere, have access to top-level social circles—and information."

Dom's pulse kicked. He'd already decided to take the promotion and settle in Lyon. He couldn't subject Natalie to the uncertainties and dangers associated with his cur-

rent occupation. But deep inside he'd been dreading the monotony of a nine-to-five job.

"Cultural attaché?" he murmured. "What exactly would that involve?"

"Whatever you wanted it to. And you'd be based here in New York, surrounded by family. Which may not always be such a good thing," Jack added drily when one of his daughters grabbed a fistful of her sister's hair and gleefully yanked.

"No," Dom countered, watching Natalie scoop the howling twin into her arms to nuzzle and kiss and coo her back to smiles. "Family is a very good thing. Especially for someone who's never had one. Tell your soon-to-be boss that the Grand Duke of Karlenburgh would be honored to accept the position of cultural attaché."

Yesterday was one of the most memorable days in my long and incredibly rich life. They were all here, my ever-increasing family. Sarah and Dev. Gina and Jack and the twins. Dominic and Natalie. Zia, Maria, even Jerome, our vigilant doorman who insisted on escorting the Brink's couriers up to my apartment. I'm not ashamed to admit I cried when they uncrated the painting.

The Canaletto my husband gave me so long ago now hangs on my bedroom wall. It's the last thing I see before I fall asleep, the first thing I see when I wake. And, oh, the memories that drift in on gossamer wings between darkness and dawn! Dominic wants to take me back to Hungary for a visit. As Natalie and Sarah delve deeper into our family's history, they add their voice to his. I've said I'll return if Dom will agree to let me formally invest him with the title of Grand Duke at the black-tie affair Gina is so eager to arrange.

Then we'll settle in until Zia finishes her residency. She works herself to the bone, poor darling. If Maria and I didn't force her

to eat and snatch at least a few hours' rest, she'd drop where she stands. Something more than determination to complete the residency drives her. Something she won't speak about, even to me. I tell myself to be patient. To wait until she's ready to share the secret she hides behind her seductive smile and stunning beauty. Whatever it is, she knows I'll stand with her. We are, after all, St. Sebastians.

From the diary of Charlotte
Grand Duchess of Karlenburgh

* * * * *

THE TEXAN'S
ROYAL M.D.

BY
MERLINE LOVELACE

To Neta and Dave: friends, traveling buds and the source of all kinds of fodder for my books. Thanks for the inside info on research grants and nasty bugs, Neta!

Prologue

I seem to have come full circle. For so many years my life centered on my darling granddaughters. Now they're grown and are busy with lives of their own. Quiet, elegant Sarah has an adoring husband, a blossoming career as an author and her first child on the way. And Eugenia, my carefree, high-spirited Eugenia, is the wife of a United Nations diplomat and the mother of twins. She fills both roles so joyously, so effortlessly.

I do wish I could say the same of Dominic, my impossibly handsome great-nephew. Dom still hasn't adjusted to the fact that he now carries the title of Grand Duke of Karlenburgh. I've caught him rolling his shoulders as though he itches for his previous life as an undercover agent. Then his glance strays to his wife and his restlessness fades instantly. Natalie's so demure, so sweet and so startlingly intelligent!

She quite astonishes us all with the depth of her knowledge of the most arcane subjects—including the history of my beloved Karlenburgh.

These days I live vicariously through Dom's sister, Anastazia. I'll admit I played shamelessly on our distant kinship to convince

Zia to reside with me during her pediatric residency in New York City. She's only a few short months away from finishing the grueling three-year program. She should be feeling nothing but elation that the end is in sight. Yet I sense that something's troubling her. Something she doesn't wish to talk about, even with me. I shan't force the issue. I don't condone unwelcome intrusiveness, even by the most concerned and well-meaning. I do hope, however, that the vacation I've engineered for the family over the coming holidays eases some of the worry Zia hides behind her so bright, so lovely smile.

From the diary of Charlotte,
Grand Duchess of Karlenburgh

One

Zia almost didn't hear the shout over the roar of the waves. Preoccupied with the decision hanging over her like an executioner's ax, she'd slipped away for an early-morning jog along the glistening silver shoreline of Galveston Island, Texas. Although the Gulf of Mexico offered a glorious symphony of green water and lacy surf, Zia barely noticed the ever-changing seascape. She needed time and the endless, empty shore to think. Solitude to wrestle with her private demons.

She loved her family—her adored older brother, Dominic; her great-aunt Charlotte, who'd practically adopted her; the cousins she'd grown so close to in the past few years; their spouses and lively offspring. But spending the Christmas holidays in Galveston with the entire St. Sebastian clan hadn't allowed much time for soul-searching. Zia only had three more days to decide. Three days before she returned to New York and…

"Go get it, Buster!"

Sunk in thought, she might have blocked out the gleeful shout if she hadn't spent the past two and a half years as a pediatric resident at Kravis Children's Hospital, part of the Mount Sinai hospital network in New York City. All those

rewarding, gut-wrenching hours working with infants and young kids had fine-tuned Zia's instincts to the point that her mind tagged the voice instantly as belonging to a five- or six-year-old male with a healthy set of lungs.

A smile formed as she angled toward the sound. Her sneakers slapping the hard-packed sand at the water's edge, she jogged backward a few paces and watched the child who raced through the shallows about thirty yards behind her. Red haired and freckle faced, he was in hot pursuit of a stubby brown-and-white terrier. The dog, in turn, chased a soaring Frisbee. Boy and pet plunged joyously through the shallow surf, oblivious to everything but the purple plastic disc.

Zia's smile widened at their antics but took a quick downward turn when she scanned the shore behind them and failed to spot an adult. Where were the boy's parents? Or his nanny, given that this stretch of beach included several glitzy, high-dollar resorts? Or even an older sibling? The boy was too young to be cavorting in the surf unsupervised.

Anger sliced into her, swift and icy hot. She'd had to deal with the results of parental negligence far too often to view it with complacency. She was feeling the heat of that anger, the sick disgust she had to swallow while treating abused or neglected children, when another cry wrenched her attention back to the boy. This one was high and reedy and tinged with panic.

Her heart stuttering, Zia saw he'd lunged into waves to meet the terrier paddling toward shore with the Frisbee clenched between its jaws. She knew the bank dropped off steeply at that point. Too steeply! And the undertow when the tide went out was strong enough to drag down full-grown adult.

She was already racing back to the boy when he disappeared. She locked her frantic gaze on the spot where his

red hair sank below the waves, crashed into the water and made a flying dive.

She couldn't see him! The receding tide had churned up too much sand. Grit stung her eyes. The ocean hissed and boiled in her ears. She flung out her arms, thrashed them blindly. Her lungs on fire, she thrust out of the water like a dolphin spooked by a killer whale and arced back in.

Just before she went under she caught a glimpse of the terrier's rear end pointed at the sky. The dog dove down at the same instant Zia did and led her to the child being dragged along by the undertow. She shot past the dog. Grabbed the boy's wrist. Propelled upward with fast, hard scissor kicks. She had to swim parallel to the shore for several desperate moments before the vicious current loosened its grip enough for her to cut toward dry land.

He wasn't breathing when she turned him on his back and started CPR. Her head told her he hadn't been in the water long enough to suffer severe oxygen deprivation, but his lips were tinged with blue. Completely focused, Zia ignored the dog that whined and pawed frantic trenches in the sand by the boy's head. Ignored as well the thud of running feet, the offers of help, the deep shout that was half panic, half prayer.

"Davy! Jesus!"

The small chest twitched under Zia's palms. A moment later, the boy's back arched and seawater spewed from his mouth. With a silent prayer of thanksgiving to Saint Stephen, patron saint of her native Hungary, Zia rolled him onto his side and held his head while he hacked up most of what he'd swallowed. When he was done, she eased him down again. His nose ran in twin streams and tears spurted from his eyes but, amazingly, he gulped back his sobs.

"Wh…? What happened?"

She gave him a reassuring smile. "You went out too far and got dragged in by the undertow."

"Did I…? Did I get drowned?"

"Almost."

He hooked an arm around his anxious pet's neck while a slowly dawning excitement edged out the confusion and fear in his brown eyes. "Wait till I tell Mommy and Kevin and *abuelita* and…" His gaze shifted right and latched on to something just over Zia's shoulder. "Uncle Mickey! Uncle Mickey! Did you hear that? I almost got drowned!"

"Yeah, brat, I heard."

It was the same deep baritone that had barely registered with Zia a moment ago. The panic was gone, though, replaced by relief colored with what sounded like reluctant amusement.

Jézus, Mária és József! Didn't this idiot appreciate how close a call his nephew had just had? Incensed, Zia shoved to her feet and spun toward him. She was just about to let loose with both barrels when she realized his amused drawl had been show for the boy's sake. Despite the seemingly laconic reply, his hands were balled into fists and his faded University of Texas T-shirt stretched across taut shoulders.

Very wide shoulders, she couldn't help but note, topped by a tree trunk of a neck and a square chin showing just a hint of a dimple. With her trained clinician's eye for detail, Zia also noted that his nose looked as though it had gotten crosswise of a fist sometime in his past and his eyes gleamed as deep a green as the ocean. His hair was a rich, dark sorrel and cut rigorously short.

The rest of him wasn't bad, either. She formed a fleeting impression of a broad chest, muscular thighs emerging from ragged cutoffs, and bare feet sporting worn leather flip-flops. Then those sea-green eyes flashed her a grateful look and he went down on one knee beside his nephew.

"You, young man," he said as he helped the boy sit up,

"are in deep doo-doo. You know darn well you're not allowed to come down to the beach alone."

"Buster needed to go out."

"I repeat, you are *not* allowed to come down to beach alone."

Zia shrugged off the remnants of the rage that had hit her when she'd thought the boy was allowed to roam unsupervised. She also had to hide a smile at the pitiful note that crept into Davy's voice. Like all five- or six-year olds, he had the whine down pat.

"You said Buster was my 'sponsibility when you gave him to me, Uncle Mickey. You said I had to walk him 'n feed him 'n pick up his poop 'n…"

"We'll continue this discussion later."

Whoa! Even Zia blinked at the *that's enough* finality in the uncle's voice.

"How do you feel?" he asked the boy.

"'Kay."

"Good enough to stand up?"

"Sure."

With the youthful resilience that never failed to amaze Zia, the kid flashed a cheeky grin and scrambled to his feet. His pet woofed encouragement, and both boy and dog would have scampered off if the uncle hadn't laid a restraining hand on his nephew's shoulder.

"Don't you have something you want to say to this lady?"

"Thanks for not letting me get drowned."

"You're welcome."

His uncle kept him in place by a firm grip on his wet T-shirt and held out his other hand to Zia. "I'm Mike Brennan. I can't thank you enough for what you did for Davy."

She took the offered hand, registered its strength and warmth as it folded around hers. "Anastazia St. Sebastian. I'm glad I got to him in time."

* * *

The sheer terror that had rocked Mike's world when he'd spotted this woman hauling Davy's limp body out of the sea had receded enough now for him to focus on her for the first time. Closer inspection damn near rocked him back on his flip-flops again.

Her wet, glistening black hair hung to just below her shoulders. Her eyes were almost as dark as her hair and had just the suggestion of a slant to them. And any supermodel on the planet would have killed for those high, slashing cheekbones. The slender body outlined to perfection by her pink spandex tank and black Lycra running shorts was just icing on the cake. That, and the fact that she wasn't wearing a wedding or engagement ring.

"I think he'll be all right," she was saying with another glance at now fidgeting Davy, "but you might want to keep an eye on him for the next few hours. Watch for signs of rapid breathing, a fast heart rate or low-grade fever. All are common the first few hours after a near drowning."

Her accent was as intriguing as the rest of her. The faint lilt gave her words a different cadence. Eastern European, Mike thought, but it was too slight to pin down.

"You appear to know a lot about this kind of situation. Are you an EMT or first responder?"

"I'm a physician."

Okay, now he was doubly impressed. The woman possessed the mysterious eyes of an odalisque, the body of a temptress and the smarts of a doc. He'd hit the jackpot here. Nodding toward the colorful umbrellas just popping up at the restaurant across the highway from the beach, he made his move.

"I hope you'll let Davy and me show our appreciation by buying you breakfast, Dr. St. Sebastian."

"Thanks, but I've already had breakfast."

No way Mike was letting this gorgeous creature get away. "Dinner, then."

"I'm, uh, I'm here with my family."

"I am, too. Unfortunately." He made a face at his nephew, who giggled and returned the exaggerated grimace. "I'd be even more grateful if you give me an excuse to get away from them for a while."

"Well..."

He didn't miss her brief hesitation. Or her quick glance at *his* left hand. The white imprint of his wedding ring had long since faded. Too bad he couldn't say the same for the inner scars. Shoving the disaster of his marriage into the dark hole where it belonged, Mike overrode her apparent doubts.

"Where are you staying?"

She took her time replying. Those exotic eyes looked him up and down. Lingered for a moment on his faded T-shirt, his ragged cutoffs, his worn leather flip-flops.

"We're at the Camino del Rey," she said finally, almost reluctantly. "It's about a half mile up the beach."

Mike suppressed a smile. "I know where it is. I'll pick you up at seven-thirty." He gave his increasingly impatient nephew's shoulder a squeeze. "Say goodbye to Dr. St. Sebastian, brat."

"Bye, Dr. S'baston."

"Bye, Davy."

"See you later, Anastazia."

"Zia," she said. "I go by Zia."

"Zia. Got it."

Tipping two fingers in a farewell salute, Mike used his grip on his nephew's T-shirt to frog-walk him up the beach.

Zia tracked them as far as the row of houses on stilts fronting the beach. She couldn't believe she'd agreed to dinner with the uncle. As if she didn't have enough on her

mind right now without having to make small talk with a complete stranger!

Arms folded, she watched the terrier jump and cavort alongside them. The dog's exuberance reminded her all too forcefully of the racing hound her sister-in-law had hauled down to Texas with her. Natalie was nutso over the whip-thin Magyar Agár and insisted on calling the hound Duke—much to the chagrin of Zia's brother, Dominic, who still hadn't completely adjusted to his transition from Interpol agent to Grand Duke of Karlenburgh.

The duchy of Karlenburgh had once been part of the vast Austro-Hungarian Empire but had long since ceased to exist anywhere except in history books. That hadn't stopped the paparazzi from hounding Europe's newest royal out of the shadows of undercover work. And Dom had retaliated by sweeping the woman who'd discovered he was heir to the title off her feet and into the ranks of the ever-growing St. Sebastian clan. Now Zia's family included an affectionate, übersmart sister-in-law as well as the two thoroughly delightful cousins she and Dom had met for the first time three years ago.

And, of course, Great-Aunt Charlotte. The regal, iron-spined matriarch of the St. Sebastian family and the woman who'd welcomed Zia into her home and her heart. Zia couldn't imagine how she would have made it this far in her pediatric residency without the duchess's support and encouragement.

Two and a half years, she thought as she abandoned the rest of her morning run to head back to the condo. Twenty-eight months of rounds and call rotations and team meetings and chart prep and discharge conferences. Endless days and nights agonizing over her patients. Heartbreaking hours grieving with parents while burying her own aching loss so deep it rarely crept out to haunt her anymore.

Except at moments like this. When she had to decide

whether she should continue to work with sick children for the next thirty or forty years…or whether she should accept the offer from Dr. Roger Wilbanks, Chief of the Pediatrics Advanced Research Center, to join his team. Could she abandon the challenges and stress of hands-on medicine for the regular hours and seductive income of a world-class, state-of-the-art research facility?

That question churned like battery acid in her gut as she headed for the resort where the St. Sebastian clan was staying. With the morning sun now burning bright in an achingly blue Texas sky, the holiday sun worshippers had begun to flock down to the beach. Umbrellas had flowered open above rows of lounge chairs. Colorful towels were spread on the sand, occupied by bathers with no intention of getting wet. Patches of dead white epidermis just waiting to be crisped showed above skimpy bikini bottoms, along with more than one grossly distended male belly.

Without warning, Zia's mind zinged back to Mike Brennan. No distended belly there. No distended *anything*. Just muscled shoulders and roped thighs and that killer smile. His worn flip-flops and ragged cutoffs suggested a man comfortable with himself in these high-dollar environs. Zia liked that about him.

And now that she thought about it, she actually liked the idea of having dinner with him. Maybe he offered just what she needed. A leisurely evening away from her boisterous family. A few hours with all decisions put on hold. A casual fling…

Whoa! Where had that come from?

She didn't indulge in casual flings. Aside from the fact that her long hours and demanding schedule took so much out of her, she was too careful, too responsible—all right, just too fastidious. Except for one lamentable lapse in judgment, that is. Grimacing, she shrugged aside the memory of the handsome orthopedic surgeon who'd somehow

neglected to mention that his divorce was several light-years from being final.

She was still kicking herself for that sorry mistake when she keyed the door to the two-story, six-bedroom penthouse. Although it was still early morning, the noise level had already inched toward the top of the decibel scale. Most of that was due to her cousin Gina's almost-three-year-old twins. The lively, blue-eyed blondes acted like miniatures of their laughing, effervescent mother…most of the time. This, Zia could tell as shrieks of delight emanated from the living room, was most definitely one of those times.

An answering smile tugged at her lips as she followed the squeals to the living area. Its glass wall offered an eye-boggling panorama of the Gulf of Mexico. Not that any of the occupants of the spacious living room appeared the least interested in the view. They were totally absorbed with the twins' attempts to add blinking red Rudolph noses to the fuzzy reindeer antlers and jingle-bell halters already adorning their uncles. Dominic and Devon sat cross-legged on the floor within easy reach of the twins, while their dad, Jack, watched with diabolical delight.

"What's going on here?" Zia asked.

"Thanta's coming," curly-haired Amalia lisped excitedly. "And…"

"Uncle Dom and Dev are gonna help pull his sled," little Charlotte finished.

The girls were named for the duchess, whose full name and title filled several lines of print. Sarah's and Gina's were almost as long. Zia's, too. Try squeezing Anastazia Amalia Julianna St. Sebastian onto a computer form, she thought as she paused in the doorway to enjoy the merry scene.

No three men could be more dissimilar in appearance yet so similar in character, she decided. Jack Harris, the twins' father and the current United States Ambassador to the United Nations, was tall, tawny haired and aristocratic.

Devon Hunter's hard-fought rise from aircraft cargo handler to self-made billionaire showed in his lean face and clever eyes. And Dominic…

Ahh. Was there anyone as handsome and charismatic as the brother who'd assumed legal guardianship of Zia after their parents died? The friend and advisor who'd guided her through her turbulent teens? The highly skilled undercover agent who'd encouraged her all through college and med school, then walked away from his adrenaline-charged career for the woman he loved?

Natalie loved him, too, Zia thought with an inner smile as her glance shifted to her sister-in-law. Completely, unreservedly, joyously. One look at her face was all *anyone* needed to see the devotion in her warm brown eyes. She occupied one end of a comfortable sofa, her fingers entwined in the collar of the quivering racing hound to prevent him from joining the reindeer brigade.

Zia's cousins sat next to her. Gina, with a Santa hat perched atop her tumble of silvery blond curls and candy-cane-striped leggings, looked more like a teenager than mother of twins, the wife of a highly respected diplomat and a partner in one of NYC's most successful event-hosting enterprises. Gina's older sister, Sarah, occupied the far end of the sofa. Her palms rested lightly on her just-beginning-to-show baby bump and her elegant features showed the quiet joy of impending motherhood.

But it was the woman who sat with her back straight and her hands clasping the ebony head of her cane who caught and held Zia's eye. The Grand Duchess of Karlenburgh was a role model for any female of any age. As a young bride she'd resided in a string of castles scattered across Europe, including the one that guarded a high mountain pass on the border between Austria and Hungary. Then the Soviets invaded and later brutally suppressed an uprising by Hungarian patriots. Forced to witness her husband's execution,

Charlotte had made a daring escape by trekking over the snow-covered Alps with her newborn infant in her arms and a fortune in jewels hidden inside the baby's teddy bear. Now, more than sixty years later, she'd lost none of her dignity or courage or regal bearing. White haired and paper skinned, the indomitable duchess ruled her ever-growing family with a velvet-gloved fist.

She was the reason they were all here, spending the holidays in Texas. Charlotte hadn't complained. She considered whining a deplorable character flaw. But Zia hadn't failed to note how the vicious cold and record snowfall that blanketed New York City in early December had exacerbated the duchess's arthritis. And all it took was one mention of Zia's concern to galvanize the entire St. Sebastian clan.

In short order, Dev and Sarah had leased this six-bedroom condo and set it up as a temporary base for their Los Angeles operations. Jack and Gina had adjusted their busy schedules to enjoy a rare, prolonged holiday in South Texas. Dom and Natalie flew down, too, with the hound in tow. The family had also convinced Maria, the duchess's longtime housekeeper and companion, to enjoy an all-expenses-paid vacation while the staff here at the resort took care of everyone's needs.

Zia hadn't been able to spend quite as much time in Texas as the others. Although Mount Sinai's second- and third-year residents were allowed a full month of vacation, few if any ever strayed far from the hospital. Zia hadn't taken off more than three days in a row since she began her residency. And with the decision of whether to accept Dr. Wilbanks's offer weighing so heavily on her mind, she wouldn't have dragged herself down to Galveston for a full week if Charlotte hadn't insisted. Almost as if she'd read her mind, the duchess looked up at that moment. Her gnarled fingers tightened on the head of her cane. One snowy brow lifted in a regal arch.

* * *

Ha! Charlotte had only to look at Zia to guess what the girl was thinking! That she was so old and decrepit, she needed this bright Texas sunshine to warm her bones. Well, perhaps she did. But she also needed to put some color back into her great-niece's cheeks. She was too pale. Too thin and tired. She'd worn herself to the bone during the first two years of her residency. And worked even more the past few months. But every time Charlotte tried to probe the shadows lurking behind those weary eyes, the girl smiled and fobbed her off with the excuse that exhaustion just was part of being a third-year resident in one of the country's most prestigious medical schools.

Charlotte might not see eighty again, but she wasn't yet senile. Nor was she the least bit hesitant where the well-being of her family was concerned. None of them, Anastazia included, had the least idea that she'd engineered this sojourn in the sun. All it had taken was some not-quite-surreptitious kneading of her arthritic knuckles and one or two few valiantly disguised grimaces. Those, combined with her seemingly offhand comment that New York City felt especially cold and damp this December, had done the trick.

Her family had reacted just as she'd anticipated. Within days they'd sorted through dozens of options from Florida to California and everywhere in between. A villa on the Riviera and over-water bungalows in the South Pacific hadn't been out of the mix, either. But they'd decided on South Texas as the most convenient for both the East and West Coast family contingents. Within a week, Charlotte and Maria had been ensconced in seaside, sun-drenched luxury with various members of the family joining them for differing lengths of time.

Charlotte had even convinced Zia to take off the whole of Christmas week. The girl was still too thin and tired,

but at least her cheeks had gained some color. And, the duchess noted with relief, there was something very close to a sparkle in her eyes. Even more intriguing, her glossy black hair was damp and straggly and threaded with what looked suspiciously like strands of seaweed. Intrigued, she thumped her cane on the floor to get the twins' attention.

"Charlotte, Amalia, please be quiet for a moment."

The girls' high-pitched giggles dropped a few degrees in decibel level, if not in frequency.

"Come sit beside me, Anastazia, and tell me what happened during your run on the beach."

"How do you know something happened?"

"You have kelp dangling from your ear."

Zia patted both ears to find the offending strand. "So I do," she replied, chuckling.

The lighthearted response delighted Charlotte. The girl hadn't laughed very much lately. So little, in fact, that her rippling merriment snagged the attention of every adult in the room.

"Tell us," the duchess commanded. "What happened?"

"Let's see." Playing to her suddenly attentive audience, Zia pretended to search her memory. "A little boy got sucked in by the undertow and I dove in after him. I dragged him to shore, then administered CPR."

"Dear God! Is he all right?"

"He's fine. So is his uncle, by the way. Very fine," she added with a waggle of her brows. "Which is why I agreed to have dinner with him this evening."

Two

As Zia had anticipated, the announcement that she'd agreed to dinner with a total stranger unleashed a barrage of questions. The fact that she knew nothing about him didn't sit well with the overprotective males of her family.

As a result, the whole clan just happened to be gathered for pre-dinner cocktails when the doorman buzzed that evening and announced a visitor for Dr. St. Sebastian. Zia briefly considered taking the coward's way out and slipping down to wait for Brennan in the lobby. But she figured if he couldn't withstand the combined firepower of her brother, cousins and the duchess, she might as well not waste her time with him.

She was waiting at the front door when he exited the elevator. "Hello."

"Hi, Doc."

Wow, Zia thought. Or as some of her younger patients might say, the man was chill! The easy smile was the one she remembered from this morning, but the packaging was completely different. He'd traded his cutoffs and flip-flops for black slacks creased to a knife edge, an open-necked blue oxford shirt and a casually elegant sport coat. The

tooled leather boots and black Stetson were a surprise, however.

Like most Europeans, Zia had grown up on the Hollywood image of cowboys. Tom Selleck in *Last Stand at Sabre River*. Matt Damon in *All The Pretty Horses*. Kevin Costner in *Open Range*. Living in New York City for the past two and a half years hadn't altered her mental stereotype. Nor had she stumbled across many locals here in Galveston who sported the traditional Texas headgear. It looked good on Brennan, though. Natural. As though it was as much a part of him as his air of easy self-assurance and long-legged stride. It also lit a spark of unexpected delight low in her belly. The man was primo in flip-flops or cowboy boots.

She did a mental tongue-swallow and asked about his nephew. "How's Davy?"

"Sulking because he got cut off from TV and videos for the entire day as punishment for skipping out of the house."

"No aftereffects?"

"None so far. His mother's patience is wearing wire thin, though."

"I can imagine."

"My family's having drinks on the terrace. Would you like to say hello?"

"Sure."

"Be prepared," she warned. "There are a lot of them."

"No problem. My Irish grandfather married a Mexican beauty right out of a convent school here on South Padre Island. You haven't experienced big and noisy until you've been to Sunday dinner at my *abuelita*'s house."

Now that he'd mentioned his heritage, Zia could see traces of both cultures. The reddish glint in his dark chestnut hair and those emerald-green eyes hinted at the Irish in him. What she'd assumed was a deep Texas tan might

well be a gift from his Mexican grandmother. Wherever the source, the combination made for a decidedly potent whole!

As she led him to the terrace that wrapped around two sides of the condo, she was glad she'd decided to dress up a bit, too. She spent most of her days in a lab coat with a stethoscope draped around her neck and her rare evenings off in comfortable sweats. She had to admit it had felt good to slither into a silky red camisole and a pair of Gina's tight, straight-leg jeans with a sparkling red crystal heart on the right rear pocket. Gina had also supplied the shoes. The lethal stilettos added three inches to Zia's own five-seven yet still didn't bring her quite to eye level with Mike Brennan.

She'd clipped her hair up in its usual neat knot, but Sarah had insisted on teasing loose a few strands to frame her face. And Dom's wife, Natalie, contributed the twisted copper torque she'd found in a London shop specializing in reproductions of ancient Celtic jewelry. Feeling like Cinderella dressed by three doting fairy godmothers, Zia slid back the glass door to the terrace.

The twelve pairs of eyes that locked on the new arrival might have intimidated a lesser man. To Brennan's credit, his stride barely faltered as he followed Zia onto the wide terrace.

"Hey, everyone," she announced. "Say hello to Mike—"

"Brennan," Dev finished on a startled note. "Aka Global Shipping Incorporated." He pushed to his feet and thrust out his hand. "How're you doing, Mike?"

"I'm good," he replied, obviously as surprised as Dev to find a familiar face at this family gathering. "You're related to Zia?"

"She and my wife, Sarah, are cousins."

"Five or six times removed," Zia added with a smile.

"The degree doesn't matter," Sarah protested. "Not among the St. Sebastians." She aimed a quizzical glance at her husband. "How do you two know each other?"

"Mike here is president and CEO of Global Shipping Incorporated, the third largest cargo container fleet in the US," Dev explained. "We contract for, what? Eight or nine million a year in long-haul shipping with GSI?"

"Closer to ten," Brennan responded.

Zia listened to the exchange in some surprise. In the space of just a few moments her sun-bronzed beach hottie had morphed to cool cowboy dude and now to corporate exec. She was still trying to adjust to the swift transitions when Dev threw in another zinger.

"And now that I think about it, doesn't your corporation own this resort? Along with another dozen or so commercial and industrial facilities in the greater Houston area?"

"We do."

"I'm guessing that's why we got such a good deal on the lease for this condo."

"We try to take care of our valued customers," Brennan acknowledged with a grin.

"Which we certainly appreciate."

Devon's positive endorsement might have carried some weight with outsiders. The two other males on the terrace preferred to form their own opinions, however. Skilled diplomat that he was, Gina's husband, Jack, hid his private assessment behind a cordial nod and handshake. Dominic was less reserved.

"Zia told us your young nephew almost drowned this morning," her brother said, his dark eyes cool. "Pretty careless of your family to let him go down to the beach alone, wasn't it?"

Brennan didn't try to dodge the bullet. A ripple of remembered terror seemed to cross his face as he nodded. "Yes, it was."

Aiming a behave-yourself glance at her brother, Zia introduced her guest to Gina, Maria and Natalie, who kept a firm hand on the collar of the lean, quivering hound eager

to sniff out the new arrival. The twins regarded him from the safety of their mother's knee, but Brennan won giggles from both girls by hunkering down to their level and asking solemnly if that was a tree sprouting from Charlotte's head.

A giggling Amalia answered for her sister. "No, thilly. Those are antlers."

"Oh! I get it. She's one of Santa's reindeer."

"Yes," Charlotte confirmed as she held up two fingers, "and Santa's coming to Texas in this many days!"

"Wow, just two days, huh?"

"Yes, 'n it's our birthday, too!" She uncurled another finger. "We're going to be this many years."

"Sounds like you've got some busy days ahead. You guys better be good so you'll get lots of presents."

"We will!"

With that ringing promise producing wry smiles all around, Zia led Mike to the snowy-haired woman ensconced in a fan-backed rattan chair. He swept off his hat as Zia made the introduction.

"This is my great-aunt, Charlotte St. Sebastian, Grand Duchess of Karlenburgh."

Charlotte held out a blue-veined hand. Mike took it in a gentle grip and held it for a moment. "It's a pleasure to meet you, Duchess. And now I know why Zia's last name seemed so familiar. Wasn't there something in the papers a couple of years ago about your family recovering a long-lost painting by Caravaggio?"

"Canaletto," the duchess corrected.

Her eyelids lowered and her expression turned intensely private, as it always did when talk drifted to the Venetian landscape her husband had given her when she'd become pregnant with their first and only child.

"Would you care for an aperitif?" she asked, emerging from her brief reverie. "We can offer you whatever you wish. Or," she added blandly, "a taste of one of the finest

brandies ever to come out of the Austro-Hungarian Empire."

"Say no and make a polite escape," Gina warned. "*Pálinka* is not for the faint of heart."

"I've been accused of a lot of things," Brennan responded with a crooked grin. "Being faint of heart isn't one of them."

Sarah and Gina exchanged quick, amused glances. Downing a swig of the fruity, throat-searing brandy produced only in Hungary had become something of a rite of passage for men introduced into the St. Sebastian clan. Dev and Jack had passed the test but claimed they still bore the scorch marks on their vocal chords.

"Don't say you weren't warned," Zia murmured after she'd splashed some of the amber liquid into a cut-crystal snifter.

Mike accepted the snifter with a smile. His dad and grandfather had both been hardworking, hard-living longshoremen who'd worked the Houston docks all their lives. Mike and his two brothers had skipped school more times than they could count to hang around the waterfront with them. They'd also worked holidays and summers as casuals, lashing cargo containers or spending long, backbreaking hours shoveling cargo into the holds of cavernous bulk carriers. All three Brennan sons had been offered a coveted slot in the International Longshore and Warehouse Union after they'd graduated from college. Colin and Sean had joined, but Mike had opted for a hitch in the navy instead, then used his savings and a hefty bank loan to buy his first ship—a rusty old tub that made milk runs to Central America. Twelve years and a fleet of oceangoing oil tankers and container vessels later, he could still swear and drink with the best of them.

So he tossed back a swallow of the brandy with absolute certainty that it couldn't pack half the kick of the corrosive

rotgut he'd downed in and out of the navy. He knew he was wrong the instant it hit the back of his throat. He managed not to choke, but his eyes leaked like an old bucket and he had to suck air big-time though his nostrils.

"Wow!" Blinking and breathing fire, he gave the brandy a look of profound respect. "What did you say this is?" he asked the duchess between quick gasps.

"Pálinka."

"And it comes from Austria?"

"From Hungary, actually."

"Anyone ever tried to convert it to fuel? One gallon of this stuff could propel a turbocharged two-stroke diesel engine."

The smile that came into the duchess's faded blue eyes told Mike he'd survived his initial trial by fire. He wasn't ashamed to grab a ready-made excuse to dodge another test.

"I've made reservations at a restaurant just a couple of blocks from here," he told her. "Would you like to join us for dinner?" He turned to include the rest of the family. "Any of you?"

Charlotte answered for them all. "Thank you, but I'm sure Zia would prefer not to have her family regale you with stories about her misspent youth. We'll let her do that herself."

Once in the elevator, Mike propped his shoulders against the rear of the cage dropping them twenty stories. "Misspent?" he echoed. "I'm intrigued."

More than intrigued. He was as fascinated by this woman's stunning beauty as by the dark circles under her eyes. She'd tried to conceal them with makeup but the shadows were still visible, like faint bruises marring the pearly luster of her skin.

"I guess *misspent* is as good a description as any," she replied with a laugh. "But in my defense I only tried to op-

erate on the family dog once. My brother, unfortunately, didn't get off as easily. I subjected him to all kinds of torture in the name of medicine."

"Looks like he survived okay."

He also looked decidedly less than friendly. Mike didn't blame the man. He and *his* brothers had threatened bodily harm to any male who let his glands get out of control while dating one of their sisters.

God knew Mike's glands were certainly working overtime. Despite those faint shadows under her eyes, Anastazia St. Sebastian was every man's secret fantasy come to life. Slender, graceful and so sexy she turned heads as they crossed the marble-tiled lobby and exited into the six acres of lush gardens at the center of the Camino del Rey complex.

The vacation complex was only one of several projects Mike's ever-expanding corporation had invested in to help restore Galveston after Hurricane Ike roared ashore in September 2008. The costliest hurricane in Texas history, Ike claimed more than a hundred lives and did more than $37 billion in damage all along the Gulf. Parts of Galveston were still recovering, but major investments like this beautifully landscaped luxury resort were helping that process considerably.

A frisky ocean breeze teased Zia's hair as she and Mike wound past the massive Neptune fountain the landscape architect had made the focal point of the gardens. Beyond the statue were two tall, elaborately designed wrought-iron gates that gave directly onto the beach. On the opposite side of the garden, a set of identical gates exited onto San Luis Pass Road, the main artery that ran the length of Galveston Island.

"I made reservations at Casa Mia," Mike said as he took her elbow to steer her through the gates. "Hope that's okay."

"This is my first trip to Galveston. I'm more than happy to trust the judgment of a local."

Temperatures in South Texas during the summer could give hell a run for its money. In the dead of winter, however, the balmy days and sixty-five-degree evenings were close to heaven…and perfect for strolling the wide sidewalk that bordered San Luis Pass Road. Smooth operator that he was, Mike casually shifted his hold from Zia's elbow to her forearm. Her skin was warm under his palm, her muscles firm and well-toned. He used the short walk to fill in the essential blanks. Found out she was born in Hungary. Did her undergraduate work at the University of Budapest. Graduated from medical school in Vienna at the top of her class. Had offers from a half-dozen prestigious pediatric residency programs before opting for Mount Sinai in New York City.

She elicited the same basics from him. "Texas born and bred," he admitted cheerfully. "I traveled quite a bit during my years in the navy, but this area kept pulling me back. It's home to four generations of Brennans now. My parents, grandparents, one brother and two of my three sisters all live within a few blocks of each other."

She eyed the ultraexpensive high-rises crowding the beachfront. "Here on the island?"

"No, they live in Houston. So do I, most of the time. I keep a place here on the island for the family to use, though. The kids all love the beach."

"And you're not married."

It was a statement, not a question, which told Mike she wouldn't be walking through the soft evening light with him if she had any doubts about the matter.

"I was. Didn't work out."

That masterful understatement came nowhere close to describing three months of mind-blowing sex followed by three years of growing restlessness, increasing dissatisfac-

tion, angry complaints and, finally, corrosive bitterness. Hers, not his. By the time the marriage was finally over Mike felt as though he'd been dragged through fifty miles of Texas scrub by his heels. He'd survived, but the experience wasn't one he wanted to repeat again in this lifetime. Although…

His psyche might still be licking its wounds but his head told him marriage would be different with the right woman. Someone who appreciated the dogged determination required to build a multinational corporation from the ground up. Someone who understood that success in *any* field often meant seventy- or eighty-hour workweeks, missed vacations, opting out of a spur-of-the-moment junket to Vegas.

Someone like the leggy brunette at his side.

Mike slanted the doc a glance. One of his sisters was a nurse. He knew the demands Kathleen's career made on her and on the other professionals she worked with. Anastazia St. Sebastian had to have a core of steel to make it as far as she had.

His curiosity about the woman mounted as they turned onto a side street. A few steps later they reached the Spanish-style villa that had recently become one of Galveston's most exclusive spots. It sat behind tall gates with no sign, no lit menu box, no indication at all that it was a commercial establishment. But the hundreds of flickering votive lights in the courtyard drew a pleased gasp from Zia, and the table tucked in a private corner of the candle-lit patio was the one always made available to the top officers and favored clients of Global Shipping Incorporated.

"Back to subjecting your bother to all kinds of medical torture," he said when they'd been seated and ordered an iced tea for the doc and Vizcaya on ice for Mike, who sincerely hoped a slug of white rum would kill the lingering aftereffects of *pálinka*. "Did you always want to be a physician?"

"Always."

The reply was quick but not quite as light as she'd obviously intended. Mike hadn't survived all those summers and holidays in the bare-knuckle world of the docks without learning to pick up on every nuance, spoken or not.

"But....?" he prompted.

She flashed him a look that ran the gamut from surprised to guarded to deliberately blasé. "Med school's been a long and rather grueling slog. I'm in the homestretch now, though."

"But...?" he said again, the word soft against the clink of cutlery and buzz of conversation from other tables.

The arrival of the server with their drinks saved Zia from having to answer. She hadn't shared her insidious doubts with anyone in her family. Not even Dominic. Yet as she sipped her iced tea she felt the most absurd urge to spill her guts to this stranger.

So why *not* confide in him? Odds were she'd never see the man again after tonight. There were only a few days left on her precious vacation. And judging from Dev's comments about Global Shipping Inc., its president and CEO had a shrewd head on his shoulders. Granted, he couldn't begin to understand the demands and complexities of the medical world but that might actually be a plus. An outsider could assess her situation objectively, without the baggage of having cheered and supported and encouraged her through six and a half years of med school and residency.

"But," she said slowly, swirling the ice in her tall glass, "I'm beginning to wonder if I'm truly right for pediatric medicine."

"Why?"

She could toss out a hundred reasons. Like the overwhelming sense of responsibility for patients too young or too frightened to tell her how they hurt. The aching helplessness when faced with children beyond saving. The

struggle to contain her fury at parents or guardians whose carelessness or cruelty inflicted unbelievably grievous injuries.

But the real reason, the one she'd thought she could compensate for by going into pediatric medicine, rose up to haunt her. She'd never talked about it to anyone but Dom. And even he was convinced she'd put it behind her. Yet reluctantly, inexplicably, Zia found herself detailing the old pain to Mike Brennan.

"I developed a uterine cyst my first year at university," she said, amazed that she could speak so calmly of the submucosal fibroid that had changed her life forever. "It ruptured during winter break, while I was on a ski trip in Slovenia."

She'd thought at first that she'd started her period early but the pain had become more intense with each hour. And the blood! Dear God, the blood!

"I almost died before they got me to the hospital. At that point the situation was so desperate the surgeons decided the only way to save my life was to perform an emergency hysterectomy."

She fell silent as the waiter materialized at their table to take their order. Mike sent him away with a quiet, "Give us some time."

"I love children," Zia heard herself say into the silence that followed. "I always imagined I'd have a whole brood of happy, gurgling babies. When I accepted that I would never give birth to a child of my own, I decided that at least I could help alleviate the pain and suffering of others."

"But…"

There it was. That damned "but" that had her hanging from a limb like a bird with a broken wing.

"It's hard giving so much of myself to others' children," she finished, her voice catching despite every attempt to control it. "So much harder than I ever imagined."

Her doubt and private misery filled the silence that spun out between them. Mike broke it after a moment with a question that cut to the core of her bruising inner conflict.

"What will you do if you don't practice medicine?"

"I'll stay in the medical field, but work on another side of the house."

There! She'd said it out loud for the first time. And not to her brother or Natalie or the duchess or her cousins. To a stranger, who didn't appear shocked or disappointed that she would trade her lifelong goal of treating the sick for the sterile environment of a lab.

Like all third-year residents at Mount Sinai, she'd been required to participate in a scholarly research project in addition to seeing patients, attending conferences and teaching interns. Worried by the seeming increase in hospital-acquired infections among the premature infants in the neonatal ICU, she'd searched for clues via five years' worth of medical records. Her extensive database included the infants' birth weight, ethnic origin, delivery methods, the time lapse to onset of infections, methods of treatment and mortality rates.

Although she wouldn't brief the results of her study until the much anticipated annual RRP—Residents' Research Presentation—her preliminary findings had so intrigued the hospital's director of research that he'd suggested an expanded effort that included more variables and a much larger sample base. He'd also asked Zia to conduct the two-year study under his direct supervision. If the grant came through within the next few months, she could start the research as her spring elective, then join Dr. Wilbanks's team full-time after completing her residency.

"The director of pediatric research at Mount Sinai has already asked me to join his staff," she confided to Mike.

"Is that as impressive as it sounds?"

A hint of pride snuck into her voice. "Actually, it is. Dr.

Wilbanks seems to think the study I've been working on as a resident is worth expanding into a full-fledged team effort. He also thinks it might warrant as much as a million-dollar research grant."

"That *is* impressive. What does the study involve?"

Lord, he was easy to talk to. Zia didn't usually discuss topics such as Methicillin-resistant Staphylococcus aureus, aka MRSA, with someone not wearing scrubs. Especially during a candlelit dinner.

As the incredibly scrumptious meal progressed, however, Brennan's interest stimulated her as much as his quick grasp of the essentials of her study.

She couldn't blame either his interest or his intellect for what happened when they left the restaurant, however. That was result of a lethal combination of factors. First, their decision to walk back along the beach. Zia had to remove her borrowed stilettos to keep from sinking in the sand, but the feel of it hard and damp beneath bare feet only added to her heightened perceptions. Then there was the three-quarter moon that traced a liquid silver path across the sea. And finally the arm Mike slid around her waist.

She turned into his kiss, fully anticipating that it would be pleasant. A satisfying end to an enjoyable evening. She *didn't* expect the hunger that balled in her belly when his mouth fused with hers.

He felt the kick, too. Although his hat brim shadowed his eyes when he raised his head, his skin was stretched tight across his cheeks and there was a gruff edge to his voice when he asked if she'd like to stop by his place for coffee or a drink.

Or…?

He didn't have to say it. Her pulse kicking, Zia knew the invitation was open-ended. "Don't you have company?

Davy and…" She searched her memory. "And Kevin and their mother?"

"Eileen took the kids back to town this afternoon. I suspect she won't let either of them close to the water for the next five years. She wants to thank you personally, by the way. She told me to be sure and get your phone number." Laughter rumbled in his chest. "I promised I would."

Zia hesitated for all of three seconds before digging her cell phone out of her purse. "I'll text my family and tell them not to wait up for me."

Three

The brief detour to Mike's place should have allowed plenty of time for Zia's common sense to reassert itself. *Would* have, if he hadn't taken her arm again to steer her toward a barely discernible path through the dunes. His hand was warm against her skin, his body close—too close!—to hers in the silvery moonlight.

The beach house on stilts he conducted her to was obviously new. Gleaming a pale turquoise in the moonlight, it sat on a high rise that gave it an unobstructed view of both the Gulf of Mexico and the lights of Houston gleaming in the far distance. The thick pilings looked as though they went down a mile, and white-painted storm shutters framed every window.

When Mike ushered her up the stairs to the front landing and keyed the door lock, Zia still had time to defuse the situation. Once inside, she could have drifted to the wall of windows overlooking the Gulf. Could have contemplated the moon's reflection on the dark, restless sea. Could have accepted his offer of an after-dinner brandy or coffee. Against every increasingly strident warning issued by her clinical, careful self, she ignored the view and declined a drink. Weeks of stress, indecision and near ex-

haustion got lost in a rush of biological need. For what was left of the night, she didn't want to think. Didn't want to do anything but give herself up to the hunger pulsing through her in slow, liquid rolls.

And Brennan didn't waste time repeating the offer. Tugging off his hat, he skimmed it carelessly toward the nearest chair and cupped her face in his palms.

"You are *so* gorgeous."

His thumbs brushed her cheeks, her lower lip. An answering need turned his forest-glade eyes as dark and restless as the sea. Zia felt another wild leap as she sensed the iron control that held him back. He was leaving it to her to dodge the bullet hurtling at them in warp speed...or step in front of it. She chose option B.

Dropping the stilettos she'd carried into the house, she hooked her arms around his neck. "So are you."

"Me? Gorgeous?" He looked startled, then amused. "Not hardly, darlin'."

The drawl came slow and rich, and the laughter in his eyes raised goose bumps of delight. That, and the quick, confident way he claimed her mouth. He was much a man, this Michael Brennan.

Very much a man, as she discovered when he lowered his hands to her waist and drew her into him. He hardened against her hip even as his lips moved over hers with dizzying skill. He'd been married, she remembered, and had learned well how to stoke a woman's fire. She was panting when he raised his head. Eager for his touch when he fumbled the clip from her hair. The heavy mass tumbled free, and Brennan buried his hands in it, holding her steady while he explored her mouth again.

With every nerve in her body alive and clamoring, Zia conducted her own avid exploration. Her palms planed his broad shoulders. Her fingers found the lapels of his sport coat. She peeled it back, forcing him to break contact long

enough to wrestle free of it. He reached for her again but
felt compelled to offer a gruff caveat.

"Just so you know, I don't make a habit of trying to finesse women I've just met into bed."

"Nor," she murmured, her acquired New York twang
slipping away a little more with each word, "do I allow
myself to be finessed."

The blood of her Magyar ancestors thrummed hot in her
veins. She felt as wild as the steppes they'd swept down
from on their fast, tireless ponies. As fierce as winds that
howled through the mountains and valleys they'd eventually settled in.

"But tonight I shall make an exception, yes?"

"*Hell*, yes!"

He scooped her up almost before the words were out
of her mouth. Cradling her against his chest, he headed
in what she assumed was the direction of the bedroom.
She used the short trip to attack the buttons on his crisp
blue shirt.

She got the top two open and was nipping at the cords in
his neck when he elbowed a door open. She gained a vague
impression of wide-plank floorboards, sparse furnishings
and framed posters of ships filling one wall. Then he was
lowering her to a king-size bed covered in thin, buttery-
soft suede.

Mike shed his shirt, boots and jeans with minimal
motion and maximum speed. A real trick, considering
that every drop of blood had drained from his head and
was now pooled below his waist. He couldn't believe he'd
managed to get the exotic, intriguing doc in his bed, but
he sure as hell wasn't about to give her time for second
thoughts.

Yet he dredged up enough self-control to strip her slowly,
item by tantalizing item. The silky camisole. The thigh-
hugging jeans with the sparkly red heart that had drawn

his eyes to her butt every time she'd walked in front of him. Her half bra and thong were mere scraps of lace and easily disposed of. Then he made the near fatal mistake of pausing to drink in the sight of her long, slender curves. She gleamed like alabaster against the pearl-gray bedcover. Her hair spilled across the suede, as silky and erotic as the dark triangle at the apex of her thighs. Mike almost lost it then. Probably would have, if he hadn't gritted his teeth and held back the raging tide with the promise of exploring every slope and hollow of that luscious body.

Thank God he kept an emergency supply of condoms in the nightstand. The cache was a year old. Maybe more. With the demand for super-container ships skyrocketing and his fleet expanding almost faster than he could keep up with it, Mike hadn't had all that many opportunities to dip into this private stash. He intended to make up for those missed opportunities now, though.

If he could find the damned things! Muttering a curse under his breath, he rifled through the drawer. Where the devil had all this junk come from? With another muffled curse, he finally resorted to dumping the contents on the bed. Two dog-eared paperbacks, a handful of loose change, a spare set of keys, several socks and a plastic fire truck tumbled out.

Zia pushed up on one elbow and eyed the hook and ladder. "I've seen all kinds of sex toys during my years in med school," she said with a grin. "Some were put to rather remarkable use. But that's a new one."

"Dammit, I told Kevin and Davy to stay out… Ah! Thank God." He gave a huff of relief and held up two foil packets. "I caught the boys making water balloons out of them four or five months back but was sure I'd salvaged a few."

Four or five months back? Zia digested that little tidbit of information as he used his teeth to rip into one of the

packets. Brennan must not bring many female friends to his beach house. The thought surprised her. And added another bubble to the cauldron that erupted into a furious boil at the sight of him sheathing himself.

He made quick work of it. A snap, a roll, and he tumbled her back onto the suede. He followed her down, bracing himself on his elbows to kiss her again. And again. And again. Her mouth. Her throat. Her aching breasts. Her quivering belly. When he eased a hand between her thighs, Zia went taut as a bow.

Yes! This was what she needed. What both her mind and her body craved. This wild pleasure. This dizzying spiral of excitement that contracted the muscles low in her belly. With each kiss and stroke of his busy fingers, the spasms got tighter, faster.

"Wait."

She clenched her jaw, tried to clamp down on the soaring sensations.

"Mike. Wait." She scrunched deeper into the velvety suede and reached for him. "Let me… Oh!"

Before she could do more than wrap her fingers around his rock-hard length the sensations spun into a white-hot core. Groaning, Zia gave up trying to stop the climax that shot up from her belly. She couldn't have held back if she'd wanted to. It came at her like an out-of-control freight train.

Neck arched, spine bowed, she rode it to the last shuddering sigh. When she collapsed onto the covers and opened her eyes, she saw Brennan watching her.

"Sorry," she murmured. "It's, ah, been a while."

"Oh, sweetheart." He was still hard and rampant against her hip. His shoulders were still taut, his tendons tight. Yet his grin contained nothing but smug male satisfaction. "You wouldn't be sorry if you had any idea how glorious you just looked."

Zia had studied human sexuality and the reproductive

process, of course. She could put a name to each stage of her body's response. Desire. Arousal. Lubrication. Orgasm. Satisfaction. She also knew the female of the species could generally repeat the cycle faster than the male. Still, she was surprised at *how* fast. All it took was for Mike to lean down and feather his lips over hers. The kiss was so tender—and such a contrast to the tension still locking his muscles—that Zia kicked into high gear again.

He filled her. Stroked her. Pushed her to another peak. She hung on this time and refused go over the edge without him.

Gasping and limp with pleasure, Zia knew she should get up, get dressed and go home. *Should* drifted into *later* when Mike defied conventional science by proving he could repeat the cycle after only a minimal break.

If the first round was fast and urgent, the second round was exquisitely slow. So slow, Zia had more than enough time to explore his hard, muscled body. The corded tendons, the washboard ribs, the flat belly, the five-inch scar on his left shoulder. She'd set enough stitches during her ER rotation to know a knife wound when she felt one.

"How did you get this?"

"Hmm?"

He shifted, obviously more interested her body than his own

"This scar?" she persisted. "How'd you get it?"

"It was just a slight misunderstanding."

"Between?"

"Me and a one-eyed, foul-breathed Portuguese. He was a pumper on the tanker I shipped out on the summer before my senior year in high school."

"And?"

"Let's just say Joachim didn't appreciate smart-assed

kids pointing out he hadn't grounded himself before opening the feed nozzle. Now…"

His hands cupped her butt and scooted her up a few
inches.

"Let's get back to more important matters."

Zia hadn't planned to zone out. Grabbing twenty or thirty
minutes to recharge in the residents' lounge had pretty much
become a way of life. All she'd intended was a brief cat-
nap between the sheets with her head nestled in the warm
angle between Brennan's neck and shoulder. So when she
blinked awake to a blaze of sunlight spilling through the
wide windows she gave a small yelp.

"Oh, no!"

She jerked upright and pushed her hair out of her eyes. A
quick glance around confirmed her hazy impressions from
last night. The flooring *was* wide oak planking polished
to a rich sheen. One wall *did* sport a collection of framed,
poster-size photographs of oceangoing vessels. And she
huddled amid a welter of silky cotton sheets topped by a
cloud-soft suede cover. Naked. With what felt like a good-
size patch of beard burn on her left cheek.

Oh, for heaven's sake! She was an adult. Responsible
and unattached. She had no reason to feel guilty or uncomfortable about explaining a whisker scrape to her family.
Or the fact that she'd spent the night with an interesting,
attractive man.

A man who evidently knew his way around a kitchen.
She discovered that after she'd made a trip to the bathroom,
scrambled into her clothes and followed the scent of frying
bacon. Mike had a small feast laid out on a glass-topped
breakfast table with a breath-knocking view of the Gulf.
Her surprised glance slid over the juice, sliced melon and
basket of croissants to lock on a tall carafe.

With a melodramatic groan, she made her presence

known. "Please tell me that's coffee," she begged, nodding to the carafe.

Mike angled around, spatula in hand, and grinned. "It is. Help yourself."

She did, but one sip had her gasping. "Good Lord!"

"Too strong?"

"Strong doesn't begin to describe it. This makes the black tar in the resident's lounge taste good by comparison."

"Sorry. I try to remember not everyone likes navy swill. Guess I didn't water it down enough. Why don't you run another pot?"

"That's okay. I'll just doctor this one."

Several ounces of milk and two heaping spoons of sugar made the coffee marginally more palatable. Sipping cautiously, Zia leaned her hip against the marble-topped island and watched the man work. She couldn't help noting how his faded University of Texas T-shirt molded his broad shoulders and his chestnut hair showed glints of dark red in the morning sunlight. She also noticed that he wielded the spatula with easy confidence.

The bacon cooked, he drained the grease and swiped the pan with paper towels before offering her a choice. "I've got the makings for a Spanish omelet and French toast. We can do either or both."

"You don't need to go to all that trouble. I'm fine with just coffee and a roll."

"I'm not," he countered, a smile in those sexy green eyes. "We burned up the calories last night. I need sustenance. So...omelet or French toast or both?"

"Omelet. Please."

Zia settled onto one of the stools lined up at the island, a little surprised she didn't feel even a trace of morning-after awkwardness. Not that the absence should surprise her. Mike Brennan had proved an easy, attentive companion

at dinner last night. She'd opened up to him about doubts and worries she hadn't even shared with Dom yet.

Which reminded her...

She'd carried her purse into the kitchen with her. She fished out her cell phone, so glad she'd sent that text last night so Dom wouldn't have the police out searching for her maimed and mutilated body. She skimmed over the list of messages and saved them to be read later before sending a brief text saying she'd be home soon. That done, she refilled her coffee cup and watched a master at work.

"Where did you learn to cook?" she asked, marveling at his chopping, browning and omelet-flipping skills.

"That one-eyed Portuguese I told you about? Joachim Caldero? He pulled doubled duty as pumper and cook. Bastard jumped ship in Venezuela. Since I was the junior crew dog aboard, the captain stuck me with galley duty." He slid the first omelet onto a plate and poured the remaining egg mixture into the frying pan. "It was either dish up canned pork and beans all the way back to Galveston or teach myself a few basic skills."

She admired the perfect half oval. "Looks like you learned more than the basics."

"I added to my repertoire over the years," he admitted with a shrug. "My ex-wife wasn't into cooking."

Or anything else that didn't involve exclusive spas and high-end boutiques. Mike didn't look back often. Nor did he wallow in regrets. But as he added diced peppers and onions to the second omelet, he had to force the memory of his soured marriage out of his head. The outing took surprisingly little effort with this stunning, dark-haired beauty watching him with admiring eyes. Playing to his audience, he flipped the omelet into a perfect crescent and let it firm before sliding it onto a plate.

"Bring your coffee," he instructed as he added bacon strips to each plate and led the way to the breakfast table.

* * *

Mike already knew he wanted more time with Dr. Anastazia St. Sebastian. Arranging a follow-up assignation turned out to be a challenge, however.

"I need to spend time with my family," she said when he proposed getting together later. "It's Christmas Eve," she added when the significance of the day failed to register with Mike.

"Oh, hell. So it is."

No way he could duck the mandatory family gathering. With its dense Hispanic concentration, the four-block area of Houston where his grandmother lived still clung to the old ways. The entire Brennan clan would gather at her house this afternoon for food and games. Come dusk, they'd troop outside to watch the traditional *posada*. Local teenagers had been chosen to portray Mary and Joseph, and the whole parish would follow with lit candles and paper lanterns.

After the procession, it was back to his *abuelita*'s to hoist the star-shaped piñata. The seven-pointed star held all kinds of religious significance, most of which Mike had forgotten. There were devils in there. He remembered that much. They had to be beaten out with a stick, with the reward being the candy that showered down on shouting, squealing kids. After that came a feast of gargantuan proportions. Tamales, *atole, buñuelos*, and *ponche*—the potent hot drink brewed from spiced fruits.

Then the Irish portion of Mike's heritage would take over. He would accompany his parents and assorted siblings to midnight Mass. Go home with them for the inevitable last-minute toy assembly and gift-wrapping. And crash until the entire clan reconvened at his parents' house Christmas morning for an orgy of present opening followed by the traditional turkey dinner.

Mike had always enjoyed the nonstop celebrations. Even when his ex-wife was at her worst. Jill had alienated every-

one in the family, but she'd never managed to destroy their enjoyment in the traditions they celebrated year after year.

Tradition was one thing, Mike thought as he eyed the woman seated across the table. Anastazia St. Sebastian was another. He'd met her less than twenty-four hours ago. Still, he would cheerfully abandon any and all family rituals for a chance to spend another evening with her.

Oh, hell! Who was he kidding? He wanted more than an evening. He wanted another entire night. Or two. Three.

"What about tomorrow? After all the presents have been opened and everyone's feasted? You might need a break from the family. I know I will."

"Tomorrow's full. It's Christmas and the twins' birthday."

"The day after?"

He was pushing too hard. He knew it. But he hadn't gotten where we was today by conceding defeat without a fight. And he still had an ace in the hole.

"Actually, I have an ulterior motive for wanting to see you again."

Her inky-black brows drew together. "Ulterior?"

He could see her turning that over in her mind. Maybe wondering if she'd walked into something here. She had, but Mike didn't want to scare her off.

"Last night at dinner you told me a little about the research you're doing. I'd like to know more."

The groove in her forehead deepened. "Why?"

"GSI has an entire division dedicated to studying and implementing technological improvements. Most of our efforts focus on the petroleum and shipping industries, of course, but we've funded research in other areas, as well."

"Medical research?"

He leaned forward, all business now. "We were part of a study last year to look at the exposure of crew members to carcinogenic agents on the decks of crude oil tankers.

It assessed the effects of the lead chromate paint used in cargo holds. I've also got my people looking at ways to contain the spread of norovirus. It doesn't hit only cruise ships," he admitted wryly.

"But I'm looking specifically at MRSA and its rate of incidence in newborn infants."

"You might be interested to know two Galveston seamen sued the owners of the *Cheryl K* for two million dollars a few years back. They claimed the owners failed to inform them of an allegedly high presence of bacteria on the vessel. Both seamen became infected with MRSA."

Mike had actually forgotten about that incident until Zia mentioned the virulent virus last night. He'd hit the internet this morning, though, and was now armed with specific details.

"The men reportedly suffered multiple infections to their extremities, backs and other parts of their body. Their suit accused Cheryl K Inc. and its namesake ship of general maritime negligence, unseaworthiness and failure to pay maintenance and cure."

He'd snagged her. He saw the interest spark in her eyes and slowly, carefully reeled her in.

"If you could squeeze out an hour or so, you could talk to the head of our Support Division. He's the one who manages our technology and research divisions."

"I would love to but I fly back to New York on Friday."

"Then we'll have to do it today or tomorrow."

"You wouldn't make your man come in on Christmas Eve!"

"Actually, he's my brother-in-law. Trust me. Rafe will grab at any excuse to escape the chaos for an hour or two."

She chewed on her lower lip, obviously torn. "How about I call you after I talk to my family and see what the plans are?"

"That works." He grabbed a pen and scribbled his cell

phone number on a napkin. Once she'd tucked it in the pocket of her jeans, he pushed away from the table. "If you're ready, I'll walk you back to the resort."

"You don't need to do that."

"Sure I do." He took her hand and tugged her out of her seat. "I also need to do this."

She came into his arms so easily, so naturally. The satisfaction that gave Mike didn't come close to the jolt that hit him when she tipped her head and returned his kiss, though. The taste of her, the feel of her, raised an instant, erotic response in every part of his body. And the little purr in her throat damned near doubled him over.

He spent the entire walk back to the resort plotting ways to delay Dr. St. Sebastian's return to New York.

Four

Zia key-carded the condo's main entrance and braced herself for the inquisition ahead. To her profound relief, the male half of the St. Sebastian clan had already departed for a round of golf. The females were lingering over cups of coffee and tea before a girding up for a final shopping foray. The adult females, anyway. The twins, Gina informed Zia before she pounced, were down at the resort's kiddie playground with Maria and the hound.

"So tell us! Was Brennan as yummy in bed as he is in person?"

"Really, Eugenia." The duchess sent her granddaughter a pained look. "Do try for a little more refinement."

"Forget refinement," Sarah interjected, crossing her hands over her belly. "We want details."

Even Natalie endorsed the demand, although she prefaced it with a solemn promise *not* to share those details with Dom.

"There's not much to tell," Zia answered, grinning. *"Vidi, vici, veni."*

Despite her bubbly personality and careless tumble of curls, Gina was no dummy. She picked up immediately

on the variation of Caesar's famous line and gave a hoot
of delight.

"No way you're getting away with just that, Zia Mia. We
need more than 'I saw, I conquered, I came.'"

"Eugenia!" The duchess issued a distinct huff. "If
Anastazia wishes to explain why she spent the night with
a complete stranger, she will."

"I didn't intend to," Zia admitted with a sheepish grin as
she dropped into an empty chair. "We had a lovely dinner
and talked about…about all kind of things."

The duchess didn't miss the brief hesitation. Charlotte
cocked her head, her shrewd gaze intent on her great-niece's
face, but kept silent. She disapproved of casual sex with all
its inherent dangers and complications. Not that she hadn't
indulged in one or two liaisons during her long years as a
widow. The brief affairs couldn't erase the pain of losing
her husband, of course, but they had helped to lighten it.

Just as last night appeared to have lightened some of the
shadows in her great-niece's eyes. Seeing the smile that
now filled them, Charlotte gave the absent Mike Brennan
her silent stamp of approval.

"Then after dinner," Zia continued, "when we were
walking home in the moonlight, he kissed me."

Gina pursed her lips in a long, low whistle. "That must
have been some kiss."

"It was. Believe me, it was."

That produced several moments of silence, which the
irrepressible Gina broke with a snicker. "So you tumbled
into bed and did the happy dance. What happens now? Are
you and Mike going to see each other again?"

"He wants to. But it's Christmas. Like me, he's got family obligations. And I'm flying back to New York Friday
morning, so…"

"So nothing! Much as we love you, cousin of mine, we'll

understand if you decide to absent yourself for a couple of hours. Or," she added with a wicked grin, "nights."

"Thanks," Zia said wryly. "Nice to know I won't be missed. But there's no point in getting together with Mike again, as hunky as he is. He's based here in Texas, I'm in New York. For the next few months, anyway. After that..."

"After that, you'll stay in the States," Gina finished firmly. "Your family lives here. Dom and Natalie, all of us. And you're already getting offers from children's hospitals all across the country. Any of them would be lucky to have a physician with your smarts. Who knows?" she added with a gleam in her blue eyes. "You may end up here in Houston. So, yes, you should most definitely steal away with the hunk for another few hours."

To everyone's surprise, it was the duchess who settled the matter. She'd picked up on Zia's vague reference to the future and watched her face during Gina's declaration. Folding her hands on the top of her cane, she held her great-niece's gaze.

"If I've learned nothing else in my eighty plus years, Anastazia, it's that one must trust one's instincts. As you must trust yours."

She knew, Zia realized. Maybe not the exact parameters of the decision she'd been struggling with. But the duchess had obviously guessed something was weighing on her heart. Chagrined, Zia leaned over and kissed the papery skin of her cheek.

"Thank you, Aunt. I will."

Mike answered on the second ring. He didn't try to hide his satisfaction when she told him she'd like to take him up on his offer to learn more about his company's research programs.

"I can slip away for a few hours today if that doesn't mess up your plans for Christmas Eve."

"Not at all. I was just about to shut down the beach house and head into Houston. I'll pick you up."

"Then you'll have to drive all the way back out to the island."

"Not a problem."

Maybe not, but Zia had some serious showering and makeup repairs to attend to. "Also not necessary," she said firmly. "I've got a whole fleet of rental cars at my disposal. Give me the address of your corporate offices and a good time to meet you there."

Zia pulled into the underground parking lot of the steel-and-glass tower housing the corporate headquarters of Global Shipping Incorporated a little before two that afternoon. Following Mike's instructions, she found the GSI guest parking slots and took the elevator to the three-story lobby dominated by a monster Christmas tree. Bubbling fountains and a rippling stream cut through a good half acre of marble tile, serenading her as she checked in at the security desk.

The uniformed guard wished her happy holidays and checked her ID. "I'll let Mr. Brennan know you're here," he said, handing her a bar-coded guest pass. "Take the first elevator on the left. It'll shoot you right to the GSI offices."

"Thanks."

The express elevator opened to a reception area with an eagle's-eye view of the Houston skyline. An electronic map of the world took up one entire wall, with flashing lights designating GSI's ships at sea. Zia's eyes widened at the array of green and amber dots. The legend beside the map tagged the green dots as cargo ships and the amber ones as oil tankers.

She was trying to guesstimate the total number when Mike emerged from an inner office accompanied by the individual she presumed was his brother-in-law. Both wore

jeans and open-necked shirts but the similarity stopped there. Where Mike was tall, tanned and green-eyed, the man with him had jet-black hair, a pencil-thin mustache and a smile that emitted at least a thousand kilowatts of wow-power.

"Hello, Zia."

They strode forward to greet her, presenting a double whammy of pure masculinity.

"This is Rafe Montoya, GSI's VP for Support Systems. The poor guy's married to my sister Kathleen."

"It's a pleasure to meet you, Dr. St. Sebastian."

"Please, call me Zia."

"Zia it is." He took her hand in both of hers. "The whole family's still shaken over Davy's near miss yesterday. You have our deepest gratitude."

"I'm just glad I was there."

"So are we." Releasing her hand, he cut right to the reason they'd congregated in the empty office building. "I understand you're an expert in bacterial infections."

"Not an expert, by any means, but I'm compiling statistical data on the increasing incidence of infectious diseases in newborn infants."

"A disturbing trend, certainly. As is the increasing incidence of both bacterial and viral infections among crews at sea. Would you like to see some of the data we've collected?"

"Very much."

"I set up my laptop in Miguel's office."

"Miguel?" she echoed as Mike gestured to the set of double doors leading to the inner sanctum.

"Miguel, Mick, Mickey, Mike, Michael. I answer to any and all."

"Don't forget your sisters' favorite," his brother-in-law interjected, pitching his voice to a reedy falsetto. "Mike-eee."

With a good-natured grimace, Mike-eee ushered her

into a spacious, light-filled office. It was surprisingly un-cluttered. The desk was a slab of acrylic on twin, bow-shaped arcs of bronze. A matching conference table was positioned beside the windows to take advantage of the distant view of Houston's busy docks. Above the credenza that ran the length of one wall was another map, this one depicting global shipping lanes. The computer-generated routes crisscrossed cobalt-blue oceans in a spaghetti tangle of neon red, gold, green and black.

Zia noted with interest the eclectic collection of items Mike had obviously picked up in his travels. An elaborately carved boomerang that looked big enough to take down an elephant occupied a triangular frame made of some exotic wood. A three-foot-high Maori tiki god painted persim-mon red sat on a pedestal, his face screwed into a ferocious grimace and his tongue stuck out, presumably to deride would-be enemies. And standing in a corner like a fourth attendant at the meeting was a tan canvas dive suit topped by a dented brass helmet.

"I made coffee," Mike told Zia, "but there's tea or soft drinks or water if you'd prefer."

"Water would be great, thanks."

"Wise decision," Montoya commented as he powered up his computer. "Miguel's coffee has the flavor and con-sistency of bilge water."

"I had a sample this morning," Zia replied, laughing. "It would certainly rank up there with some of the bile we resi-dents down to stay awake during a thirty-six-hour rotation."

Montoya hiked a brow but he was too well mannered to follow up on her admission that she'd shared morning coffee with his brother-in-law. Instead, he tapped a couple keys on his laptop. The computerized wall map faded to a blank screen.

"As you can imagine, the health of the crews that man our ships is an ongoing concern. The IMO—International

Maritime Organization—has set guidelines for conducting pre-sea and periodic fitness examinations for all crewmembers. Despite this medical screening, however, we've noted disturbing trends in recent years.

"Part of that stems from the fact that seamen constitute a unique occupational group. Their travel to different parts of the world exposes them to infections and diseases at a rate comparable only to that of airline crews. And, like airline crews, they generally remain in port for relatively short time periods."

"But wouldn't a short turnaround mitigate their risk of exposure?"

"You'd think so, but that doesn't prove to be the case. In fact, seafarers report an incidence of certain diseases eight to ten times higher than the international average."

Montoya brought up the first slide. Its no-nonsense title—Infectious Diseases—riveted Zia's attention instantly.

"GSI maintains a database of all medical issues that impact our crews, but I extracted the data Mike indicated you might be particularly interested in."

The title slide gave way to a series of graphs that tracked GSI's reported incidents of HIV, malaria, hepatitis A, B and C, and tuberculosis against the international average. As Montoya had warned, the numbers were significantly higher than those Zia was familiar with.

"Although GSI is below the maritime average in every category, we're concerned by the worldwide upward trend in both malaria and tuberculosis. As a result we've funded or contributed heavily to a number of research projects targeting those diseases."

The next slide listed five studies, the company or institute that conducted them and the dollars GSI had contributed. The string of 0's on each study made Zia blink.

"Mike said you're focusing specifically on MRSA-related incidents," Montoya commented.

"That's right."

"We track that data, too."

She leaned forward, her interest riveted once again as he brought up the next slide. It showed the number of MRSA incidents by year and then by ship.

"Damn," Zia muttered. "You're seeing an across-the-board increase, too."

"Unfortunately."

"That's one nasty bug," Mike put in.

"Yes, it is. And becoming more and more resistant to antibiotics."

"Which is why we'd be interested in the results of your study," Montoya continued.

Startled, Zia started to protest that she'd focused on the very controlled world of neonatal nurseries. She couldn't imagine an environment farther removed from a massive container ship or oil tanker until she stopped, backed up and thought about it for a moment. The grim fact was that MRSA was on the rise in hospitals, nursing homes, homeless shelters, military barracks and prisons. All places where people were crowded and confined. Crews on ocean-going vessels certainly fell into that category.

"I'd be more than happy to share my findings, as limited as they are."

GSI's chief executive officer and VP for Support Systems exchanged a glance.

"Mike mentioned the possibility you might expand your research," Montoya said. "If so, GSI might be in a position to help with a grant."

Zia's jaw sagged. No way she would have imagined that a casual dinner date with a near stranger could lead to funding for the kind of in-depth study Dr. Wilbanks had talked to her about.

"Are you serious?"

"Very much so. We'd have to see a proposal that includes

all the standard criteria, of course." He ticked them off with knowledgeable ease. "A comprehensive rationale for the study. An assessment of the resources required. A detailed budget for the initial start-up, along with an estimated budget for the entire project. Biographical sketches of the people on your team, what you hope to accomplish and so on."

"Right."

Her mind whirled. Global Shipping Inc. had just made the question of whether she should switch from hands-on medicine to research ten times more difficult. Up to this point the possibility of participating in a major research effort with big-dollar funding had been just that—a possibility. Suddenly it had moved into the realm of probable. *If* she chose to go in that direction.

"Would you make me copies of these slides?"

She needed to study the data and think about the possibility of cross-fertilization with her research.

"Certainly."

He hit a key on his laptop. A sudden whir sounded from the printer on the sleek credenza behind Mike's desk. While he went to retrieve the copies, Montoya extracted a slim case from his shirt pocket.

"Here's my card. Please let me know if and when you're ready to put your proposal together. I'll be happy to take a look at it and provide input from this end."

Zia nodded, her mind still churning, and slipped his business card into her purse.

"Now, if you'll excuse me, I'd better get back to *abuelita*'s before the kids have Kate pulling out her hair." He shut down the laptop and tucked it under his arm. "It was good meeting you, Zia. Mike explained that you're pressed for time, but if you can squeeze out another hour or two I know the rest of the family would like to meet you, too."

"Particularly Davy's mom," Mike added. "Eileen called

just before you arrived with explicit instructions to bring you by the house if at all possible."

"Well…"

Zia checked her watch, surprised to find the session with Rafe Montoya had lasted a mere forty minutes.

Sarah, Gina and Natalie hadn't left to go shopping until almost noon. They'd taken the twins with them to give Maria and the duchess some downtime. Zia suspected both women were on the balcony, their feet up and eyes closed for an afternoon snooze.

The men would have finished their golf game by now but would no doubt hit the clubhouse before returning to the condo. Nothing formal was planned until this evening, when the family would follow the age-old Hungarian custom of celebrating *Szent-este*, or Holy Evening, with carols and a Bethlehem play using nativity figures.

Once the girls were in bed, the adults would indulge in a little stronger Christmas Eve cheer. Tomorrow would bring church services, the extravagant Christmas buffet at the resort's tony restaurant and the twins' birthday party later in the day. If Zia was going to meet the other members of the Brennan family, it had to be this afternoon.

"I guess I could stop by for a quick visit," she told Mike.

"Great." He grabbed his hat and settled it low on his forehead. "Everyone's congregated at our grandmother's house. It's only a few miles from here."

"I'll follow you."

Those few miles took them out of the canyon of downtown skyscrapers into what was once obviously a working-class neighborhood of small stucco houses. Property values must be shooting up, though, as newer and much larger residences appeared to be replacing the older homes.

Red, pink and white oleander bushes defined front- and backyards, while hundred-year-old live oaks dripping with

Spanish moss formed dense canopies. A heavy Hispanic flavor showed in storefront signs and churches with names like Our Lady of Guadalupe and Saint Juan Diego. Mike turned onto a tree-lined street and pulled up behind a string of vehicles parked curbside in the middle of the block. Zia parked behind him and got out, careful to avoid a hot-pink bike lying on its side in the middle of the sidewalk.

"This'll be Teresa's," Mike said as he whisked the bike up and out of the way. "She's Davy and Kevin's sister and the bane of their existence, the way they tell it. Here, let's go around to the patio. Everyone's usually out back."

As they followed a winding path, Zia admired the skillful way the original one-story stucco house had been expanded. The stone-fronted second story added both living space and architectural interest, while a glassed-in sunroom extended the first floor and brought the outdoors in.

"Does your grandmother live here alone?"

"She did until recently. My youngest sister and her new baby have moved in while her husband's in Afghanistan. We're negotiating with *abuelita* what'll happen when Maureen moves back out."

"How many brothers and sisters do you have again?"

"Three sisters, three brothers. Between them they've produced fifteen offspring...so far. And from the sound of it," he added, cocking his head as high-pitched shrieks of laughter emanated from the rear of the house, "they're pretty much all here."

Even with that warning, the noise and sheer size of the crowd in the backyard made Zia blink. Three little girls clambered in and out of a plastic castle while two others and a toddler made good use of a swing set. Several boys of varying ages played a game of tag with two joyously barking dogs. One was a large mixed breed, the other the small wirehaired terrier Zia remembered from yesterday morning. His owner, Davy, appeared to be suffering no af-

tereffects from his dunking as he raced after an older, near carbon copy, who had to be his brother, Kevin.

Additional family members crowded the glass-topped tables and lounge chairs set under a pergola draped with red and green lanterns. Kids occupied one table, adults another, both groups involved in noisy board games. The rhythmic beat of "Feliz Navidad" rose above the dogs' barking, shrieks of laughter and buzz of conversation. The music pulsed through a screen door that must lead to the kitchen, Zia guessed as she breathed in the tantalizing scents of roasting pork and spicy chipotle marinade.

One of the board players glanced up and caught sight of the newcomers. Pushing away from the table, the brunette jumped out of her chair and rushed across the lawn.

"Mike called and said you were stopping by, Dr. St. Sebastian. Thank you!" Disdaining formalities, she enveloped Zia in a fierce hug. "Thank you so much!"

"I'm just glad I was in the right place at the right time."

"Me, too! I'm Eileen, by the way. Eileen Rogers."

"And this is her husband, Bill," Mike said, introducing yet another of his brothers-in-law. This one didn't come anywhere close to either Mike *or* Rafael Montoya on the hotness index, but his warm brown eyes signaled both sincerity and a keen intelligence.

"You have my thanks, too, Dr. St. Sebastian. From the bottom of my heart."

"You're welcome. Both of you. And please, call me Zia."

"That's short for Anastazia, right?" Eileen hooked arms with her son's rescuer. "I looked you up on the internet," she admitted as she tugged Zia toward the others. "You're Hungarian, graduated from med school in Vienna and are just about to finish a residency at Mount Sinai."

"I think Zia knows her pedigree," Mike drawled from behind them.

Eileen ignored him. "You're also the sister of the yummy

Grand Duke of Karlenburgh, whose face was plastered all over the tabloids last year. Kate, Maureen and I all drooled over his picture."

"Thanks," her husband said with a mock groan. "Just what the rest of us mere mortals needed to hear."

His comment almost got lost in a chorus of excited shouts. The kids—all ten or twelve or fifteen of them—had noticed the newcomers' arrival. Like a human tsunami, they surged past Zia and Eileen emitting shrill squeals.

"Uncle Mickey! Uncle Mickey!"

They swamped him. Literally. Hung on his arms and wrapped around his legs. He crab-walked past the two women with kids dangling from every extremity. Zia laughed, but Eileen's chuckle ended on a low, almost inaudible mutter.

"Damn that bitch."

Zia sent her a startled glance. "Excuse me?"

"Sorry." Color rushed into the other woman's cheeks. "I shouldn't have let that slip out. It's just…"

"Just what?"

Eileen bit her lip, her gaze on the shrieking tangle of humanity a few yards ahead. "Mike is so good with them. With all of them. He'd make such a fantastic father."

A sudden, queasy sensation hit Zia. She had a feeling she knew where this was going. Her stomach muscles clenched, preparing to ward off the blow that Eileen Rogers delivered like a roundhouse punch.

"I probably shouldn't air our family's dirty laundry, but…" Eileen's voice flattened. Hardened. "It broke our hearts when his bitch of an ex-wife announced she didn't want children. Broke Mike's heart, too, although he would never admit it."

Five

Mike could sense the change in Zia. The signs were subtle—a slight dimming of the smile in her exotic eyes, just a hint of reserve in her responses to his family's boisterous welcome. He shouldn't have been surprised, given how many there were of them!

Interesting, though, that he'd become so attuned to this woman's small nuances after only one night together. He did his best to wipe the erotic mental images out of his head as he introduced her around. Her every move got to him, though. Each time she hooked a strand of hair behind her ear or bent to catch something someone said or just glanced his way, Mike felt a tug. And each tug only increased his determination to get to know Anastazia St. Sebastian a whole lot better.

She renewed her acquaintance with Davy and his terrier before Mike introduced her to his parents. He could see her relaxing a little as they welcomed her. It would be hard not to relax around Eleanor and Big Mike Brennan, given that they were two of the most unpretentious and genuine people on God's green earth. And, of course, Zia had snatched their grandson from the treacherous waters

of the Gulf. That put her right at the top of their list of can-do-no-wrong human beings.

The shamrock-green eyes Big Mike had passed to six of his seven of his children beamed his gratitude. "You need anything, Doc, anything at all, you just call. What Mickey here can't do for you, Eleanor or I or one of the others will."

Zia looked a little overwhelmed by the offer but accepted it graciously. "Thank you."

She connected with Mike's middle sister, too. Not surprising, since the two women shared a common bond. Jiggling her nine-month-old on her hip, Kate expanded on that link. "I don't know if Mickey told you that I'm a cardiovascular surgical nurse at St. Luke's, here in Houston."

"He mentioned that you're a nurse, but not your specialty. Cardio's a tough area."

"It can be," Kate admitted cheerfully. "My husband, Rafe, said you're doing a research study on MRSA. Obviously, I have a vested interest in hospital-acquired infections. I'd love to sit down and talk with you about your study sometime. Maybe we could do lunch after the craziness of the holidays?"

"I wish we could. Unfortunately, I'm flying home to New York the day after tomorrow."

"Too bad." Her gaze turned speculative. "My brother hasn't shown much interest in any of the women Eileen and Mo and I have thrown at him the past three years. Not enough to bring them home to meet the family, anyway. You've obviously made an impression."

"Obviously," Mike's youngest sister chimed in, joining the group. Like Kate and most of the other Brennan siblings, Maureen had inherited their father's shimmering green eyes, but her red hair was at least a dozen shades lighter and brighter than the others'.

As though uncomfortable with the turn the conversa-

tion had taken, Zia smiled and redirected it. "I understand your husband's in the military."

"That's right. He's army, despite Colin and Mickey's attempt to browbeat him into going navy."

"Colin being the most obnoxious of my brothers," Mike warned with a grin as he shepherded Zia toward the men waiting their turn. "Right after Sean and Dennis."

He made quick work of the intros to the rest of the clan. Brothers, sisters-in-law, kids all got a brief acknowledgment before Mike whisked Zia away to meet the clan's matriarch.

Consuela Brennan's unlined skin and calm black eyes belied her age. To Mike's admittedly biased minds, his grandmother still exuded an aura of quiet beauty and the convent-bred serenity that had captivated his rough-and-tumble Irish grandfather so many years ago.

"So you are the one who saved our little Davy." She framed Zia's face with her palms. "I lit a candle this morning to thank God for His grace in bringing you into our lives. I will light another each day for a year."

"I...uh...thank you."

"And now, I think, you should sit here in the shade with Eleanor and me and tell us about your country. Miguel says you're from Hungary. I must confess I know little about it."

Zia chatted with Consuelo and Eleanor Brennan for a good twenty minutes or more. The mother- and daughter-in-law were very different in both age and interests but shared an absolute devotion to each other and to their families. Under any other circumstances, Zia would have thoroughly enjoyed getting to know them better.

Yet she couldn't help sneaking an occasional side glance, observing Mike interact with his siblings and in-laws. Noting, as well, how his nieces and nephews all seemed to adore him. Cries of "Uncle Mickey, watch me!" and "Come push me, Uncle Mickey!" peppered the air. Each shout,

every giggle and squeal of delight, seemed to reinforce his sister Eileen's earlier comment. Mike Brennan would make a fantastic father.

The thought twisted like a small knife in Zia's chest. She shrugged the familiar pain aside as she said her goodbyes and wished everyone merry Christmas but it was still there, buried deep, as Mike walked her to her car.

"You have a wonderful family," she said, smiling to cover the ache. "I thought mine was big and lively, but yours wins the prize."

"They keep life interesting."

She fished out the keys of the rental and clicked the lock, but Mike angled between her and the door.

"I want to see you again, Zia. Sure you can't slip away again tonight or tomorrow?"

She wanted to. God, she wanted to! With him leaning so close, his smile crinkling the tanned skin at the corners of his eyes, his body almost touching hers, all she could think of was how his hands had stroked her. How he'd kissed and teased and tormented her. How she'd given more of herself to this man in one night than she'd ever given before.

She had a sneaking suspicion she could fall in love him. So easily. He was smart, handsome, fun, unpretentious and devoted to his family...which was the one thing she *couldn't* give him.

"I'm sorry, Mike. I need to spend tonight with my family. And tomorrow isn't just Christmas, it's also the twins' birthday. Gina wants to make a big deal of it since the girls won't have any of their friends from preschool to play games and blow out candles with, so we'll all be doubly..."

He laid a finger on her lips. "Leave it to me. I'll find a way to make it happen."

Not if she didn't answer her phone or return his calls. Trying to convince herself it was better to cut the cord now,

before they got in any deeper, Zia shook her head. "Best to just say goodbye now."

He looked ready to argue the point but gave in with a shrug.

"Okay."

Bending, he brushed his lips over hers. The first pass was light, friendly. The second set her heart thumping against her sternum.

"Goodbye, Zia. For now."

He didn't call to press the issue. Although Zia had made up her mind to end things between them before they could really get started, she had to admit she was surprised. Okay, maybe a little miffed.

She spent Christmas Eve enjoying the twins' almost giddy eagerness over Santa's imminent arrival and the fact that they would share their birthday with Baby Jesus the next day.

The evening blended so many traditions, old and new. With her eye for color and genius for party planning, Gina made the most of all of them. The tree, the carols, the twins' construction-paper daisy chains draped like garlands at the windows. Stockings hooked above the marble fireplace for every member of the family, the hound included. White candles giving off just enough heat to gently turn the five-tiered nativity carousel, a reminder of the duchess's Austrian roots and a precious memento from Sarah and Gina's childhood.

They celebrated the Hungarian side of the St. Sebastian heritage, as well. Zia and Natalie spent a fun hour in the kitchen baking *kiffles*, the traditional Hungarian cookie made from cream cheese dough and filled with various flavors of pastry filling. Delicate and sinfully rich, they made a colorful holiday platter in addition to supplying the required treat to leave for Santa.

The highlight of the evening was the Bethlehem play orchestrated by Zia and Dom. The original folk tradition went back centuries, when children dressed in nativity costumes would go from house to house. Carrying a crèche, the young shepherds and wise men accompanying Joseph and Mary would sing and dance choreographed versions of the birth of Christ. Their performance would be rewarded with a treat of some kind at each house.

The tradition had gone through many different variations over the centuries. Most Bethlehem plays these days were performed at churches or schools. So Dom and Zia had to improvise costumes and staging and conscript the other adults for various roles. The performance delighted the twins, however. So much so that everyone was exhausted by the time Gina and Jack finally got them to bed.

The next morning the hyper-excited twins roused everyone before seven, the hound included. Gina and Jack were determined the girls should experience all the joy of Christmas morning, so their follow-up birthday celebration wasn't planned until late that afternoon…a timetable Mike Brennan exploited very nicely.

The call came after the family returned from church services and had all trooped down to the resort's elegant restaurant for the Christmas buffet. They were waiting to be seated when Dev's cell phone pinged. He checked caller ID and shot Zia a glance before answering.

"Hey, Brennan. What's happening?" He listened a moment, his brow hiking. "Yeah, she's right here."

To everyone's surprise, he handed the phone to Gina instead of Zia. She took it with a bewildered look. "Hi, Mike. Yes," she said after a brief pause. "Around four."

Another pause, punctuated by a wide smile.

"The twins would love that! If you're sure it's not too

much trouble. Yes. Yes, by all means! Great! We'll see you then."

Grinning, she hung up and addressed a phalanx of questioning faces. Her brightest smile went to Zia. "How sweet of you to tell Mike that you couldn't pass up the girls' birthday party to see him again."

"I…well…"

"So he's coming to the party," she said happily. "With a piñata and a pony and a half-dozen nieces and nephews, all close to the girls' age. He said he knew the twins' friends were all back home, so he thought they might like to share their special day with new ones."

Zia could only stare at her, openmouthed, and left it to the girls' father to inquire drily how they were supposed to accommodate a pony in the condo.

"Mike suggested we have the party in the play area. He's already spoken to the resort manager. The entire playground is ours for the duration." She hunkered down to address her wide-eyed daughters. "What do you say, girls? Do you want pony rides and a piñata at your party?"

Amalia stamped both feet and clapped her hands enthusiastically. "Yeth!"

Wide-eyed, serious Charlotte had to ask, "What's a piñata?"

By six-thirty that evening, Zia's suspicion that she could fall in love with Mike Brennan had solidified into certainty. She'd never met any man more suited to a brood of nosy, lively children. Children she could never give him, she reminded herself with a slice of pain.

And then, when the last of the kids had driven off with their respective parents and Zia's family had retreated to the condo, it was just her. Just him.

The salt breeze fluttered the ruffles of the cinnamon-colored overblouse she'd changed into along with jeans

and a pair of sandals more suitable to a playground party. Mike had changed, too, and was once again in his beach persona of shorts and flip-flops. Trying to decide which version she liked best, Zia ached to lose herself in the smile she saw in his eyes.

"Thank you. You made this day so special for the twins. For all of us."

"It's not over yet." He tilted his head toward the surf rustling against the deserted shoreline. "Walk with me?"

Zia's precise mind tabulated an instant list of reasons not to let this man burrow deeper into her heart. Just as quickly, she countered them with the same arguments she'd trotted out yesterday. She was leaving tomorrow. Flying back to cold, snowy New York. She'd most likely never see him again. Why not make the most of these stolen hours?

"Sure."

As they tracked a path of side-by-side footsteps in the damp sand, his hand folded around hers. His grip remained loose, his voice easy as they swapped stories from their childhood and tales of Christmases past. By contrast, a tight, delicious tension gathered in the pit of Zia's stomach. It had knotted into a quivering bundle of need by the time the pale turquoise silhouette rose above the dunes directly ahead.

"I know you must be tired," Mike said as they approached the beach house, "but I don't want the day to end. How about we have that drink I offered last night but we never quite got around to?"

"A drink sounds good."

He'd closed the shutters after Zia had left yesterday morning. No light spilled through them as they took the path through the dunes and mounted the zigzagging staircase. Once inside the beach house, she sniffed the faint scent of trapped salt air. Mike made quick work of folding

back the shutters protecting the French doors in the high-ceilinged living room, though, and opened them to let in the sea breeze.

"Would you like coffee or something a little stronger?"

"No offense, but your coffee should be registered with the EPA as a class II corrosive."

"True." Grinning, he acknowledged the hit. "But ironic coming from the woman whose great-aunt serves *pálinka* to unsuspecting guests."

"I tried to warn you."

"Yeah, you did. I think I have a less explosive brandy."

The banter was relaxed, the Courvoisier he poured into two snifters as smooth as sin. And with each sip, the need to touch him grew more critical. She fought the urge, determined to stretch their time together for as long as possible, and carried her drink out to the deck.

The wraparound, multilevel deck was banded by a railing of split boards spaced close enough to keep young nieces and nephews from wiggling through and plunging to the dunes below. The top rail was wide and flat and set at just the right height for adults to lean their elbows on. Zia took advantage of the ledge, cradling the heavy snifter in both hands while she absorbed the vista of foaming surf and the sky purpling out over the Gulf.

"You know," Mike mused as his elbows joined hers on the weathered shelf, "the NMC is working on a program that would allow mariners to upgrade or renew their credentials on demand from any cyber location in the world."

She angled to face him, not sure where he was going with that conversational gambit. "NMC?"

"Sorry. The National Maritime Center. It's a US Coast Guard agency, under the auspices of the Department of Homeland Security. The center is responsible for credentialing US mariners. The process is complicated and time-consuming now, but the NMC's new program would let

crews access the system electronically, just like they access their bank accounts or withdraw cash from an ATM."

"Sounds reasonable."

"GSI provided input into the initial system architecture."

"Oh-kay."

She still couldn't guess where this was heading, especially with the swiftly falling darkness painting Mike's face in shadows.

"NMC's presenting a status update briefing at the Maritime Trades Association's executive board meeting in mid-January. I was supposed to be in Helsinki and hadn't planned to attend but now I'm thinking I might. The meeting's in New York. Not," he added with an exaggerated drawl, "that I need an excuse to come callin'."

She wasn't expecting the sudden zing of excitement at the prospect of seeing him again. It took every ounce of Zia's resolve to squelch it.

"I've enjoyed our time together, Mike, as brief as it's been. But…" She pulled in a breath. "I don't think it's a good idea for us to try to build on it."

"Funny, I think it's a hell of an idea."

She had a dozen convenient excuses she could have thrown out. She was supervising four interns, conducting team meetings, examining patients, doing chart reviews—and all this less than two weeks away from presenting the results of her research study. She also owed Dr. Wilbanks an answer when she got back to New York.

But dealing with patients and anxious relatives had taught Zia it was best to be honest. She usually softened a harsh truth with sympathy, but sometimes it was stark and unavoidable. This was one of those times.

"I like you, Mike. Too much to let either of us get in over our heads."

"Okay, that needs a little more explaining."

"The other evening, during dinner, I told you about… about the skiing trip in Slovenia that ended in disaster."

Now it was his turn to look as though he wasn't sure where the conversation was going. "I remember."

"I watched you with your family yesterday. With my family today. You're so good with the children." She dragged in another breath and carefully centered her snifter on the broad ledge. "You don't need to get involved with a woman—*another* woman—who isn't going to give you any."

"Well, Christ! Which one of my loving sisters told you about…?" He shook his head, exasperated. "Never mind. It doesn't matter. What does matter is that we're a long ways yet from getting in over our heads."

"Which is why I say…" She caught her accent slipping and forced a correction. "Why I *said* we should stop now, before either of us gets hurt."

He angled his head, studying her in the deepening twilight. She couldn't see the expression in his eyes, only the purse of his lips as he weighed her comment.

"How about we strike a deal here?" he said after several long moments. "I'll tell you if and when I approach the hurting stage, and you do the same."

Rendben! Oké! She'd warned him. Made it perfectly clear they could never become serious. So…

"All right."

"All right?"

"I accept the deal." She hooked a hand behind his neck, tugged him down to her level. "And just to seal the bargain…"

Mike was careful not to let his quick, visceral triumph flavor the kiss. He hadn't lied. He *was* a long way yet from getting in over his head. But he was navigating in that direction and had no intention of charting a different course. Zia St. Sebastian fascinated and challenged and aroused

him in ways he hadn't been fascinated or challenged or aroused in a long, long time.

Her revelation the other night at the restaurant that she couldn't have children had given him pause for maybe ten, fifteen seconds. It had also brought back some bitter memories. Right up until he reminded himself there was a whole passel of difference between *couldn't* and *wouldn't*.

Zia wasn't Jill. The two women might have been bred on different planets. Different universes. And right now, all Mike wanted to do was revel in those differences. Like the way Zia's mouth molded his with no coy pretense of having to be coaxed. The fit of her tall, slender body against his, so perfect he didn't have to stoop or contort to cant her hips into his. The lemony scent of her shampoo, the smoky taste of Courvoisier on her lips, the way the skin at the small of her back warmed under his searching fingers when he tugged up the hem of her blouse. Every touch, every sensory signal that raced along his snapping nerves, made him raw with wanting her.

He managed to keep from tugging the ruffled blouse over her head and baring her to the night. But he did circle her waist and perch her on the wide ledge. The move put her nose just a few inches above his and gave him easy access to the underside of her chin.

"You know," he said as he nibbled the tender skin, "you're a hard woman to please. I had to call a dozen stables before I found someone who would deliver a pony this afternoon."

"That was your idea, not mine," she reminded him, threading her fingers through his hair. "And totally unnecessary, I might add. The piñata and kids were more than enough. But I appreciate the trouble you went to."

"Yeah, well, since you brought it up…"

"*You* brought it up."

"I'm talking about your appreciation."

"Is that right?" She used her hold on his hair to tilt his head back. "What about it?"

"Well, it just seems to me there are a number of ways you might show it."

Her eyes glinted with amusement. "Just what did you have in mind, cowboy?"

He answered her question with a quick barrage of his own. "What time's your flight tomorrow?"

"Eleven-twenty."

"From Houston Hobby or George Bush Intercontinental?"

"Houston Hobby."

"And how long will it take you to pack?"

"Thirty minutes. Maybe less. *Why*?"

"Hold on." He settled his hands on her hips and pretended to conduct a series of rapid mental calculations. "Okay, the way I figure it we have fifteen and a half hours. Should be just enough time for me to go through my entire repertoire of moves and send you back to New York a happy woman."

"Good Lord!" The amusement bubbled into laughter. "Fifteen and a half hours going through your repertoires and I won't be able to walk, much less board a plane."

Which was pretty much the idea. Mike didn't share that thought, choosing instead to scoop her off the rail and into his arms.

"Better call back to the condo," he suggested as he carried her, still grinning, into the house. "Your brother wasn't looking all that friendly this afternoon."

"Are you worried what Dom might think?"

"More what he might do," Mike admitted wryly. "Which is probably exactly the same thing I would if any of *my* sisters spent fifteen and a half hours engaged in the kind of activity I have planned for you, Doc."

Six

Zia slept for the entire flight from Houston to LaGuardia. Hardly a surprise, given that Mike had made good on his promise to keep her busy for an astonishing portion of their stolen interlude.

When she exited the terminal, the icy air hit like a slap in the face. Luckily, she'd worn her UGGs and fleece-lined parka on the flight down to Texas. They protected her now while she stood in the taxi line, but the howling wind sliced into the tiger-striped leggings Gina had given her for Christmas and her nose dripped like a faucet by the time she tumbled into a cab.

After a week of sun-washed beaches and balmy days, the dirty slush and nasty gray sky should have been a shock to her system. Yet as the taxi rattled over the Robert F. Kennedy Bridge and headed for Manhattan's Upper West Side, the hustle and bustle of her adopted city grabbed her. She loved its pulsing rhythm, its cultural diversity, its kitsch and class. Of course, her perceptions were skewed by the fact that she now lived in one of the city's most famous apartment buildings.

As the cab pulled up at the entrance to the Dakota, Zia couldn't help thinking how much the multistory Victorian-

era complex reminded her of her native Budapest. Gabled and fancifully turreted, the Dakota stood out from the modern structures crowding it on three sides and drew the eye with the same regal dignity as the iconic spires of Hungary's parliament building.

Charlotte St. Sebastian had purchased her fifth-floor, seven-room apartment after an odyssey that included her escape from the Soviets and short stays in both Vienna and Paris. Her title and the jewels she'd converted to cold, hard cash had won her acceptance by the Dakota's exclusive enclave that over the years had included such luminaries as Judy Garland, Rudolph Nureyev, Leonard Bernstein, Bono and John Lennon, who was tragically murdered just steps from the front entrance.

Zia knew the duchess had almost been forced to sell her apartment not long ago. The apartment and her determination to educate her granddaughters in the manner she insisted was commensurate with their heritage had drained her resources. Bad investments by her financial advisor had sucked away most of the rest.

When Sarah married her handsome billionaire, she'd known better than to offer to pay her grandmother's living expenses. The duchess's pride would never allow it. But Charlotte *had* allowed Dev to sink what little remained of her savings in several of his wildly successful business ventures. And Gina's husband, Jack, had added to the duchess's financial security with investments in blue-chip stocks. Charlotte could now live in splendid luxury for the rest of her life.

This development pleased the uniformed doorman who made his stately way to help Zia from the taxi almost as much as it did the St. Sebastians. Sarah and Gina considered Jerome one of the family. He'd treated them to candy and ice cream during their schoolgirl years, scrutinized their

high school dates with steely eyes, attended their weddings and delighted in the lively twins.

He'd taken Zia under his wing, too, when Charlotte had invited her to live at the Dakota. As kind as he was dignified, Jerome had acquainted the new arrival with such intricacies as subway schedules, jogging paths and the best pastrami this side of Romania. Which is why Zia made sure she paid the cab fare even before the driver pulled up at the curb. There was no way she would keep Jerome standing in the icy wind.

"Welcome home, Doctor."

He would no more think of dropping her title than he would Lady Sarah's or Lady Eugenia's. But his smile was warm and welcoming as he held the door and ushered her into what was once the *porte cochère*.

"How was your Christmas?"

"Wonderful."

"And the duchess? Maria? They're enjoying being out of this ice and snow?"

"Very much so, although I suspect they'll be happy to come home after another two weeks of sun and sand."

"I suspect so, too. And if I may be so bold," he added as he escorted her to the bank of elevators, "may I say it's good to see you smiling again."

"Was I so glum before?" Zia asked, startled.

"Not glum. Just tired. And," he said gently, "somewhat troubled."

Jézus, Mária és József! Was she so transparent? Surely she did a better job of sublimating her inner self when working with patients.

"You hid it well," the doorman hastened to assure her. "But a keen eye and an ability to assess character comes with this job." He paused, searching her face. "Did you find the solution to whatever was distressing you in Texas?"

She had to hide a smile at the slight but unmistakable

emphasis on the last word. New York born and bred, Jerome would find it hard to believe the answer to anyone's problems couldn't be found right here in the city. And to tell the truth, Zia wasn't quite sure how those stolen hours with Mike had lifted some of the weight of the decision that still hung over her like an executioner's ax, but they had. They most definitely had.

"Not the solution, perhaps," she said as the elevator door pinged open, "but a very potent antidote."

Propping the door with one hand, she took her bag in the other and leaned in to kiss the doorman's cheek.

"Just so you know," she added, "the antidote plans to make a trip to New York in the next week or so. His name's Brennan. Michael Brennan."

"I'll be sure to ring the apartment the moment Mr. Brennan arrives," Jerome replied with a twinkle in his eyes.

Strange, Zia thought as she keyed the front door and let herself into the black-and-white-tiled foyer. She still faced a wrenching decision. Yet now opting for research instead of hands-on medicine didn't feel like such a traitorous act. The possibility of a substantial grant from GSI to underwrite that research had given it impetus. She could be part of a team that pinpointed sources of deadly infections. Reduced risks to hospital patients. Saved lives.

First, though, she had to draft the proposal Rafe Montoya had outlined. She'd get on the computer, she decided as she dropped her bag in her bedroom and went to the bathroom. Right after she'd soaked long enough to ease her aching hip and thigh and calf muscles. Mike Brennan, she acknowledged with a rueful grin, had given her a lesson in anatomy unlike any she'd taken in med school.

She was at the hospital early the next morning. Those residents who'd worked through Christmas greeted her return with relief.

"Hope you're rested and ready to go," Don Carter warned. Happily married and totally stressed, he couldn't wait to shed his stethoscope for a long-anticipated New Year ski trip to Vermont. "We've been slammed with the usual spike in heart attacks and acute respiratory failures."

Zia nodded. Contrary to the popular misperception that the sharp increase in holiday deaths was driven by substance abuse, family-related homicides or depression-driven suicides, she now knew other significant causes came into play. A major contributing factor was that people who felt ill simply put off a trip to the hospital, choosing instead to be with their families over Christmas or New Year's.

Holiday staffing was also an issue, especially at Level 1 trauma centers, where seconds could mean the difference between life and death. Recognizing that fact, Mount Sinai's various centers, schools and hospitals paid careful attention to staff levels during this critical period.

Even with the controlled staffing, however, the holidays kept everyone hopping. Zia quickly fell back into the hectic schedule of morning team meetings, patient exams, family-centered rounds, chart reviews, one-on-ones with her interns and day-end team sessions. She still had two weeks in the Pediatric Intensive Care Unit before she completed that rotation. And, as they always did, these desperately ill kids tugged at her heart. Some cried, some screamed, but others showed no reaction to the catheters and IVs and high-dosage drugs that made them groggy or nauseous or both.

This was particularly true of the five-month-old admitted the second day after Zia's return. The infant lay listless and unmoving, his skin sallow and his eyes dull. She said nothing while one of her interns read aloud the admitting physician's chart notations. Nor did she offer an

opinion or advice while he examined the patient under his parents' worried eyes.

When her small group had adjourned to the hall outside the nursery however, she quizzed the intern. "Did you note any anomaly in Benjamin's penis?"

She always referred to her patients by first name to insure neither she nor her students ever forgot they were treating living, breathing humans.

"I…uh…" The intern looked from her to his fellow students and back again. "No."

"It appeared elongated to me. Combined with his low birth weight and failure to thrive, what does that suggest to you?"

The intern bit his lip and searched his memory. "Low-renin hypertension?"

The genetic defect was rare and difficult to diagnose. She didn't blame the intern for missing it on the first go-around.

"That's what it looks like to me. I would suggest you have the lab measure his renin level and compare it to his aldosterone."

"Will do."

"If the ratio's too low, as I suspect it may be, let's get a consult from the Adrenal Steroid Disorders group before we discuss his condition with his parents."

Relief and respect reverberated in the fervent reply. "I'll take care of it."

Jézus! Had she ever been that young? Ever that terrified of doing more harm than good?

Of course she had.

That thought stayed with her as she crossed the catwalk connecting the Kravis Children's Hospital with the tower housing the school of medicine's research center. As head of the world-renowned facility, Dr. Wilbanks and his staff occupied a suite of offices with a bird's-eye view of Central

Park. Zia confirmed her appointment with the receptionist, then stood at the windows to admire the landscape. From this height, the frozen reservoir, rolling fields and bare-branched trees were a symphony in gray and icy white.

The buzz of the intercom brought her around. The receptionist listened for a moment and nodded to Zia. "Dr. Wilbanks will see you now."

Roger Wilbanks's physical stature matched his reputation in the world of pediatric research. Tall, snowy haired and lean almost to the point of emaciation, he greeted Zia with a burning intensity that both flattered and intimidated.

"I hope you've come to tell me you've decided to join our team, Dr. St. Sebastian."

"Yes, sir, I have."

As soon as the words were out, a thousand-pound boulder seemed to roll off Zia's shoulders. This was right for her. She'd known it somewhere deep inside for months but hadn't been able to shake the feeling that she would be abandoning the youngest, most helpless patients.

That guilty sense of desertion, of turning her back on her young patients, was gone. Part of that was due to Dr. Wilbanks's validation of her initial research. And part, she realized, was due to Mike Brennan. He'd triggered an interest in a world outside of pediatric medicine. She was light-years from expanding her research to the wider population of ships' crews and prison populations, but Mike had opened whole new vistas that gave the sterile environment of a lab new, exciting dimensions.

The possibility GSI might contribute to her research sparked an interest on the part of Dr. Wilbanks, as well. "Global Shipping Incorporated?" he echoed, his brows soaring above his rimless half-glasses. "They suggested they might fund a study of hospital-acquired infections in newborn infants?"

"They're interested in any research that might pinpoint

sources of infection. Apparently MRSA is as much a worry in the maritime world as it is in hospitals."

His brows remained at full mast while Zia walked him through the paper copies of the slides Rafe Montoya had printed out for her. The chart listing the studies GSI had funded or contributed to proved especially riveting. By the time she finished, she could almost see the dollar signs gleaming in her mentor's eyes.

"When do you present your current study to the faculty?" he asked.

"The second week in January. I don't have a specific day or time yet, but..."

"I'll take care of that. In the meantime, you need to get to work on a proposal for an expanded study. I'll have one of the senior research assistants work with you on that. You also need to talk to someone in the comptroller's office. Unfortunately, requesting and acquiring grants has become a complex process. So complex we often use the services of consultants. The comptroller will help you there. In the meantime, you can count your work with us as an elective and complete your residency on schedule."

He pushed away from his desk and came around to lay a collegial hand on her shoulder.

"I don't need to tell you research is the heart and soul of medicine, Dr. St. Sebastian. The public may hail Albert Sabin and Jonas Salk as the heroes who conquered polio, but neither of those preeminent scientists could have developed their vaccines without the work done by John Enders at Boston's Children's Hospital. God willing, our research into the molecular genetics of heart disease, the pathogenesis of influenza and herpes and, yes, the increasing incidence of MRSA among newborns, will yield the same profound results."

Zia couldn't have asked for a more motivational speech. Or a more ringing endorsement of her shift to full-time

research. Buoyed by the increasing certainty she'd made the right decision, she traded hours with another resident so she could have dinner with Natalie and Dom the evening they flew in from Texas.

They'd come back a week before the duchess and Maria were scheduled to return. The New Year celebrations were over, the slush had morphed to grime, and the city shivered under an Arctic blast. Hunched against the cold, Zia took a cab to their apartment in the venerable old 30 Beekman Place building. It was less than a block from UN Headquarters, where Dom was still trying to adjust to his mission as cultural attaché.

The tenth-floor condo boasted plenty of room for entertainment and a million-dollar view of the Manhattan skyline. More important, as far as Natalie was concerned, it was only steps from a dog run, where she and the liver-and-white-spotted Magyar Agár exercised twice a day.

Natalie and the hound were just returning from their evening constitutional when Zia climbed out of the cab. The whipcord-lean hound greeted her ecstatically, Natalie with a hug and a smile.

"I was so surprised and excited when you called and told us you were switching to pediatric research," her sister-in-law said. "I hope you get as much fulfillment from your field as I do from mine."

"I hope so, too." She had to ask. "How did Dom react to the news that I won't be practicing hands-on medicine?"

"Oh, Zia! Your brother wants whatever you want." Her brown eyes brimmed with laughter. "You could dance naked down Broadway and Dom would flatten anyone who so much as glanced sideways at you. And speaking of dancing naked…"

She hit the elevator button and spun in a slow circle to unwind the leash wrapped around her calves.

"Mike Brennan stopped by the resort before we left."

"Why?"

"He *said* he wanted to talk to Dev about a fleet of new cargo ships his company is thinking about acquiring. But he and Dom spent quite a bit of time out on the balcony, one-on-one."

This was news to Zia. She and Mike had iMessaged each other a few times. Like most texts, they were short and only hinted at the activities cut off by her departure from Houston. Yet they also managed to convey an unsaid but unmistakable desire to pick up where they'd left off. None of Mike's iMessages had mentioned a one-on-one with her brother, however.

"How did they get along? Was any blood spilled? Bodily harm inflicted?"

"Let's just say your brother isn't making any more 'Cossack-y, I'll carve out his liver with a saber' noises."

Zia had to smile. Dom talked a good game. She couldn't count the number of dates she'd had to bring by the house so he could scope them out. Or the friends he'd subjected to intense and, to them, nerve-racking scrutiny. Yet he'd always respected Zia's intelligence and, more important, her common sense. He'd never interfered or second-guessed her choices. Not an easy task for the older brother who'd raised her from her early teens.

"By the way," Natalie said casually as the elevator arrived and the hound dragged her inside, "we expect you to bring Mike to dinner when he's in New York for that conference he's suddenly decided to attend."

"How did you...?" Laughing, Zia followed her sister and the hound into the elevator. "Never mind."

The two women exchanged a wry smile. Dominic St. Sebastian might have put his days as an undercover agent behind him. He kept a hand in the business, however. Or at least a finger.

* * *

Zia didn't exactly count the days until Mike showed up in New York. She was too busy with rounds and teaching and preparing the presentation of her MRSA study to the faculty and her fellow residents. In between, she snatched what time she could to work on the proposal for the expanded study.

Per Dr. Wilbanks's instructions, she used National Institutes of Health guidelines to draft the proposal. The first step was to describe the greatly expanded research project and what it was intended to accomplish. After that she interviewed prospective team members, detailed their credentials and ran her choices by Dr. Wilbanks for approval. Once she had the team lined up, she used their collective expertise to refine the objectives and nail down the resources required. They also put together a projected budget for the estimated life of the study. The "one million, two hundred thousand" bottom line made Zia gulp.

It caused the school's assistant comptroller to suck a little air, too. A busy, fussy type with salt-and-pepper hair and a string of framed degrees on her office wall, the financial guru felt compelled to deliver a lecture about the acquisition and disbursement of grant monies.

"I'm sure you understand that we have to be very careful, Dr. St. Sebastian. Especially with a grant in the amount you're requesting. We have an excellent record here at Mount Sinai, I'm very happy to say. But recent audits by the National Institutes of Health have uncovered waste and, in some cases, outright fraud at other institutes."

"That's why I'm here, Ms. Horton. I want to be sure we do everything by the book."

"Good, good." She glanced over the figures in the proposed budget again. "I doubt you'll pull in half of what you're requesting."

She hesitated, her lips pursed.

"We use the services of two excellent consulting firms that specialize in searching out and securing grant monies. I'll give you the contact information for both, but in this tight economy…"

She shook her head discouragingly. Zia debated whether to tell her about the GSI connection. She decided to wait until the expanded study had been approved and the hunt for funding actually got under way.

A few clicks of the assistant comptroller's keyboard produced a printed list of "grant consultants." Zia tucked it in the black Prada messenger bag Gina and Jack had given her for Christmas. It was exactly the right size to carry her iPad mini, her phone and all the paraphernalia she needed for work.

The dollars were still on her mind when she emerged from the subway at 72nd and Broadway just after seven o'clock. The Arctic cold front had finally blown itself out, but the air was still frosty enough for her to keep her head down and her shoulders hunched as she hurried the two blocks to the Dakota.

Jerome had gone off duty at six. The new night doorman, whose name Zia had to struggle to recall, intercepted her on the way to the elevators. "Excuse me, Doctor. A courier delivered this for you a short time ago."

With a word of thanks, she examined the plain white envelope he handed her. The outside contained only her name. The inside, Zia discovered with a delighted grin, contained an IOU for one carriage ride through Central Park, redeemable tonight or anytime tomorrow. Her pulse skipping, she dialed Mike's number.

"When did you get in?"

"A couple of hours ago."

"Why didn't you call me?"

"I knew you were working. So what's the deal? Are you up for a carriage ride?"

"It's freezing out there!"

"I'll keep you warm."

The husky promise sent a shiver of delight dancing down Zia's spine. She tried to remember if she'd seen any carriages during her dash from the subway. The new mayor had vowed to ban them, citing traffic safety and animal protection issues. She didn't think the ban had gone into effect but didn't remember noticing any carriages on the street.

"Why don't we decide what we'll do when you get here?"

"Fine by me. I'll grab a cab. See you shortly."

"Wait! How shortly?"

Too late. He'd already disconnected. She headed for the elevator again and keyed the door of the duchess's apartment with a fervent prayer she had time for a shower and to do something with her hair.

She didn't. The intercom buzzed while she was soaping herself down. She almost missed it over the drum of the water. Would have if she hadn't kept an ear tuned for it.

"Damn!"

She grabbed a towel but left a trail of wet footprints as she dripped her way from the bathroom to the hall intercom. "If that's Mr. Brennan, send him up."

"Yes, ma'am."

Back in the bedroom she yanked her closet doors. She was reaching for the comfortable sweats she spent most evenings in but stopped with her hand in midair. When she answered the front door a few moments later, she was wearing only the towel and a smile.

He, on the other hand, was wearing leather gloves, a charcoal cashmere overcoat and his black Stetson. Tipping the brim back with two fingers, he gave a low whistle.

"If this is how you New York City gals answer the door," he drawled as his gaze made a slow, approving circuit from

her neck to her knees and back again, "I'll have to make a few more executive board meetings."

"I'm only a temporary resident," she reminded him.

"So this is a Hungarian custom?"

"Actually, it is. Public baths have been popular in my country for several thousand years. The Romans loved to luxuriate in the bubbling hot springs in and around Budapest."

"That so?" He waggled his brows in an exaggerated leer. "You have to hand it to those Romans."

Laughing, she backed into the foyer. "Are you going to just stand there and gawk or do you want to come in?"

"I not sure I can move. I'm a little weak at the knees."

"Mike, for heaven's sake! I'm getting goose bumps in places no woman should. Come in."

Seven

For the next forty minutes the towel proved superfluous. So did Mike's overcoat, suit, shirt and tie.

He'd intended to display a little couth this time. Show Zia his smooth, sophisticated side as opposed to the barefoot beach bum and everyone's favorite uncle. The two of them had been so pressed for time in Galveston, so surrounded by their loving but in-the-way families. Despite having stolen her away for two memorable nights, he hadn't had time to show her that he could be as comfortable in her world as he was in his own.

Time wasn't the only issue that had factored into his decision to go for more suave and less hot and hungry. As every one of his sisters had tried to hammer home to their brothers and spouses, women need romance. Wooing. Candles and flowers and, yes, heart-shaped boxes of chocolates.

Mike had considered various strategies to up the romance quotient on the flight from Houston. New York offered all kinds of possibilities. A carriage ride in the park, an elegant dinner for two at the latest in spot, a Broadway show. He'd even been prepared to man up and take her to a concert or opera if she'd preferred.

Then she had to open the door and drain every drop of

blood from his head. He'd damned near had a coronary right there in the hall. The hour that followed would remain etched in Mike's mind for the next hundred years.

Now they were lazing side by side on a sofa angled to catch the heat of a roaring fire, both of them more or less fully clothed. She was in warm, well-washed sweats and fuzzy slippers. He'd pulled on his shirt, pants and shoes. He liked the way her head rested on the arm he'd stretched across the back of the sofa. Was glad, too, that they'd decided to order Chinese instead of going out in the cold. Empty cartons littered the coffee table and surrounded a half-consumed bottle of California cabernet.

Mike played with a strand of her hair and let his appreciative gaze roam the elegant room. The duchess's salon, as Zia had termed it, featured parquet floors, antiques and a ceiling so high it was lost in the shadows. Flames danced in a fireplace fronted with black marble, and a tiny Bose Bluetooth speaker filled the room with the haunting strains of a rhapsody. Liszt's "Hungarian Rhapsody No. 5," Zia had informed Mike. One of nineteen he'd composed based on folk music and Gypsy themes.

"This is nice," he announced, wrapping a finger around the silky strand of hair. "Much better than a carriage ride. We'll have to go that route next time I'm in New York, though."

She tipped her face to his. The firelight added a rosy glow to her cheeks but didn't do anything for the shadows under her eyes. Mike found himself wishing he could banish them by keeping her in bed for the next week or month or decade.

"Is this a horse fetish," she wanted to know, "or just a Texas thing?"

"Neither. My secretary pulled up a list of the ten most romantic things to do in New York."

"You're kidding."

"Nope. A carriage ride through Central Park was near the top of the list."

"Not in January!"

The laugh accompanying the protest was easy, natural. But when she tugged her hair free of his loose hold and sat up to retrieve her wineglass, he could feel the subtle withdrawal.

Well, hell! He'd overplayed his hand. The doc had let it be known back in Galveston she didn't want to get in too deep, too fast. Yet he'd just pretty well let drop that *he* was already in up to his neck.

With deliberate nonchalance, he redirected the conversation. "How's the proposal coming?"

The ploy worked. Groaning, she dropped back against the sofa.

"I had no idea getting a major research project approved was such a complicated process. I'm on the third draft of the proposal now and have yet to finalize the lab protocols. And I still have to meet with one of the consultants the hospital recommended. Evidently there's a whole subspecialty of 'grant professionals' out there who make their living seeking out and securing funding for studies like this."

Mike nodded. "We've worked with a few of them."

"I'm going to make an appointment tomorrow. If nothing else, they can give me a reality check on the dollar figures."

"Want me to take a look at them?"

"Would you?" She hesitated and bit her lip. "Or would that be a conflict of interest? If we come to GSI for funding, I mean."

He flashed her a grin. "Not unless you intend to skew your study to show that GSI operates the cleanest, most bacteria-free ships at sea."

"Not hardly." She laughed again, once more relaxed. "I don't even know how I got interested in the incidence of

MRSA aboard ships in the first place. Wait! Yes, I do! You and Rafe reeled me with all those statistics."

Some women were wowed by money, Mike thought wryly. Others by extravagant romantic gestures. The way to Anastazia St. Sebastian's heart, apparently, was through a germ.

"Get your draft and let me take a look."

She pushed off the sofa and retreated down a tiled hall. When she returned, she flipped on the overhead lights, killed the music and deposited a thick file secured by a paper clip on the coffee table.

"I'm assuming you're not interested in the list of publications or bibliography."

"You assume right. Let me see the description of facilities and resources, then we'll take a look at the budget."

Nodding, she slid off the paper clip. "The research center at Mount Sinai is state-of-the-art. We'll use the computers there to collect and analyze data. Also to test samples."

"Good."

"Here's the estimate of start-up costs and first-year operating budget, broken out by personnel, equipment and overhead. The second and third pages project the costs out for an additional two years, assuming the initial results warrant continuation."

As Mike skimmed the neat columns, her commentary took on a hint of nervousness.

"I ran the figures by the hospital's assistant comptroller. She sucked some serious air when she saw the bottom line. That's when she suggested I talk to a grant professional."

"I'm not surprised. One-point-two million isn't exactly chump change in today's environment." He flipped to the next page, studied the numbers, returned to the summary. "You may want to take another look at your ratio of direct to indirect costs in year two. You show a shift to more field

sampling at that point, so your direct costs will increase more than you project here."

Frowning, she leaned in for another look. "Damn! You're right. I've worked these numbers until I was cross-eyed. How did I miss that?"

"Because you worked the numbers until you were cross-eyed."

"Yet you caught it on the first pass."

"Unfortunately, I spend most of my time these days looking at numbers and not nearly enough with salt spray in my face."

He lazed back against the sofa, enjoying the way the firelight shimmered against the glossy black of her hair.

"Which brings me to another item on the top-ten list. Not as romantic as a carriage ride in Central Park maybe, but a lot more exciting."

"Mmm." The deep crease between her brows told him she was still crunching her numbers. "What's that?"

"Next month's Frostbite Regatta, hosted by the New York Yacht Club. A friend of mine is a member. He and his wife have been inviting me... Correction. They've been *daring* me to come up and help crew for years. I'll tell them I will if I can bring along a third mate."

He had her full attention now. Incredulous, she glanced from him to the draped windows and back again.

"Let me get this straight. You're inviting me to go sailing? On the open sea? In *February*?"

"Actually, we'd be sailing Long Island Sound, not the open sea but..." He rubbed his chin and appeared to give the matter some thought. "I can see how that might not appeal as much as the midwinter races in Kauai. I'd rather do those, too, if you can get away for a week."

"Kauai, like in Hawaii? Oh, Mike! You know I can't. I've got too much going on right now."

"Yeah, I figured that was out. But circle Saturday, Feb-

ruary thirteenth, on your calendar. That's the date of the Frostbite Regatta. And as an added incentive, everyone who survives the regatta will rig themselves out in long gowns or tuxes for the big Valentine bash at the 44th Street Club-house that evening."

She was getting that cautious look again. Pulling back. He could feel her retreating into herself. Away from him.

"I don't know my February schedule yet."

"No problem. Just give me a call when you do and we'll plan accordingly." He kept it easy, casual, and made a show of looking at his watch. "I'd better head back to the hotel."

"But you…" She stopped, restarted more slowly. "You could stay here."

"I've got two fat notebooks to review before the board meeting tomorrow morning. Besides…" He brushed a fin-gertip under the sooty-black lower lashes of her left eye. "You look whipped. Get some sleep, and I'll see you tomor-row evening. We'll go out for dinner, this time."

He shrugged into his suit jacket and pulled on his over-coat before issuing a final word of warning. "Just don't answer the door in a towel again. My system can't take another shock like that."

Zia flipped the locks behind him and shuffled slowly back down the tiled hall. She wasn't sure her system could take another shock like the one that had hit her when she'd opened the door, either.

The jolt of delight had come fast and cut deep. She shouldn't have ignored that warning. Shouldn't have en-gaged in the silly exchange about the Romans and laughed at his admission of going all weak at the knees. And she most definitely shouldn't have enticed him into bed again. Not that he'd required much enticing.

She wandered back into the salon and gathered the empty cartons to carry to the kitchen. The possibility she'd wor-

ried about in Galveston was now looking all too probable. She'd thought then she could fall in love with Mike Brennan. She knew now it was more than a mere possibility.

The old hurt, the one buried deep in her heart, sent out a familiar stab of pain. Dropping the cartons in the trash, Zia flattened both hands on the kitchen counter and fought back.

Why *not* take the tumble, dammit? Why *not* let herself start imagining a future that included Mike? He knew she couldn't have children. She'd shared that agonizing reality with him their first night together. She still couldn't quite believe she'd opened up to a stranger the way she had but even then, when they'd only known each other for a few hours, he'd called to something inside Zia. His humor, the intelligence behind his easy smile, his obvious affection for his nephew and Davy's for him…

Her raging inner debate stopped dead. As her flattened palms curled into fists, all she could hear was an echo of his sister's bitter revelation. Mike's ex-wife refused to give him children…and had broken his heart in the process.

"A francba!"

Thumping the counter with her fists, she whirled and stalked out of the kitchen.

She woke the next morning prey to the same wildly conflicting emotions. She wanted to have dinner with Mike that evening. She even wanted to be crazy stupid and go sailing with him in the dead of winter, then feel his hands and his mouth and his body covering hers in the coming weeks and months. Years!

Yet wanting wasn't enough. Was it?

What about Mike? His needs, his desires? Did she have the right, the incredible selfishness, to tie his future to her past?

She was still torn between waiting and wanting when

she hit the hospital. As always, she sublimated her personal life to the hectic routine. Team meetings, patient exams and family-centered rounds consumed most of her morning, but she used a late lunch break to review the list of consulting firms the assistant comptroller had given her yesterday. As much as she hated to divert any of her project's potential funding to consultants, their success rates in securing that funding overcame her initial reluctance.

The head of the first firm she contacted was out of town until the following week. His office manager offered to set up an appointment with an assistant but given the amount of money involved, Zia opted to wait for the main man.

She tried the second firm, Danville and Associates, and was put through to the boss himself. As brief as their conversation was, Zia's description of her proposal fired Thomas Danville's interest.

"Sounds like you've done a lot of preliminary work, Dr. St. Sebastian." He spoke fast, his words staccato and filled with energy. "But one of the key services we provide is a thorough scrub before a draft proposal goes final. We're very skilled at nuancing research projects to make them more salable to private foundations and corporations."

Judging by the successes posted on their website, Zia could believe it. But given the interest Mike and Rafe Montoya had already expressed, did her proposal need nuancing?

Danville sensed her hesitation and jumped on it. "You have some reservations about working with a consultant, right? Understandable. Look, why don't we get together and I'll explain exactly what we can do for you?"

"It'll have to be soon. I want to get this in the works."

"Not a problem. In fact…I'm having dinner with another client at La Maison tonight. It's just a few blocks from the hospital. I could swing by and meet with you beforehand.

Or, better yet, you could join us for dinner. Get a firsthand testimonial from a satisfied customer."

"I'm sorry, I have other plans for dinner tonight."

"Drinks, then. It'll be easier to talk at the restaurant than at the hospital."

That was true enough. Her beeper never seemed to stop going off here at work.

"What time do you finish your shift?" Danville asked.

He was certainly persistent. Probably not a bad trait for a grant professional.

"I should be done by seven."

"Perfect. That'll give us an hour before my other client arrives. I'll see you then."

Feeling as though she'd just been swept along on a high-energy tide, Zia tried to reach Mike. She guessed he was still in his board meeting and sure enough, her call went to voice mail.

"About dinner tonight. I'm getting together with a grant consultant at seven o'clock at La Maison on East 96th. He's hooking up with another client at eight, so you could meet me then and we'll go from there."

Mike wasn't in the best of moods when the Maritime Trades Association executive board meeting finally adjourned.

The US Coast Guard had presented an excellent update on their new electronic credentialing program. Mike and most other ship owners hailed it as a welcome advance, one that would allow the crews manning their ships to apply for recertification via any computer in any country in the world.

Unfortunately, someone had gotten to the reps from the Seafarers International Union. Citing growing concerns over government surveillance of electronic communications, they'd dug in their heels. They wanted a detailed

account of built-in safeguards to protect personal, medical and psychological information. Not an unreasonable demand but the resulting exchange was as exhaustive as it was acerbic. As if any system could guarantee 100 percent protection, Mike thought grimly as he retrieved his voice mails.

When he spotted Zia's name and number in his recent calls list, his gut tightened. She wanted to cancel dinner. He would bet money on it. The woman was so wary, so cautious. So damned worried about this baby thing. As if his interest in her depended on her reproductive abilities!

Thinking he might have to step up his campaign to convince her otherwise, Mike hit Play. His gut unkinked as he listened to her invitation to meet her at La Maison. He checked his watch and saw he had just enough time to go back to his hotel to shower. Better scrape off his five-o'clock shadow, too, he thought, scrubbing a palm over his chin. What he had planned for Dr. St. Sebastian tonight involved some very sensitive patches of skin.

Mike had been in business long enough to know as many deals were cut over drinks or dinner as they were in boardrooms. He hadn't thought twice about Zia meeting this consultant at what turned out to be a very small, very elegant restaurant on the Upper East Side…right up until he walked into the dimly lit bar and he spotted the slick New Yorker in the thousand-dollar suit crowding her space. Ignoring the fact that his own suit and tie had been hand tailored in Italy, Mike started toward them.

The consultant caught sight of him first. In one narrow-eyed glance he assessed the newcomer's style, size and attitude. As a result, he didn't need either Zia's warm greeting or the quick, proprietorial kiss Mike dropped on her lips to understand he was skirting dangerously close to

territorial waters. He acknowledged as much with a cool smile when he stood to shake hands.

"Good to meet you, Brennan. We were just talking about you."

"That right?"

"Zia…Dr. St. Sebastian…says your corporation is a source of funding for her research project."

"A *potential* source," she corrected, shooting Mike an apologetic glance. "Actually, I was relating some of the statistics you and Rafe shared about the rate of MRSA incidents among ships' crews."

"A correlation worth exploring," Danville said smoothly.

Too smoothly. Mike concealed his instinctive dislike behind a polite nod.

"I agree. I've reviewed Dr. St. Sebastian's draft proposal, but my VP for Support Systems will have to do an in-depth analysis of the final before he brings a recommendation for funding before our board."

"Of course."

Zia picked up on the chill in the air. Her brows rose, but her smile stayed in place as she rose and hooked her coat off the back of her chair.

"I appreciate you squeezing in time to meet with me, Tom. I'll email the draft proposal to you tomorrow."

"I'll look for it."

Yeah, Mike just bet he would. He didn't comment, though, until he had Zia in a cab and she turned to him with an exasperated look.

"What was that all about?"

"I didn't like the guy."

"Obviously. Care to tell me why?"

"He was too smooth. And he was poaching. Or trying to."

"Poaching? What on earth do you…? Oh."

"Yeah. Oh."

Her mouth opened. Closed. Opened again. "Please tell me you're not serious."

The irritation he'd clamped down on in the restaurant gathered a whole new head of steam. Dammit all to hell! He backed off every time Zia turned all wary and skittish. Folded himself almost in half trying not to push her into something she wasn't ready for. There was only so much a man could take, however.

"Sorry, sweetheart. I'm dead serious."

"I don't believe this. I assumed… I thought…"

She broke off, shaking her head in disgust. Mike should have let it go at that point. Given them both time to cool down. Perversely, he fanned the fire.

"You thought what?"

"I thought this Texas cowboy stuff was just another layer! One of the many that make up Michael slash Mike slash Uncle Mickey."

He had to smile. "You forgot Miguel. He's in there, too. Probably the most anachronistic part of the mix."

"Anachronistic?" Ice dripped from every syllable. "Or chauvinistic?"

"They're pretty much the same thing where I come from."

"And that's supposed to make me feel better?"

"No," he replied, realizing too late that he needed to tread carefully, "it's not supposed to do anything but put you on notice."

Her chin came up. A dangerous glint lit her dark eyes. "Of?"

Mike knew it was too soon. He'd intended to give her time. Calm her doubts. Let her get used to the course he was steering. But the angry set to her jaw told him he'd just run out of windage.

"Remember the deal we made back in Galveston?"

Anger gave way to the wariness that hit him like a right cross. "I remember," she said cautiously. "Do you?"

"Every word. I said I would tell you if and when I approached the hurting stage."

He reached for her hand. She resisted but he folded it between both of his. Was that a slight tremor in her fingers or the hammer of his own pulse? He didn't know, didn't care.

"I'm there, Zia. I'm in love with you, or so close it doesn't matter."

The admission came easy and felt so right he asked himself why the hell he'd waited this long. He got his answer in the quick flare of panic in the dark eyes locked on his face.

"Mike, I…uh…"

"Relax." He forced a grin. "This isn't a race. Doesn't matter who gets where first. And," he said when the panic didn't subside, "you don't need to come up with an appropriate response right this minute. You've got a whole month to think it through."

"A whole month?"

"Okay, three weeks and some change. Until the Frostbite Regatta," he added in answer to her blank look.

"Holy Virgin!" Her expression went from blank to incredulous. "You're not really planning to participate in that insanity, are you?"

"Not unless you do. Although I have to say…" His grin widened. Curling a knuckle under her chin, he tipped her face to his. "My sisters all insist I look pretty hot in a tux."

Her disbelief melted into a reluctant laugh. "Do they?"

"Word of honor." He puffed out his chest. "Be a shame if you didn't get to see me in all my splendor."

"And I can't do that without freezing my ass off aboard a sailboat as it cuts through the icy waters of Long Island Sound?"

"Nope. That's the deal. You, me, wind and waves." His voice softened. Caressed. Challenged. "C'mon, Doc. Live dangerously."

Eight

Despite her unrelenting schedule, Zia was thrilled when the duchess and Maria finally returned from their Texas sojourn the last week in January. She'd rattled around in the empty apartment during her hours off for well over a month. The week in Galveston and Mike's brief visit had provided welcome diversions. She'd also had lunch or dinner with her brother and Natalie several times during the interval. But she was ready for the companionable presence of the duchess.

Thankfully, the vicious Arctic cold and damp that had caused Charlotte's bones to ache so badly had loosened its grip on the city. The temperature hovered at a balmy forty degrees the evening Charlotte, Maria, Gina and the twins arrived home. Jack was in Paris for some high-level diplomatic meeting, while Sarah and Dev had flown back to LA.

That left Dom and Natalie and Zia to greet the remainder of the Texas contingent when they drove in from the airport. The three St. Sebastians waited in the lobby with Jerome, who'd lingered an additional forty minutes after his shift ended to greet the travelers.

"We can't stay," Gina said as she hopped out of the limo to distribute hugs all around, including a big one for the

delighted doorman. "The girls are tired and cranky. I need to get them home to bed. I'll see you this weekend, Grandmama, after you've rested and recovered."

She hopped back in and left it to the welcoming committee to escort the duchess inside. Zia noted with some concern that Charlotte leaned heavily on her cane as they crossed the lobby. So did Jerome. The doorman and Zia exchanged a speaking glance but neither wanted to spoil the homecoming by commenting on her uneven gait.

Yet after everyone else had dispersed and it was just the duchess and Zia settling in for a chat before the fire, Charlotte's first concern was for her great-niece. When Zia delivered the aperitif her aunt insisted on, the duchess's paper-thin skin of her palm stoked her cheek.

"I hoped to find the shadows under your eyes gone, Anastazia."

"It's been crazy here, Aunt Charlotte. I've been so busy."

"I can imagine." She accepted the snifter Zia handed her. "How did your presentation to the faculty go?"

"Great! Fantastic! Really, really good!"

Chuckling, the duchess hefted her glass in a salute. "Tell me."

Trying not to sound too self-congratulatory, Zia gave a quick recap of the nerve-racking session in front of the faculty and her fellow residents.

"They all found the statistics detailing the increase in Methicillin-resistant Staphylococcus aureus infections in neonatal facilities sobering."

"I should think so!"

"And no one challenged my correlation between the increasing number of MRSA incidents and staffing levels in neonatal intensive care units. Or," she added with deliberate nonchalance, "the need for more intensive study of MRSA in controlled environments similar to NIC units."

"Such as crew compartments on seagoing vessels?"

She shot the duchess an incredulous look. Charlotte chuckled and took a sip of her brandy. "Don't look so astonished. Mike Brennan paid me several visits after you left."

"He did?"

"He did. I suspect," she added drily, "he holds the mistaken impression I wield as much influence over my family as his *abuelita* does over his."

The comment struck Zia the wrong way. She couldn't believe Mike hadn't told her about these visits. Or that he might be conducting some kind of an end run by enlisting the duchess to exert her influence.

"Is that what he did? Ask you to plead his case for him?"

"Of course not. He's too intelligent for that. We discussed your research proposal…among other things."

"*What* other things?"

The abrupt demand had the duchess lifting a haughty brow. Skewered by that regal stare, Zia issued a quick apology.

"I'm sorry. It's just…Mike didn't tell me he'd spoken with you when he was here a few weeks ago."

"I'm not surprised," Charlotte returned. "Reading between the lines, I gather the time you two have spent together has been…" She paused. "Shall we say, intense."

Coming from the duchess, the delicate wording put spots of heat in Zia's cheeks. She took a few moments to regain her composure by downing a healthy gulp of *pálinka*. "I guess that's as good a description of our time together as any," she admitted.

The duchess's eyes might be clouded with age but they lingered on Zia's face with disconcerting shrewdness. "The man's in love with you, Anastazia. Or so close to the edge you could push him over with a single poke." Her voice softened, and her face folded into fine lines. "Why aren't you poking?"

"It's complicated."

"Tell me."

"I…"

"Tell me, dearest."

The quiet command broke the dam. Abandoning her chair, Zia dropped to her knees beside the duchess. The private pain she'd shared with no one but her brother—and Mike Brennan!—spilled out in quick, disjointed phrases.

"I had a hysterectomy. When I was in college. They had to do it to save my life. And now…now I can't have children."

She dropped her forehead. The words came more slowly now, more painfully.

"You saw Mike. He loves kids. He's terrific with them. He deserves someone who can give him the family he—"

"Bull!"

Zia's head jerked up. "What?"

"You heard me," the duchess retorted. "That's total and complete bull."

Her eyes snapping, she took her great-niece's chin in a firm grip.

"Listen to me, Anastazia Amalia. You're a sensitive, caring physician and a brilliant researcher. Far more important, you have a wonderful man who's in love with you. You should be grabbing at the future with greedy hands. Instead you're wallowing in self-pity. Stop it," she ordered briskly. "Now! This very instant!"

Zia reared back, or tried to. Charlotte refused to release her chin. Their eyes locked, faded blue and liquid black. One woman with a lifetime of great joy and great sorrow behind her, another just embarking on that perilous, exhilarating journey.

She was right, Zia realized with a crush of self-disgust. She'd been so worried about what she and Mike *couldn't* have that she'd refused to let herself focus on everything they *could*.

"Okay," she said on a shaky laugh. "I'm done wallowing."

"Good." The duchess didn't release her firm hold. "Now be honest with me. Do you love him?"

She couldn't deny it any longer. Not to Charlotte. Not to herself.

"Yes."

"Ahh." The quiet sigh feathered through the duchess's lips. Her cheeks creasing in a smile, she gave her greatniece's chin a little shake. "Then put the poor man out of his misery! Tell him how you feel."

"All right! I will."

The duchess released her grip but not her tenacious hold on the subject under discussion. "When?" she demanded.

Surrendering, Zia sank back on her heels. "He's flying in to New York for Valentine's weekend. He wants to take me sailing. In something called the Frostbite Regatta."

"Good heavens. That sounds perfectly dreadful."

"Exactly what I said!"

"Then again," Charlotte mused as she reached for her brandy and took a delicate sip, "I seem to recall that a sailboat rocking on a choppy sea can be rather erotic. If you're curled up in a bunk with the right person, of course."

Zia didn't share the duchess's musings with Mike when he called later that night to make sure the travelers had all returned home safely. She did, however, tell him that Charlotte had mentioned his visits.

"I enjoyed getting to know her a little better. She's a fascinating woman."

"She said pretty much the same thing about you."

"Not only fascinating, but very discerning." He let that hang for a moment before changing the subject. "So, where are you on your proposal?"

"It's signed, sealed and delivered. The research center's executive review committee meets tomorrow."

If...*when*...they gave the expanded study their stamp of approval, Danville and Associates would go out for funding. And if the financial gods were kind, the project would be up and running within weeks.

"Let me know what the committee decides," Mike said.

"I will."

"And I'll see you soon. I'm flying into New York the afternoon of the twelfth. I want to make sure we have time to suit you up for the regatta the next day."

"Right," she said slowly.

"You're not chickening out, are you?"

"What if the boat tips over? Do you know how quickly we could succumb to hypothermia?"

"Not gonna happen, Doc. It's been a while since I exercised my sea legs, but sailing's like riding a bicycle. It's easy once you learn the ropes."

"Oh, that's reassuring! You might be interested to know ERs treat more than three hundred thousand kids for bike injuries every year."

"Crap." He paused, no doubt thinking of his hyperactive nieces and nephews. "That many?"

"That many."

He mulled that over for a few moments before tossing out the one argument she couldn't counter. "I guess you'll just have to trust me to take care of you."

"I guess so. I'll see you on the twelfth."

Zia was conducting chart reviews with her interns when Dr. Wilbanks buzzed with word that the executive review committee had green-lighted her proposal.

"Congratulations," he said in his brusque way. "You're the first resident to have a study of this scope and magni-

tude approved. Who are you working with to secure funding?"

"Danville and Associates."

"Have we used them before?"

"They were on the list Ms. Horton gave me."

"Then I suggest you get with them as soon as possible and tell them to start the ball rolling."

"Yes, sir."

Zia made the call as soon as Dr. Wilbanks disconnected. Tom Danville added his congratulations, along with the suggestion that Zia come to his office so she could meet the others on his staff. She checked her schedule and set the appointment for three the following afternoon.

Danville and Associates occupied a suite of offices on the thirty-second floor of Olympic Tower on Fifth Avenue. Zia stepped out of the elevator into a sea of Persian carpets and gleaming mahogany. She cringed a little at the thought that the cost to maintain these expensive surroundings came from the commissions Danville and Associates made off proposals like hers. She'd included their commission in her budget but still…

A smiling receptionist confirmed her appointment and reached for her phone. "We've been expecting you, Dr. St. Sebastian. I'll let Tom know you're here."

Danville appeared a moment later. Zia wasn't intimately familiar with men's apparel, but the European in her had no trouble identifying the leather loafers and silk tie as Italian.

His eyes bright and brimming with high-voltage energy, he escorted her to his office. "I had my people scrub your proposal. They've lined up a hit list of potential funding sources. I think you'll be impressed."

He made quick work of the intros. Two men, one woman, all dressed as expensively as their boss. And all sporting

very impressive credentials, Zia knew, from her study of Danville and Associates' website.

Elizabeth Hamilton-Hobbs took the lead. A trim brunette in a black Armani suit and a butterscotch silk blouse, she held a BS and a master's from the Wharton School of Business. Zia's field might be medicine, but even she knew Wharton was private, Ivy League and one of the top-ranked business schools in the US.

"My colleagues and I are very impressed with your proposed research project, Dr. St. Sebastian. You're investigating a dangerous trend impacting medical facilities, but you left room to explore other occupational areas, as well. As a result—"

"As a result," Tom Danville jumped in, scrubbing his upper lip in his eagerness, "we have the perfect in with the big shipping companies like MSC, COSCO and GSI. Also with state and federal agencies looking at the spread of infectious disease among their prison populations."

Hamilton-Hobbs waited for him to finish before continuing her presentation "We've prepared a target list of private corporations and health-oriented foundations. Now that your study's been approved, we'll get the solicitations in the works and—"

"Dr. St. Sebastian doesn't want to hear 'in the works,'" Danville huffed, scrubbing his upper lip again. "Neither do I."

Zia went cold. Stone-cold. She didn't need the quick glance the brunette exchanged with her colleagues to guess what lay behind it.

Their boss was flying high. Soaring. That wasn't his upper lip he was itching. That was the underside of his nose.

An irritated septum was one of the classic symptoms of cocaine snorting, right along with the fever-bright eyes and hyperactivity. Zia couldn't believe she'd missed the warning

flags at their first meeting. She didn't miss them now, however. Danville must have cut a line right before she arrived.

Her glance shot from him to Hamilton-Hobbs. The other woman had to have seen the dawning realization and disgust in her client's expression. She held Zia's gaze with a steely one of her own.

"I'll be handling the solicitations personally, Dr. St. Sebastian. They'll go out this afternoon, and I promise I'll follow up on each one myself."

When Zia hesitated, the brunette laid her professional reputation on the line.

"Danville and Associates has one of the highest success rates in the country. I guarantee we'll secure the one-point-two million you require for your study."

Medicine, Zia had learned, was knowledge multiplied by experience compounded by instinct. So was life. She could get up, walk out and start over again with the next grant professional on the comptroller's list. Or she could trust Elizabeth Hamilton-Hobbs.

She nodded. Slowly. Not bothering to disguise her reluctance. "I want to be kept in the loop. Please copy me on each solicitation you send out and every response you receive."

Danville voiced an instant objection. "We'll send you weekly status reports. That's our standard policy. But we don't…"

His subordinate cut him off with a knife-edged smile.

"Not a problem, Dr. St. Sebastian. I'll keep you in the loop every step of the way."

Elizabeth held to her word. She cc'd Zia on every solicitation that went out and forwarded copies of every response that came in. In a remarkably short space of time, Danville and Associates secured more than eight hundred thousand dollars from three foundations and four private corpora-

tions....including a quarter million promised by GSA over the projected two-year life of the study.

Rafe Montoya called Zia personally with the news. He caught her at work, busy preparing for the weekly discharge conference. It was one of Children's Hospital's most popular sessions. Attended by faculty and staff alike, the conference focused on patients with unusual diagnoses or diseases difficult to treat. One of Zia's patients would be discussed at this session—a five-year-old who'd presented with retinitis pigmentosa, mental retardation and obesity. She'd tested him for a dozen different possibilities before diagnosing the extremely rare Bardet-Biedl Syndrome. She was preparing to lead the discussion of his case, but took Rafe's call eagerly.

"Thought you might want to know GSI's executive board voted unanimously to help underwrite the study."

"Really? That's fantastic!"

She couldn't resist a little happy dance. The gleeful two-step set her stethoscope bobbling and her interns gaping. But when the initial thrill subsided, she had to ask.

"Just out of curiosity, how many members of GSI's executive board are related to the CEO?"

"Seven of the twelve," Rafe admitted with a chuckle. "If it makes you feel any better, though, the remaining five all have extensive backgrounds in the shipping industry. Your proposal struck a chord with them, Zia. Especially after I dropped a casual reminder of the multimillion-dollar MRSA suit brought by the crew of the *Cheryl K*."

"Thanks, Rafe. I really appreciate your support. I'll do my damnedest to make sure our research justifies GSI's investment."

"That's all we can ask. And it wasn't just me pushing this," he added. "Mike's been behind this project from the start. Okay, not just the project. He believes in you, Zia."

* * *

Rafe's ringing endorsement was still front and center in Zia's mind when Mike called to advise her of his arrival time on February twelfth. He caught her in the hospital cafeteria. She'd missed lunch and had dashed down to grab a frozen yogurt and a much-needed break. She was just dousing the creamy ice-cream substitute with chocolate sprinkles when her cell buzzed. She fished the iPhone out of the pocket of her white coat and balanced it between her shoulder and ear while signing the chit for her yogurt.

"Wheels down at five-fifteen," Mike announced as Zia carried her treat to an empty table. "I'll be at my hotel by six-thirty. Seven at the latest. Plan on dinner at eight, with several hours of uninterrupted quality time to follow. Or," he said with a husky laugh that raised shivers of anticipated delight, "quality time first and dinner to follow. Your choice, Doc."

"Wrong," she countered with a quick lick of her spoon.

"Which part?"

"The choice part. Anyone who can squeeze a quarter-of-million dollars out of his board of directors to study germs deserves first pick."

It was a joke. A lighthearted attempt to thank him for his support. Yet Zia sensed instantly the joke had fallen flat.

"Is this something we need to talk about?" he asked. "Our personal relationship vis-à-vis our professional responsibilities? I don't have a problem keeping them separate, Zia."

"Neither do I. I was just kidding, Mike. Although..."

Now that it was out there like the proverbial elephant in the room she couldn't ignore it.

"Is it really possible to separate them? Would you have endorsed my study if you didn't...if we weren't...?"

"Lovers?" he supplied when she fumbled for the right word. "Friends? Acquaintances?"

"Involved."

That was greeted with a dead silence that thundered in Zia's ears, drowning out the rattle of the trays two candy stripers had just placed on the cafeteria's conveyor belt.

"Okay," Mike said after that pregnant pause. "Looks like we're going to have to sit down and have a long talk about tax credits and incentives for corporations to invest in research and development. They vary greatly at national, state and local levels."

"I know that."

"Did you also know Texas possesses four of this country's busiest deep-water ports? Galveston, Beaumont, Houston and Corpus Christi."

"No," she replied, a little put off by the lecturing tone.

"Houston is the tenth busiest port in the *world* in tonnage. So yes, GSI invests heavily in research we think may positively impact our industry and, oh, by the way, earns us almost as much in tax breaks as our original investment. Does that answer your question?"

"No," Zia snapped back, annoyed now. "I know how much GSI invests in research. Rafe briefed me on the figures in your office, yes?"

She could hear her accent thickening, feel the temper stirring behind it.

"My question was…and still is…would you have supported this particular project if you and I were not *involved*?"

"Dammit, woman, is that the best you can up with to describe where we are together?"

He still hadn't answered her question, but he now singed the airways. She gripped the phone and started to bite back. Would have, if she hadn't remembered her recent conversation with the duchess.

She owed Mike the truth. She might have given it if he hadn't just come down on her with both feet. Gritting her teeth, she forced a cool reply.

"Do you not think this is something we should discuss in person?"

"No," he shot back, as irritated now as she was. "I told you I wouldn't push you. I also remember saying this isn't a race. But I think I need some indication of whether you're even on the track."

"Jézus, Mária és József!" Goaded, she spit out the truth she'd owned up to so recently. "I love you! There! Is that what you wish to hear?"

The pause this time was longer. Moments instead of seconds.

Embarrassed by her heated outburst, Zia glanced around to see if any of the other cafeteria customers had tuned in. None had, and despite her simmering irritation she found herself holding her breath until a slow drawl came across the airwaves.

"Oh, yeah, darlin'. That's exactly what I wanted to hear. Maybe not quite in that tone, but I'm not complaining."

She could hear the laughter in his voice. And something deeper, something that locked her breath in her chest.

"Care to repeat it?" he asked, a caress in each word. "Without the attitude this time?"

How in God's name did he do this? Spark her temper one moment and make her melt the next? Sighing, Zia stabbed her spoon into the melting yogurt.

"I love you."

"There now. That wasn't so hard, was it?"

"Yes, it was! I was going to wait until this weekend to tell you, in the proper setting."

"Aboard a sailboat while we're freezing our asses off?"

"No, you fool. Before that. Or at the ball afterward."

She gave a hiccuping laugh. "I hadn't nailed down the specifics."

"Tell you what. You decide on the venue and we'll do this again in person. Deal?"

A smile spread across her heart. "Deal."

Nine

To Zia's infinite relief, she didn't get to experience the thrill of chopping through the icy waters of Long Island Sound. A front rolled in Friday afternoon, bringing with it a dense fog. Every airport on the East Coast shut just hours before Mike's private jet was scheduled to land. He had to divert to Pittsburgh and wait it out.

The impenetrable mist continued to blanket New York well into Saturday morning, forcing the yacht club to postpone their Frostbite Regatta. The Valentine Ball, however, remained on schedule for that evening. Mike promised he'd arrive by plane, train or rental car to escort her to the big bash.

The duchess took advantage of the delay to arrange a shopping expedition. Zia had already called Gina to ask if she could borrow one of her many gowns, but Charlotte dismissed that with a wave of one hand. "Nonsense. You have a very distinct style, quite different from Gina's."

"I've lived in white coats and sweats for almost three years," Zia protested. "If I had a distinctive style, it's dead and buried."

"Then we shall have to resurrect it."

Conceding defeat, Zia buzzed down and asked Jerome

to hail a taxi. It was waiting curbside when the two women emerged into the gray, drizzly afternoon a little past one o'clock.

The doorman opened the rear door with a flourish. "Where shall I tell the driver to take you, Duchess?"

"Saks Fifth Avenue."

"Of course."

The cabbie zipped through the light weekend traffic and pulled up less than thirty minutes later at the mecca for shoppers with discriminating tastes and the money to indulge them. Saks's flagship store first opened in 1924 and now covered an entire city block. Its seventh-floor café looked down on the spires of St. Patrick's Cathedral. Every floor above and below offered an array of tempting, high-end goods.

Charlotte had been forced to dispense with the services of a personal shopper during the lean years. Since Sarah married and her husband had taken over management of the family's finances, however, she was once again able to indulge in one of life's more decadent luxuries.

The ponytailed personal attendant had been alerted by a phone call from Jerome and was waiting curbside to help his clients out of the cab. "What a delight to see you again, Duchess."

"And you, Andrew."

"How may I assist you today?"

"This is my great-niece, Dr. Anastazia St. Sebastian. She requires a ball gown, shoes and an appointment at the salon."

"A pleasure to meet you, Dr. St. Sebastian." The shopper measured Zia's lithe figure and distinctive features with something approaching ecstasy. "I'm sure we can find just what you're looking for."

Mere moments later he had them ensconced in a private viewing room on the fifth floor. Crystal flutes shared

a silver tray with iced champagne and bottles of sparkling water.

"May I ask if you have a particular style or color in mind?" Andrew asked as he poured champagne for Charlotte and a Perrier for Zia.

"No frills," the duchess pronounced. "Something sleek and sophisticated. In midnight blue, I think. Or..." She cocked her head, assessing Zia with the discerning eye that had once filled her closets with creations from the world's most exclusive designers. "Red. Shimmering, iridescent red."

"Oh, yes!" Andrew almost clapped his hands in delight. "With her ebony hair and dark eyes, she'll look delicious in red. Emily! Madeline!" A snap of his fingers made the two waiting saleswomen jump. "What do we have that might fit the bill?"

"It's Valentine's week," the older of the two women reminded him. "We're swimming in red."

"Well, show the duchess and Dr. St. Sebastian what we have."

The women disappeared and returned mere moments later with an array of designer originals. Each, Zia noted, was more expensive than the last. Not that she was particularly concerned about the price tag. Charlotte had flatly refused to let her contribute to household expenses for the past two and a half years. She'd insisted instead that her great-niece's company in the big, empty apartment was more than enough recompense. So Zia had banked her entire salary and could well afford to splurge on something outrageously expensive.

She tried several designs and labels, but the moment she slithered into a tube of screaming scarlet, she knew that was the one. The front bodice was cut in a straight slash from shoulder to shoulder. The back, however, plunged well below her waist. And every step, every breath, set off

tiny pinpricks of light from the sparkling paillettes woven into the fabric.

Three-inch stilettos and a clutch bag in silver completed the ensemble, but the duchess wasn't done. After high tea at the seventh-floor café with its magnificent views, the two women hit the salon. They emerged three hours later. Charlotte's snowy hair was arranged in a regal upsweep. Zia wore hers caught high behind one ear with a rhinestone comb, falling in a smooth black wing over the other.

It was almost six when they returned home. Mike had called to let Zia know he'd made it into the city okay and would pick her up at seven. That left a comfortable margin to freshen up, shimmy into her gown and apply a little more makeup than her usual swipe of lip gloss. She was adding mascara to her thick lashes when the duchess tapped lightly on her bedroom door.

"Oh, my dear!" Charlotte's blue eyes misted a little as she had Zia perform a slow pirouette. "You've inherited the best of the St. Sebastian genes. There's Magyar in your eyes and high cheekbones, centuries of royal breeding in your carriage. You do the duchy of Karlenburgh proud, my dear."

Charlotte's praise stirred a glow of pride. Zia had indeed inherited a remarkable set of genes. The fierce Magyars who'd swept down from the steppes on their ponies…the French and Italian princes and princesses who'd married into the St. Sebastian family in past centuries…the Hungarian patriots who'd fought so long and so hard to throw off the Soviet yoke… They'd all contributed to the person she was. She felt the beat of their blood in her veins and a wash of surprise when the duchess pressed a small velvet box into her hand.

"These are part of your heritage, and my gift to you."

Zia flipped the lid on the box to reveal a pair of ruby

earrings nested in black velvet. Each red oval dangled from a smaller but similarly cut diamond.

"Oh, Charlotte! They're beautiful. I'll certainly wear them tonight, but I won't keep them. You should give them to one of the twins."

"I've managed to preserve a few pieces for my great-grandchildren. And Dev, clever boy that he is, has helped me reclaim some I was forced to sell over the years. These," she said with a sniff of disdain, "were apparently purchased by an extremely vulgar Latvian plutocrat for his mistress. I didn't ask Dev how he recovered them, although I understand Jack had to step in and exercise some rather questionable behind-the-scenes diplomatic maneuvering. Now," she finished firmly, "they're yours. Let's see how they look on you."

Zia thought they looked magnificent.

So did Mike when he arrived a few moments later.

When Zia met him at the door, what looked like an acre of pleated white shirtfront and black tuxedo filled her vision. He carried his overcoat over his arm, his hat in his hand and an awed expression on his face.

"Wow. You, Dr. St. Sebastian, are stunning."

"It's the earrings." She bobbed her head to set the rubies dancing. "Charlotte gave them to me, insisting they're part of my heritage."

"Trust me," he growled when she turned to precede him through the foyer, "it's not the earrings. You sure that dress won't get us both arrested?"

She was laughing when she left him to say hello to the duchess while she fetched her wrap…and thoroughly surprised for the second time that evening when she exited the lobby to find a black carriage with bright yellow wheels drawn up at the curb. The driver wore a top hat and volu-

minous red coat. A jaunty red plume decorated his horse's headpiece.

Zia came to a dead stop. "You've *got* to be kidding."

"Nope. I decided to do it up right this evening."

"You do know it's February, right? There's still frost on the ground."

"Not to worry. Natalie sent along a warm blanket. And your brother provided this." He fished a thin silver flask out of his pocket and held it up with a smug grin. "It's not *pálinka*, but Dom guarantees it'll warm the cockles of your heart. Whatever the hell those are," he added as he took her elbow to help her climb aboard.

"The ventricles," Zia murmured while he settled beside her. "From the Latin, *cochleae cordis*. When did you see Natalie and Dom?"

"Right before I came to pick you up." He draped the blanket over her knees and settled his hat on his head before stretching an arm across her shoulders to keep her close for added warmth. "All right, Jerry. Let's go."

The driver nodded and checked over his shoulder for traffic before clicking to his horse. Still slightly dazed to find herself clip-clopping down Central Park West, Zia felt compelled to ask.

"Did you stop by Natalie and Dom's just to pick up a blanket and brandy?"

"Pretty much. Although *abuelita* suggested it would be a smart move to let your brother know I intended to ask you to marry me. I wasn't too keen on the idea," he admitted with a grimace. "At best, Dominic considers me a half step above a freebooter. But I figured I…"

"Wait! Back up!"

"To what? Freebooter? It's an old Dutch term for pirate." He attempted to look innocent but the gleam in his eyes gave him away. "Or do you mean the part of about telling Dom I intend to propose?"

"You know very well that's what I mean!"

"Well, I have to say His Grace wasn't all that happy about his sister hooking up with a lowlife Texas wharf rat. But after some abject begging on my part and several comments from Natalie about *his* lifestyle prior to marriage, Dom conceded it was your decision."

Zia's mind whirled with images of swashbuckling pirates and Dom assuming his haughtiest grand duke demeanor and Mike trying his best to appear abject. She was still trying to sort through the kaleidoscope when he used the arm draped across her shoulders to angle her into a close embrace. His breath warmed her cheek, and his eyes smiled down into hers.

"Why look so surprised? What did you think was going to happen after you threw that bombshell at me over the phone?"

"I *thought* we were going to talk about it this weekend, at a time and venue to be decided."

"We could talk, I suppose, but it makes more sense to me to cut right to the chase. I love you. You love me. What else matters, Anastazia Amalia Julianna St. Sebastian?"

"Did Dom make you memorize all my names?"

"No, that was Natalie. Your sister-in-law," he added with a touch of awe, "is a powerhouse packed in a very demure, very deceptive package. I'm not sure I want to get her and my sisters in the same room at the same time. The males on both sides of our respective family trees might never recover."

A thousand questions had swirled through Zia's mind. Where would they live? How would marriage affect her appointment to Dr. Wilbanks's research team? When, if ever, would she return to her homeland? But his comment about family trees pushed everything else out of her head.

"We *do* need to talk, Mike." She threw a quick glance at the driver and dropped her voice. "We're making a life

decision here and I don't even know how you feel about adoption. Or fostering. Or using a surrogate or…or not having children at all."

"Look at me."

His eyes lost their teasing glint and he, too, lowered his voice to give her gut-wrenching worry the seriousness it demanded.

"I'm good with *any* of those options, Zia. As long as we make the decision together."

"But your family…your sisters…"

"This isn't about them. It's about us. You and me, spending the rest of our lives together. I want to sail the Pacific with you and show you my world. Tag along behind you at the hospital to learn more about yours. When and if we decide to bring children into the world we create together, we'll figure out the best way to do it. All that's required at this moment is a simple 'yes.'"

The old hurt, the sense of loss Zia had carried since that long-ago ski trip, was still buried deep in her psyche. She suspected it would never fully disappear. But a burgeoning joy now overlaid the ache. The duchess was right. She had to reach out and grab the future with both hands.

Literally *and* figuratively. Sloughing off her doubts, she hooked both hands in the lapels of Mike's overcoat and tugged him closer. "Yes, Michael Mickey Miguel Brennan. Yes."

When he moved in to seal the deal with a kiss, Zia knew she would always remember this snapshot in time. Whatever came, whatever the future he'd sketched for them brought, she would feel February's nip. Hear the horse's hooves clacking on the cold pavement, the carriage wheels rattling out their winter song.

Then he surprised her with another memory to tuck away and savor. This one included a jeweler's box. Her second of the night, Zia thought with a wild thump of her

heart. She raised the lid, her fingers a little shaky, and gasped when the pear-shaped diamond caught the glow of the streetlamps.

"I had to guess at your ring size," he confessed as he plucked the ring out of its nest and eased it over her knuckle. "The fit looks pretty good to me, though."

Not just the fit. The size and clarity and the fact that it adorned her finger had Zia swinging between delight and disbelief. She'd met this man less than two months ago and now wore his ring. It was only a symbol. A *very* expensive token. Yet it shouted to the world she and Mike intended to make a life together. She'd never appreciated the awesome power of symbols before.

She tucked her hands under the blanket and fingered the ring throughout the ride. The raised mounting and sharp, V-shaped prong protecting the pear's pointed tip had almost drawn blood by the time they arrived at the New York Yacht Club.

Hemmed in on three sides by towering skyscrapers, the club was a bastion of old Manhattan now immortalized as a National Historic Landmark. Light poured from the huge windows fronting West 44th Street. Fashioned to resemble the elaborate transoms of Spanish galleons, the windows gave tantalizing views of an immense interior room lined with scale models of members' yachts.

Hundreds of scale models, Zia discovered after she and Mike had checked their coats and joined the glittering crowd. Thousands! Some with sails furled, some in full rigging. They were mounted on lit shelves that filled almost every inch of the fantastic room's walls, leaving space only for a monstrous white marble fireplace decorated with tridents and anchors and an oval painting of a ship in full sail. Zia rested her arm lightly in the crook of Mike's arm and craned her neck to take in all the nautical splendor.

"Mike!"

A short, sturdy fireplug of woman with iron-gray hair and leathery skin cut through the crowd. A distinguished and much taller gentleman trailed in her wake.

"That's Anne Singleton," Mike advised as the woman plowed toward them. "Her husband and I served in the navy together."

Zia appreciated the brief heads-up, especially after Anne latched on to Mike's lapels and hauled him down for a loud, smacking kiss. She broke the lip-lock but hung on to his tux.

"Can't believe we finally got you up here to the Frostbite Regatta and the damned thing gets postponed! Promise you'll come when we reschedule."

"We'll see."

"If you're done with him, Annie, mind if I say hello?"

The mild exposition came from the man Zia assumed must be Singleton's husband. His wife relinquished her hold and used the brief interval while they shook hands to inspect Zia from head to toe. All of a sudden she let out an earsplitting whoop.

"He did it!" Her leathery face creased into a wide grin. Eyes alight, she jabbed an elbow into her husband's side. "Harry! He did it!"

"I see," he replied, wincing.

Zia didn't, until Mike explained. "After cooling my heels so long in Pittsburgh this morning, I wasn't sure I'd get here in time to pick up the ring. Tiffany's said they would courier it to my hotel, but just to be safe I called Anne and asked her to pick it up, then meet me at the airport."

"Which I was so thrilled to do! You have no idea how many women I've tried to hook this man up with in the past three years. I've run through every one of my single, divorced and widowed friends, the *daughters* of those friends, the *friends* of those…"

"I think she's got the picture, Anne."

"Oh hush, Harry! You paraded a few past him, too. Remember that bottle blonde you invited to the races in Newport? Worst weekend of my life," his wife confided with a shudder. "The woman had a laugh that could strip the paint from a steel hull."

"True," her husband conceded good-naturedly.

They were so different, Zia thought. One so tall and elegant in his tux, the other wearing what was probably a ten-thousand-dollar designer original with complete disregard for the way it hitched up on one shoulder and bunched around her sturdy hips. Yet the affection between them was obvious and heartwarming.

"I'm Harry Singleton, Dr. St. Sebastian. I don't know if Mike told you, but he and I go way back."

"Please call me Zia. And, yes, he mentioned that you served in the navy together."

"Did he also mention that he saved my ass when I went overboard in the Sea of Japan during Typhoon Ito?"

"No."

She threw Mike a questioning glance, but Anne Singleton waved an impatient hand. "You can bore her with your war stories later. Right now we need to toast this momentous occasion."

She detached Zia from Mike, caught her arm and hauled her toward a table groaning with crystal and china bearing the yacht club's distinctive insignia etched in gold. Two other couples lingered by the table, cocktails in hand. While her husband signaled to one of the hovering attendants, Anne introduced Zia to their obviously close circle of friends.

"That's Alec, former conductor of the Lincoln Center Orchestra," she said, stabbing a finger at each of the four in turn. "Judy, his wife and the lawyer you want if you're ever charged with tax evasion. Helen, mother of five and the world's greatest cook. Dan, who's yet to miss one of

Helen's meals. Okay, now listen up, crew. This is Zia St. Sebastian. She and Mike are about to hook the bight."

Zia's puzzled look generated grins all around and several equally unintelligible phrases.

"Fit double clews," Harry supplied, his eyes twinkling.

"Get spliced," the retired conductor put in.

"Also," Judy drawled, "known as getting hitched." She rounded the table and took both of Zia's hands in hers. "I know protocol says you're supposed to congratulate the man in this situation, but I think everyone at this table will agree you've won a real prize."

Zia didn't need to hear Mike's low groan to know his friends had acutely embarrassed him. She, on the other hand, was delighted to discover yet another dimension to his multifaceted personality. A side of him this group obviously cherished. A side she was suddenly, voraciously eager to explore.

The rest of the evening passed in whirl of color and music. The seven-course dinner was a gourmand's delight. The live band provided dreamy music during and after the meal. What kept Zia laughing, though, were the personal recollections that grew more incredible and less believable as the night progressed. Interestingly, there was only one mention of Mike's previous plunge into stormy matrimonial waters. It was couched in an obscure nautical term that dropped Zia's jaw when Anne whispered a translation.

Her sides were still aching when she and Mike collapsed in the backseat of a taxi well past one in the morning. By unspoken consent they went to his hotel. And, again by mutual consent, they called the duchess the next morning to ask her permission for a family gathering at the apartment later that afternoon.

Natalie and Dom showed up. So did Gina and Jack and the twins. Maria made a special trip in, and even Jerome managed to pop up for a quick glass of champagne.

After the toasts and hearty congratulations, Dom engineered a few moments alone with Zia. They stood at the windows overlooking Central Park, two foreigners with unbreakable ties to America…and Americans.

"This is what you want?" he asked softly in their native Hungarian.

"Yes."

"It's not easy to blend two worlds, two nationalities."

"You and Natalie don't seem to have had any problems."

"We haven't," Dom agreed, his gaze drifting to his wife. "But Natalie is altogether unique."

"So is Mike."

His glance came back to Zia. The love in his eyes flooded her heart. "Then I wish you all the joy that I've found, little one."

"Thank you."

An hour later, Zia kissed Mike goodbye. She hated to see him go. This separation loomed so much larger than their previous weeks apart. It also resurfaced her concerns about where they'd live and how they'd merge their very different careers.

"We'll work it out."

"Before or after we're married?"

"Whenever."

"Mike…"

Her snort of exasperation made him smile, but his eyes turned dead serious as he curled a knuckle under her chin.

"We Texicans are thickheaded as hell, darlin'. Stubborn, too. But I've been down this road before. Nothing and no one matters to me more than you do. We'll work out the minor details."

Mike made pretty much the same declaration to his family when he returned to Houston and announced his engagement. Eileen took considerably more convincing than the

rest. Probably because she'd seen him at his lowest point after his divorce.

Mike hadn't been happy then, when his sister had tracked him to one of Houston's sleaziest waterfront dives. And he wasn't happy now, when she marched into his office unannounced and uninvited. It didn't faze his sister that he was on a teleconference with Korea. She planted a hip on the corner of his desk, crossed her arms and waited.

"I like Zia," she said the moment he disconnected. "I do! And I get down on my knees every night to thank God she was there to drag Davy out of the undertow. But you've known her for what? Six weeks?"

Mike set his jaw, but she ignored the warning.

"That's two weeks less than you knew The Bitch before you waltzed her to the altar."

"Eileen…"

"I don't want to see you hurt again, Mike. None of us do." Tears filmed her eyes. "Please tell me you know what you're doing."

The tears took the sting from his anger. He pushed out of his chair and came around to drape an arm across her shoulders.

"Jill was heat and hunger and lust. Zia's…" He searched for the impossible words to describe her. "Zia's what you and Bill have," he said finally. "What Kate and Maureen and our parents and *abuelita* all found. What I need."

His sister heaved a resigned sigh. "Since you put it that way…"

He thought he was home free after that. Right up until the middle of March, when Rafe came into his office just hours after Mike's return from a three-day meeting in Seoul. A frown creased his brother-in-law's forehead and his dark eyes telegraphed trouble. Still, Mike wasn't prepared for his uncharacteristically hesitant opening salvo.

"You remember the bottom line on Zia's MRSA study?"

"One point two mil and some change." A knot formed low in Mike's belly. He'd worked with Montoya long enough now to read his VP for Support System's unspoken signals. "Why?"

Rafe scowled at computer printouts in his hand and framed a slow, careful reply. "The change seems to have multiplied since the original proposal. And I'm damned if I can figure out why."

Ten

With Rafe's words hanging heavy in the air, Mike got out from behind his desk. "Let's take this to the conference table. You need to show me exactly what's got you concerned."

The table was a slab of thick glass supported by a bronze base. It seated twenty and had hosted too many high-level negotiations and contract signings for Mike to count. Those billion-dollar deals weren't on his mind as Rafe spread out his pencil-annotated reports, however. What concerned him was a specific project that GSI had helped fund to the tune of a quarter-of-a-million dollars.

"The study's direct costs track," Rafe said, spreading out a series of documents. "Zia's initial report accounts for every hour her team spent refining their objectives and setting up their base of operations. Ditto expenses for supplies and equipment, hours logged on the center's computers and fees paid to their outside funds consultant."

Mike frowned as he skimmed the fees charged by Danville and Associates. The total was on the high side, but not out of the ballpark compared to those charged by other firms that specialized in securing and managing grant mon-

ies. He just couldn't get past his instinctive and purely personal gut reaction to Danville himself.

"The discrepancy's in the indirects," Rafe was saying as he flipped several pages.

Well, hell! Mike had warned Zia to check her indirects.

They were tricky at best. A soft area encompassing overhead expenses like administrative support, utilities and depreciation for buildings and equipment. Usually the parent institution—in Zia's case Mount Sinai's school of medicine—negotiated with the United States Department of Health and Human Services every four years or so to determine its indirect cost rate. Unfortunately, those negotiations weren't based on any hard-and-fast mathematical formula. They had to take into consideration such intangibles as the school's academic standing, salary levels of their professors compared to other institutions, and so on.

"As you know," Rafe said, echoing his thoughts, "indirect rates can vary anywhere from twenty to forty percent depending on the reputation of the institution involved. And even when HHS agrees to a rate, there's still considerable flex in the process."

He flipped to another printout. This one showed the amounts contributed by private foundations and corporations.

"Not all of Zia's investors funded her indirects at the same percentage. These two didn't fund the indirects at all."

Mike zeroed in on a single entry. "But GSI did."

"Yes, we did. We also approved the formula the university uses to determine how much of the money we send them goes into their general operating fund and how much goes back to Zia's project."

Rafe paused and stroked a fingertip along his pencil-thin mustache. An unconscious habit, Mike knew. One that suggested he'd damned well better sit up and pay attention.

It also usually indicated he wouldn't like what his VP for Support Systems was going to say next.

"That redistribution doesn't happen automatically. The project manager has to request it."

"What are you telling me? Zia hasn't requested her indirects?"

"Yeah, she has. Or rather, the agency managing her project funds has."

"Danville and Associates."

"Right. But…" Rafe frowned at his penciled notes. "As best I can tell, they're using a different formula than the one we approved."

Mike bit down on a curse. Whatever the discrepancy— *if* there was one—this was Zia's project. When she signed her name on the bottom line of her proposal, she'd accepted full responsibility for how the money expended on the project was used.

"I'm sure Zia can explain the difference," he said with a shrug.

He checked his watch, saw it was almost three-thirty New York time and pulled out his cell phone. When his call went to her phone's voice mail, he left a message asking her to call him back, then tried the number she'd given him for her new work area at the research center. That call was answered by one of the other researchers working the project.

"Dr. Elliott."

After more than a month of communicating with Zia via email, FaceTime and phone—and one very eye-opening visit to the research center—Mike was now on a first-name basis with most of his fiancée's team.

"Hi, Jordan. This is Mike Brennan. I'm trying to reach Zia."

"She's still at lunch. I expected her back before now but it's a working session. Must be running longer than expected."

"Must be."

"I'll be happy to take a message. Or you could contact Danville and Associates. I'm sure Tom's secretary can tell you where he and Zia are having lunch."

Mike didn't skip a beat, but he could feel his fist tightening on his phone. "Just ask her to give me a call, would you?"

"Sure thing."

"Thanks."

He cut the connection and gave Rafe a quick update. "She's having a late lunch. Why don't you leave your notes and I'll go over them with her when she calls back?"

"Sure. In the meantime, I'll keep scrubbing the numbers."

Mike pushed away from the conference table but didn't return to his desk after Rafe left. Jamming his hands in his pants pockets, he faced the windows and stared unseeing at the haze belched out by Houston's millions of vehicles and dozen or so oil refineries. ExxonMobil's Baytown facility—the world's largest—processed more than five hundred thousand barrels a day. It also contributed heavily to GSI's profit margin. Even from where he stood, Mike could see two GSI tankers negotiating the bays and bayous leading to Exxon's giant facility. Yet the sight of their distinctive green-and-white hulls barely registered on his consciousness. He was still trying to understand his gut-level reaction to hearing Zia had yet to return from an extended lunch with Tom Danville.

Hell! What was the matter with him? He wasn't some Neanderthal. A throwback to the Middle Ages, jealously guarding his property. What he was, he reminded himself, was ass over end in love with a smart, savvy professional woman. One who couldn't be more different from his ex-wife if she tried. And yet...

He still remembered Jill's reaction when he'd told her

he was filing for divorce. He'd be a long time erasing the memory of her face as it twisted into a mask of fury. Or the string of affairs she'd tossed at him in retaliation. Or her snarling admission that she'd counted the hours until he'd left on another of his endless business trips. Or her shouted obscenities when he'd walked out the door for the last time.

Mike had never told anyone about that sorry scene. Not his family. Not his friends. Maybe because he knew the debacle was as much his fault as Jill's. He *had* used his rapidly expanding business interests as an excuse to escape her endless complaints. He *had* picked up more than one subtle hint that there might be more to his wife's jaunts to Vegas than casinos and high-end malls. And he'd experienced nothing but relief when their marriage was finally over.

What he had now, with Zia, represented the opposite end of the spectrum. From the moment he'd met her on the beach at Galveston, he'd felt nothing but admiration for her dedication, her brilliance, her unshakable belief that her research might make a difference. And, yeah, the woman inside those sweats and lab coats was pretty spectacular, too.

Now her research could be in trouble. Rafe hadn't come right out and mentioned fraud or mismanagement. He didn't have to. Mike didn't believe in the old saw that money was the root of all evil, but he'd seen it corrupt too many people too often. His jaw set, he whirled and strode to the outer office.

"Clear my schedule for the rest of the week, Peggy. I'm going to New York."

"Tomorrow?"

"This afternoon—or as soon as they can get the Gulfstream turned around."

The jet would have to be serviced after the flight back from Seoul and a new crew called in. Mike would be lucky to be in the air by five, in New York by ten Eastern time. Although he wasn't jet-lagged from the Korea trip, he knew the time warp would hit with a vengeance somewhere over

Ohio. He should probably wait until tomorrow to fly but couldn't shake the need to work through this problem—whatever it was—with Zia.

Half a continent away, Zia was prey to the same itchy feeling of impatience. Against her better judgment, she'd yielded to Tom's argument they could get more done at a restaurant than at his office, where his phone rang incessantly and other clients demanded his attention. She'd also accommodated his busy schedule by agreeing to a late lunch.

His solo appearance at this cozy French bistro on Broadway and 58th had irritated her no end, however. So had his insistence that they eat before getting down to the nitty-gritty. She'd picked her way through half of her Salad Niçoise but now pushed her plate to the side and voiced her annoyance.

"I've communicated directly with Elizabeth Hamilton-Hobbs for the past month. She's my primary contact at your firm. I don't understand why she couldn't make this meeting."

"That's one of the reasons I wanted this face-to-face." Danville dabbed his mouth with his napkin and folded his expression into unhappy lines. "I know how well you and Elizabeth connected. But…well…I had to let her go."

"What! When?"

"This morning."

Zia jerked back, her shoulders slamming the padded booth. She'd worked so closely with Elizabeth these past weeks! Had come to appreciate the woman's droll sense of humor almost as much as her business acumen. When GSI approved that quarter-million-dollar grant, Zia and Elizabeth had celebrated with a bottle of Chilean Malbec. And when the rest of the funding came through, they'd treated each other to an orgy of Godiva chocolate. Now she was gone?

"What happened? Why did you let her go?"

"I really can't..." Danville paused and scrubbed a finger under his nose. "I'm sorry, Zia. I have to follow certain rules of confidentially in situations like this."

"Situations like *what*, dammit?"

"I can't say. I really can't. But I can tell you this. From now on I'll manage your funding personally."

Oh, sure! Like she was going to trust a crackhead to oversee her project's finances? She started to tell him so but pulled up short when she remembered the contract she'd signed with Danville and Associates.

How binding was it? Did she have an out? Any grounds to terminate? She'd better find out, and fast.

Grabbing her purse and hooded wool jacket, she squeezed out of the booth. "I'm not happy about this, Tom."

"Neither am I. I trusted Elizabeth."

He rose and helped her on with her coat. Zia murmured her thanks and raised her left hand to tug her hair free of the hood. The sight of her engagement ring sparked a now-familiar refrain.

"I hope your fiancé knows what a lucky bastard he is."

"I hope so, too."

He caught her hand and angled it so the pear-shaped diamond caught the light. "If any your project funding falls through," he said with a cynical twist of his lips, "you could always hock this."

She tugged her hand free and pinned him with an icy stare. "Let's hope it doesn't come to that. For *both* our sakes."

"Whoa!" He held up both palms. "Just kidding, Doc."

He'd damned well better be! Her mind churning, Zia left the restaurant and headed for the subway stop on the corner. A quick glance at her phone showed a short list of missed calls, including one from Mike. She decided to wait until she was back at the hospital to return it along with the others.

She exited the subway at Lexington and 96th and cut

over to Mount Sinai's four-block campus. Spring was still just a vague hope. Trees and bushes had yet to put out any buds and the hospital's brick-and-glass towers looked stark against the unforgiving sky.

The sounds and smells of the Children's Hospital greeted her. She'd finished her neonatal ICU rotation and now spent the majority of her time in the research center. The familiar scent of antiseptic followed her as she hurried past the labs with their gleaming equipment and ongoing experiments to the modular unit set up to house the MRSA study. The only member of the team present at the moment was Jordan Elliott, a microbiologist with a specialty in infectious diseases. Petite and vivacious, she glanced up from her computer and flashed a smile.

"Hey, Zia. How was lunch?"

"Long. Unproductive. Worrying."

"Huh?"

"Elizabeth Hamilton-Hobbs isn't with Danville and Associates anymore."

"You're kidding! When did that happen?"

"This morning, evidently. Tom wouldn't tell me why he and Elizabeth parted ways. It's some kind of confidentiality thing." Frowning, Zia shed her coat and hooked it over the back of her chair. "I need to review our contract with Danville and see what our options are."

Jordan's brows lifted but she didn't comment. This wasn't her first research study. She knew funding was a complex and multilayered process. Even more complicated with outside sources like GSI in the mix. Which reminded her...

"I almost forgot. Mike called. He wants you to call him back."

"I will," Zia promised, her gaze locked on the contract scrolling up on the computer screen.

The legalistic phrasing didn't reassure her. If she was interpreting it correctly, the only way out of the contract

was if Danville and Associates failed to meet one of their stated objectives. Elizabeth had aced them all so far, not least of which was soliciting and securing every penny Zia had requested.

Only a fraction of those funds had been disbursed to date, though. Just what they'd needed to cover the start-up. Computers, furniture, subscriptions to medical and commercial databases, the first month's salaries for team members…six pages worth of direct costs. The total looked ginormous to Zia, but she knew it would climb even higher when they factored in the indirects.

With a moue of disgust, she clicked through the dizzying array of figures again before listening to her messages. The one from Mike requested a callback. He didn't answer his cell, though, so she tried his office.

"Hi, Peggy. It's Zia. I'm returning Mike's call."

"Sorry, Zia. He's already left for the airport."

"Left? I thought he just got back."

"Didn't he let you know? He's on his way to New York. They should be wheels up, um, right about now."

Surprised and delighted, Zia thanked her and tried Mike's cell again. The call went through this time, although about all she could hear was the roar of revving engines.

"I just heard you're headed this way," she shouted over the noise. "What's the occasion?"

"Do we need one?"

"I can barely hear you."

"I said… Never mind. Hang loose and I'll call you back when we're airborne."

Mike waited for the sleek ten-passenger executive jet to slice through the haze and hit open sky to make the return call. When he picked up his phone, however, the instrument buzzed in his hand and Rafe's office number popped

up on the screen. He took his brother-in-law's call and had his world rocked for the second time that day.

"Have you talked to Zia?" Montoya wanted to know.

"Not yet. We've been playing telephone tag. I was just about to call her back."

"You may want to hold off on that."

The reply turned Mike's insides cold. "Why?"

"Remember I told you I was going to keep scrubbing the numbers on her indirects."

"What'd you find?"

"A disbursement code that wasn't in the original proposal. It's buried in a subset of indirects relating to utilities. But instead of linking to the university's general operating fund, the code links to a separate bank routing number."

Mike's knuckles turned white where they gripped the phone. "Bottom line this for me, bro."

"That's just it. I can't. When I tried to trace the routing number, I hit a wall. Or more precisely, a damned near impenetrable firewall."

"Oh, hell. It's a blind?"

"That's what I'm thinking."

Rafe fell silent. Mike knew there was more, though. When his brother-in-law sank his teeth into something, he didn't let go.

"You said damned near impenetrable. Did you get in?"

"No, but I did poke around enough to generate a call from a friendly FBI agent."

"Christ!"

"He's with what used to be the white-collar-crimes division, Miguel. He wanted to know why we're digging into that particular account."

"Did you tell him I'm on my way to New York? That I plan to check into this very issue myself?"

"Yeah, I did. He says he needs to talk to you first. In fact, he offered to fly up from DC tomorrow and meet you

in New York. I told him I'd check with you and see if that's how you want to handle it."

Mike scrubbed a hand across his jaw. He could feel the jet lag from his trip to Seoul crawling over him now. Combined with the tension Rafe had just piled on, he felt as though he'd been hit with a pile driver.

"Mike?"

"Yeah, I'm here. Set up the meeting."

Before returning Zia's call he signaled the steward. The Gulfstream crew didn't normally include a cabin attendant on short hops within the States. Graham hadn't checked out after the transatlantic flight, however, and at this moment, Mike was happy to make use of his services.

"Would you bring me a Scotch, Gray? Neat."

"Sure thing."

The Glenlivet went down with its usual smoky fire, but the heat didn't dissipate the cold spot in Mike's stomach. Whatever way he looked at it, he couldn't see a good ending to what was smelling more and more like fraud.

Although he didn't for a second believe Zia had a hint of anything questionable in the works, she was the project manager. She'd put the proposal together. She'd signed off on the grant solicitations. She was responsible for proper distribution of funds. At the very least, a fraud investigation would hang a cloud over her project. At the worst, her reputation in the tight-knit world of pediatric research would take a hit. Not the best way to kick-start a new career.

Mike tossed back the rest of his Scotch, powered up his phone and hit the speed-dial number for Zia's cell.

"Sorry it took so long to get back to you. I had another call."

"No problem. So how was Korea?"

"Busy and productive. GSI's going to acquire six new Triple-E class super-containers over the next three years."

"Super-containers, huh? I'm getting a mental picture

of hundreds of those shipping containers piled one on top of each other."

"Try thousands. Eighteen thousand, to be exact."

"On each ship?" she asked incredulously.

"On each ship."

"Okay, I'm officially impressed." She paused before changing the subject. "I'm really glad you're flying in tonight, Mike. Something's come up. I'd like to talk to you about it."

"Personal or otherwise?"

"Otherwise."

Hell! He had to ask. "Is this related to your working lunch with Tom Danville?"

"How did you know about lunch?"

Surprise and just a hint of wariness colored the question. She obviously hadn't forgotten Mike's reaction to Danville when they'd met at La Maison.

Or was it something else?

No, dammit! He was letting this FBI business spook him! Whatever the hell was going on, there was no way Zia could be involved. Deliberately, he put a shrug in his reply.

"Jordan mentioned where you were when I called earlier."

"Oh." Another pause. "What time do you think you'll be in?"

"Late, I'm afraid. After midnight."

"You have to be dead, considering you were on the other side of the world this morning. Get some sleep tonight and I'll take off early tomorrow afternoon to welcome you home in style."

"Define style," he said with a smile, relaxing for the first time since Rafe's call.

"We could do the ballet," she teased, well aware of how he felt about it. "Or the opera. Or maybe just snuggle in with a pizza and a movie."

"Now you're talking. Your place or mine?"

"Well…" Her voice dropped to a provocative purr. "The duchess doesn't particularly care for pizza."

"This is sounding better by the moment."

She laughed and agreed. "Where are you staying this time?"

"Let me check." He pulled up the travel docs Peggy had loaded to his phone. "The W New York."

"Okay, here's the deal. I'll call you when I'm on the way with pizza. You pick the movie. But nothing X-rated," she instructed sternly. "Maybe not even R. We wouldn't want to overstimulate your poor, jet-lagged brain."

"Can't happen, kid. You walk into the room and my brain shuts down anyway. All that's left is pure, unadulterated…"

"Lust? Greed?"

"I was going to say love, but lust and greed are right there in the mix, too."

He disconnected, still smiling. Rafe's call a few minutes later wiped the smile off his face and put the kink back in his gut.

Eleven

"It's set," Mike's brother-in-law announced tersely. "Tomorrow, 9:00 a.m., at the FBI's New York office. Ask for Special Agent Dan Havers."

"Got it. Although I've got to tell you, Rafe, I don't like keeping Zia in the dark about all this."

"I understand, but…"

"But what?"

"I'm beginning to think there's more to the situation than we suspect, Miguel. I can't see a DC-based FBI agent jumping on a plane and meeting you in New York just to talk about fifty thousand in misdirected grant money."

"I've been having those same thoughts," Mike admitted grimly. "They're the only reason I didn't tell Zia about this FBI contact. The more I can find out from this guy tomorrow, the better I can help her navigate through whatever the problem is."

"Keep me in the loop, too."

"Will do."

Mike had the steward pour him another Scotch and nursed it for the rest of the flight. He nursed more than a few doubts, as well. He knew he was setting himself up for some potentially tense moments with Zia if he told her

about the FBI meeting after the fact. But he also knew he was in a better position to elicit information than she was at this point. GSI was only one of several corporations contributing to the MRSA study but it had provided significant funding. Naturally Mike would want to investigate any apparent anomalies in the distribution of those funds. Especially if the person ultimately responsible for the disbursement was his fiancée.

The FBI would view Zia in a more cautious light. She was a foreign national in the United States on a work/study visa. What's more, she had close ties to some very high viz personalities. Jack Harris, Gina's husband, was the US Ambassador to the UN. And Sarah's husband, Dev, operated half the damned civilian transports in the country.

Then there was the duchess. And, Mike thought with an inner grimace, the grand duke. He didn't know much about Dominic's years as an undercover agent for Interpol. Just enough to appreciate that the FBI might be understandably wary of crossing agency lines. Looking at it from that angle made Mike feel marginally better about his 9:00 a.m. meeting.

Any delusion that the FBI was the least bit concerned about Zia's personal situation or connections shattered ten minutes after Special Agent Dan Havers met Mike in the lobby of the FBI's New York office at 26 Federal Plaza.

Havers was an athletic-looking thirty-six or -seven, with wrestler's shoulders and a tree-trunk neck that strained his white shirt and navy suit jacket. The lines etched deep around his eyes suggested white-collar crime was something other than sport, however.

"Thanks for coming in, Brennan."

Mike took the hand Havers thrust out and braced for a bone cruncher that didn't come.

"Let's get you ID'd and badged. We've got a conference room reserved. We'll talk there."

They kept small talk to a minimum until Havers ushered Mike into the twenty-third-floor conference room. Four others—two men, two women—were waiting his arrival. Three clustered around the coffee and pastries at the far end of the room. One stared moodily through the blinds at the Manhattan skyline.

Mike's chest got tighter with each introduction. One of the women was Havers's New York counterpart, a special agent working white-collar crime. The other was from the International Operations Division. The two men were from the Counterterrorism Division.

"Coffee?" Havers asked. "A bagel or Danish, maybe?"

"I'm good."

"Okay, then let's get to it."

The group drifted to the table. Mike claimed a seat with his back to the windows. It was a small power play, just one of the many any negotiator worth his salt might employ, but it gave him the advantage of facing away from the bright sunlight.

He didn't derive much satisfaction from the maneuver. Not when he faced two counterterrorism agents. They left it to Havers to lay whatever cards they intended to share on the table.

"Here's the deal, Brennan. Your guy Montoya set off all kinds of alarms with his probe into that blocked account yesterday. We had to decide fast what to do about it. Especially when Montoya said you were on your way to New York. So we ran both of you through our computers. Every wrinkle, every wart."

"Find anything interesting?"

"Montoya is an open book. You read more like a tabloid."

"That so?"

"We know about the knife fight with the Portuguese cook when you were a ten-dollar-a-day deckhand," Havers commented. "We know about the navy medal you were awarded after diving into the Sea of Japan to save a crewmate who'd been swept overboard. We know you bought a rust bucket after you got out of the service and parlayed it into a multinational corporation. We know about your friends, your family, the divorce."

"What's your point?"

"My point is we wouldn't be talking to you today unless we knew we could trust you."

"Right now I can't say I feel the same. Cut to the chase. What's this all about?"

Havers angled his bull-like neck a few degrees to the right and nodded to one of the counterterrorism agents. Sandy haired and squinty eyed behind his wire-rim glasses, the other agent took the lead.

"What this is about is a guy named Thomas Danville and his five-thousand-dollar-a-week habit, which he feeds by skimming from his clients."

Mike felt his insides go tight but kept his voice even. "And?"

"And how this guy Danville buys his drugs from an international consortium. One that just happens to be headed by a terrorist organization whose stated goal is to wipe Israel—and its evil ally, the United States—off the face of the earth. You've heard of Hezbollah?"

Mike didn't alter his expression, didn't blink, but they'd just confirmed his worst-case scenario. Zia had gotten caught up in something a whole lot deeper and uglier than fraud.

"Yes, I've heard of Hezbollah."

"Then you might also have heard it has a substantial connection to the Mexican cartel Los Zetas. Two years ago we got an indictment in absentia against one of the mid-

dlemen acting on behalf of Hezbollah, a Lebanese drug lord by the name of Ayman Joumaa. Bastard conspired to smuggle more than 9,000 tons of cocaine into the US. In the process, he laundered over $250 million for the cartels.

"Look," he continued. "We don't give a shit about Danville. He's small change. Wouldn't even constitute a blip on our radar except for this drug connection. Nor would we be talking to you this morning if you hadn't started nosing around one of Danville's blind accounts. We need you to back off, Brennan. Now. Today."

Havers picked up the ball again. "We've been tracking Danville ever since one of his employees tipped us to his extracurricular activities. Problem is, he fired that employee yesterday."

Mike's eyes narrowed. "So you're worried Danville could be spooked."

"He could be," Havers conceded. "Though that's not all bad. Spooked guys make mistakes. Sometimes they run. Sometimes they turn to their big, bad pals for something to calm their jittery nerves."

"And sometimes," Mike said coldly, "they take innocent people down with them."

"Exactly. That's why we need you to back off. We've got taps on Danville's home, office and cell phones. We'll know if and when he makes a wrong move. Let us handle him, Brennan. Don't get in the middle of it."

"You're welcome to him. Like you, I don't give a shit about Danville. I do, however, care about—"

"Your fiancée. Yeah, we know."

Havers pursed his lips, as if debating whether to continue. The act didn't fool Mike for a moment. He sensed what was coming. Still, it hit hard.

"Danville and Dr. St. Sebastian enjoyed a three-hour lunch yesterday. According to one source, they got real close. Some might say cuddly."

Mike's reply came fast and flat. "For someone who wants my cooperation, you just went in exactly the wrong direction. This meeting is over."

He shoved back from the table and strode for the door. Havers had to scramble to catch up with him.

"Hold on, Brennan!"

He reached for Mike's arm. A low, savage warning halted his hand in midair.

"You really don't want to do that."

"Okay." He dropped his arm. "Look, I obviously pushed the wrong button there. I'm sorry."

Mike didn't bother to respond, just made for the elevator.

"Brennan! Wait. I have to escort you out."

He tried again to apologize but the elevator arrived too quickly. All he could do was follow Mike inside and ride down in silence. When they hit the lobby, though, he reached into his suit pocket.

"Here's my card," he said as they approached the security checkpoint. "Call me if there's anything else you want to talk about."

Mike came within a breath of telling him where he could shove the stiff, sharp-edged cardboard. He swallowed the urge, stuck the card in his wallet and tossed his visitor's pass on the security desk.

He used the rest of the morning to work the fury out of his system. A brutal workout in the hotel's exercise center helped. A long session in the steam room sweated out the rest. Showered and under control, he called Rafe with an update. His brother-in-law listened without interruption. At the end his only comment was a succinct and very graphic curse.

"Yeah," Mike drawled. "My sentiments exactly."

"How much of this are you going to tell Zia?"

"All of it."

"The FBI okay with that?"

"I didn't ask."

"I guess you probably didn't need to. They have to know you're not going to let her get in any deeper with this bastard Danville."

Let, Mike acknowledged wryly after he'd hung up, was the wrong verb. If he'd learned nothing else from living with three sisters and a moody ex-wife, it was to be extremely careful with that particular verb.

He shoved his hands in his pockets and wandered across the sitting room of his twentieth-floor suite. The wall-to-wall window offered an unimpeded view of One World Trade Center and, farther out, the Statue of Liberty. Mike let his gaze drift from one to the other, thinking of the jihadist pumping drugs into the United States, determined to destroy it one way or another. Thinking, too, of the thousands of little people caught in his poisonous web.

Like Danville.

And this employee Danville had reportedly fired.

And Zia.

Now him.

He'd charged right in, suspecting there was more to that blind account than mismanagement or misdirection of funds, and firing up like an Aegis missile when Havers and company confirmed it.

The more he thought about that visceral reaction, the more it bothered him. He didn't want to admit it sprang from that crack about Zia and Danville getting cuddly. He couldn't get around the implanted image, though. Not after Zia's wariness when Mike had told her he knew about the long lunch. Which, he remembered grimly, had come right on the heels of her saying she needed to talk to him. Maybe she already knew about Danville skimming his client's funds. Or maybe...

Christ! He had to stop chasing his tail like this. He'd

wait for Zia, talk it out with her, lay what he knew on the line and get it behind them both.

So he was more than ready when she called a little past three o'clock. "I'm just getting ready to leave the hospital. Are we still on for pizza and a movie?"

"I am if you are."

"Good. I skipped lunch so I'm starved. There's a John's Pizzeria right around the corner from the W. I'll call ahead and have a large regular crust waiting for pick up, all hot and gooey. What do you want on it?"

"Everything but anchovies or anything that resembles fruit."

"Got it. See you in forty-five minutes or so. In the meantime, you could check out the movies. I'm in the mood for something light and silly."

"Light and silly it is. See you soon."

Smiling in anticipation, Zia hit the off button and grabbed her coat.

"Pizza and a movie, huh?"

She glanced up to find Jordan Elliott smirking across the top of her computer terminal. The microbiologist's eyes reflected both mischief and envy.

"Sounded more like a little afternoon delight to me."

"What happens at the W, stays at the W."

"Oh, sure! Rub it in. You know very well the closest I've come to sex in the past month is watching bacteria multiply in a petri dish."

"I also know," Zia shot back, "there's a certain radiologist who's offered to fix that problem. Several times."

"Ugh. I'd rather cozy up to the bacteria. Hang loose a sec. I need to go over to the Infectious Diseases center. I'll walk out with you."

They exited the school of medicine and took the sidewalk that cut diagonally across Mount Sinai's sprawling

campus. Spring was still weeks away, although the afternoon sun offered a hint of warmer temperatures and a sudden burst of greenery.

Zia was just about to peel off and make for the subway when her phone buzzed again. It was a text message from Tom Danville.

"It's Danville," she told Jordan, skimming the message. "He needs to talk to me ASAP about Elizabeth."

The two women exchanged quick glances. The Wharton School of Business grad's firing had shocked them both. Maybe now they'd discover what was behind it. When Zia called Danville, however, he didn't want to talk over the phone.

"It's an extremely sensitive issue. I need to discuss it with you in private."

"I don't have time now, Tom. I'm on my way to an appointment downtown."

"It'll just take a few minutes. You really need to know the mess Elizabeth's landed us both in."

She hesitated, chewing on her lower lip. "Where are you now?"

"At the office."

"All right. I'm just leaving the hospital. I'll swing by there on my way downtown."

Mike expected Zia by four. At four-thirty he hit the speed-dial number for her cell phone. When the call went to voice mail, he tried her office.

Her associate picked up and responded with a throaty chuckle when he identified himself. "Hi, Mike. Don't tell me you and Zia have already, uh, finished your pizza."

"We might have, if she'd showed up with it."

"She's not there? Wait. Scratch that. Of course she's not, or you wouldn't be calling."

"So she's not still at the hospital?"

"She left a couple of hours ago. I walked out with her, in fact."

"Did she take the subway?"

"That was the plan, but she got a call from Tom Danville. He said he needed to talk to her privately, right away, so she told him she'd swing by his office on the way downtown."

"I'll call you back."

"Wait! What's—"

He stabbed the end button and did a Google search for Danville and Associates. His jaw was tight and the cords in his neck as taut as hawsers. He knew what he would hear even before Danville's secretary confirmed that her boss had left the office several hours ago.

"Was Dr. St. Sebastian with him?"

"No," she replied in some surprise. "I'm looking at Tom's schedule now. He didn't have an appointment with her. Shall I—"

Mike slammed the phone down to search his wallet for Special Agent Havers's card. The FBI agent answered on the third ring.

"Havers."

"This is Brennan. Where are you?"

"On my way to the airport, getting ready to head back to DC. Why?"

"My fiancée was supposed to meet me at my hotel an hour ago. She hasn't showed."

"Have you—"

"She was on her way," Mike cut in savagely. "An associate walked out with her. The same associate just informed me that Zia got an urgent call from Danville. He needed to talk to her. Privately. At his office. But he left, and she never showed."

The pregnant silence that followed torqued his jaws so tight he could feel his teeth grinding.

"Listen to me, Havers. She's not having an affair with Danville. Nor is she in any way involved in his schemes."

When the agent still didn't reply, Mike pulled out every ace in the deck.

"My next call is to Dr. St. Sebastian's brother. He won't hesitate to tap his former sources at Interpol. Then I'm contacting Ambassador Harris at the UN. Then…"

"Hang up. Sit tight. Wait for me to call you back."

Mike's lips curled back in a snarl. "The hell I will. I'm going to hold on the line while you do the following. First, you contact your pals in the New York office. Second, you have them run a GPS trace on Danville's mobile phone. Third, you tell me where the bastard is."

"We warned you this morning to stay out of this, Brennan. We'll handle it."

"Call your pals, Havers. Now!"

Twelve

Zia just had to wait him out.

She'd stopped kicking herself for agreeing to meet Danville at his office. Gotten past the surprise of finding him in the lobby and ushering her into the elevator, only to send it down to the parking garage instead of up to his office. She'd also worked through her shock when he'd pulled out a small, lethal-looking pistol and aimed it at her heart.

Once her stunned mind reengaged, she'd recognized the signs. The fever-bright eyes. The agitation. The desperation. She'd seen it in patients, read about it in hundreds of case studies. Danville was in the panic stage. It usually set in several hours after the user's last hit. He would feel himself coming down and go frantic with the need to make sure he could score another hit.

If he didn't have a supply on hand, he'd beg, borrow or steal for it. Patients had reported pawing through their own and their parents' houses for something, *anything*, to pawn or sell. Others had robbed convenience stores, fast-food restaurants, even busy mall stores. The withdrawal is so intense, the craving so frantic, that they work themselves into a frenzy of need.

Danville was there. Jerky. Desperate. Paranoid. As he

forced her to get behind the wheel of the flashy red Porsche parked in his assigned slot, he kept mumbling they would kill him.

"Who, Tom? Who's going to kill you?"

"Drive! Just drive!"

She did. Up Madison Avenue, across 106th, down 2nd Avenue, with the pistol jammed into her side the entire time. She'd tried to talk him down. Tried to calm and soothe and assure him she'd get him help, but he was still locked in that hard, panicky shell. Checking his watch constantly. Flinching at every sound, every distant siren or screech of tires. And phones. Zia's. His. The buzzing must have ricocheted around in his mind like a loose ball bearing.

She'd considered crashing the Porsche into a street sign or traffic light, but she couldn't take the chance the airbags would explode in Danville's face before he pulled the trigger. So she'd followed his instructions until her shoulders ached with tension and her mind screamed with the need to do something, anything, to end the situation.

"There! Turn in there!"

She had to brake to take the ticket from the automatic dispenser at the entrance to the underground garage. Two lanes over, a bored attendant sat in his booth with his back turned so he could service exiting vehicles. Zia willed him to turn around, begged him to send just one glance her way. When he remained facing the other direction, she calculated her chances of yanking the door open and throwing herself out. Not very good with Danville's pistol bruising her ribs.

"Go down to the bottom level," he rasped at her.

She followed the winding ramp down five increasingly less crowded levels. The last was almost deserted.

"Pull into that space. The one beside the pillar."

The concrete column was square and fat but not difficult to maneuver around with so many empty spaces. Zia barely had time to wonder why he'd chosen that particular

slot before she realized the pillar screened them from the security camera mounted in the corner.

Danville had been here before. Used this same parking slot. The realization hit like a balled fist to her chest. Fighting for calm, she cut the engine and angled toward him. He twisted in his seat, too, planting his back against the door, pulling the gun back with him. The bruising pressure on her ribs eased, but the barrel was still terrifyingly close.

"What now, Tom?"

"We wait."

She let her hand drop to her thigh, clenching and unclenching her fist as though driven by nerves. Which she was! But if she could keep him talking, keep his eyes on her face, she might be able to inch her hand into her tote, finger her iPhone, tap 911. The bag was in the space between their seats, just behind the gearshift console. So damned close.

"What do we wait for?"

"Not what. Who." He shot another look at his expensive watch. "They'll come," he muttered, more to himself than her. "Now that I can pay, they'll call off the dogs and deliver."

His suppliers, she guessed as the knot in her chest pressed hard against her sternum. She flattened her palm, eased it over the outside of her thigh.

"You cannot do this." She spoke evenly, slowly, but she could hear the American accent she'd acquired over the past two and a half years slipping away. "You cannot kidnap me, make me drive to this place, and think to get away with it."

Anger and a smirking bravado leaped into his face. Not a good mix with the desperation.

"Shows what you know! I've been getting away with it for years. Five thousand from one client, ten K from another. Eighty, a hundred thousand a year funneled into a special account the auditors never got a whiff of until that bitch started sniffing around it."

"Are you...? Are you speaking of Elizabeth?"

"Yes, Elizabeth." His lips curled back in a sneer that didn't quite match the fear and paranoia behind it. "She sicced the FBI on me. My...my associates found out about it. I don't know how. But they took care of her and now I have to cut and run. Today. Tonight."

Zia's stomach heaved. She'd ascribed his frenetic mood and barely controlled panic to crack. Now she knew it was due to something much worse, much uglier.

"How do you mean, they 'took care of her'?"

"It doesn't matter. She doesn't matter. *That's* what matters."

His gaze dropped like a stone and locked on the hand she'd slipped closer to her bag. For a frozen instant Zia thought he'd detected her cautious moves. Then she realized he'd focused on her engagement ring.

"I can't go back to my place. The FBI is probably watching it. I don't dare use my laptop or phone or credit card to withdraw the cash I need to pay my associates. But I can use that." He made a short, choppy motion with the gun. "Take it off."

"This is all you want from me?" she asked incredulously. "The ring?"

"Take it off."

She played the fingers of her right hand over the pear-shaped diamond. The faceted stone sat high in its mount. The surface was smooth, the tip sharp against her nervous fingers.

"You can have it, Tom. It is only a stone. Then will you let me go?"

He wouldn't meet her eyes, wouldn't answer her question. She knew then he would feed her to the dogs as cold-bloodedly as he had Elizabeth.

He had not the courage to do it himself, Zia thought on a burst of contempt. The men he waited for. They came not

just to bring him the cocaine he craved. They would dispose of yet another problem female for him.

She twisted the band, tugged it toward her knuckle, pretended to have trouble getting it over the joint. "It's too tight. I…I meant to have it sized but have not had time."

"You'd damned well better get it off," he snarled, "or my friends will do it the hard way."

"So they are now your friends?" She couldn't keep the disgust from her voice as she twisted the band again. "A moment ago they were merely associates."

"It's none of your business wh—"

He broke off, his head cocking. Above the jackhammering of her heart, Zia caught the rumble of an engine. A vehicle was descending from the level right above them. A large, heavy vehicle.

"About damned time," Danville muttered, glancing over his shoulder at the ramp.

This was her chance! Her only chance! She didn't stop to think. Didn't weigh the odds. Fired by fear and utter desperation, she flayed out her arm and knocked the gun barrel aside. The violent action triggered an equally violent response. Shots exploded inside the sports car. One. Two. With blinding flashes. Concussive waves of sound. The searing burn of nitrate and the nauseous stink of sulfur.

Even before the shock waves died, Zia whipped her arm back. Ears ringing, eyes streaming, she curled her fist and put every ounce of her strength into a blow aimed for Danville's face. The force of it sank the sharp tip of her diamond deep into his left eye.

His eyeball exploded almost as violently as the shots had. Vitreous solution spewed in a clear arc. Blood gushed as Zia wrenched her wrist down and ripped through the lower lid. Howling, Danville dropped the pistol and slapped both hands to his eye.

She scrabbled for the gun with her bloody hand, but it

had fallen behind her seat. Not daring to wait another second, she shoved her door open and lunged out onto the oil-stained concrete. Her ears screaming, her cheek burning, she took a dizzy second or two to reorient herself. God help her if she ran up the down ramp and met Danville's *associates* head-on.

The brief hesitation proved a fatal mistake. A huge black SUV with darkened windows careened off the ramp less than thirty yards away. Zia whirled, then felt a scream rise in her throat when she saw Danville had crawled out of his car. Using the roof of the Porsche, he dragged himself upright. One hand still covered his oozing eye. The other gripped the pistol he'd recovered from the floor of the car.

Then everything happened in a blur. The SUV streaked by. Zia jumped back, barely avoiding its fender. It fishtailed to a screeching halt, and she dodged for the concrete pillar. Before she reached it, the SUV's passenger door flew open and Mike launched himself at the Porsche.

Danville whirled to meet this new threat, but the eye injury threw off his aim. The bullet hit the pillar just inches from Zia's head. Vicious bits of concrete bit into her still-burning cheek as the two men went down on the far side of the Porsche.

When Zia raced around the rear of the car, Mike was slamming his fist into Danville's already bloody face. She couldn't hear a thing above the screaming in her ears, but she saw his nose flatten and more blood gush through the shattered cartilage. Then a big, bull-like man rushed up and kicked the pistol away.

"Brennan! Enough."

He caught Mike's arm and hauled him off the now-unconscious Danville. Chest heaving, Mike shoved to his feet and spun around.

"Zia! Jesus!"

She saw his lips move but heard only a muted echo of

his words. She clung to him, her heart pumping fear and relief in equal measures until he caught her arms and gently eased her away. An oozy mix of blood and vitreous fluid now splotched the front of his saddle-tan leather jacket.

"Are you hurt?" His gaze raked her, searching for injuries. "Zia, tell me where you're hurt."

She saw his lips moving again, heard the words as a tinny echo this time and shook her head. "I'm okay. This…." She had to gasp for breath. "This is Danville's blood."

And some of her own, she realized as she fingered the bits of concrete embedded in her cheek. Her hand came away filthy with body fluids and gunpowder residue.

The hulking man next to Mike said something. He was huge, with a loud, rumbling voice that was completely drowned out by the squeal of tires as what looked like an entire fleet of black-and-white patrol cars screeched down the ramp and onto their level.

She grabbed Mike's lapels and shouted to make herself heard. "Danville was expecting his…his suppliers. Here. Any moment."

"Hell!"

The next thing she knew she was being bundled into the back of a squad car.

"Get her out of here," the big man barked at the uniformed officer behind the wheel, then shouted to two others. "And get this bastard to a hospital. Then the rest of you disperse. Now! Tune to my frequency for additional instructions."

The ringing in Zia's ears had subsided enough for her to distinguish his roared commands. She also heard the one he threw at Mike.

"You go with the doc, Brennan. This is our operation."

"It was." His mouth grim, Mike scooped up Danville's

pistol. In one smooth move, he hit the release, popped out the magazine and snapped it back in. "It's mine now."

The squad car Zia had been thrust into sped past the openmouthed booth attendant and took up a position a block away. Then they waited.

The ringing in her ears had lessened in volume but now had a sharp, shrill pitch. Tinnitus, she diagnosed. Not a concern in and by itself, but the accompanying numbness and tingling could signal a possible perforation of the middle ear. She fisted her hands and tried to ignore the metallic pinging while she waited. It couldn't have been more than a half hour but it felt like five before the radio squawked.

"Operations terminated. Four men in custody. All other units will be back in service."

"It's over?" she asked the uniformed officer.

"Yes, ma'am."

"Please, take me back to the garage."

He put the car in Park at the entrance and Zia waited anxiously for Mike to emerge from the dark tunnel. The moment she spotted him, she hammered on the Plexiglas partition.

"Let me out!"

Light-headed with relief, she threw herself at Mike for the second time that afternoon. As before, he held her gently. Too gently. She ached for the feel of his arms around her, but he eased her away and frowned at her cuts and powder burns.

"We need to get you to the ER."

"I'm…I'm supposed to wait and give a statement."

"The authorities can come find you."

By the time they reached the hospital her tinnitus had subsided to a bearable level. Enough, anyway, that she could hear the ER physician's diagnosis when he confirmed her own.

"You've sustained sensorineural damage in both ears.

The numbness and tingling in your right ear indicate moderate to severe nerve irritation. The ringing in your left may be temporary, but you should consult an audiologist as soon as possible."

"I will."

He rolled his stool back, looking as tired at the end of his long shift as Zia had so often felt. "We need to clean the debris from your cheek and swab it. Then, I'm told, the FBI wants to talk to you. There's an agent waiting outside."

She nodded but turned a surprised face to Mike after the door to the exam room closed behind the ER physician. "Did he say FBI?"

"Yeah, he did."

"How did the FBI get involved?"

"It's a long story. I'll tell you later."

The big, burly man from the SUV identified himself as Special Agent Dan Havers. He spent a good forty minutes walking Zia through her ordeal, from Danville's call to his gut-wrenching admission in the garage.

"He said that?" Havers demanded. "He said his friends had 'taken care' of Elizabeth Hamilton-Hobbs?"

Sick at heart, she could only nod. The FBI agent gestured for her to go on. She related the rest of the conversation, the momentary distraction of the vehicle on the floor above, her frantic swipe at Danville's arm, the ring she'd stabbed into his eye.

"Jesus!"

Havers shot Mike a quick glance but he didn't see it. His face was set in savage lines and his gaze had dropped to the gore still staining Zia's left hand. She couldn't tell whether he was pleased the engagement ring had proved so lethal or shocked she'd used it as a weapon.

She got her answer when he reached for her hand and

eased the ring over her knuckle. Face grim, he tossed it into the plastic-lined trash can beside the gurney.

"Hey!" Havers grabbed a glove from the box mounted on the near cabinet and shoved his beefy fist into it. "That's evidence. We need to preserv—"

"Preserve whatever you want. Then you can toss the thing in the East River, for all I care. Come on, Zia. I'm taking you home."

After a brief stop at the front desk to sign the necessary paperwork, he hustled her into a cab. Her ears were still tinny and every street sound seemed magnified a hundred times over. Still, she tried to dissuade him from calling ahead to alert the duchess.

When he insisted, the call resulted in exactly the chain reaction Zia feared. Charlotte alerted Dominic and Natalie, who arrived at the Dakota mere moments after Zia and Mike. Gina and her husband had been en route to a black-tie charity event and showed at almost the same time, Jack in his tux and Gina dripping sapphires. The duchess had even called Sarah, who'd begged for an update as soon as Zia and Jack explained everything.

The concern, the questions, the straining to separate their voices from the high-pitched ringing in her ear proved too much for Zia. With a pleading look, she turned to Mike.

"I need to wash and change. You tell them what happened."

Her departure left a stark silence in the sitting room. Mike squared his shoulders and faced her family. They were arrayed in a semicircle, Dom and Jack standing, Gina on the sofa holding Natalie's hand, the duchess in a high-backed chair gripping the head of her cane. Even Maria had come in from the kitchen to hear the details. All wore almost identical expressions of shock and concern.

Mike debated briefly where to start, then jumped right

to the heart of the issue that concerned them most—Zia's abduction.

"I don't know if Zia told you that she was working with a consultant to secure and manage the funding for her grant."

"Yes," Dom said shortly. "We know about that."

"Turns out this consultant—Thomas Danville—was skimming from his clients' accounts to support a cocaine habit. Evidently Danville was obtaining his coke from thugs working for a drug cartel with direct links to a known terrorist organization."

"What cartel?"

"Los Zetas. Which supposedly has ties to—"

"Hezbollah," Dom supplied, his jaw working. "And through them to Iran."

Hissing, he spit out something in Hungarian that whipped the duchess's head around. She said nothing, however, as he continued in a low growl.

"The Iron Triangle of Terror. And Zia got caught in the middle of this?"

"One of Danville's associates—a woman by the name of Elizabeth Hobbs—evidently became suspicious and contacted the authorities. Danville's suppliers got wind of it somehow and…"

A muscle worked in the side of Mike's jaw. He had to force himself to continue.

"According to Danville, his pals took care of Hobbs. At that point he panicked. He knew the authorities had to be on to him, tapping his phones, tracking his finances. He planned to skip the country but needed cash. And, apparently, another fix."

The grim account didn't get any easier with telling. An iron band seemed to tighten around Mike's chest as he finished in short, terse bursts.

"Danville contacted Zia. Arranged to meet her around three this afternoon. He pulled a gun on her, then forced

her to drive to an underground garage. He intended to parlay her engagement ring into cash and coke. She used it instead to put out the bastard's eye."

The silence this time ranged from stunned to incredulous to furious. Gina broke it by pounding a clenched fist on her thigh. "I wish she'd jammed it down his throat!"

"Zia's face," the duchess put in. "The blood on her clothes. She was injured?"

"Danville got off a couple of shots at close range. One hit a concrete pillar mere inches from Zia's face, and her ears are still ringing from the percussive impact. The doc at the ER diagnosed the ringing as tinnitus but wants her to schedule an appointment with an audiologist for a more thorough check."

The family looked from one to another, still stunned, still processing the incredible information.

"Why didn't you call me?" Dom wanted to know. "Or Jack?"

"There wasn't time."

"The hell there wasn't. You just told us my sister went missing in midafternoon. You had hours to get hold of us. Unless…" Dom's eyes narrowed. "What *aren't* you telling us, Brennan?"

The razor-edged question brought Jack Harris out of his chair. Frowning, he stood shoulder to shoulder with his wife's cousin. "Cut the bull, Brennan. What do you know that we don't?"

Tension raced like a tsunami through the room. The force of it stiffened the duchess in her high-backed chair and caused her to rap out an imperious command.

"Sit down!"

She enforced the order with a vigorous thump of her cane. The solid whack pivoted the men around. Three bristling males who'd stormed or stolen their way into her heart. Jack so tall and tawny haired and sophisticated.

Dominic, her great-nephew, the grand duke, so dark and dangerous looking. And Michael, with his wide shoulders braced for battle and his green eyes refusing to yield so much as an inch.

Charlotte couldn't have asked for a more impressive set of genes to infuse the St. Sebastian family line. She wouldn't admit that to them, of course, any more than she would permit them to behave with such a lamentable lack of manners in her presence.

"I must ask you not to ruffle your feathers and scratch the dirt like fighting cocks in my sitting room. Sit down. Now, if you please."

They obeyed. Slowly. Reluctantly. Charlotte tipped her chin and waited until they were seated to pin Mike with a cool stare.

"I, too, would like an explanation of why it took so long for Zia's family to be apprised of the danger she faced from this…this Danville person. Why didn't she tell us?"

"She didn't know the full extent of it until he abducted her this afternoon."

"But you knew?" The duchess's snowy brows arched. "You must have, to have enlisted the FBI's aid so quickly."

"An agent contacted GSI yesterday," Mike admitted, his jaw working. "I met with them this morning."

"A fenébe is!" Dominic shoved to his feet again, his eyes blazing. "You knew about Danville, and yet you let Zia walk into his trap?"

"I didn't let—"

"What was she?" His fists balled. "Bait? A lure to bring the bastard crawling out of the woodwork?"

"No."

Mike understood the man's fury. The same anger boiled in his gut. He should've told Zia about the call from the FBI last night. Failing that, he should've insisted she accompany him to Havers's office this morning. Instead, he'd

kept his damned mouth shut and she'd ended up fighting for her life. He'd never forgive or forget that monumental error in judgment.

Neither would Zia's brother. St. Sebastian moved on Mike, ignoring the duchess's gasp and his wife's quick word of warning.

"The FBI needed her, didn't they? To help nail their terrorist. *You* needed her, to recover your quarter million."

The charge was absurd. St. Sebastian knew that as well as everyone else in the room. Yet Mike didn't argue. Just waited for the punch *he* would have thrown if it had been one of his sisters in that dim, cavernous garage.

St. Sebastian ached to deliver it. Mike saw the primal urge in the man's bunched shoulders, read it in the flared nostrils. Then Dominic's dark eyes shifted to the right.

Mike followed the look and saw Zia standing in the arched entrance to the sitting room. She'd scrubbed her hands, combed back her hair and changed into sweats. Confusion and disbelief chased across her face.

"Did I hear right? The FBI contacted you *yesterday*? And you didn't tell me?"

Thirteen

Mike had only himself to blame for Zia's close brush with death. He couldn't escape that burden and didn't try. It sat like a stone on his chest as he related the sequence of events that had led him to the FBI.

First, Rafe's discovery of the overpayment of indirects. Then their suspicion funds were being diverted to a blind account. Mike's abrupt decision to fly to New York to discuss the discrepancy with Zia. Rafe's call relating the grim news that his probe had resulted in a call from the FBI. The request for Mike to meet with the agent this morning in New York.

His audience listened in stony silence. Zia, the duchess, Dom and his wife, Gina and her husband. The St. Sebastians had closed ranks, protecting their own, shutting him out. Mike's family would have done the same.

"I could have told you about it last night," he said to Zia. "I started to. Then…"

"Then?"

The single word was edged with ice.

"Then I played the odds," Mike admitted with brutal honesty as she entered the room. "I figured they had to know your background. I figured they'd also know yours,"

he said, meeting Dominic's stare head-on. "Europe's new-est royal. Cultural Attaché to the UN. Former undercover agent. You think the Bureau didn't consider the possibility Interpol might come crashing down on them?"

His gaze shifted, pinned Jack Harris.

"Then there's you, Ambassador. Doesn't take a genius to grasp the political fallout if word leaked that the FBI was asking questions about your wife's cousin. And you, Duchess. You've become a celebrity. Again," he amended as her chin tilted.

"What has my aunt's status or that of anyone in my fam-ily got to do with your decision to talk to the FBI and not me?" Zia asked coldly.

"I thought they would talk to me more openly without all the heavy guns your family could bring to bear. The plan was to scope out the extent of the threat before I told you about it."

"*Would* you have told me if Danville hadn't abducted me and forced your hand?"

"Yes! Hell, yes!"

"How do I know that?" The frost didn't leave her voice, thick now with her native accent. "How do I know you do not think to protect me always? How do I know you won't shield me from everything that is dangerous or cruel or merely unpleasant?"

He opened his mouth, snapped it shut again. He wanted to assure her that he was modern enough, mature enough, to respect her as both an adult and a professional. Yet he couldn't deny the instincts imprinted in his DNA. Or was it RNA?

Hell, who cared? All Mike knew was that he was driven by the same need to shield his mate as every other living creature. He'd be lying if he denied it, so he pulled in a breath and spoke straight from his heart.

"I love you, Zia. I respect your drive and can't even begin

to appreciate your intelligence. But I'll always, *always*, try to protect you from harm."

That was met with dead silence. Mike thought he detected a glimmer of understanding in Jack's eyes, maybe even Dom's. The duchess looked cautiously noncommittal. But Zia had heard enough.

"I can't speak more about this now." She lifted trembling fingers to her bruised and cement-pitted cheek. "My face hurts and I still hear tinny cymbals in my ear. I'll call you, yes?"

When she turned away, Mike stretched out a hand. "Zia…"

"I'll call you!"

She whirled and left the room. To Mike's surprise, Dom rose and crossed slowly to where he stood. His dark eyes, so like his sister's, held marginally less hostility than they had before.

"I understand why you did what you did. I don't like the results, but I understand."

Mike snorted. "Can't say I'm real happy with the results, either."

"I know my sister. She won't be pushed or prodded. Give her time. Wait for her to call."

"And if she doesn't?"

"Then I would advise you to go back to Texas and forget her."

Yeah, Mike thought as he gathered his stained leather jacket and made for the door. Like that was going to happen.

Zia emerged from her bedroom into the stillness of the night, enveloped in the familiar comfort of her sweats and fuzzy slippers. An *un*familiar and unrelenting sense of loss sat like a stone on her chest as she negotiated the darkened apartment and shuffled into the kitchen. She flipped on the lights and filled the teakettle. While she waited for the

water to heat, she rested both palms on the counter and stared blindly at the backsplash.

Her parents' death had shattered her. If not for Dom, she might still be mired in grief. He'd been her anchor then, and again during those long days after she'd nearly died herself. He'd buried his pain to help her work through hers. Brought her slowly, inevitably back to an appreciation of the joys life had to offer.

Yet Zia sensed—she *knew*—she couldn't turn to her brother to ease this hurt. He wouldn't understand how deep it cut. He couldn't. Although Dom would never admit it, he was every bit as possessive and territorial as any of their sword-wielding ancestors. Luckily he'd married a woman with the smarts and humor to tame those atavistic tendencies.

But Zia didn't want to "tame" her chosen mate. She wanted an equal. Was sure she'd found one. The realization Mike regarded her as someone to be coddled and protected blasted crater-sized holes in that erroneous assumption.

"Are you making tea?"

Lost in her thoughts, Zia hadn't heard the duchess's cane tracking toward the kitchen or the gentle swish of the swinging door. Her great-aunt stood on the threshold. She was wrapped in the fleecy blue robe Sarah had given her for Christmas and leaned heavily on her cane.

"I'm so sorry. Did I wake you?"

"Unfortunately not," Charlotte replied drily. "Sleep becomes extraneous when one reaches my age. May I join you?"

"Of course. The water's about to boil. Shall I make a pot of decaffeinated Spiced Chai?"

"Yes, please."

With the ease of long familiarity, Zia measured the fragrant tea into the infuser in Charlotte's favorite Wedgwood pot and added boiling water. While the tea steeped and re-

leased the tantalizing scent of ginger and cloves and cardamom, she filled a tray with two delicate china cups and saucers, a matching sugar and creamer, napkins, spoons and fresh lemon wedges.

She carried the tray to where the duchess waited in the breakfast room just off the kitchen. During the day, the room's ivy-sprigged wallpaper, green seat cushions and tall windows seemed to reflect Central Park at its joyous summer best. Even this late on a cold March night, the room served as a cheerful beacon in the gloom.

"There's something so soothing, so civilized about tea," Charlotte mused as she stirred milk into her cup. "Especially after such a brutal day."

Zia nodded and opted for lemon instead of milk.

"Are your ears still ringing?"

"Not as badly as before."

"And your face? Your lovely face?"

"The cuts will heal."

"Yes, they will." Carefully, the duchess replaced her spoon on the saucer. "Most hurts do, eventually."

"And some go deeper than others." Zia looked up from the dark swirl in her cup. "I'm not a child. Although Dom still tries to play the big brother, I declared my independence some years ago. I respect his concern for my welfare but I don't need him to protect me. I don't need any man to protect me. I thought Mike understood that."

"Forgive me, Anastazia, but that's twaddle."

"Excuse me?"

"Twaddle," the duchess repeated. "You're a physician. You know the male of the species better than most women. Their instincts, their idiosyncrasies. One of which is the belief that they're supposed to beat their chests and protect their females from all poachers."

The duchess's choice of words hit home. Mike had used the same word to describe Tom Danville after their first

meeting. The noun ruffled Zia's feminist feathers almost as much now as it had then.

"Of course I know men are driven by primal urges. So are women. That doesn't mean we can't control them." She frowned, surprised by the direction the conversation had taken. "I thought you of all people would understand how I feel. You're the bravest, most courageous woman I know. You would never let someone wrap you in cotton wool and shield you from the realities of life."

"Oh, but you're wrong! You can't imagine how many times I wished for that cotton wool. For someone to block at least a little of the ugliness. And," she added with a sigh, "share the beauty."

"So what are you suggesting? That I should let Mike decide what to block and how much to share?"

"You must *both* decide. That's what marriage entails. Learning to respect each other's wants and needs and boundaries. It doesn't happen overnight."

"It certainly didn't happen today."

"Oh, Anastazia." The duchess stretched out a hand and folded it over Zia's. "I believe Michael only intended to… how did he phrase it? Scope out the threat. I also believe he planned to tell you as soon as he'd done that. Don't you?"

"I… Yes."

"And, my dear, I think you're forgetting one rather salient fact." She gave Zia's hand a brisk pat. "You're hardly a weak, helpless female. You didn't sit around and wait to be rescued. You incapacitated your attacker and escaped."

Those terrifying moments in the garage replayed in Zia's mind. Each graphic sequence, every desperate move. Including the heart-stopping seconds when Mike lunged across the Porsche.

"That's not entirely true," she said slowly. "I did incapacitate Danville and managed to get out of the car, but he

still had his gun. Mike wrestled it away from him before he pounded the bastard into the pavement."

"He did that? Good for him!"

"He didn't tell you?"

"No."

Zia's surprise must have shown on her face.

"I suspect," Charlotte said drily, "he was more prepared to accept the blame for what happened than any credit." She let that sink in for a moment, then grasped her cane. "It's late and you've had a horrific day. You should get some rest."

"I will, I promise. As soon as I finish my tea."

"All right. Sleep well, dearest."

When the quiet thump of her cane faded, the apartment settled into silence. Zia cradled her cup in both hands and breathed in the last whiff of ginger and cloves from her cooling tea. The final moments in the garage kept playing and replaying in her mind.

"Dammit!"

Cutting off the mental video, she pushed away from the table.

The call dragged Mike from a restless doze. He'd hit the rack an hour ago and spent most of that time with his hands behind his head, staring up at the ceiling. After what seemed like hours, he'd finally drifted off.

When his cell phone buzzed he fumbled it off the nightstand. The number marching across the incoming display had him swinging his legs over the side of the bed and jerking upright.

"Zia? All you all right?"

"No. We have to talk."

"Now?"

"Yes, now. What's your room number?"

"My...?" He shook away his grogginess. "You don't need to come all the way downtown. I'll come there."

"Too late. I'm in the lobby. What's your room number?"

"Twelve-twenty."

"Got it. Now tell security to keycard the elevator for me."

After Mike gave his okay, Zia came back on the phone with a crisp, "I'm on my way up."

He pulled on his jeans, his thoughts grim. She'd told him to wait for her call. It had come a hell of a lot sooner than he'd anticipated. Too soon, his gut told him. She was still angry, still hurt. And very possibly suffering a delayed reaction to the traumatic events of the afternoon. He'd have to be careful, measure every word, or he'd screw this up worse than he already had.

He shagged a hand through his hair and made a quick trip to the bathroom. He barely had time to splash water on his face before she rapped on the door to his suite. He flicked the dead bolt, prepared for a kick to the gut when he saw her cut-and-bruised cheek. He *wasn't* prepared for the red-and-white cardboard carton she balanced on the palm of her hand.

"No anchovies or anything resembling fruit," she announced as she sailed past him with the carton held high. "I hope you have wine or beer in your minibar."

He stammered for a moment but finally managed, "I'm pretty sure there's both."

"Then I'll take wine. Red, not white."

She plopped the carton onto the counter that separated the living area from a small kitchenette and flicked on the overhead lights. The canned spots illuminated both the cuts and the determination in her face.

Mike was damned if he could interpret her confusing signals. Pizza and that lethal "we need to talk." Wine and utter resolve. Still wary, he uncorked a red and filled two wineglasses. She accepted hers with a cool word of thanks.

Ah, hell! He'd never been one for sailing at dead slow speeds. Might as well get the water roiling. Raising his glass, he tipped it toward hers.

"What should we drink to?"

She thought that over long enough to have him sweating.

"To us," she finally answered, "with certain caveats."

He brought his glass down. Slowly. Carefully. "I think I'd better hear what those caveats are before we drink to them."

"Smart man." She deposited her wine on the counter beside the pizza box and folded her arms. "Okay, here's the deal. I love you. You love me. But, as you no doubt learned from your previous marriage, love isn't always enough."

She had that right. Although Mike now wondered if he'd ever really loved Jill. Whatever he'd felt for her had certainly come nowhere close to this driving need to keep Zia in his life.

"So what do you propose?"

"First of all, no more scoping out situations on your own. No more independent threat assessments. We need to talk things out. Everything! The big issues, the little annoyances. Our families, our dreams, our fears."

"You want to talk all that out tonight?"

He was half teasing, half scared she meant it. Thankfully, his question elicited a muffled laugh.

"I supposed we can stretch out the discussion period."

The reluctant laugh told Mike he hadn't totally blown it. He moved closer, relief washing through him. "Stretch it out for how long?"

"Ten years?"

"Not long enough."

"Thirty?"

"Still too short." He caged her against the counter and felt himself falling into those dark, exotic eyes. "I'm thinking forty or fifty."

"Hmm," she murmured, sliding her arms around his neck, "that sounds about right."

A raw, gaping hole had ripped open when he'd almost lost her—literally and figuratively. She filled that emptiness now. The feel of her, the taste of her, was like coming home.

Sighing, she rested her forehead against his chin. "I was so terrified this afternoon."

"Who wouldn't be in that situation?"

"I wasn't scared for me! Well, yes, for me but for you, too. My heart stopped when you threw yourself at Danville."

"I was just the cleanup crew. You did the hard work."

She shuddered, and Mike wished savagely that he could have another ten minutes alone with Danville.

"You know," he said, to take her mind off the horror of the afternoon, "there's something we need to discuss that can't wait ten or twenty years."

She tipped her head back. "What's that?"

"When and where we're getting married. I vote for city hall, this weekend."

"This weekend!"

"As soon as we can get the license and blood tests done," he confirmed. "Your friends at the hospital lab ought to be able to help us out there."

"But city hall…"

"Or St. Patrick's or the chapel at your hospital or the top of the Empire Building. You pick the place, I'll take care of the arrangements."

"You can't! I mean, we can't. Gina would have a fit."

"What's she got to do with it?"

"Gina's an event coordinator! She does only a few select events now that she has the twins, but she's still one of the best in the business."

"Fine. Ask Gina to arrange it. For this weekend."

She leaned back in his arms. "This is your idea of talking things out?"

"Well…" He tried to sound apologetic but couldn't pull it off. "Pretty much."

"I'll get together with my cousin," she said, holding his eye sternly, "and come up with a list of options for us to discuss. You. Me. Together."

Mike had no problem with that. He'd achieved his primary objective of getting her mind off the horror of this afternoon. Even more important, he had her thinking when, not if.

"Fine. Now let's talk about whether we're going to eat pizza or go to bed. You. Me. Together."

She melted into a smile. "Bed. Now. End of discussion."

Fourteen

Gina pulled out all the stops and coordinated two separate events.

The first was a May wedding that took place in Galveston a week after Zia completed her residency. They did it Texas style, with Mike's male relatives and friends in either formal Western wear or Spanish-style suits. The women wore lacy dresses in a rainbow of colors. Even the New York contingent got in the spirit of things, with the duchess looking especially regal in a tall ivory comb and exquisite white lace mantilla purchased for the occasion.

The Camino Del Rey resort erected a portable pavilion that stretched from the dunes almost down to the water's edge. Filmy bows with sprays of bluebonnets decorated the white chairs. Long, fluttering white ribbons tied additional clusters of bluebonnets to the pavilion's tall poles.

Mike's three brothers stood shoulder to shoulder with his brothers-in-law. His three sisters joined Gina and Sarah and Natalie on the other side of the dais. Little Amalia and Charlotte made prim, dainty flower girls, in direct contrast to the fidgeting, reluctant ring bearers, Davy and his brother, Kevin.

Mike's parents and *abuelita* sat with the duchess in the

front row of seats. Aunts, uncles, cousins, friends and acquaintances of both families filled the rest. But Mike had eyes for no one but his bride when she walked down the aisle on the arm of her brother.

She'd caught her ebony hair back and crowned it with a garland of white roses, but the sea breeze played with the ends. The glossy black tendrils danced around her face as she and Dom matched their steps to Franz Liszt's "Liebestraum No. 3." Or maybe it was one of his nineteen rhapsodies. Mike figured he'd learn which was which in the next ten or twenty or thirty years.

Then he took Zia's hand in his and refused to let his gaze linger on the spot where she'd worn the diamond. She hadn't wanted another engagement ring. Just the wide gold band he'd had inscribed with what had become their personal mantra. With a smile in his heart, he recited the words to her now.

"You. Me. Together. Forever."

Gina coordinated a second event that took place less than a week later, just before the start of Zia and Mike's extended honeymoon trip to all her favorite haunts in Hungary and Austria. This event took place on a rocky promontory guarding a high Alpine pass between those two countries, with the ruins of Karlenburgh Castle forming a dramatic backdrop.

The number of people in attendance was considerably smaller than the Galveston event. Just Zia and Mike. Dom and Natalie. Sarah and Gina and their husbands. The twins, bundled against the cool mountain air. And the Grand Duchess of Karlenburgh.

It was the first time she'd returned to her homeland since she'd fled it more than sixty years ago. She stood alone, both hands resting on the head of her cane, the ruins behind her, the sun-dappled valley far below. She didn't seem

to notice the wind that molded the skirt of her pale green traveling suit to her hips and fluttered the scarf she wore around her neck in a fashionable double loop. Her gaze was fixed on the distant horizon. Her family could only guess what she saw in those lacy clouds.

"She must be remembering the first time she came here as a bride," Gina murmured, maintaining a firm grip on Amalia while Jack kept Charlotte corralled. "She was so young. Barely eighteen. And so much in love."

"Maybe she's thinking of the balls she and our grand-father held here," Sarah said softly. "How I wish we had a photo or portrait of her in sables and the St. Sebastian diamonds."

"Or she may be remembering Christmases past," Dom put in quietly. "The last time Natalie and I were here, we talked to an old goatherd. He still remembered the tree-lighting ceremony in the magnificent great hall. Everyone from the surrounding villages was invited."

Zia folded her hand into her husband's, aching for the woman she'd come to love so fiercely. Zia and Mike were just beginning their life together. So much of Charlotte's was past and shrouded with sadness.

The duchess's eyes drifted shut for a few moments. Her right hand lifted a few inches, moving in a small, almost imperceptible wave. Then she regripped the ebony head of her cane and squared her shoulders. When she turned to face her family, her chin was high and her eyes clear.

"Thank you for talking me into returning to Karlen-burgh. I shall always remember this moment and I'm more grateful than you can ever imagine that I was able to share it with all of you. Now for pity's sake, let's go down to the village. I could use a good, stiff *pálinka*."

Epilogue

What an amazing summer this has been. My darling Sarah
has given birth to the most exquisite baby girl. Dev is beyond
thrilled and sends me detailed and rather exhaustive reports
on her gurgles, her burps, her every hiccup. Gina and Jack stood
as her godparents, then just weeks later Natalie and Dom announced that they, too, would be adding to the ever-increasing
St. Sebastian clan.

Anastazia and Michael are so very busy with his business
and her work. Her research, I'm quite pleased to note, has expanded to such an extent that she travels extensively to other
universities and hospitals around the country—most often to
University General Hospital in Houston, I must note.

She and Michael talked about starting a family. I took great
care not to insert myself into that discussion, of course. But
it couldn't have been more than three weeks later that Maria
called, frantic with the news that she'd found a toddler wandering down her street wearing only a soiled diaper. Anastazia
rushed over immediately to examine the child. It's a crack baby,
as addicted to drugs as its mother must have been when she

abandoned him. The authorities took custody of the child and Anastazia has become his fierce and very protective advocate. I suspect it won't be long before she becomes his mother.

When I look back at all these astonishing events I realize yet again what a rewarding life I live. I wake every morning eager to see what the day will bring. And every night before I drift to sleep I let my gaze linger on the Canaletto hanging in my bedroom. The painting takes me back to Karlenburgh—the sorrows, the joys, the memories I'll hold in my heart forever.

From the diary of Charlotte,
Grand Duchess of Karlenburgh

* * * * *

MILLS & BOON®
By Request

RELIVE THE ROMANCE WITH THE BEST OF THE BEST

A sneak peek at next month's titles...

In stores from 19th October 2017:

- **Romance in Paradise** – Joss Wood, Sarah Mayberry *and* Avril Tremayne

- **Dreaming of You** – Michelle Douglas, Margaret Way *and* Beth Kery

In stores from 2nd November 2017:

- **A Very Fake Fiancée** – Fiona Brand, Nancy Warren *and* Andrea Laurence

- **Her Highland Boss** – Marion Lennox, Jessica Gilmore *and* Annie O'Neil

1017/05